DRAWN
IN BLOOD

ANDREA KANE

DRAWN IN BLOOD

WILLIAM MORROW
An Imprint of HarperCollins*Publishers*

DRAWN IN BLOOD. Copyright © 2009 by Rainbow Connection Enterprises Inc. All rights reserved. Printed in the United States of America. No part of this book may be used or reproduced in any manner whatsoever without written permission except in the case of brief quotations embodied in critical articles and reviews. For information address HarperCollins Publishers, 10 East 53rd Street, New York, NY 10022.

HarperCollins books may be purchased for educational, business, or sales promotional use. For information please write: Special Markets Department, HarperCollins Publishers, 10 East 53rd Street, New York, NY 10022.

FIRST EDITION

Library of Congress Cataloging-in-Publication Data
Kane, Andrea.
    Drawn in blood / by Andrea Kane. – 1st ed.
        p.   cm.
    ISBN 978-0-06-123680-8
    I. Title.
PS3561.A463D73   2009
813'54—dc22   2009002109

09 10 11 12 13   OV/RRD   10 9 8 7 6 5 4 3 2 1

To Mischief Mini, whom we all adore. Thank you for bringing a new and renewed love into our hearts and our home. You are truly a blessing.

ACKNOWLEDGMENTS

The researching and writing of *Drawn in Blood* took me one level deeper into the multifaceted world of the FBI. Even after all I learned when I was writing *Twisted*, this sequel introduced me to new units of the Bureau and broadened my knowledge of those units I'd already explored. I was launched into the complexities and danger of undercover work, the fascinating world of art theft, and an entirely different, but equally gripping, dimension of Asian and Eurasian organized crime.

One aspect of my research didn't change, and that's the caliber and commitment of the FBI professionals with whom I consulted. Their dedication, consistent availability, and depth of knowledge are inspiring. I can't thank them enough for helping me make *Drawn in Blood* the kind of thriller I always strive to create—accurate, exciting, and alive with three-dimensional characters who draw my readers in and make them part of their stories.

The following people deserve special thanks. Many of them are experts I have turned to time and again for information, explanations, and answers. Miraculously, they always come through for me:

Angela Bell, public affairs specialist at FBI Headquarters. Angela, you were as instrumental in the creation of *Drawn in Blood* as you were in its predecessor, *Twisted*. Thanks to you, I met and worked with the best of the best (you rank high up there among them), and you coordinated my Bureau-related contacts and my research requirements every step of the way. You define the phrases *top-notch, rapid response,* and *caring dedication.* In other words, you're the best, and I couldn't have written *Drawn in Blood's* FBI foundation without you.

Special Agent Robert Wittman, an incomparable senior investigator of the Art Crime Team, but most of all, an even more incomparable human being. Bob, when it comes to art crime, you're the ultimate source—but that's just the tip of the iceberg. Your people skills and diversity of expertise stretch far beyond the art world, as does your compassion for others. Thank goodness your humility makes you totally unaware of just how awesome you are. Retire? Never. Just begin anew.

Special Agent Konrad Motyka, who never ceases to astound me with his in-depth knowledge of organized crime and of the world as a whole. Besides giving me a deeper understanding of the investigations of the Asian Criminal Enterprise Task Force (C-6) and Asian organized crime as a whole (including their international as well as their national operations), you expanded my education to include Albanian organized crime (C-7), the cultural and historical elements of eastern Europe and the Far East, not to mention giving me an A-plus crash course in submachine guns. Konrad, you are truly indispensable. Thank you for being so generous with your time, your prompt responses, and your detailed explanations.

Supervisory Special Agent James McNamara of the FBI's Behavioral Analysis Unit. Understanding human behavior and incorporating that into the complex knowledge base we laypeople know as "profiling" is just one layer of your specialized skills and wealth of experience. Thanks to you, I gained an understanding of the different prototypes and motivations of art thieves, the different cultural composites of various Chinese provinces and villages, and most important, what makes different criminal minds tick. Jim, as the essence of integrity, judgment, dependability, and initiative, you embody the slogan "Once a marine, always a marine."

Margaret Young, who taught me the culture and dialect of the Loong Doo, and who was a sheer delight to meet and to work with.

Special Agent Sherri Evanina of the Newark Field Office, my type A wizard.

Despite an increasingly hectic schedule, you always came through for me, making arrangements, setting up contact meetings, and knowing the answers to just about everything—or finding me someone who did. Working with you is a joy.

Bonnie Magness-Gardiner, the art-theft program manager. Thank you for opening the door to the Art Crime Team for me, for giving me a finer appreciation of art, and for giving me the basic knowledge of the structure and responsibilities of the team—all of which paved the way for my research.

Special Agent Jerria Williams, media representative in the Philadelphia Field Office. I so enjoyed working with you—your enthusiasm and professionalism made me feel both informed and welcome. And I'll thank you forever for setting up my first meeting with Bob; it's no easy task to pin down a man who zooms around the world!

Special Agent James Margolin of the New York Field Office, who once again always found time to get me the answers I needed and to connect me with all the right people. Jim, you multitask to the max and make it all work, despite having to handle the overwhelming job of being the media contact at the busiest, most densely populated FBI Field Office in the country.

Special Agent Jim Wynne, one of the longtime, invaluable senior investigators of the Art Crime Team, whom SA Jim Margolin arranged for me to speak to. SA Wynne has the daunting job of interviewing suspects and handling the Big Apple's countless major theft investigations.

Special Agent Jody Roberson (now retired, but still more vital than a twenty-year-old) and Special Agent Mike Adams, the two principal firearms instructors at Fort Dix. Thanks to Mike, I can now hold, load, and fire an MP5. (And if you think that handling a heavy subgun is easy, just give it a try. Your muscles won't speak to you for a week.) And thanks to Jody, my skills with the MP5 and the Glock 22 have been honed, with Jody pushing me to, but not beyond, my limits.

Kurt Crawford, public affairs specialist at Quantico, who came through for me when I needed to find an expert firearms consultant ASAP, and who guided me via phone to the FBI Academy when my driver and I got lost on the extensive grounds of Quantico.

Defensive Systems Unit Chief William Kozacek, the expert firearms consultant Kurt connected me with, who knew every single detail about every single weapon imaginable, and who was kind enough to share his knowledge with a novice.

Everyone at FBI Headquarters in Washington, D.C., who welcomed me during my first official visit. Thank you for your hospitality, your enthusiasm, and your introduction to the nucleus of the Bureau. Congratulations on your one-hundred-year anniversary!

The New York, Newark, and Philadelphia Field Offices for their ongoing cooperation.

I truly hope I haven't omitted anyone, since everybody I dealt with at the FBI was an integral part of the creation of *Drawn in Blood*. An added thanks to all of you at the Bureau who read the manuscript for accuracy and then provided me with your invaluable feedback.

As always, I take full responsibility for any unintentional errors that might have slipped by and for any literary license I took. I only did so when absolutely necessary.

With the integration of the NYPD in *Drawn in Blood*, I must once again thank my ongoing consultant, Detective Mike Oliver, who exemplifies the street smarts and allegiance of the NYPD, who never seems to have to say "I don't know" to any of my endless questions, and whose sense of humor never fails to lift my spirits and make me laugh—even when I'm on deadline and running on empty.

Many thanks to my editor at HarperCollins, Lucia Macro, for all she does on my behalf.

A special thanks to my agent, Andrea Cirillo, for our long and flourishing partnership, for weathering the storms along the way, and for always making the sun come out. And welcome to the team, Christina!

Most significant of all, a huge thank-you to my family, for all the love, support, and teamwork we share, and always seem to discover and rediscover, despite life's obstacles. Your input is invaluable. The spot you fill in my heart and my life is irreplaceable.

DRAWN
IN BLOOD

CHAPTER ONE

The front door of the apartment was open a crack. That meant Matthew was home.

Generally, Rosalyn Burbank preferred being the first one through the door at night. It gave her time to unwind, to transition from work to home. To savor a glass of wine and a hot shower before starting to think about dinner.

But tonight she was just as happy her husband had beaten her to their Upper East Side apartment. The two of them needed to talk.

Something was weighing on her husband's mind, and had been for weeks. She'd waited for him to approach her and broach the subject. He hadn't. That was way out of character. Matthew wasn't big on secrets. Neither was Rosalyn. It was probably one of the reasons their marriage had endured for thirty-three years. And what made this situation worse was that whatever Matthew was keeping from her was significant. He wasn't himself. He was quiet and pensive, and he tossed and turned all night, every night.

Rosalyn was really starting to worry.

Tonight she planned to clear the air.

"Matthew?" She elbowed the front door open the rest of the way and stepped inside, shutting it behind her. "It's me. You forgot to close the door behind you again. Not the smartest idea. One day, someone's going to—"

She never finished her sentence.

She heard the footsteps rush up behind her a split second before a pair of strong arms grabbed her. A rag was stuffed in her mouth, and a rough sack was pulled over her head.

Instinctively, Rosalyn fought back. Enveloped by darkness, she struggled like a wild animal, even when she was backhanded so hard that her head snapped around and she lost her footing, nearly toppling to the floor. She managed to stay upright, regained her balance, and swung out blindly with her fist.

Her knuckles connected with what felt like her attacker's jaw, and she heard his grunt of stunned surprise.

She took advantage of the moment, delivering a second punch, hoping to do some serious damage. But this time she missed and her attacker grabbed her arms, pinning them behind her and anchoring them so her movements were restricted. She still didn't cave, but continued to battle him with sharp defensive jerks of her body and as many clumsy kicks as she could manage.

When her knee connected with his groin, she knew she'd gone too far.

He swore viciously, then barked out a terse, unintelligible command in another language—some Asian tongue. Pounding footsteps ensued, and a second intruder burst out from wherever in the apartment he'd been. The two men started arguing in a guttural Chinese dialect. An instant later, Rosalyn was dragged through the foyer and into another room—Matthew's office, if her sense of direction wasn't completely off. There, she was shoved into a chair, her wrists were bound behind her, and her ankles were tied together on the floor.

She tried to let out a scream but only succeeded in gagging on the rag that was crammed in her mouth. The garbled sound that emerged was muffled by the burlap sack. Before she could try again, a heavy, solid object struck her head, and pain exploded through her skull.

She saw stars and heard herself whimper. Pinpoints of light flashed behind her eyes. The voices . . . just two? No, maybe three. Male voices. All speaking in the same rapid Chinese. Dazed, she found herself wishing she'd joined Matthew and Sloane all those years ago when they'd taken their trips to the Far East. Then maybe she could have deciphered what was being said. As it was, all she could make out was the urgency of their tones, mixed with the sound of slamming drawers and what was probably a lifetime of possessions being hauled off.

With her tongue, she managed to maneuver the rag to one side—far enough so she could scream.

That was a mistake.

A drawer thudded to the floor. A whiz of motion. And then another blow that connected solidly with the side of her head.

This one was too much.

Blinding pain. Then, dark silence.

———

It had started to drizzle when Matthew got out of the taxi and paid the driver—a cold autumn drizzle that left you feeling chilled inside and out.

Matthew didn't notice it.

He didn't notice anything.

He was paralyzed with shock and worry.

He'd walked into a Chinatown restaurant to meet his partners, men who also happened to be his oldest friends. It wasn't a social dinner. It was a strategy session. *All* their necks were on the line—even the two of them who hadn't been at the crime scene—and it had been crucial that they nail down the details of the story they'd be giving to the FBI during their individual interrogations. No hesitations. No deviations. It was the only way.

Matthew had arrived late and on edge.

But he'd left panicked, punched in the gut with the very basis for this meeting, and sucked into a memory he'd long since buried—or had tried to. Suddenly, the past was the present. No. Worse. Because now what he feared for was his life.

He'd stepped out for a smoke. The Mercedes had pulled up to the curb, parking directly in front of the Cadillac Escalade, not fifteen feet from where

Matthew stood. Two Mediterranean guys, who looked like thugs and were built like linebackers, had gotten out of the Escalade and waited on the sidewalk as the driver of the Mercedes, burly and Asian, hurried around to open the back door for his passenger.

The man had emerged, emanating power, despite being dwarfed in size by the linebackers. He'd greeted them with a nod, waited for his driver—who was clearly a bodyguard—to be glued to his side, and then led the way, keeping his head down as he walked.

He raised it just as he reached Matthew. He stopped. A long moment of eye contact. The recognition had been mutual and indisputable.

It was more than enough to tell Matthew he was living on borrowed time.

He was barely aware of greeting the doorman at his building or entering the high-rise on York Avenue and Eighty-second Street. On autopilot, he summoned the elevator, then rode upstairs as he berated himself for being a prisoner to his own stupidity.

The elevator doors slid open, and he headed toward the apartment. Never had he needed a drink more than he did right now.

He unlocked the front door and flipped on the light as he stepped inside. His gaze swept the living area, and he froze in his tracks.

The place was trashed, furniture shoved aside, empty recesses left where the flat-screen TV and entertainment center had been. Kitchen drawers were dumped upside down, minus all the unique Art Deco silverware they'd contained. Two handcrafted sculptures that Matthew had bartered for in Thailand were missing, as was the Monet that had hung over the sofa, and the one-of-a-kind ivory chess set he'd bought in India. And one of Rosalyn's diamond stud earrings was lying in the corner, clearly having been dropped. That meant they'd been in their bedroom and cleaned out her jewelry box.

None of that meant jack. It was the other painting. That's why they'd come. The rest was just bonus. They'd broken in because of the painting.

Not the Monet. It was one of his lesser known works, not one of his masterpieces. But the Rothberg. Not the painting itself, but its paperwork. *That* was what was invaluable. And timely. Especially after Matthew's encounter tonight.

He flung down the portfolio he'd been holding and raced to his office—where he'd find his answer.

He found a lot more than that.

Rosalyn was crumpled on her side in a corner of the room. She was bound to a toppled chair—hands and feet—and her head was half-covered by a cloth sack. One of the heavy wooden bookends he kept on his mantle lay beside her. A pool of blood was oozing from inside the sack, staining the Oriental rug beneath his wife's head. She wasn't moving. Her unnatural stillness was terrifying.

"Roz." Wild with panic, Matthew dashed over, squatting down and easing the sack off her head, dreading what he'd find.

She was breathing. He released his own breath when he saw that. Thank God. She was alive. The shallow rise and fall of her breasts confirmed it. So did the thready but definite pulse at her wrist.

To hell with the Rothberg.

He pulled the rag out of her mouth and untied her wrists and ankles, scrutinizing her as he did. There were nasty gashes just above her ear where the blood was seeping from. Whoever had done this had struck her at least twice with the bookend. Hard.

"Roz!" Matthew gripped her shoulders and shook her, realizing he was being an ass. He shouldn't be jarring her, shouldn't be wasting precious seconds before calling 911. But he needed a sign, *any* sign—a word, a flicker of recognition—*anything* that told him she was okay.

He got both.

After his second "Roz! Honey, can you hear me?" she cracked open her eyes.

"Matthew?" she managed, blinking up at him. She stirred, then moaned, sinking back into the carpet and squeezing her eyes shut at the pain.

"Don't talk. Don't move. I'll get help. It'll be okay." Matthew knew he was reassuring himself more than his wife, who'd slipped back into unconsciousness.

Groping in his jacket pocket, he snatched his cell phone and punched in 911.

"This is Matthew Burbank," he announced the instant the emergency operator answered. "I live at 500 East Eighty-second, at the corner of York. Apartment 9B. My home's been broken into. My wife is hurt. I need an ambulance—fast." His gaze was darting around, taking in the wreck of his office as he spoke. "She was struck on the head. At least twice. I don't know how bad it is. She's bleeding, but she's alive. Please . . . hurry." Dazed, he supplied the other customary answers, then hung up.

He forced himself to scan the room, taking in the ransacked drawers of his myriad file cabinets. Even though he didn't label the cabinets themselves, he had a system, and he knew which cabinets were which. So he knew exactly where to direct his scrutiny. The cabinet that was thoroughly trashed, with a specific drawer pulled out to the max, was the one holding his pre-electronic business records of promising modern artists.

Neatly placed across the open drawer was a now-empty file folder. No surprise as to which one. A. *Rothberg's Dead or Alive* was printed on the tab. And resting on top of the folder like some kind of menacing paperweight was a fortune cookie. He picked it up. The fortune was sticking out from inside the cookie. Matthew eased it free.

Devote tomorrow to silent reflection, it read.

Bile burned Matthew's tongue. It wasn't a suggestion. It was a threat. This is what they'd come for. Not his possessions.

Matthew stared at the objects in his hands. Then, he shoved the empty file folder, fortune cookie, and fortune into the inside pocket of his trench coat.

The cops couldn't see these. If they did, the whole situation would explode wide open.

It was already too late for him.

But now his whole family was in mortal danger.

CHAPTER TWO

The evening rush hour had come and gone, but the cars were still rumbling through the Midtown Tunnel, making the apartment vibrate and sleep impossible.

Fortunately, sleep was the furthest thing from Sloane Burbank's mind.

Lying alone in Derek's bed, she pulled the sheet up higher, gripping it tightly in her fists, and wondering for the dozenth time if she was jumping the gun, making a huge mistake. Was this happening too fast? Was it premature? Would it solidify things or blow them apart?

The step she was making was huge. How did she know if it was right?

She was still pondering that when the key turned in the front-door lock, and Derek's voice reached her ears, accompanied by the sound of racing paws. An instant later, three bright-eyed dachshunds scrambled into the bedroom, dragging their leashes behind them. They pounced on the bed and on Sloane with a vengeance, licking her face and burrowing in the pillows.

"Hey." Sloane greeted Moe, Larry, and Curly—or "the hounds," as she affectionately called them—with alternating scruffling of their necks. Their enthusiasm was infectious, and she had to grin as Larry stuck his head inside one pillowcase and emerged with two feathers on his snout. She plucked them off, pivoted to her side, and propped herself on one elbow. "That's quite a greeting, you three. And you've only been gone a half hour."

"It feels like a lot longer." Derek Parker entered the room, shrugging out of his lightweight jacket and hanging it neatly over one of the two suitcases near the bedroom door. "We jogged half a mile up Second Avenue. I think we marked every fire hydrant along the way twice—once going and once coming back."

Sloane laughed, sitting up to unsnap the hounds' leashes. Curly was panting the least. Then again, he was her little frankfurter, with almost no hair to weigh him down. Larry was curly haired, and little Moe—actually, Mona, the only female of the trio—was long-haired and silky. She was panting the most, and took the opportunity to gaze at Sloane and emit a plaintive whimper.

"Oh, cut it out," Derek muttered as he stepped into the galley kitchen to refill their water dishes. "You're such a drama queen. You were the one who dragged us into that mud puddle to play—and refused to leave for five minutes. So cut the violins-playing-in-the-background act."

Moe gave a pointed snort and jumped off the bed, leaving to join the others for a long drink.

"Thanks for taking them out," Sloane said to Derek. "You know that when I'm in the country I take them for a jog every morning and night. But I hate running in the city."

"Not a problem."

Sloane watched as Derek guzzled a bottle of water, then stripped off his shirt and tossed it in the hamper nearby. That was the one good thing about a small apartment—everything was within reach.

The man had a great body. There were no two ways about it. From his broad, muscled shoulders to his six-pack abs, he was as hot as they come. And he didn't owe that body to the FBI. He owed it to the military. As a former Army Ranger, Derek still rose at dawn and worked out like a demon. When the rest of the world—and the sun—was rising, Derek was finishing up a workout that would knock most people on their asses for a week. No collapsing for him. After the workout, Derek showered, ate a PowerBar, and drove down to the FBI's New York Field Office to start his workday.

Tonight the two of them had cut short their regular workaholic hours. They'd quit work by six and headed over to Derek's apartment to pack. The packing had been minimal. They'd spent most of the past few hours in bed.

Now, Derek was bare to the waist, and, knowing the effect they had on each other, Sloane held up her palm. "Much as I'd love to see the rest of the striptease, it'll have to wait. I ordered up Italian. It should be here in ten."

Derek gave her that sexy grin that made her insides melt. "We've burned up the sheets in five," he reminded her. "And that included getting our clothes off. You're already naked, and I'm halfway there. Plus, we both love a challenge." His smile faded. "Of course, we also know that's not the problem. The problem is you've used the past half hour to freak out and consider changing your mind about my moving in to your place. Kind of puts a damper on the mood."

Sloane blew out her breath. She wished he didn't know her so well. "Guilty as charged," she admitted. "And it's not because I don't want to live together. I just don't want to screw things up—again."

"We weren't living together when things fell apart," he reminded her. "And you know damned well that, even if we had been, living together would have had nothing to do with what happened. We shut each other out. We let our pride outweigh our love. We won't make that mistake twice."

"No," Sloane agreed softly. "We won't."

She was being ridiculous. She knew it. It had been six months since they'd found their way back to each other. They'd worked out the obstacles—at least the big ones. What they had together was unique. She loved him. He loved her. An emotional connection like theirs was rare as hell in today's world.

Which was why she was terrified.

But, as Derek had just said, she loved a challenge. Living together was going to be a biggie. It meant relinquishing another piece of her freedom and lowering another protective wall.

He was worth it. *They* were worth it.

The buzzer sounded, sending the hounds into a barking frenzy.

"Dinner's early." Derek walked over, tipped up Sloane's chin, and kissed her—not just a kiss, but one of those slow, deep kisses she felt down to her toes. "Pity. We could have put those ten minutes to good use."

Her eyes were smoky. "I'll owe them to you. We'll tack them on to dessert."

"Deal." Derek yanked his T-shirt back on. "I'll get the food."

Sloane scooted over to get out of bed. "I'll set the table."

"Don't bother. We'll eat out of the tins. Fewer dishes to wash, more time to pack. And whatever." With a wink, Derek went to buzz the doorman and tell him to let the delivery kid upstairs with their food.

Pulling one of Derek's oversize sweatshirts on, Sloane combed her fingers through the layers of her dark shoulder-length hair, and then padded into the kitchen to grab some forks and knives. She took an extra minute to pour two glasses of Chianti.

The wine wasn't meant to be savored. Not tonight.

Her cell phone rang.

Pausing for a quick sip of Chianti, Sloane retraced her steps to the bedroom. One of her clients, no doubt. With something that couldn't wait until morning. She was used to that. As an independent consultant with credentials as a former FBI agent and crisis negotiator, she had a client list that consisted of law enforcement agencies and companies that needed round-the-clock availability. So, adaptability in her personal life was the name of the game.

She wondered what tonight's interruption would be.

Scooping her phone off the nightstand, she flipped it open. "Sloane Burbank."

"Sloane, it's me."

"Dad?" Her brows drew together. It wasn't that hearing from her father was unusual. She and her parents touched base a lot more since they'd moved back north to Manhattan from their Florida condo. But her father's tone, which was normally smooth and upbeat from all his years in sales, was shaky and strained. Not to mention the disturbing background noises Sloane could make out through the phone. The institutional bustle. The clear, unwelcome echo of a doctor being paged. The sounds were sickeningly familiar.

Her father was calling from a hospital—a setting she'd had more than her fair share of experience in.

Her gut clenched. "Dad, what's wrong?" she demanded. "You're in a hospital. Why?"

A hard swallow. "It's your mother. She's been hurt."

"Hurt—how?" Sloane was already shrugging out of Derek's sweatshirt and rummaging around for her clothes. "And how bad is it?"

Another swallow, as her father struggled to keep himself together. "Our apartment was robbed. Your mother must have walked in and surprised the intruders. She was tied up and knocked unconscious. The good news is that, by the time the ambulance got us to the emergency room, she was coming around."

"So she's conscious?" Sloane wriggled into her bra and snapped the front clasp with her free hand, then stepped into her thong, and reached for her slacks and sweater.

"Conscious, and in pain. I'm waiting for an update from the doctors now."

"Which hospital?"

"New York Presbyterian."

"I'll catch a taxi and be there in ten minutes."

"Wait." Matthew interrupted her. "Ten minutes? Where are you?"

"At Derek's place."

"That's what I was afraid of." An uncomfortable pause. "Sloane, I need you to come alone. Not with Derek. Not with anybody. The NYPD is already handling the break-in. They've got detectives here asking me a hundred questions—most of which I have no answers to. The last thing I need is to escalate the situation by having an FBI agent join this three-ring circus. Your mother needs her rest. She also needs you. So do I. Please, come alone."

"All right." Something about her father's request didn't sit right. Sloane sensed it, despite her shock and worry over her mother. She just couldn't pinpoint what it was—not yet.

But now wasn't the time to argue.

She grabbed her pocketbook. "I'm on my way."

"Alone?"

"Yes, Dad. Alone."

She snapped the phone shut and finished pulling on her sweater and buttoning her slacks. She was halfway through the bedroom door when she collided with Derek, who'd come to announce that dinner was served.

He frowned, taking in her drawn expression and the fact that she was fully dressed. "What's going on?"

"My mom's in the hospital. I've got to get over there."

He snapped into take-charge mode. "Is it serious?"

"Someone broke into their place. She surprised them. They knocked her out. That's all I know."

"I'll go with you." Ignoring the trays of lasagna, Derek headed for the door.

"No—wait." Sloane stopped him, shrugging into her coat as she spoke. "My dad asked me to come alone. He sounds really upset. The cops are in his face, asking questions. I think he and my mom have had all they can take."

Derek went very still. "I'm not going to interrogate them. I'm going to offer my support. And to be there for you."

This was going to be tough. "I realize that," Sloane carefully replied. "And I'm grateful. But think of it from my dad's point of view. Right now, he doesn't see you as my boyfriend. He sees you as yet another law enforcement official. I don't want to upset him any more than he already is. So I'll do it his way. He and my mom are right here at New York Presbyterian. I'll be there in a flash. And I'll call you with updates."

"Fine." Derek wasn't happy. But he didn't argue. "My doorman will hail you a cab."

"Thanks for understanding."

"I don't. I'm accepting."

"That works, too." Sloane's gaze flitted to the kitchen table. "Go ahead and eat. I'll warm mine up when I get back."

"Right. Sure. Send my best to your folks."

"I will." Sloane was already halfway out the door, waiting only until Derek had reined in the hounds before she took off.

Derek shut the door behind her. He parked himself at the kitchen table but ignored the food. He wasn't hungry. He was bugged. Sloane had a hell of a poker face. But he knew her. Something was up. What had her father divulged about the break-in that he wanted kept under wraps? It couldn't have been too detailed, given the brevity of the conversation. Regardless, he'd managed to convey that he didn't want Derek around. And Derek wasn't buying in to that I'm-too-overwhelmed excuse. There was more to this whole scenario than that.

He was still brooding when his phone rang.

Hoping it was Sloane, he snapped up the receiver. "Parker."

"It's me."

The "me" in question wasn't Sloane. It was fellow agent Jeff Chiu, Derek's friend and squad mate on the Asian Criminal Enterprise Task Force.

"Listen," Jeff continued in his no-BS tone. "The squad just picked up a weird conversation from our wiretap on Xiao Long's phone. Something about finalizing a deal with an old art dealer on East Eighty-second."

"Shit." Derek's fist struck the kitchen table.

"So I *am* right. I remember your mentioning that Sloane's parents live on the Upper East Side and that her father's a retired art dealer."

"Not so retired."

"Meaning this involves him. And you don't sound surprised. What do you know?"

"Only that the Burbanks' apartment was just hit. Sloane got a call from her father a little while ago. He's at New York Presbyterian with his wife. Evidently, she interrupted the burglary. She was roughed up and knocked out."

"Just knocked out?"

"Yup. That means she didn't see Xiao Long's guys, or she'd be dead. That's all I know—at least until I hear from Sloane. She's over at the hospital now. I'm assuming C-6 will be getting official details soon. In the meantime, from what Sloane said, it sounds like the Nineteenth Precinct is all over this."

"I'll have one of our task force detectives contact them and make sure they're aware we have bigger fish to fry. But I doubt that'll come as big news. The NYPD knows we're closing in on Xiao Long. He's the Dai Lo. His gang members are superfluous. If the cops want to make a couple of independent arrests, so be it."

"I doubt they'll find enough to do even that. I'd bet money that Rosalyn Burbank never saw her assailants, or she wouldn't be alive to say otherwise. That eliminates a description or an ID. And, based on the previous break-ins, there'll be no physical evidence. All that adds up to nothing."

"Yeah." A pause. "But from what Xiao Long said on the phone—this break-in wasn't random."

"No," Derek repeated darkly. "It wasn't."

CHAPTER THREE

Matthew Burbank was pacing the floor of the waiting room when Sloane burst in.

"How's Mom?" she asked.

"Better." Matthew reached out and squeezed his daughter's arm. "She's talking a bit, and her memory is intact. The doctors want to keep her overnight just as a precaution. Hopefully, they'll release her tomorrow."

Sloane blew out a relieved breath. "Can I see her?"

"In a little while. The doctor just finished his examination." An uneasy pause as Matthew glanced down the hall toward his wife's room. "Now the cops are with her. After that, she's got to rest."

"I'll wait till the police leave. Then I'll poke my head in." Sloane studied her father's ashen complexion and the tight lines around his mouth. There was sweat beading on his forehead, and he couldn't seem to stand still.

She hadn't been imagining things. Something was wrong, something more than what she already knew.

"Dad?" She sought his attention, drawing his gaze to hers. "What is it?"

Another swift glance down the hall. "Let's go for a walk outside," he suggested. "I need the fresh air. And we need the privacy."

"All right." Sloane didn't question him. She just rode down in the elevator beside him, left the building, and waited until they were seated on a bench in a more secluded section of the hospital grounds before she spoke. "Talk to me."

Matthew was trembling. "I never wanted to drag you or your mother into this. I really thought it was over. Then the FBI got involved. And now the whole thing's unraveling."

Sloane turned to face him. Taken aback as she was, she called upon her training, making her questions direct and keeping her approach calm and sans accusation. "What is 'it'? And why is the Bureau involved?"

Staring at the ground, Matthew spoke. "First, I need to know you'll keep everything I tell you between us." He reached into his pocket and pulled out a dollar bill, which he tucked into Sloane's hand. "You're still licensed to practice law in New York. So that should buy your silence."

Sloane's gaze lifted from the dollar bill to her father's face. "I was a prosecutor, Dad, not a defense attorney. And that was before I joined the Bureau. But, yes, my license is current. So privilege does apply. I'm also your daughter. So I won't repeat anything you tell me. You have my word."

"Not even to Derek?"

A hard swallow. "Not even to Derek."

Matthew nodded. "You know how far back the art-partnership guys and I go."

"Of course. You've been tight since college." Sloane had grown up among the group of men her father was describing. Leo Fox, Phil Leary, Ben Martino, and Wallace Johnson. The five of them, including her father, had met at NYU, formed a lifetime friendship and an equally long-standing poker game, and eventually combined their individual talents to form an art partnership that ended up making each of them comfortably successful. Wallace—formally C. Wallace Johnson III—had put up the initial capital, being that he could afford it. He came from money and had increased his wealth through his career as a successful investment banker.

"Right." Matthew was talking again. "Well, a little over fourteen years ago we were lucky enough to buy an Aaron Rothberg—a pretty renowned one, called *Dead or Alive*. Then, we got a handsome offer for it from a dealer in Hong Kong. So we flew over there to finalize the transaction—all of us except Ben and Wallace. Ben's father had just suffered his stroke, and Wallace was tied up with a major acquisition. That didn't present a problem. The three of us could handle it."

"Go on."

"We made the exchange. The dealer, Cai Wen, was impressed with us. He asked us to meet him the following evening at his Hong Kong office in the Kowloon district to discuss future deals. We were delighted. We showed up at the arranged time. As we arrived, we saw a young man leaving the building. He was carrying the Rothberg under his arm."

"A pretty quick turnover," Sloane observed.

"That's what we thought. We soon found out otherwise." Matthew drew a ragged breath. "The office door was open. We let ourselves in. Cai Wen was lying on the floor. Half his head had been blown away, and blood was everywhere. There was never any doubt he was dead. And the only ones at the scene were the three of us—all Americans. We had to get away—fast. We had families, lives to protect. So we took off. We agreed never to discuss it again."

Sloane was processing this nightmare as quickly as she could. "Obviously something happened to reverse your decision."

"The FBI happened. Several months ago, two copies of Rothberg's *Dead or Alive* appeared on the U.S. art scene—both presumably authentic. One was up for auction at Sotheby's. The other showed up in Christie's catalog before they learned about the discrepancy and pulled it."

"I remember reading about this in the paper," Sloane said, her eyes narrowing. "Although I didn't pay much attention at the time. I had no idea any of this affected you. I take it the Christie's painting was the forgery."

"Right. The Sotheby's painting was authenticated."

"And which was the painting you sold?"

"You tell me. There are gaping holes in the provenance of both paintings. They changed hands numerous times. Receipts are missing, sales went undocumented. That's all too typical in my business. So I have no idea if the painting we sold to Cai Wen was genuine. Or if that's what got him killed. I only know that we believed our painting was authentic and that we had nothing to do with the murder." Matthew rubbed the back of his neck. "The FBI's investigation is coming to a head. Each of the guys in my partnership is being interviewed by an agent with the Art Crime Team. I'm up first. Tomorrow."

"Do they know about the murder?"

"Murders are rare in Hong Kong—then and now. So I doubt it slipped by them. Whether they suspect us of being involved, I don't know."

Sloane placed her hand over her father's. "Tell them the truth."

"It's not that simple."

"Why not?" Sloane's forehead creased. "You're not going to be prosecuted for a murder that took place in Hong Kong. Plus, you didn't do it."

"But I know who did."

Sloane went very still. "You'd better explain."

"I don't know his name. But I saw his face—clearly. We all did. It was early evening. The sun was just starting to set. There was more than enough light. Like I said, we thought Cai Wen had turned over the painting to a buyer he'd already secured. It turned out the buyer was a killer." A pause. "It also turned out he was smart. When news of the forgery got out, he did his homework."

"Which led him to you."

"Right."

"So he knows your investment group sold Cai Wen the painting."

"He also knows we saw him take it—and under what circumstances. That's why he had your mother's and my apartment broken into tonight. It was a threat to keep my mouth shut." Matthew fumbled in his trench coat's pocket, pulled out the empty file folder and the fortune cookie, complete with message. "He left me these."

Sloane glanced over all the items, concentrating on the ominous fortune that had been placed inside the cookie. "What about the rest of your friends? Did they get similar threats?"

"Doubtful. I haven't gotten any frantic phone calls since I saw them a few hours ago. But that doesn't surprise me. Even though the killer's aware that the art investment group had a handful of members, the signature on the bill of sale between us and Cai Wen was mine. Lucky me. I chose that particular opportunity to sign as a member of the partnership."

"So you're the only one he could trace."

"I think so. And it gets worse." Matthew turned toward his daughter, his eyes filled with fear. "Sloane, he doesn't just know my name on paper. He saw my face that night. I was never sure. But I am now."

That was the last thing Sloane wanted to hear. "How?"

"When I met with the guys earlier this evening, it was to coordinate our stories. We had dinner in Chinatown. I stepped outside the restaurant for a cigarette while Ben and Phil were settling the check. A black Mercedes pulled up to the curb where I was standing. The man who got out—it was him. It might be fourteen years later, but I'll never forget that face. He looks older, but otherwise unchanged. It was definitely him. He had a bodyguard with him, and he met up with two Mediterranean guys who looked like bouncers. But his choice of meeting places was no coincidence. He knew I was there. He'd arranged a 'chance encounter' so I could see him, and he could emphasize what I was about to find at home. He was less than five feet away before he raised his head and looked me in the eye. I had no time to think, much less duck back inside the restaurant. Besides, I couldn't move. It's like I was frozen in place. Which gave me plenty of time to stare at him. And he definitely knew who I was."

"Maybe he recognized you from a photo that appeared in one of the articles you've written over the years—"

"He remembered *me*, Sloane," Matthew interrupted her. "Not from some random photo. From that night. I saw the look in his eyes. It was stark recognition. Only he wasn't shocked. I was. And he witnessed the full extent of my shock. That was the nail in my coffin. If I'd only had time to hide my reaction . . . but I didn't. He realized I could identify him. He's a killer. I'm a threat. What do you think that adds up to?"

"A dangerous situation." Sloane raked her fingers through her hair. "Did he speak to you?"

"Not a word. He just stood there for maybe thirty seconds, watching me. Then he passed by with his goons, and they walked into another restaurant.

He was like some kind of pack animal letting me know he was about to tear out my throat. And it's not just me I'm worried about—not anymore. I'm terrified for your mother, for you. Sloane, I don't know what to do." Matthew leaned forward, holding his head with unsteady hands.

Sloane fell silent. She'd never seen her father like this. It's not that he was a rock. He wasn't. But he'd always been the positive force in the family, the extraverted optimist. Even though her mother was the family powerhouse—'the Barracuda,' as she was known in the publishing world—there was a quality about her father that made him her mother's stabilizing foundation. Sloane felt the same way. She'd inherited her aggressive nature from her mother, and it was her father who made things right. He loved life, and life loved him. To see him fall apart this way—albeit for a very real and terrifying reason—made Sloane feel ill. Ill and responsible for finding a solution to this ordeal.

For a long moment, she desperately tried to separate the daughter in her from the professional. It was a pretty tall order. Life-threatening danger was part of *her* world, not theirs. She was a trained FBI agent. She was also an expert in Krav Maga—"contact combat," as it translated into English—a self-defense technique so forceful and effective that it was used by the Israeli Defense Forces. Plus, she was thirty-one years old. Her parents were in their late fifties. She was young, strong, and vital—mentally, physically, and psychologically.

And her parents?

They were regular people with regular lives. They'd lived and worked in Manhattan. Two years ago, they'd tried retirement. They'd bought a condo in Florida and taken up golf. That lifestyle didn't last long. They'd both missed the New York scene. So they'd moved back.

To this.

"Sloane?" her father prompted, seeking something she wasn't sure she could provide.

She stared straight ahead, keeping her emotion well in check. "You and Mom are going to need protection."

"Your mother doesn't know anything about this. She thinks the break-in was just a random burglary."

"Then it's time you told her. It's her life, too. This isn't a secret you can keep anymore."

"I shouldn't have kept it at all. I just wanted to forget."

"Yes, well, forgetting doesn't work. Neither does hiding things from law enforcement. The cops are questioning Mom about the break-in. The Bureau is investigating the art theft. How long do you think it's going to take before they connect the two?"

"There's no reason they ever should—unless you tell them." Her father's barb found its mark. "As far as the FBI knows, my investment group and I are persons of interest. Nothing more. I already told you there are huge gaps in the provenance of *Dead or Alive*. Anyone who's smart enough to kill and whose actions are so deliberate is smart enough to destroy any paper trail that leads to him. That leaves things wide open, with no proof of what we saw. We're not even sure if we sold a fake or an original. How much more guilty can we look?"

"So when the FBI interviews you, you plan to leave out the part about witnessing the murder. Oh," she added, holding up the file and fortune cookie. "And now you're withholding physical evidence."

"It's the only way. Especially after what happened tonight. If I open my mouth, I'll be the subject of an investigation, and our family will be the target of a murderer. I won't do it. Robberies happen every day of the week. No one's going to connect the break-in to the Rothberg. It's not like I owned the painting." Matthew paused, looking like a cornered rat. "Did I do the right thing by calling you? Or are you going to go to the FBI? They're your former employer. I'm your father. My future—our whole family's future—is in your hands."

There it was, pure and simple, laid out in the most basic way possible.

She'd tried. She'd failed. The whole situation sucked. But, in the end, there was no choice to make.

She had to protect her family.

"I have contacts in the private security sector. I'll call them."

Stark relief flashed across Matthew's face. "Thank you."

"Don't thank me. Gut instinct tells me I'm not doing you any favors. But I won't betray you. Let's just hope my instincts are wrong, and we're not making things worse." Sloane paused, drawing a sharp breath. "In any case, like I said, I have contacts. They'll keep an eye on the apartment—and more important, on you and Mom."

"And you?"

"I can take care of myself. Besides, I doubt any criminal would mess with me. Your murderer's research must have revealed my credentials—and my connection to the FBI. The last thing he'd want is to open that door. Things might get ugly."

"You're tough, Sloane, but you have your vulnerabilities," Matthew reminded her quietly.

Automatically, Sloane glanced down at her right hand. The sight wasn't pretty. The scars from the knife assault, and the three successive surgeries performed to save her life and her hand, were still prominent.

Her injury was her Achilles' heel. Everyone who knew her knew that.

"The murderer doesn't have me in his sights," she told her father. "He has you. As for Mom, the good news is that she didn't see your killer's hired hands. So I'm less worried about her—unless they decide to use her as leverage against you. That's why I want bodyguards on you both." Sloane flipped open her cell phone. "I'll make arrangements right away. After that, I want to go inside and see Mom. Oh, and I'll spend the next few days in the city, so I can be close by and keep an eye on you."

"What are you going to tell Derek?" Her father asked the million-dollar question.

A heartbeat of a pause. "Whatever the cops tell me. Nothing more."

FOUR

BILBAO, SPAIN

Dressed in white coveralls, the team of Albanian gunmen kept their heads lowered as they pushed the maintenance carts across the plaza. They looked like custodial workers—nondescript, virtually invisible to the patrons exiting the museum. Their caps were pulled down low, concealing their faces. No one noticed the stocking masks they'd yanked on moments earlier—masks that now completely distorted their facial features and hid their Mediterranean coloring.

The choice of museums had been deliberate.

The nearby Guggenheim Museum got all the attention. A prominent landmark, it had been targeted by the ETA, a Basque separatist group with a propensity for violence. In October 1997, just before the museum's grand opening, a guard had been killed there. As a result, the Guggenheim was packed with armed guards, making it too risky.

In contrast, security at the Museo de Arte Moderno was light. Just a few guards with batons, a couple of docents, and a curator. Very peaceful and serene—especially near closing time, which was only minutes away.

The gunmen reached the entrance. They grabbed their MP5Ks from inside the canvas utility carts where they'd been hidden. Bursting through the doors, they instantly overpowered the startled security guard, seized his baton, and ordered the frightened attendant to remain silent. In complete control, they forced their captives away from the entrance and shoved them through the museum at gunpoint. With speed, purpose, and an extensive knowledge of the floor plan, they made their way to the second level.

A minute and a half later, they were there.

Footsteps. Another security guard turned the corner. Using the just-confiscated baton, one muscular gunman dealt a punishing blow to his head. The guard's knees buckled, and he sank to the floor, unconscious.

Right on schedule, the well-trained team entered the display of nineteenth- and twentieth-century paintings. They headed first for the Cassatt. The tallest gunman pulled out a pair of wire cutters and snipped the wires that suspended the painting from the ceiling. He then turned to the adjacent wall and repeated the process, releasing the Bacon from its mounting wires. With both paintings safely in their possession, they headed to the other room and the works of those artists who inspired great national pride: Miró and Picasso.

An unexpected guard appeared on the scene and spotted them. He pulled his baton from its holster, lunging at the thieves and shouting, "*¡Ustedes! ¡Para!*"

They had no intention of stopping.

The team leader turned, releasing an explosive spray of bullets from his submachine gun. The first shots ripped the baton from the guard's hand, send-ing the baton tumbling to the ground and severing two fingers in the process. Bullets also pierced the guard's torso, puncturing his chest and shoulder. He screamed, lurching forward in agony. Instinctively, he reached over to clutch his mangled hand, dropping to his knees as he did. Another burst of fire and he was dead.

The other gunmen had already gone on to complete their mission. Once they'd secured the Miró and the Picasso, they turned to their leader for further instructions. He motioned for them to leave.

Blood was oozing from the dead guard's body and pooling around him, the last of his screams still echoing through the expansive building as the team of gunmen raced off. They passed stunned onlookers, who were frozen with fear as they tried to assess what had just happened. Once outside the museum, the gunmen dashed across the plaza with the four paintings and jumped into a white Mercedes Sprinter that had been waiting, engine running. The van screeched off, heading toward the A-8 and Santurtzi, where a cargo ship was departing tonight for the Philippine province of Cebu.

———

Derek shoved aside the foam cup on his desk. There was nothing left except the dregs of his third cup of morning coffee.

The coffee was foul. The weather was foul. And his mood was foul.

Swiveling around in his chair, Derek stared broodingly off into space. He'd waited for hours last night for Sloane to come home. She'd called twice from the hospital, both times giving him brief updates on her mother's condition, both times cutting the conversation short. When she'd finally gotten back to his place, she'd looked like hell—exhausted and stressed out. She'd greeted him and the hounds, taken a few halfhearted bites of lasagna, and provided him with details about the break-in that he already knew or could read in today's newspaper. A half hour later, she'd crawled into bed and fallen asleep.

This morning had been no better. She'd been asleep when he left for the gym, and gone when he returned, leaving a note saying she'd gone to the hospital to visit her mother, and hopefully, to expedite her release.

Sloane's worry over her mother was genuine. But it was crystal clear to Derek that she'd learned something else—something that her father had shared with her, and that she had no intention of sharing with him.

The worst-case scenario was that Matthew Burbank had done something illegal that linked him to Xiao Long, and that Sloane was protecting him. But that theory didn't fly. Sloane would never agree to hide information that kept organized criminals in business. Especially when it was Asian organized crime, the very gangs Derek was trying to bring down. Sure, Matthew could have lied to Sloane about who the players were or about the extent of his involvement. But Sloane was way too smart for that. If her father had fed her a line of crap, she'd see through it.

Besides, Matthew was an art dealer—well established, financially comfortable, with a clientele who was educated and affluent. What possible link could he have with a Dai Lo?

Xiao Long was a thug, not an art connoisseur. So maybe Derek was walking down the entirely wrong path. Maybe Matthew's career had nothing to do with this. Maybe he'd witnessed something he wasn't supposed to, something he didn't even recognize as significant until last night's robbery had shoved his nose in reality. Maybe he had no idea who he was dealing with, or, if he'd figured it out, what Xiao Long was capable of.

Finding his wife bound, gagged, and knocked unconscious would be a major eye-opener. It would certainly explain why Matthew would panic, and why he'd turn to his daughter rather than the cops. If he felt threatened, his first instinct would be to protect his family.

That had to be the explanation—not just for Matthew, but for Sloane. Her loyalty to her father, and her own independent pigheadedness, would spur her into action. She'd get whatever facts her father had, including any he might have omitted from his official police report, and then run with this alone.

She had no clue what kind of danger she'd be walking into.

That did it. Derek was going to insert himself in the situation—*now.*

Gripping the arms of his chair, he shoved himself around to face his desk. He'd finish up his critical work here, and then head over to the hospital, or the Burbanks' apartment if Rosalyn had already been released. He'd respectfully check on her recovery. And then, he was going to get Sloane alone and pry information out of her.

Reaching for his keyboard, he nearly knocked over his almost-empty coffee cup and a pile of paperwork.

Son of a bitch. His desk was a disaster. He didn't have a minute to organize it—not today. But, damn, he hated clutter.

The paradoxical thought almost made him laugh aloud. Clutter and the far corner of the twenty-second floor, where C-6's squad was located, went hand-in-hand. Boxes of confiscated goods—from fake Rolexes to equally fake Nike sneakers—were stacked everywhere. Getting from point A to point B meant weaving your way around the crap and through the aisles.

Derek always got a kick out of watching FBI shows on TV. In the Hollywood versions, the New York Field Office was usually a tall glass building that was a dead ringer for Trump Tower and that took up half a city block. Modern, expansive, and grand—it didn't even slightly resemble the perpetual construction zone that was 26 Federal Plaza. And the FBI's home in that building? Just eight floors in all. Too bad reality didn't emulate fiction. Bureau employees would be in hog heaven inside one of those TV buildings— glass-walled offices and spacious cubicles, all decorated with sleek, streamlined furnishings instead of what looked like rejects from a scratch-and-dent sale at a used furniture outlet.

So, C-6—or the Asian Criminal Enterprise Task Force, as it was formally known—existed in its old, cluttered splendor. On the plus side, at least there was a great view of the Brooklyn Bridge. And the ten agents and two NYPD detectives who constituted the squad were great to work with.

"Hey." Jeff poked his head over the top of Derek's cubicle. "What happened with Sloane last night? Did she say anything?"

"Yeah." Derek grimaced. "'Good night.'"

"You're kidding. No guess as to why her parents' place was broken into?"

"Nothing except the party line—that it was no secret that Matthew had collected some expensive pieces from his travels, that he and his wife were fairly well off, and that they both worked long hours—leaving an empty apartment that was a perfect target for thieves."

"Nice logic. Except for the fact that there's a full-time doorman there to dissuade thieves, and that we know it was Xiao Long's guys who did the breaking and entering."

Jeff's comment was greeted by silence.

"Are you going to confront her?" Despite the potential blowup that provoking Derek might elicit, Jeff wasn't ready to back off. "Or do you plan to let things slide and see what you can draw out of her without clueing her in to your motives?"

Derek slapped his hands on his desk, using the leverage to shove back his chair. "Tony's asked me that same question three times already," he retorted, referring to their boss, Supervisory Special Agent Antonio Sanchez.

"And?"

"And I'll tell you what I told him. We have no proof Matthew Burbank is involved in anything. He could be a target, not a criminal. As for Sloane, she's way too smart for games. Whatever her father told her, she's not about to be fooled by supposedly subtle attempts to pump her for information. She's also not about to spill her guts if she chooses not to—with or without a confrontation. One thing's for sure—if she planned to tell me what her father said, she would have done so last night." Derek got to his feet. "I need more coffee." He walked around Jeff and snaked his way down the aisle.

He was irked at the situation, worried about Sloane, and pissed off for being in the position he was in. His whole squad had been eyeing him speculatively since they arrived. They all knew what the wiretap on Xiao Long's phone had revealed last night. They all knew about his relationship with Sloane. And they all knew it was her parents' house that had been robbed.

He couldn't look at their curious expressions anymore.

He poured a cup of coffee and kept walking. He hoped one of the interviewing rooms was empty. It was either that or a men's room stall. He really needed to be alone or he'd explode. And this situation warranted logic, not emotion.

Easier said than done.

He rounded the corner to the interviewing rooms. The first one was occupied. So was the second. He was about to turn away when he happened to glance inside—and what he saw made him stop dead in his tracks. There, deep in discussion with his subject, was SA Rich Williams.

Rich was the senior agent on the Art Crime Team, and one of the SAs Derek most respected. Silver-haired and distinguished, Rich handled cases of art theft, art fraud—you name it. He'd been doing it for decades, since long before the Art Crime Team was officially formed several years back. He often worked undercover, especially when the case he was cracking was international in scope.

He and Derek had met more than twelve years ago, during Derek's initial training at Quantico, when Rich had given a guest lecture on interstate trafficking of stolen property. Derek had been so impressed by the colorful agent—his knowledge and insights—that he'd waited until after the lecture and introduced himself, asking half a dozen questions. Rich had been generous with his time, and was as impressed by Derek's big-picture mentality as Derek was by Rich's experience and expertise.

Since then, they'd stayed in touch, especially after Derek was transferred to Rich's home turf—the New York Field Office. They caught a drink together when Rich's time permitted, and talked Bureau politics, world events, and life in general. They also made sure to good-naturedly one-up each other on the subject of the military, since Derek was a former Army Ranger and Rich was a former marine.

The Art Crime Team was part of the Major Theft Squad, which was also on the twenty-second floor. So seeing Rich interviewing a subject here wasn't what startled Derek. What startled him was the man being interviewed.

Matthew Burbank.

For a long moment, Derek peered through the glass, watching Matthew's body language as he answered Rich's questions. He was definitely unsettled. Then again, Rich had a way of doing that to people. With his laid-back demeanor and that great poker face, he usually threw people off and found a way to make them talk.

Filled with questions of his own, Derek turned away long enough to stop a computer tech who was passing by. "Hey, Gus, do me a favor," he said. "Poke your head in there and ask Agent Williams to step outside for a minute. And don't mention my name in front of the guy he's interviewing, okay?"

Gus looked perplexed, but he nodded. "Okay." He walked over, knocked on the door, and went inside long enough to follow Derek's instructions.

Without a flicker of reaction, Rich came to his feet. "Excuse me," he said to Matthew. "This will only take a moment." He buttoned his blazer and left the room, shutting the door behind him.

He spotted Derek right away, even as Gus explained that it was Agent Parker who wanted to see him.

"That's fine, Gus. Thanks." Rich looked more intrigued than surprised to see Derek. He waited until the computer tech had continued on his way before speaking his mind. "That was fast. How did you find out I was interviewing Burbank?"

"I didn't." Derek's reply was equally as direct. "I just happened to walk by and see you." His gaze flickered from Rich's face to inside the room where Matthew was fidgeting. "What's this about?"

"Long story." Concisely, Rich filled Derek in on the two copies of *Dead or Alive* and the sketchy provenance his team had pieced together on each. "Given your relationship with Burbank's daughter, I planned to run all this by you after I heard what Burbank had to say. If any additional facts or perspective exist that you can provide, I want them. As of now, I have no reason to suspect the man of anything, other than being in the wrong place at the wrong time."

"But the wrong place happened to be in Hong Kong," Derek muttered, frowning as he contemplated what Rich had told him. "And the wrong time happened to be when a murder was committed there, in a region where murders are rare. That's one too many coincidences to me, in light of what happened last night."

"Last night?"

Derek told Rich about the burglary, and about the tidbit C-6 had picked up on Xiao Long's wiretap.

"Interesting." Rich ingested that thoughtfully. "Burbank never mentioned the break-in. I'll bring up the subject, and ask him about that omission as soon as I go back in there. He's probably just shell-shocked. And, other than the nationality of the criminals, there's nothing linking the two incidents, and nothing tying Burbank and his investment group to the murder."

"His group sold the murder victim one of the Rothbergs."

"Yes, but the paper trail tells us they sold Cai Wen the original, not the fake. That eliminates motive. And Cai Wen wasn't exactly squeaky clean. We're still investigating him and his clientele, but it looks like it runs the gamut—from trustworthy to questionable. Any of the questionables could have been involved. There's also a gap in the provenance. No sales records for the painting from when Cai Wen was killed in 1995 until the painting resurfaced five years later in the private gallery of a Dutch collector."

"Did you question the collector?"

"He died of natural causes a few years ago, and his heirs recently submitted *Dead or Alive* to Sotheby's for auction. The painting showed up in their current catalog at the same time the forgery showed up in the Christie's catalog. That's where we came in."

"So whoever killed Cai Wen stole the painting and sold it to an anonymous source."

"Where it could have changed hands any number of times before finding its way to the Netherlands."

"Talk about complicated." Derek whistled, and rubbed the back of his neck.

"Welcome to my world." Rich gave a tight-lipped smile. "For what it's worth, I've spent the last hour interviewing Burbank, and I'd be really surprised if he's involved with organized crime. If this Xiao Long is targeting him, it's probably because he saw or heard something he shouldn't have. But I tell you what. I'll find a way to drop in your Dai Lo's name, just to see if Burbank reacts. If there's a connection, I'll spot it. And I'll stop by your desk afterward to fill you in."

"That works."

Rich had just turned to go back into the interviewing room when another agent from the Major Theft Squad strode over. "Rich. Sorry to interrupt, but you've got an urgent phone call from Interpol. The Museo de Arte Moderno in Bilbao was just hit. The story is already breaking on Fox News and CNN."

"On my way." Rich was already in motion. "Do me a favor," he directed his coworker. "I'm interviewing someone—Matthew Burbank—in there." He jerked his thumb in the direction of the interviewing room. "Would you just tell him something urgent came up, and ask him to please wait. Tell him I'll be in as soon as I can." A quick glance at Derek. "Somehow I doubt you want to do it."

"You got that right."

Rosalyn Burbank sank back in one of the pebbled chocolate leather sofas in her living room. Gratefully, she accepted the cup of tea her daughter had brought her, at the same time turning her trained smile on Derek.

"I appreciate your dropping by, Derek. I also apologize for the mess. The cleaning team I hired is still putting things back in order. But, as you can see, we're almost there. Myself included." Gingerly, she rubbed the side of her head. "No permanent damage. Certainly nothing that won't return to normal in a few days."

"I'm glad to hear that." Derek stood against the far wall of the living room, his arms folded across his chest, his body language conveying that he had no intention of making this a long visit. "Sloane said you defended yourself like a pro. Maybe you should take up Krav Maga and give your daughter a run for her money."

Amusement flickered in Rosalyn's eyes. "I don't think so. Not at this stage of my life. But, you never know. I did knee one of those animals in the groin. I hope he's doubled over for weeks." Her smile vanished. "I just wish I'd understood what they were saying. I should have joined Sloane on those trips she took to the Far East with her father. Then maybe I could tell the police something useful. As it is, all I'm sure of is that the thieves sounded like they were young—early twenties. And they weren't speaking Mandarin; I have a feel for that from hearing Matthew on the phone. Their phrases sounded way too guttural. Not that that's helpful. There are more Chinese dialects than I can count. And frankly, my main focus was on keeping myself alive. So I couldn't give the detectives much to go on."

"I'm sure you told them whatever you could." Derek felt Sloane's probing stare. It didn't take a genius to figure out that she was trying to gauge his real reason for dropping by. And if that reason was to pry information out of her mother, she'd be applying the brakes—forcibly.

Derek could have saved her the aggravation. Whatever information he wanted, he wanted from her, not her mother.

Purposefully, he straightened. "I'm sure the NYPD launched a full-scale investigation. They'll come up with answers. I'm just glad to see you looking so well," he concluded, his brows lifting in question. "Actually, I was wondering if I could borrow Sloane for a while—if you feel up to sparing her."

Realization flashed in Rosalyn's eyes. "This is the week you're supposed to move into the cottage." She shot Sloane a rueful look. "I'm sorry. I forgot all about it. This must have caused a major chink in your plans."

"Not at all." Derek answered before Sloane could. "Given the circumstances, I assumed Sloane would want to be here with you. Besides, moving's a bigger hassle than I thought, especially since I'm practically married to my job. So I'll spend my evenings driving boxes over to New Jersey. Sloane's welcome to stay at my place until you're fully recovered."

"Nonsense." Rosalyn waved away the idea. "Matthew hired a private nurse until my hospital recheck at the end of the week. After that, it'll be business as usual. Now go." Another wave, this time toward the door. "Both of you. Stop by your place and pick up the hounds. Take them for a walk. Then plan your move. I'm absolutely fine."

Sloane hesitated, clearly not eager to talk to Derek alone.

"Go on," Rosalyn reiterated, shooing her daughter off. "Your father's due home soon anyway. He had an early morning meeting. And Lana, my nurse, is in the kitchen, getting my pain medication. So I'm in excellent hands."

"Okay." Sloane relented, scooping up her jacket. "But I'll be back later to check on you."

Ignoring her mother's protests, Sloane led Derek out of the apartment. She made sure to double-lock the front door.

The elevator ride was silent, and there was definite tension in the air.

Sloane turned up her jacket collar as they stepped outside and began to walk. "It's cooler than I realized."

"Don't," Derek stated flatly.

"Don't what?"

"Patronize me with small talk. It's not going to work. Something's going on. And you're going to tell me what it is."

Sloane blew out a breath. "If this is about your moving in, I'm not getting cold feet. Just be patient for a few more days, a week tops. Once my mother's gotten the green light from her doctor . . ."

"Cut it out, Sloane. I mean it. I'm not talking about the move. It's waited this long. It can wait another week. This is about whatever's going on with your father."

"Their place being robbed and my mother being knocked unconscious isn't enough?"

"It's plenty. But you're keeping something from me. We're not going that route—not again. So I'm asking you straight out—what is it?"

Sloane stopped dead in her tracks, ignoring the pedestrian traffic that parted to get around them, and the glares of the people as they passed by. She turned to face Derek. "Fine. I won't patronize you. And I won't lie to you. I'll just say that I'm not at liberty to discuss this. It's confidential. Which is no different than it would be with any other client."

Client privilege. So she was playing it that way.

Derek was almost relieved. At least she was being straight with him, even if she was ducking his question with a ridiculous excuse. "I understand."

Surprised darted across Sloane's face. "Do you?"

"Better than you think."

"And you're going to just leave it at that?" she asked warily.

"Now *that* I didn't say. I *do* understand. I don't like it, but I understand. So I'll follow your rules and be just as vague as you're being."

"Meaning?"

"Meaning you'll never guess who I spotted at the New York Field Office an hour ago. Then again, I'm sure you already know. That must have been where his morning meeting was."

Sloane didn't flinch. "Fine. So you saw my father."

"Last I heard, it was the NYPD who handled routine burglaries. Then again, this wasn't about the burglary, was it?"

No response.

"Did I ever mention to you that I have a close colleague at the Major Theft Squad? Actually, he's the senior agent on the Art Crime Team."

This time, Sloane started.

"Ah. So you get my drift. Any idea what the Art Crime Team wants with your father? Because I'd much rather hear it from you than the other way around."

Sloane's eyes began to blaze. "Why are you so interested in this?"

"Because I think you're in over your head. And I don't think even you know how far."

CHAPTER FIVE

Xiao Long, or "Little Dragon," as his street name translated into English, crossed the street with his driver, who also served as his bodyguard. The driver unlocked the doors of Xiao's Mercedes sedan, and Xiao slid into the backseat. He popped a couple of aspirin in his mouth, swallowing them with a gulp of bottled water. His head ached from the effort of carrying on a conversation in unbroken English. His client, the rich collector Wallace Johnson, was a world traveler, so he spoke some Mandarin and Cantonese, but not enough to conduct a whole business exchange. So they used English. As for Xiao's native dialect of Fukienese? That was far too low-class for Johnson. *Xiao* was too low-class for Johnson. The old man treated him like a stupid delivery boy. Which, in his eyes, he was.

The irony of that was almost funny. Education didn't make a man smart, only well read. Xiao was smart. It was *he* who was the spider, and Johnson the fly. The pathetic old fool had no idea who he was dealing with, or the power he wielded.

He'd shudder if he knew the lengths Xiao had gone to in order to secure his position. And he'd be terrorized if he knew how far Xiao would be willing to go to preserve and increase his power.

Success was his. He was already the Dai Lo of the Red Dragons, hand chosen and sent to the United States by the triad's Dragon Head himself. And that was just the beginning. He'd come from nothing, clawed and killed his way to something, and stood on the brink of becoming the supreme leader.

And Johnson? He was on his way to hell.

Xiao ordered his driver to go. The bodyguard obeyed instantly, inserting the key in the ignition and turning over the motor. The car hummed to life. Xiao gazed across the street at the sprawling manor as they pulled away from the curb. Then, he plucked the disposable cell phone out of his jacket pocket. It had been purchased for him by one of his Red Dragon kids this morning.

The first call he made was to the bank. This time speaking in Cantonese, he confirmed that the wire transfer was complete. All of the five hundred thousand dollars that had been deposited in his Cayman Islands account earlier this week had been transferred to the designated account in Hong Kong. Ten percent of the full five million the Cassatt was worth when it hung in the Museo de Arte Moderno. An excellent price for a stolen masterpiece that would be far too recognizable to sell. Then again, the world would never see this painting again. Its buyer had other plans.

The second call Xiao Long made was to Hong Kong. For that call, he spoke in the unique dialect of the Loong Doo region of Guangdong. He'd learned it for a reason. And that reason was at the other end of the phone.

Xiao Long provided the facts. The deal had gone off as always. Clean. No hitches. No attempts to renegotiate. One week after the museum theft, Johnson had his painting, and the Dragon Head's bank account had received payment in full.

That was all the Dragon Head needed to know. Until further instructions were issued, the rest was Xiao Long's problem. And he'd handle it any way he had to.

He was far too shrewd not to have noticed a change in Johnson. The procedure they'd just gone through might have been the same, but the mood that went with it was different. Johnson had been nervous. It was no secret why. The FBI and their fucking investigation. Johnson being on their interview list. The fact that Jin Huang, Xiao Long's enforcer, had paid Johnson a visit, warning him to keep his mouth shut. And the knowledge that the art collection Johnson owned could send him to jail. There was plenty to make the old guy nervous.

Doubtful that Johnson would crack. He hadn't even been there. And to tell any more of the truth would mean screwing himself or getting himself killed.

But it would also mean screwing them. And the Dragon Head wouldn't tolerate that. Especially not at Johnson's hands. Nor would the Dragon Head forgive.

It was Xiao Long's future on the line. He'd ensure it at all costs.

With that in mind, he picked up the phone again to make a quick call to Jin Huang.

Words were one thing. Pain was another. A small reminder of the consequences was needed.

Soon, a reminder wouldn't suffice. The Dragon Head would be finished toying with Johnson. He'd order him killed. His partners, as well. Xiao would personally carry out those orders, inflicting the greatest amount of pain possible before ending their lives.

The pleasure would be all his.

Sloane let herself into Derek's apartment, simultaneously tossing her tote bag into the closet and shrugging out of her jacket.

Long, hard day. Cranky human resources manager who wasn't a big fan of consultants, their seminars, or their steep rates. Although she had been interested enough to stick around while Sloane trained the staff of Adler and Berber, the prominent security company that had hired her to educate them in the newest techniques of crisis negotiations. That HR exec was singing a different tune by the time Sloane left.

It was a win-win. Sloane did her job, the company was satisfied, and she had time to check in privately with the first shift of the security team she'd hired to protect her parents. The relief team was on the job now, and she checked in with them by phone.

So far, so good. No one else following her father or mother around, and no subtle visitors hanging around the apartment.

That had to be good news. It meant that, more than a full week after her father had been interviewed by the FBI, he wasn't being regarded as an immediate threat—not to the Chinese killer and not to the Bureau.

Who was she kidding, she thought with a frown. That whole line of thinking was a crock.

She was swimming with sharks and she knew it.

Her father and his art group colleagues were convinced that they'd come through their respective FBI interviews unscathed.

She knew better, even without having been there.

FBI agents were pros at questioning. If every member of that investment group had parroted the exact same story, while no doubt fidgeting and worrying about blowing his lines, then red flags would be raised. She'd tried to counteract that. She'd talked her father into calling all the other guys after his own meeting, to urge them to vary their exact recollections of what had happened so they wouldn't sound so rehearsed. Had they pulled it off? Doubtful. They weren't actors. They were frightened men.

Her father also had no clue that Derek had seen him at the Field Office on the day he was questioned. If she'd told him, he would have been even more scared—which was the last thing he needed to be right now. He had to stay calm, act normal, and focus on keeping himself and her mother safe. That meant following their normal routines and making sure to stay in plain sight of the security guards Sloane had hired.

But she was worried. She'd heard the gravity of Derek's warning, seen the intensity in his eyes. He'd all but told her he had an inside track—one that put him a step ahead of her and clued him in to the fact that whatever her father was hiding was putting her family in danger.

That could only mean that there was a link to Asian organized crime. But how strong a link? If whoever killed Cai Wen was affiliated with a gang Derek's squad was investigating, then they'd be one step closer to putting her father at the scene of the crime.

And that would put him one trigger-pull away from being killed.

"Hey."

Sloane nearly jumped out of her skin as Derek appeared in the bedroom doorway.

"Hi." She went for honest; lying would be pointless and stupid. He'd already seen her reaction at the sound of his voice. "You scared the hell out of me."

"Why? I live here—for now." Crossing over, Derek poured two glasses of the Chianti they had yet to drink, and offered her one. "Here. You look like you could use this."

"You're right. I could." Sloane took the proffered glass. Her first sip was more like a gulp. Her right hand trembled a little, and she transferred the goblet to her left.

Derek's sharp gaze took in the motion. "Bad day with your hand?" he asked, genuine concern in his voice.

"A grueling OT session this morning," Sloane replied, referring to the occupational therapy she still religiously, and rigorously, endured.

The Hospital for Special Surgery at New York Weill Cornell Medical Center was the best, and so were Dr. Charles Houghton, her surgeon, and Constance Griggs, her hand therapist.

"Connie's determined to push me right back into the Bureau—right hand first," Sloane added wryly. "Then again, she's always been an optimist."

"Maybe you're ready."

A dubious shake of her head. "My dexterity's still not where it needs to be. Sure, I can fire my weapon now. It would be pretty sad if I couldn't, since I'm at Fort Dix weekly getting firearms training."

"That's a huge step for someone who couldn't hold a pistol two months ago."

"Fine. I've made progress. But my aim is mediocre when it comes to rapid fire, and my trigger finger's still weak. I'm pushing myself as hard as I can, and then some. But I'm just not there."

"You will be."

Derek was always so damned sure—when it came to them, and when it came to this. She couldn't make that claim. Sometimes she waffled. Sometimes she was terrified. And sometimes the bitterness ate away at her. Then again, she was the one who'd lost a chunk of her life doing the job that she loved, being with the man she loved.

And for what? Lousy judgment. Doing a hell of a job defusing a hostage crisis in a bank barricade, and then blowing all her hard work by acting like a stupid newbie. Not waiting for backup. Single-handedly chasing down the one scrawny teenage punk who'd gotten away. Cornering him in an alley, and assuming the threat was eliminated once he'd dropped his weapon and was on his knees. Then finding out he was smarter than she was. He'd whipped out a knife he'd stashed in his boot, and sliced up the tendons, nerves, and flesh of her right hand.

Three surgeries and seventeen months of occupational therapy later, she still wasn't whole. Maybe she never would be.

"Cut the self-doubt," Derek instructed, reading the emotions on her face. "You suck at it. Besides, you want back into the Bureau so bad you can taste it. Combine that with the fact that you're stubborn as a mule, and you're practically a special agent again."

Sloane arched a brow. "Ya think? I'm not so sure. I mean, regaining my skills is one thing. But rejoining the Bureau? It would mean a major pay cut. Going from private consulting to federal law enforcement—it's usually the other way around, isn't it? Plus, by the time I'm ready, I'll have been out for almost two years. I'll get as many recommendations as I can, but I'll probably have to go through the whole training program again. Twenty weeks at the FBI Academy at Quantico, plus weeks of brush-up in crisis negotiations. Not to mention . . ."

"Not to mention you want it almost as much as you want me."

Sloane blinked, then dissolved into laughter. "You lend new meaning to the word 'arrogant.'"

"Yeah, but I'm incredible in bed."

"True." Sloane took another sip of Chianti. "That's why I put up with the rest."

"Put up with it at your place."

Derek's words cut through their banter like a knife.

He put down his glass and walked around to grip her shoulders. "Sloane, you can't babysit your parents forever. I know you're investigating something. And I know it involves your father. If you'd let me, I could help." *Unless he's guilty of a crime* was omitted but clearly implied. "It would make whatever this is go away that much faster."

"Maybe. But whether or not I talk to you isn't my decision." A pointed stare. "Just like filling in for me whatever details you know that might help, or at least telling me what I'm up against, isn't yours."

"Fine." Impatience laced Derek's tone. "Then let's call it a draw and move into your place."

"So we can get me far away from the danger you alluded to? So you can protect me?"

"Partly. Partly so we can live together."

"We're already living together. I've slept here every night this week."

"Out of necessity. This is a temporary hangout for you, and for us; a place to stay over when we're stuck late in the city. But a home? No way. It's a coffin with a bathroom, with the continuous rumble of Midtown Tunnel traffic for mood music. You've got a cozy cottage, seven acres, and three hounds who are about to mutiny if they're locked up in this place much longer. And I'll be joining them."

Sloane could feel herself losing this argument.

So could Derek.

"Most of my stuff is already at your place," he continued, then went in for the kill. "So's your archery range, by the way. You haven't practiced in almost a week."

Inhaling sharply, Sloane glared at him. "That was low."

"It was honest. Manipulative, but honest."

She couldn't deny that one. Archery had always been her thing. She'd been captain of every archery team she participated in since high school. She loved the focus and the self-competitive edge, the way it cleared her mind and honed her skills. And since her injury, it had been a lifesaver. It did wonders for her concentration, her aim, and her strength training. These days, her arrow was hitting the bull's-eye more often than not—or at least it had been, before this whole crisis with her father had relegated her to Manhattan.

"The clock is ticking." Sloane spoke one of her greatest fears aloud. "I'm close to finishing my hand therapy." She glanced down at her scarred palm. "Connie made it clear; two years is the limit. After that, whatever nerve damage is left will probably be permanent. So, yes, I need to get back home."

"Say the word and we're there," Derek urged quietly. "There's nothing standing in the way but you."

"I know." A pause. "I'm still going to be driving into Manhattan."

"I never assumed otherwise. You've been commuting here regularly ever since you moved to Hunterdon County—to see clients, friends, your hand therapist, and now your parents. Go wherever you want. Just come home to me."

"Okay." Slowly, Sloane nodded. "Tonight's my father's weekly poker game. I'll talk to him then. Oh, and Derek?"

"Hmmm?"

"He's not guilty of anything."

"If you say so."

Wallace took another sip of his martini. He had to head back to the city. Even if he sped, it was a two-and-a-half-hour drive. He'd be an hour late as it was. The game normally started at eight. Tonight, it was at Matthew's place. Rosalyn was venturing out for a business dinner, so she wouldn't be home. And the group of them needed to talk—alone. He had to be there.

But he couldn't leave. Not yet. He couldn't tear himself away.

He'd hung the new painting in his private gallery with the others. This Cassatt had been costly. And the risk was enormous.

But it had been worth it.

He leaned back in the leather swivel recliner that was at the center of the room. From there, he could turn in any direction and view any masterpiece in his collection—or take in the entire collection at once. Some of the paintings were high-end, like the Renoirs and the Cassatts. Others were far less pricey, often created by up-and-coming, and even local, artists. Cost wasn't the issue. Content was.

He studied the new addition to his private gallery with deep gratification. His life was a facade, the world simply a stage upon which to enact the charade.

This room was his only sanctuary.

The clock in the upstairs hallway chimed six-thirty.

Reluctantly, he rose, setting down his martini glass and taking in the exquisite painting for one long moment. Yes, acquiring this one had been worth the risk.

He climbed the stairs, flipped off the light, and shut and locked the door. This room was off-limits to everyone—family, friends, and colleagues alike.

He shrugged into his jacket and headed for the garage. He was just opening the door to his Jaguar when he sensed someone behind him.

He barely had time to turn when a foot slammed into his stomach. The impact sent him sprawling to the concrete floor. He lay there, groaning, doubled up with pain, and gazed up at his attacker.

The dark, emotionless eyes that stared into his belonged to the same brawny Asian man who'd been here earlier in the week. The threat he'd issued then had been menacingly clear. He'd shattered an antique mirror, sending shards of glass scattering all over the hall. With a gloved hand, he'd picked up the longest piece and held it to Wallace's throat. "FBI. You say nothing," he'd warned in broken English.

"I won't," Wallace had gasped. "I have nothing to tell them."

"Good."

He was gone as quickly as he'd come.

Now he pinned Wallace to the ground, one knee planted squarely across his throat, squeezing his windpipe.

"I didn't say a word," Wallace wheezed out. "I . . . swear . . ."

The dull-eyed thug leaned into him, increasing the pressure on Wallace's throat with his knee until Wallace couldn't drag air into his lungs, the other knee pressing into Wallace's bruised kidney. The agony was beyond bearing.

"I . . . can't . . . breathe . . ." he managed. "You're . . . killing . . . me . . ."

"No," Jin Huang replied tonelessly. "This not kill. This not even pain. When I kill, *then* pain. So bad you beg to die quick. But you die slow. Very slow. Tell friends tonight, don't talk. Or everyone dies—slow."

CHAPTER SIX

The poker game was in full swing when Sloane walked in.

There had been a low, tense conversation going on among the men. It came to an abrupt halt the moment she entered the living room.

Sloane wasn't surprised. It felt weird, given she'd known these men her entire life. But she got it. They weren't sure how much her father had shared with her, even if he'd reassured them he'd said nothing. And she wasn't a curious little girl anymore, or even a ballsy teenager. She was a grown woman, a former FBI agent, and a threat.

"Hi, all," she greeted them casually, pretending she hadn't noticed the lull in conversation. She plucked an apple out of the fruit bowl her mother had no doubt put out. The rest of the snacks were her father's contribution—a platter of deli sandwiches from the Second Avenue deli, bowls of mixed nuts and chips, and, judging from the half-empty bottles on the card table, a couple six-packs of Sam Adams, plus one six-pack of O'Doul's for Ben Martino, who was a recovering alcoholic. He had yet to break into the O'Doul's, but the night was young.

No shocker that her apple was the first thing missing from the fruit bowl.

"Sloane." Ben slapped down his cards and jumped up to give her a paternal hug. He was a demonstrative guy, not to mention a high-strung type A perpetual motion machine. Sloane remembered visiting his clothing manufacturing company as a child and watching him pace back and forth, doing everything from overseeing the seamstresses to reworking the patterns himself. The only time he sat in one place was during these weekly poker games, and even then he fidgeted, tapped his foot, or perched at the edge of his seat like an eagle about to take flight. He looked like an eagle, too, with his beakish nose, sharp dark eyes, and close cap of gray-white hair.

"It's great to see you," he told her, tugging a lock of her hair the way he used to when she was a kid. "It's been way too long."

Sloane smiled, struck by a wave of nostalgia. "Yes, it has."

She'd seen her father's friends occasionally these past few years, but never all together, and never at the card table. In fact, she hadn't dropped in on the poker game since her days at the Manhattan D.A.'s Office. She'd left to join the FBI, gone down to Quantico for her new-agent training, and moved to Cleveland for her first Field Office assignment. By that time, her parents had moved to Florida. They'd only moved back four or five months ago, and she'd been too busy to visit them for more than a few hours at a time.

So, yes, it had been ages since she'd dropped in on the infamous poker game. But her memories of watching, learning, and ultimately sitting in for a few hands of Texas Hold 'Em were warm and fuzzy.

She hugged Ben back. Talk about hyper. He was normally tightly strung, but tonight he was practically vibrating. "How's your new grandson?" she asked, hoping to ease the tension by bringing up his favorite subject: his family.

It worked, and Ben visibly relaxed—as much as he was capable of relaxing. "He's great. He's only four months old, and he's cutting his first tooth. Personally, I think he's also trying to talk. A real genius."

"Gurgling isn't talking, Ben," Leo Fox informed him, striving for a touch of his customary levity. "Except in your case. You talk so fast, gurgling is easier to understand." He winked at Sloane, and then averted his gaze, seemingly examining his cards before looking back at her.

Sloane noticed that his face and neck were flushed.

"You look prettier every time I see you," he claimed. "Which reminds me, your father tells me your boyfriend's moving in. That means your cottage needs a makeover. Give me a call and I'll make it happen."

"Thank you, Leo," Sloane replied, her gratitude visible and sincere. Leo was an interior designer, and a good one. He was in high demand. And since neither she nor Derek had a flair for decorating, she'd be thrilled for Leo to take over. "That's a really kind offer. And, boy, do I need it. So does Derek. He's been making some not-so-subtle comments about moving into a 'chick pad.' I'm sure he'd appreciate a few masculine touches."

"Of course he would."

After that, the rest of the men said their hellos as well.

Phil Leary, a certified financial adviser and CPA, and the number cruncher of the art group, was normally quiet. Tonight he was downright subdued, and he kept swallowing, as if there was something caught in his throat.

"I'd be happy to help you select a few art pieces." Wallace Johnson, who'd been sitting out this hand, slid forward on the sofa and picked up his bottle of beer to polish it off. He owned two art galleries; one in Manhattan, and one in East Hampton, near his suburban estate. "Some modern paintings would complement Leo's work nicely."

Wallace was the odd duck of the group. Unlike the others, who came from middle-class backgrounds, Wallace hailed from a wealthy family. His speech and demeanor carried a touch of a patrician air, as did his taste in gourmet food, fine wine, and an elegant lifestyle. But the class difference never intruded on the long-standing friendship he had with these men, or with their business partnership.

Art was their common bond. In Wallace's case, it was his passion, and always had been. But owning the galleries was his second career, one he'd started the April before last, and under tragic circumstances. He'd been an investment banker for over thirty years—until tragedy had rocked his world. His and his wife Beatrice's five-year-old daughter had been killed by a hit-and-run driver, one whose identity the police had never uncovered. It had destroyed his career, his marriage, his entire being. Little Sophie had been his heart and his soul. He hadn't been the same since he'd lost her.

He hid his grief well. But every once in a while, Sloane would see the over-whelming emptiness in his eyes. It was heartbreaking.

"Paintings from your gallery would be wonderful," she told him warmly. "Between you and Leo, the cottage will get a makeover worthy of *Architectural Digest*. Derek will be overjoyed—and spoiled rotten."

"Yeah, we don't want that to happen," her father muttered. "I expect *him* to spoil *you*, not the other way around."

"I'll be sure to tell him that." Sloane was listening, but her attention was on Wallace. She frowned as he rose, grimacing before he made his way over to the table of refreshments.

"Are you all right?" she asked.

"More or less." His voice, which Sloane had noticed was hoarse, rasped as he spoke. "Fighting a cold or the flu." He put half a roast beef sandwich on a paper plate, then leaned past the tray to grab a Sam Adams from the ice bucket. It was as if the food was for show, when all he really wanted was the beer. Which was odd, because Wallace didn't usually drink much at the poker games. Fine wine was his thing, not beer.

He must have noticed the puzzlement on Sloane's face as he turned away, because he drily added, "Your father's wine collection is sadly lacking. So I'm settling for this to ward off the chills."

Wallace was wearing a turtleneck on an autumn night that was relatively warm. And his forehead was dotted with beads of perspiration. Maybe he had a fever, or else he was as unnerved as the others.

"Go sit down," she urged, playing along with his charade. "You need more than half a roast beef sandwich if you want to fight off the flu. I'll bring you a plate." She did just that, her frown deepening as Wallace coughed and rubbed his throat before sinking down heavily onto the sofa. "Maybe you should go home to bed."

"Nonsense." He waved away her suggestion, putting the bottle of beer to his lips and taking a healthy swallow. "The game will take my mind off the annoyance of catching a cold. Besides, the aspirin Rosalyn gave me before she left are starting to kick in."

"Left?" Sloane's brows rose in supposed surprise. "Where did she go? I wanted to check on her."

"She's at a publishing dinner," Matthew supplied. "You tried to talk her out of going, remember?"

"I remember. I thought I'd won that argument."

"You know your mother better than that. She was getting cabin fever." A pointed glance, reminding Sloane not to refer to the security guard she'd hired—or anything else that might clue his friends in to figuring out she was in the loop. "Her doctor gave her the green light, if that makes you feel better."

"Okay, you got me." Sloane had planned this from the start. It was why she'd come at the tail end of their game, rather than earlier. She could accomplish everything she needed to, then take off. "Mom told me she was going to that dinner. She also told me you'd have plenty of company, since the poker game was here tonight. And, since I'd cleared my work schedule to play Mother Hen, and since Mom wasn't going to be here to put up with it, I couldn't resist dropping by to play a few hands—just like old times."

"You mean trying to clean us out—just like old times," Phil amended.

Sloane grinned. "Well, something has to pay for redecorating and accessorizing the cottage. And, by the way, not *trying—succeeding* in cleaning you out."

"Back then, we let you cheat," Ben informed her. "Not anymore. Not since you grew up and started using the strategies we taught you against us. Now it's every man—and woman—for himself."

"Sounds fair." Sloane nodded, already walking toward the kitchen. "Finish your hand. I'll grab more beers from the fridge. And then, with all due respect, you can kiss your money good-bye."

———

An hour later, the group disbanded.

The men yanked on their jackets and left, looking far more on edge about Sloane standing in the living room waiting for Matthew than they did about the cash they'd lost to her at the poker table.

"Aren't you heading home, too?" Phil turned in the doorway to ask, striving for nonchalance and failing. "It's late. And it's a long drive to that rural part of New Jersey you live in."

"Not to worry." Sloane strove for nonchalance, too. "I'm staying at Derek's apartment in the city tonight." A quick glance at her watch. "Actually, I promised to meet him for a drink in a half hour—a drink I also promised to pay for, since I knew I'd win." She gave Phil an easy smile. "I just need to talk to my father for a minute. He's the only one who'll tell me how my mother *really* feels. She tells me only what she wants me to hear."

"I understand." The way Phil's features relaxed told Sloane he believed her. "Then I'll let you two talk. And don't be a stranger."

"Yeah, but don't join the game either," Leo chimed in as he followed Phil out the door. "I've got a mortgage to pay." He squeezed her shoulder. "I expect to hear from you. Between Wallace and me, we'll make a cozy home for you and your guy."

"I'm counting on it. Thank you both. Oh, and Wallace"—Sloane stepped into the hall to speak to him—"I assume you're not driving out to the Hamptons tonight. Not with that flu coming on."

"No," he replied. "I'm staying at my place in the city." A tight smile. "I always do after our poker games—and the inferior alcohol that goes along with them."

"Good. Take care of yourself."

Sloane stepped back inside and shut the door, more convinced than ever that there wasn't a shot in hell these men had fooled the FBI agent who'd interviewed them.

"Did you get what you wanted?" Matthew demanded. "Do you believe everyone here is innocent?"

Sloane turned to face her father. "I never doubted their innocence. Their acting ability? Now that's another matter entirely."

"Meaning?"

"Meaning I walked into a freaked-out meeting of the Knights of the Round Table. Things rapidly deteriorated the longer I stayed. And that's given the fact that you told them I'm clueless about everything except the burglary."

Her father began nervously gathering up empty beer bottles. "So you don't think the FBI bought our story."

"No way. Every one of those guys is a mess." Sloane raked a hand through her hair. "I wish you'd let me talk to Derek."

"We've been over this before. The answer's still no. Look, Sloane, not one of us has been contacted again by that Special Agent Williams. So he must have accepted our story and assumed we were just nervous about being interviewed by the FBI." Matthew continued cleaning up, tossing dirty paper plates into a large trash bag. "We're no longer on their radar. Period."

"You're burying your head in the sand. FBI investigations take months, sometimes years. If they'd figured out what happened with the real and the fake Rothbergs, the story would be out. The media would be all over it. This one's juicy. A man was murdered. And, according to the provenance, you guys were the last ones to do business with him before he was killed; maybe even the last ones to see him alive."

"We didn't kill Cai Wen. They can't charge us with anything."

"Oh, come on, Dad." Sloane walked over and planted herself in his face. "You're not naive. You know that the law isn't always fair, or right. Besides, this is about more than your innocence. It's about protecting you from the real killer. You know what he's capable of. Who knows if he'll go away? Who knows if he's acting alone?"

Matthew went very still. "Why? Did you find out something? Is he part of some crime ring?"

"I'm not sure," Sloane answered honestly. "But I do know that he stole a valuable painting. I know that he traveled from Hong Kong to here, that he owns a Mercedes, and that he has the contacts to track you down. That tells me he's got money. He also has a bodyguard, hangs out with thugs, and arranged for your chance encounter to happen in an area of Chinatown that's filled with gang-run casinos and brothels. That tells me he's got power in dangerous circles. He doesn't sound like an arbitrary killer to me."

"I never thought he was. But you're not talking about just a group of thugs. You're talking about Asian organized crime."

"Yes, I am."

Sloane watched the color drain from her father's face.

"You didn't go down this path before," he said, his voice unsteady.

"It didn't automatically come to mind."

"But now it has. And you wouldn't pull it out of thin air. Which means Derek told you something."

"Nothing concrete. He can't discuss Bureau business. But I can sense he's worried. And that worries me. Because if he knows more than we do about whoever broke into this apartment, my guess is that it involves C-6. Mom said the intruders were speaking some Chinese dialect. It doesn't take a genius to put together the pieces. And if Asian organized crime *is* involved, that's even worse than our original idea that you were just being warned off by Cai Wen's killer and whoever hired him."

Matthew's jaw was working. "You think we walked into an even bigger hornet's nest."

"Yes, I do." Sloane wasn't going to sugarcoat this, not with so much at stake. "Which brings me to my next point. Derek is pressuring me about the move. I've been putting him off. I think I should stop, and let him move into the cottage with me."

Her father did a double take. "Why? If some organized crime group is after me, why would you choose now to move out of the city? I'm having a hard enough time containing your mother and convincing her she's in danger. Even after I told her the whole story, she still thinks she's invincible."

"I have the best security team there is watching both of you. And I'm moving back to New Jersey, not California. I'll drop by constantly." Sloane gave a firm nod. "I've been away from home way too much. And it's the right time for Derek and me to go forward with our plans."

Matthew's eyes narrowed. "What's really going on here? First, that whole gung ho reaction to having Leo and Wallace redecorate the cottage. Now, this uncharacteristic urgency to get Derek moved in, when you've been waffling about that decision for a month. You're in no hurry to forfeit your independence, so don't tell me you're suddenly desperate to play house. Especially under these circumstances. So why now? How is leaving the city going to help? You'll be an hour plus away from us."

"And in close proximity to Derek. In a place that distinctly separates work and play. We'll be living like a real couple. We can talk about our jobs at the end of each day and not have the blurred lines we have now. It's an important step in our relationship. And, hopefully, it'll make it easier for me to figure out what you're up against."

"You're going to spy on Derek?"

"No." Sloane's reply was adamant. "Nor am I going to manipulate him. Number one, I swore I'd never compromise our relationship again—which doing either of those things would. And number two, he's way too smart for games. He'd see right through me. I'm simply going to take this official, personal step—one I'm excited about taking, even if I am a little scared—and hope that it also provides an atmosphere where Derek is more likely to let me in."

"And if he won't?"

"Then I'll find another way to get inside information. Classified or not. Even if it means breaking the rules. And even if that means blowing my chances of getting back into the Bureau."

CHAPTER SEVEN

The Kunsthalle München was a rectangular building of concrete and glass, the perfect venue to exhibit modern masterpieces.

Near Barer Strasse, the area was filled with art galleries. But the three men who were casually pushing a twin-size baby stroller weren't interested in window shopping. They strolled toward the museum entrance, pausing to bend over the stroller, as if trying to appease two fussing infants.

All that changed when they reached the main door.

Straightening, they yanked on their black masks and exploded into the museum, waving their submachine guns and shouting orders to the security guards in Slavic-accented German. They restrained them with Flex-Cufs and, holding them at gunpoint, forced the guards to accompany them upstairs.

They reached the third floor. The guard at the entrance to the main hall was practically asleep. From beneath half-lowered lids, he spotted his comrades walking toward him. Slowly, he came to his feet—and then froze. His eyes widened with fear as he focused on the MP5K now aimed directly at his heart.

The third gunman rushed forward and quickly disarmed him, pocketing the guard's Glock inside his own inside jacket pocket. He then secured the guard's hands with another set of Flex-Cufs.

Using their terrified captives as human shields, the gunmen headed down the corridor and toward their objective.

The outer exhibition room contained the Impressionists on their list: Renoir and Sisley. Using his wire cutters, the tallest gunman made quick work of the wires holding the paintings in place. He tucked the two paintings under one arm, snatching up his submachine gun and gripping it tightly in his other hand. He and his two accomplices shoved their hostages toward the inner room that contained the two most valuable paintings: the Van Gogh and the Seurat.

As they were about to enter the room, one of the captured guards yelled out, "*Halt!*" The three guards protecting the inner sanctum instantly hit the floor facedown, as they'd been trained to do in a hostage situation. Crouched behind metal and glass display cases marking the entrance to the exhibit, two other security guards began firing handguns at the masked thieves.

They were no match for the MP5Ks.

All three gunmen opened fire. Their bullets hammered the guards and annihilated the tops of the display cases, sending shards of glass flying everywhere. Without pausing to assess the damage, they each loaded another clip into their weapons and continued firing.

The silence that followed was abrupt and eerie. The walls behind each case were splattered with blood, bullet holes, and glass fragments.

The leader motioned one of his accomplices to check the guards. The first guard was dead. A short burst of gunfire finished off the second. A quick wave signaled that the path was clear.

Without the slightest hesitation, the leader pounded the three prone guards with bullets, leaving them dead in rivers of their own blood.

The tallest gunman had been hit in the shoulder. Relieving him of the Renoir and the Sisley, the leader motioned for the other gunman to get the Van Gogh and the Seurat.

Less than two minutes later, their goal was achieved.

With the leader helping the injured gunman, and the third member of the team carrying all four paintings, they hurried downstairs, went through a fire exit in the rear of the museum, and rushed toward the waiting BMW.

The paintings were quickly wrapped in blankets. The sedan lurched from the curb, speeding down Gabelsbergerstrasse. The driver eased onto the Oskar-von-Miller-Ring, and around the center of Munich, en route to A-8 and the Austrian border.

Final destination: Budapest.

———————

Inside SSA Tony Sanchez's office, a closed-door meeting was going on.

Tony, Derek, and Rich Williams were gathered around Tony's desk, reviewing the various pieces of the C-6 case against Xiao Long, and how it might factor into the shady provenance surrounding the genuine Rothberg.

"All nine of the recent burglaries on the Upper East Side are tied to Xiao Long," Derek told Rich. "One break-in every two or three weeks. He's got a great scheme going. A nephew of his, Eric Hu, a bright kid who graduated from MIT a few years ago, has a start-up computer support company—oh, and an addiction to crack, which is an easy get for Xiao Long. Turns out Hu's company serviced the computer systems of eight of the nine burglarized apartments. Also turns out all the owners of those apartments are affluent, with lots of expensive jewelry, electronic equipment, and artwork."

"Hu's computer support team scopes out the apartments and their owners' routines," Rich surmised. "They take note of where all the valuables are, and where the lady of the house keeps her jewelry. They probably take pictures with their cell phones. That way, Xiao Long's guys know just where to go to get as much as they can, as fast as they can."

"Right." Tony tapped his pen against his leg. "We've been onto this part of Xiao Long's business for almost six months—since he started it. He's coming up in the world. He used to deal in just gambling, drugs, and prostitutes. Now he's graduated to fencing top-dollar goods."

"And finding willing buyers for the artwork," Rich noted. "Keeping that under the radar is easy, unless any of the pieces are collectors' items or famous masterpieces. Which, judging from the partial list you rattled by me, they're primarily not." A glance at Derek. "You said eight of the nine burglaries fit the profile. The ninth, I assume, is Matthew Burbank's apartment."

Derek gave a tight nod. "Burbank's not rich. He is an art dealer, so it stands to reason that he has a few decent pieces in his place. But Eric Hu never set foot in that apartment, and his company never serviced Burbank's computers. So how would they know?"

"Let's play devil's advocate. Let's say they read or overheard something that made them think Burbank had more than he did, and that they tipped off Xiao Long, who had his gang break in and rob the place."

"Fine. So they saw the Monet and ripped it off. Makes sense. Monet's famous, even though you said it wasn't one of his well-known works. But they're not connoisseurs. So they grabbed it, along with a bunch of other pieces that had more sentimental than actual value. In addition to that . . ." For the tenth time, Derek studied the list of stolen items the cops provided. "We're talking standard household stuff—a flat-screen TV, a couple laptops, a set of silverware, a pair of diamond studs, and a gold necklace. Nothing close to the haul they got from the other thefts. And what bugs me most is that the rest of what they took smacks of camouflage—a DVD player they could get for seventy-five bucks at Best Buy, a hundred-dollar men's watch they could buy on the Internet for less, and a whole slew of knickknacks. They spent more time trashing the place than robbing it."

"You think they were looking for something else."

"Yeah. And I think they were disguising that search as a burglary. Why else would our wiretap catch Xiao Long getting word about finalizing a deal with an old art dealer on East Eighty-second?"

"Could be payback for anything," Rich suggested.

"Right," Derek returned drily. "And it could be coincidence that the very next morning you had an appointment to interview Burbank about a dirty art deal."

"Which we have no reason to believe he was involved in." Rich pursed his lips. "Look, Derek, I understand how frustrated you are. But I haven't found the connection you're looking for. The painting Burbank sold was genuine. As for a link between Burbank and Xiao Long, when I slipped in Xiao Long's name during the Hong Kong portion of our interview, there wasn't a flicker of recognition. Burbank's a lousy actor, and I'm a great reader of body language. I'd know if he was hiding something."

"Unless he doesn't know what he's hiding."

Rich shrugged. "We can speculate all day. All I can say is that, if Burbank's sale of *Dead or Alive* to Cai Wen, or if Cai Wen's murder itself, is in any way tied to your investigation of Xiao Long, I can't see it. Then again, a killer and a thief isn't about to leave a sales receipt. So the gaping hole in our provenance certainly leaves room for a variety of possibilities."

"All the more reason to keep digging into Burbank's art investment group and the timing of their sale. Please, Rich. I'd consider it a personal favor."

"Fine," Rich agreed, eyeing Derek quizzically as he spoke. "I'll review each of their interviews. But, just to clarify, are you leaning toward Burbank being a pawn or a criminal? I'm getting mixed signals."

"That's because Derek's giving them off." Tony leaned forward, interlacing his fingers on his desk. "Rich, would you excuse us for a minute?"

"Not a problem. Actually, I've got to run anyway." Rich got to his feet. "I'm waiting for a call from Interpol."

"That museum heist in Munich earlier today?" Tony asked.

"Yup. Bloody and profitable. Five dead guards. And a haul including a Van Gogh worth about forty million."

Tony whistled. "You've got your hands full."

"Always." Rich headed for the door. "I'll let you know if I find anything in those interviews."

"Thanks," Derek replied.

He waited until he and Tony were alone. Then, he got right into it. "You want to discuss my objectivity where it comes to this case."

"Do you blame me?"

"Not a bit. And you're right. I've got a personal stake in this. But my loyalty is to Sloane, not her father. Which is all the more reason I want to get at the truth—whatever it is. Sloane believes her father's innocent of whatever wrongdoing he presented to her, be it real or fabricated. She also believes he's in danger. She's hired security to watch both her parents. I checked that out.

And if Burbank's lying, if he is involved with the Red Dragons, then it's not just him and his wife who are in danger. It's Sloane, too. So I might not be objective, but I've got a hell of an incentive. Which makes me the best lead agent on this case."

Tony contemplated Derek's argument, then nodded. "If I didn't know Sloane so well professionally, I'd say your argument's thin. I'd say she's an attorney acting in the best interests of her client, and that that client happens to be her father—which gives her twice the motivation to protect him from prosecution if he committed murder. But I do know Sloane. I mentored her during her hostage negotiation training in Quantico. I know how ethical she is. And, coming from me, that's objective. I'm not the one who's in love with her. So, fine, you're the lead agent on the case. Now solve it."

CHAPTER EIGHT

The one thing Derek hadn't approached Tony with was how much of the FBI's need-to-know policy still applied to Sloane. She wasn't currently a Bureau employee, but she had been and she would be again. She also consulted for them on a case-by-case basis, and had retained all her old contacts.

Talk about a gray area.

Derek leaned back against the cushion of the living room sofa in Sloane's cottage, and contemplated that delicate matter, rolling his goblet of merlot between his palms.

Being here alone felt more comfortable than he'd expected. Not that he was really alone, he noted with a grin, glancing down at the three hounds who were sprawled around him, snoozing. He'd picked them up, along with the last of his bags, around six and driven straight to the cottage. Sloane was finishing up with a midtown client, dropping by her parents' apartment, and then heading home.

That had given Derek time to grab a snack, run the hounds, and do a little unpacking. Now he was relaxing with a glass of wine and a couple of takeout menus. Even though he was still mulling over the day's events, he could do so in a quieter, less frenetic manner while deciding between Chinese and Thai food. Sloane loved both.

Half and half, he decided. An eclectic Asian meal for their first night officially living together.

Asian. How ironic.

The telephone rang, and Derek reached over to get it. "Hello?"

There was a long, awkward pause at the other end of the receiver before a man's guarded voice replied, "Hello. This must be Derek."

"It is. And you are . . . ?"

"Leo Fox." The guardedness remained as he identified himself, and Derek knew just why. He was well aware of who Leo Fox was.

"Yes, Mr. Fox, what can I do for you?" Derek had no intention of tipping his hand.

"I don't know if Sloane's mentioned me," Leo continued tentatively. "I'm a friend of her father's. I'm also an interior designer."

"Oh, sure, of course. You're the magician who's going to transform this cottage so it doesn't scream out only feminine and canine."

Leo chuckled, his relief so acute that Derek almost pitied him. "So Sloane did tell you about my offer. I was afraid she'd think I'd just made it out of obligation, given how far back her father and I go. I wanted her to know it wasn't lip service. I really do want to help you two settle in as a couple."

"Well, I appreciate that, and gratefully accept. Sloane's got great taste, but this place is designed for her, not us."

"Of course. You need to feel comfortable, make it so you can call the cottage home." A pause. "I remember the layout of the house, but I haven't been there in years. Nor have I seen the decor since Sloane moved in. I'd like to set up an appointment to drive out there when both you and Sloane are home. I can look the place over and also talk to you, get to know who you are, so I can give the right flavor to my design, and the right blend of your tastes and Sloane's."

Derek felt his lips quirk. "Makes sense. The only problem is Sloane's not home yet. But I expect her soon. Can she give you a call tomorrow? That'll give us a chance to coordinate our schedules before she sets up an appointment with you to visit the cottage and work your magic."

"Of course." At this point, Leo sounded almost relaxed. "I'll be in my office all day tomorrow. I'm really looking forward to this project."

"So am I." As he spoke, Derek heard the faint crunching sound of tires on gravel from outside. Sloane must be home. "Thank you again, Mr. Fox."

"Please—Leo."

"Leo," Derek amended. "I'll talk to Sloane tonight."

"Excellent. You have a nice evening."

"Same to you." Derek hung up the phone just as the hounds heard Sloane's key in the door and sprang to life, jumping off the sofa and scrambling toward the front hall.

Derek rose as well, setting down his glass of wine and watching as Sloane came in, dropped her briefcase and coat, and squatted down to greet the three elated dachshunds.

No matter what else was going on—even if his workday had been a nightmare, if he was dead on his feet, or if he was under massive pressure; even when the two of them weren't on speaking terms, when she frustrated the hell out of him, or when they were so at odds he wanted to punch a hole in the wall—she always had the same effect on him. One look at her and he wanted her.

"Hi, my little jumping beans," she was saying to the hounds now, affectionately scratching their ears. "What a wonderful welcome."

"I can provide an equally wonderful welcome," Derek offered, his tone half teasing, half seductive. As he spoke, he made his way over to her. "I'm just afraid of getting mowed down if I try to beat these three to the door."

Sloane rose, her eyes glinting and a warm flush starting to tinge her cheeks. The fire between them was mutual. And she was just as attuned to him as he was to her. "Be daring. From you, I'm up for a different type of welcome home."

"I like the sound of that." Derek wrapped his arms around her, pulling her against him. "And I like the sound of the word 'home.' It feels right."

"You feel right, too." Sloane slid her hands under his sweater, hiking it up as she did.

Derek yanked it off and tossed it aside, then helped Sloane unbutton her blouse, which he dragged off with her blazer.

"Which room should we initiate first?" he asked, unhooking her bra and letting it drop to the floor.

"That's a tough one." She wriggled out of her slacks, kicked them aside, and stood there in only a thong. "I think we've already initiated them all—several times over."

"Then how about right here?" He lifted her onto the hall table, shedding the rest of his clothes, and stripping off her thong in a few hot, fast motions. He moved between her legs, pushing her thighs apart, and wedging himself between them.

"Here is good." Sloane's voice was breathless, and her eyes held that familiar, smoky hunger that drove him crazy. She leaned forward and reached for him. "In fact, here is great." Her words ended in an aroused whimper, as Derek reached under her, gripping her bottom and lifting her against him.

"No foreplay?" she managed, wrapping her arms around his neck and rubbing her body against his.

"Not this time." He angled her, his erection nudging her, pushing slightly inside to see how ready she was.

She was more than ready for him.

He thrust all the way in and then some, simultaneously taking her mouth in an all-consuming kiss. His tongue mimicked the motions of his hips, plunging, stroking, retreating, again and again, and she held on, meeting him kiss for kiss, stroke for stroke.

It was over before either of them could think of prolonging it. Sloane came in hard, racking spasms. Derek spurted into her, each clench of her body milking his, drawing out his orgasm as he instinctively timed it to match hers.

An exquisite peak, and an equally exquisite plummet.

With a soft moan, Sloane went limp, her head dropping forward until her forehead was resting against Derek's chest.

"Wow," she said in broken pants. "Quite an initiation."

"Just a prelude." Derek's ability to speak wasn't much better.

"Your heart's racing."

"Your legs are quivering" was his hoarse reply.

She nodded against his damp skin. "I don't think I can walk. Or stand."

"Then don't." He lifted her, his body still lodged inside hers, and carried her toward the living room. "We've got a lot more initiating to do."

———

It was hours later when they lay draped across each other in Sloane's bed, replete with that utter, bone-melting peace that was the result of one of their marathon lovemaking sessions.

"Did I miss any rooms?" Derek muttered into her hair.

Sloane's lips curved. "Definitely not. You were very thorough. We covered every room in the house—even the laundry room. Making love on a washer and dryer—that's one I never thought of."

"You loved it. You came twice."

"No arguments. I'll just never be able to think of it as a laundry room again. Guess you'll be doing the wash from now on."

"Touché." Derek chuckled.

"I'm starved," Sloane announced.

"Me, too. I was about to order a combo dinner—Thai and Chinese—when you walked in. Once that happened, all I wanted was this."

"I don't blame you. It was my first choice as well."

"But now that I've worn you out, you'd like some sustenance."

"Exactly." Sloane eyed him with a wry expression. "And wipe that smug grin off your face. I gave as good as I got. You look like a train wreck."

"True." Derek wasn't the least bit put off. "I feel like I was hit by an eighteen-wheeler, even though it came in a very small and sexy package. As for the Thai and Chinese, I could eat everything on both menus."

Sloane sat up, squinting at the clock. "Well, we'd better hurry. We'll get in just under the wire. The restaurants here close by nine. Ten if you're lucky." She gave Derek a playful poke as she reached for the phone. "Get used to the country, city boy. This isn't Manhattan. No twenty-four/seven food."

"It's worth the sacrifice. The perks are good."

———

Forty minutes later, Derek returned with their food. They ate in bed, right out of the cartons. The hounds, having been fed and taken out, were clustered around them, nibbling on their own treats.

"If we make a ritual out of this initiation process, I'll never have the strength to work," Sloane commented between bites.

"Right." Derek was shoveling in mouthfuls of General Tsao's chicken, having long since abandoned his slower and more cumbersome chopsticks in favor of a fork. "Like anything could keep you from working."

Sloane considered that, and nodded. "Good point. Although I kind of like being a part-time sex goddess. But, the rest of the time—watching soaps and reading *Home and Garden* wouldn't do it for me."

The unlikely description was amusing. But it also made Derek remember a subject he was eager to broach.

"Speaking of *Home and Garden*, Leo Fox called just before you got home. He asked if you'd call him back tomorrow. He wants to set up an appointment to come over and check out the cottage—and me." Derek's lips quirked again at the memory. "I think he's trying to get a handle on my aura so he can do justice to our new, unified decor."

"That's Leo," Sloane acknowledged with a twinkle in her eye. "An artist through and through. But he is incredibly talented. You'll like what he comes up with." A pause as she tapped her fork against her lips. "Let's see. He'll probably start with a sign on the front door saying 'Rangers Lead the Way.' Then he'll add a vintage G.I. Joe collection on the coffee table. Oh, and let's not forget a wall-to-wall ruler on the floor of your half of the bedroom closet, to make sure your shoes are lined up just so and with equal space between pairs."

"Yeah, but how is he going to incorporate that with a bathroom overflowing with hair-care products, file cabinets that are about to explode at the seams, and a lifetime's collection of bows and arrows that would put Robin Hood to shame and that takes up half the guest room?" Derek countered.

"Are you suggesting I'm a slob?"

"Nope. I'm suggesting you're a pack rat. I'm a minimalist. It should be interesting to see how Leo melds the two." Derek set his empty carton down on the night table and leaned back against the headboard, interlacing his fingers behind his head and studying Sloane. "Leo sounded nervous when I answered the phone. My voice must be a lot more intimidating than I realize, because he was definitely edgy, and he doesn't seem like the introverted type."

Sloane shrugged, polishing off her shrimp in black bean sauce. "Maybe having you answer the phone caught him off guard. It is a little awkward, talking to a live-in boyfriend you've never met."

"Maybe. Although artists are usually the most open-minded people in the world." Derek's gaze was steady, and there was no longer any banter in his tone. "So there's no other reason I'd make him uncomfortable?"

"None that I can think of. Unless you made an aura joke. That would offend him. He takes his craft very seriously."

"Nope. No aura jokes. Just Special Agent Derek Parker, being himself."

The comment was too pointed for Sloane to ignore.

She raised her head and met his gaze. "Is there something you wanted to ask me?"

"Dozens of somethings. But I respect your position. So I'll get my own answers—for now."

"What kind of answers?" Sloane demanded. "And why are you grilling me about Leo?"

"You're way too intelligent not to have figured that out."

Sloane sucked in her breath. "If you honestly believe this is part of a bigger picture . . ."

"I do."

"And if that bigger picture causes you to worry about my safety . . ."

"It does."

"Then don't I deserve some kind of explanation—some forewarning?"

"Yes—unless you plan on sharing it with your father."

A weighty pause.

"I won't," Sloane replied at last. "Not unless it puts him at risk, either legally or physically."

"Ah. Therein lies the rub. I can't promise you that unless you tell me what you know. And you can't tell me what you know unless I promise you that. A catch-22, if ever there was one."

"Dammit, Derek." Sloane raked a hand through her hair. "You know my hands are tied. I've told you my father's innocent of any major crime that you or your friend on the Art Crime Team could be investigating. That's all the wiggle room I have. You have a lot more latitude on your end about what you can or can't say."

"You're right. And, for the record, I've spoken to Tony. I'm the lead case agent on the C-6 investigation that I'm concerned might be tied to your father. I think Tony might ease up on the need-to-know directive where it comes to you. But not if there's a blatant conflict of interests. You're representing your father. That's both a legal and a personal conflict. I'm not sure how to get past it. But I'm trying."

Sloane nodded. "I appreciate that. And, for the record, at my end, I've pushed my father to opt for full disclosure. I'm still hopeful that will happen. But you're not the only one who worries about me. He does, too."

"I realize that. I also realize that worry is reciprocated. Since the break-in, you've hired round-the-clock security on both your parents."

Grim lines tightened around Sloane's mouth. "So you know about the bodyguards. Did you share that information with Tony?"

Derek had no intention of lying. "Yes."

"And, from that, you both deduced there's a big conspiracy going on. How about deducing that the security stems from precaution, not from my father's potential guilt?"

"Doesn't fly. Uncharacteristically overreactive on your part. That is, *if* the burglary at your parents' apartment was really just a simple burglary. Which we both know it wasn't."

Sloane didn't avert her gaze. "Don't put me in this position."

"I don't want to. But when it comes down to a question of your safety or your father's freedom, there's no choice to make."

———

Xiao Long received the telephone call that night. It came in on his throw-away cell phone.

He was being summoned. All the necessary arrangements had been made.

He had only to pack a bag. A car would be waiting to take him to the airport.

The morning after next, he'd be in Hong Kong to see the sunrise.

CHAPTER NINE

Something was bugging Rich Williams.

The past two days, from dusk till dawn, he'd been buried in meetings and exchanging phone calls with Interpol, with the Bundeskriminalamt, or BKA—the German federal police—and with the regional headquarters of the Bundespolizei in Munich. There was no doubt that the heist at the Kunsthalle München fit the same pattern as the others. It was a trademark performance of the Black Eagles, a brutal gang from Lezhë, Albania. Interpol had been hunting them down since their early days as gunrunners to Kosovo. By now they'd grown in size and strength, evolving into a major art-theft ring. Violent and ruthless, they operated without a shred of remorse or emotion.

They'd do anything, kill anyone, for money.

A plan was being formulated to break them up. At the drop of a hat, Rich might be required to go undercover and fly to Europe.

Coordinating strategies posed by various international government agencies had dominated his life these past few days. But those discussions weren't what was bugging him now.

After a hectic forty-eight hours of work, he'd been too wound up to sleep.

And since his mind was now free to focus on other things, it kept flitting back to Derek's certainty that Matthew Burbank's involvement in the Rothberg sale went deeper than just an innocent transaction.

Rich had known Derek since he was a NAT—a new agent in training. He'd spotted Derek's sharp instincts from their first conversation. And, given he was like a dog with a bone on this one, maybe it did warrant a closer look. Not to mention, Rich had given him his word.

The Field Office was quiet as the first rays of sunlight rose over Manhattan. Rich went out, bought himself an extra-large cup of coffee and a bacon-and-egg sandwich. He munched on breakfast and drank his coffee at his desk. At the same time, he carefully reread each of the interviews he'd conducted with the five members of Burbank's art group.

Phil Leary's accounting records were in perfect order. The purchase of *Dead or Alive* for $125,000 at a reputed Manhattan art gallery in 1990 had been confirmed by the gallery owner, and Leary's bookkeeping entries coincided with the date and amount on the original receipt. Matthew Burbank had produced that original receipt, along with catalog photos of the painting and written correspondence between Wallace Johnson and the gallery owner arranging for the transaction. Johnson had been shrewd enough to recognize Rothberg's genius when he was still a relative unknown. Three years later, that same painting would have sold for twice the price.

It had sold five years later for even more.

Leary's records on the sale of *Dead or Alive* were as meticulous as those on the buy. Cai Wen, a wealthy Hong Kong art dealer, had snatched up the painting, willingly paying $375,000 for what he recognized as a prime investment.

The financial records were precise, right down to the last date and dollar.

So what was bugging Rich?

He turned his attention back to the interview with Leary, rereading it sentence by sentence. The arrangements. The transactions. The records. The files.

That was it. The files were the inconsistency.

In his nervous recounting, Leary had explained the way their group worked. Leary was the numbers guy. Johnson was the art connoisseur, with the knowledge and the means to spot the high-value paintings, and to bid on them. Fox and Martino were the local guys. Fox was an interior designer, making him an artist in his own right. He had an eye for budding talent. Martino had a clothing manufacturing business, with dozens of contacts who knew, or were related to, struggling artists just looking for a break.

And Burbank was the art dealer, the one who negotiated deals full-time, and the glue that held them all together.

As precise as Leary's financial records were, that's how thorough Burbank's files were. He kept every item of provenance available on the paintings—from photos to newspaper clippings to certificates of authenticity. He also kept duplicate receipts—not just on the buys but also on the sales.

He'd produced all that with regard to the Rothberg purchase. What he *hadn't* produced was a duplicate receipt for the sale. In fact, he'd produced nothing on the sale whatsoever, allowing Leary's financial records to stand alone as proof.

Normally, that would be fine, since the buyer would have all the original paperwork. But if what Leary said was true, the absence of a thick file—or *any* file—on the sale was an anomaly for Burbank. Add to that the fact that their buyer had turned up murdered the day after the transaction, and all sorts of new questions were raised.

Was it possible that Burbank's group had switched the genuine Rothberg for a fake, and then, when Cai Wen figured it out and confronted them, they'd killed him? Nope. Despite the gaping holes in the provenance of both the genuine and the fake Rothberg, the paper trail of the fake didn't begin until 1997, when it was sold at an absurdly low price by an amateur collector—now nowhere to be found—to a gallery in Macao. In contrast, Burbank's art investment group had conducted their transaction with Cai Wen in October 1995.

The next potential scenario was that Burbank, Fox, and Leary had tried to screw Cai Wen, or vice versa, and they'd wound up killing him.

Anything was possible, but if those three men were murderers, then Rich would eat his hat. Aside from Ben Martino's misdemeanor DWI, none of them had a police record. None of them had brought a lawyer to the interview—not even Matthew Burbank, who had Sloane as free legal counsel. None of them was shrewd enough to realize that having total recall *and* providing near-identical details of a sale that happened fourteen years ago screamed rehearsed. And none of them was the hotheaded type.

They'd been total wrecks about being questioned by the FBI over a case of art fraud. If they'd killed a man, they would have passed out at Rich's feet.

Still, there was that discrepancy over Burbank not producing a file on the Rothberg sale.

Rich pulled out his paperwork on Burbank's interview to double-check. Yup. Memory had served him correctly. Not only hadn't Burbank produced the comprehensive file Leary had alluded to, he'd never mentioned, much less emphasized, his thorough file-keeping system. And he'd certainly never broached the subject of a duplicate receipt.

This warranted further investigation—along with the proper venue and the element of surprise. It was the only way to catch Burbank off guard, throw him into a panic, and corner him into producing his other files.

Rich picked up the phone and dialed Derek's number.

———

It was Derek's second call of the morning.

Both calls had sucked.

The first one came before dawn, when Jeff called to report that something weird was going on with Xiao Long. He hadn't been seen in Chinatown for the past two nights, nor had C-6 reported any comings or goings from his house in Long Island or his hangouts in the city. He hadn't made or received any phone calls. It was as if he'd dropped out of sight. And that couldn't mean anything good.

Derek's stomach had clenched as he closed his cell and glanced at Sloane sleeping next to him. The timing of Xiao Long's disappearance sucked. It made Derek only more suspicious that whatever was going on was somehow linked to the Bureau's investigation of a connection between Xiao Long and Matthew Burbank.

So much for phone call one.

Derek had just finished his morning workout, during which he'd managed to convince himself that Xiao Long could just as easily be sick in bed as he could be hiding out, planning something sinister or letting the heat die down, when Rich's call came in.

Afterward, Derek wrapped a towel around his neck and sank down on the bed. He had to think—and he didn't have a lot of time to do it in. Sloane was out running with the hounds. She'd be back in a few minutes. And by the time she walked in, Derek had to have a plan to keep her busy and out of contact with her parents—at least for the morning.

In other words, he had to manipulate her.

With a muttered oath, Derek tossed the towel into the hamper and went to take a quick shower.

It took very little arm-twisting to persuade Leo Fox to push up their original appointment next week and to drive out to the cottage that morning. He seemed to be chomping at the bit to transform the place into the perfect love nest for Derek and Sloane. As for Sloane, her morning schedule was light, and after the intensity of the last two nights, Derek had no trouble convincing her that he did want to leave his mark on what was now their home—or why. Getting Leo there ASAP seemed like the most natural reaction in the world.

And Derek felt like the biggest SOB arranging it.

Leo arrived armed with stacks of fabric samples, decorating catalogs, and a burst of fanfare.

He was an average-size man with a long, thin face, a sallow complexion, and a shock of black hair. He reminded Derek of Bert from Sesame Street, except more expensively dressed and without the scowl. Leo was all smiles, carrying in his wares, tentatively greeting the hounds—although he drew the line at letting them sniff his samples—and pumping Derek's hand when Sloane introduced them.

"It's a pleasure to meet you," he said, scrutinizing Derek as subtly as he could—but not so subtly as to escape Derek's notice. "Let me start out by telling you what a lucky man you are. I've known Sloane since she was a precocious little girl who climbed trees and roughhoused with the boys because the girls didn't play hard enough. She was, and is, beautiful, smart, and afraid of nothing. I hope you can keep up."

Derek found himself grinning as he pictured a miniature Sloane beating the crap out of the boys. "I can try."

"Oh, for pity's sake." Sloane rolled her eyes. "Derek is a former Army Ranger, Leo. He's been an FBI agent for a dozen years, and he's worked every kind of grisly violent crime you can imagine. Believe me, he can keep up. His morning workouts alone would kill me."

"And your Krav Maga?" Leo inquired politely.

Sloane's lips twitched. "That would kill him."

"So you're evenly matched." The decorator beamed.

"We think so." Derek looped an arm around Sloane's shoulders. "As for knowing how lucky I am, I do. That's why I'm so eager to get settled. I want to solidify what I've got."

"Excellent. Then let's get right to it." Leo glanced around the hallway. "Where shall I set up?" he asked, indicating everything he'd brought along, which was currently perched on the hall table.

"How about the living room?" Sloane suggested. "There's lots of room there to spread out."

Leo glanced in the direction she indicated. "Perfect." He was already halfway to his destination. Forget Bert. This guy was more like Road Runner, except as tightly wound as Wile E. Coyote right before he inevitably went over the cliff.

"I'll leave all this in here while we take our walk-through," Leo was continuing. "Sloane, give me a tour of the cottage as you've decorated it. Derek, I'll ask you some questions as we walk. By the time we sit down, I'll have a very good idea of what to show you."

And I'll have a very good idea of what you're about, Derek thought. *Because there's a lot more to this visit than a decorating consultation.*

Fred Miller had been working security for twenty years. He was a pro. He'd familiarized himself with every detail of Rosalyn Burbank's routine. He also checked in with her twice a day to ensure she kept him apprised of her schedule.

This morning, she had a business breakfast to attend. He'd be picking her up outside her apartment in his navy Ford Explorer.

He arrived half an hour early, as always. And, as always, he checked to make sure his counterpart, Matthew Burbank's security guard, was posted outside the building. Yup. Jake Lambert was right there. Jake handled the night shift, which meant that Tom O'Hara would be arriving soon to relieve him.

As Fred pulled up to the building, he and Jake exchanged impersonal nods. The doorman spotted Fred immediately, and gestured that, per instructions, he could leave his car right out front.

That done, Fred walked over to the Starbucks on East Eightieth and York to get a cup of coffee.

The pedestrian traffic was typically congested on a weekday morning. Fred bought his coffee and stepped outside, nudging his way through the crowd to cross over and head back to his car. He stopped at the corner, waiting on the sidewalk for the light to change. He didn't notice the stocky Asian man who came up behind him. His mind was running through the day's schedule.

The light changed. The pedestrians began to cross.

That's when Fred felt the searing pain of the switchblade as it plunged straight into his back.

The rest happened quickly. The Asian man moved before Fred could cry out, before his legs buckled under him, before the blood soaked through his suit. He grabbed Fred's arm and shoved him into a waiting sedan, his motions that of a colleague who was helping his associate grab his ride before the driver was forced to move on or be pounded by traffic.

The sedan pulled away and drove off.

No one noticed the incident, or thought it anything but business as usual.

No one knew that Fred Miller bled to death in the sedan, or that his lifeless body was dumped in the East River.

CHAPTER TEN

Rosalyn was in a hurry. Business tote in one hand, file folder in the other, she was skimming through her notes as she left her apartment and made her way over to the Explorer. As usual, her mind was in a dozen places at once. She didn't wait for Fred to come around and help her in. She never did. She was far too impatient. She simply yanked open the back door, placed her tote on the seat, and slid in after it.

"Good morning, Fred," she greeted him, never glancing up as she shut the door and continued reading her notes. "Please find a way to get around this traffic. I've got to be in midtown in twenty minutes, rush hour or not."

Her driver muttered a good morning along with a grunt of acknowledgment, and pressed the button that activated the automatic door locks. Then, he pulled into the stream of traffic.

It wasn't until a chunk of time had passed that Rosalyn got the niggling feeling they'd been driving for way too long. Her head came up, and she blinked when she saw where they were.

"Fred? What are you doing? We're in Harlem, practically in the Bronx." She leaned forward as she spoke, searching the rearview mirror to see Fred and hear his explanation.

The flat, emotionless gaze that looked back at her did *not* belong to Fred. Nor did he say a word.

Rosalyn froze. "Who are you? What do you want?"

The menacing Asian man still didn't answer. He just continued driving over the Willis Avenue Bridge into the Bronx.

Rosalyn wasn't stupid. She knew this wasn't a case of a mix-up in drivers. This had been planned. And it was linked to the murderer who was threatening Matthew.

Alarmed as she was, she forced herself to outwardly keep her cool. "Where are you taking me?" she demanded. "And why? What do you plan on doing this time?"

The driver veered off into a lousy section of the Bronx. "Your husband has visitor on the way," he stated. "FBI. More questions. Burbank weak. He talk. Stupid. Dangerous. We warned. He not listen. We punish. You die."

Die? So much for Rosalyn keeping her cool.

"You're wrong," she responded, confused and desperate. "The FBI's not coming by. And, even if they do, Matthew wouldn't say a word. He didn't last time. He won't this time."

"No trust. Too many talks between him and FBI. No more."

The finality in his tone was absolute. There was no reasoning with this animal.

That did it. Rosalyn lunged forward, scrambling to climb into the front seat and wrestle away control of the steering wheel. As she did, she spotted the long, open switchblade on the passenger seat, and shuddered. The knife was covered with blood. She forced her gaze away, trying to climb over the center console, groping and clawing at the driver's thick arm to break his concentration and yank his hand off the wheel.

He grabbed hers instead, bending her forearm sideways until blinding pain shot through her and she could hear the crunching sound of bones. She cried out, struggling to escape his grasp.

"Stay in back," he ordered, shoving her off the console. "You can die quick. Or you can die slow. Your choice." He released her arm, sending her sprawling into the back.

Rosalyn slid back into her seat. Her arm was throbbing horribly. Her life was on the line. And she had no idea how to save it.

Fate intervened.

The Explorer approached a red light. Her intended killer accelerated to run it. As he did, the wail of an ambulance siren reached their ears. An instant later, the emergency vehicle appeared and sped through the intersection.

Rosalyn's abductor slammed on the brakes, swearing in Chinese. He and Rosalyn both lurched forward.

She didn't miss a beat or pause to regain her bearings. Manually, she pressed open her door lock, yanked the handle, and flung open the door. She hit the ground running, heading for the first crowd of people she saw—a bunch of teenage boys shooting hoops.

Hands trembling, she unhinged the gate and rushed inside, slamming the gate as if it were some kind of protective wall.

The basketball game stopped. A half-dozen tall, muscled teens turned in her direction. A half-dozen pairs of wary eyes stared at her. She twisted around, peering back at the street and the unmoving Explorer. The driver had leaped out and dashed around to the open rear door. Suspicious passersby, recognizing a stranger on their turf, were already pausing on the sidewalk to scrutinize him. He scanned the area for a minute. Then, he slammed the rear door shut, ran back around to the driver's side, got in, and gunned the engine, disappearing around the corner.

Rosalyn sank down on the cracked and broken ground, leaning her head against the fence and trembling from head to toe. The pain in her arm was so sharp, she could scarcely breathe.

"Hey, lady, you all right?"

She looked up and gazed blankly at the sweaty teenager holding a basketball, who had come over when he saw her collapse.

"All right?" Her laugh was hollow.

"You on something?" he asked, seeing her glazed expression.

Oh, how she wished she were. "No." She managed to shake her head, simultaneously reaching for her tote bag and remembering it was still in the car with her file. "A hospital . . . I need a hospital. My arm . . ." She winced. "My cell phone's gone. Could you . . . ?" Her voice trailed off.

"Here." He groped in his pocket and pulled out a cell phone. "Use mine."

Kindness and charity still existed, and thank heaven for it.

"Thank you," Rosalyn said gratefully, reaching out with her good arm and taking the phone. "Thank you so much."

———

Matthew Burbank was reading the morning paper and drinking a mug of coffee when the doorbell of the apartment gave a quick ring.

He folded the newspaper and set it down with his mug, rising to head over and answer the door. It had to be Sloane. Roz had left a little while ago for a breakfast meeting. Anyone but her or Sloane would have been announced by the doorman.

Reflexively, he peeked through the peephole. His hand, already on the door handle, froze.

There was a distinguished-looking silver-haired man in a suit standing outside—one he recognized right away. It was Special Agent Richard Williams, the FBI agent from the Art Crime Team who'd interviewed him about the Rothberg.

What the hell was he doing here?

Fighting a surge of panic, Matthew inhaled slowly, trying to calm himself. When he felt sufficiently composed, he opened the door. "Agent Williams. This is a surprise."

Williams's brows rose quizzically. "Is it a bad time?"

"No, of course not. I just wasn't expecting you."

"Well, don't blame your doorman. I showed him my ID, and he let me up without a formal announcement. I hope that's all right."

"Yes . . . of course . . . it's fine." It occurred to Matthew that Special Agent Williams was still standing in the hallway. Hastily, he moved aside and gestured for him to enter. "Please, come in."

"Thank you." Williams stepped into the foyer. "I noticed your bodyguard hanging out outside the building. A very formidable-looking fellow. I'm sure he'll scare off any additional, or returning, intruders."

Matthew swallowed hard to keep down his coffee. How did Williams know about the bodyguards? And what did he mean by "returning intruders"?

"My wife hasn't been herself since the burglary," he tried, realizing that lying about the security guy could do nothing but hurt him. "Knowing we have some kind of protection puts her mind at ease."

"Of course." Williams seemed to buy the explanation. He glanced around. "Is your wife home now?"

"No. She's at a client meeting."

"I see. In any case, I had some business on the Upper East Side, so I took the liberty of dropping by here afterward." He reached into the inside pocket of his sport jacket and extracted a note pad and pen. "I reviewed all the interviews I conducted regarding the provenance of *Dead or Alive*, and a few loose ends presented themselves. I'll just need to ask you a couple of additional questions."

"No problem." Heart pounding, Matthew showed Williams into the den and gestured at the settee. "Make yourself comfortable." Even as he extended the invitation, he could hear the unsteadiness in his own voice, feel sweat dripping down his spine. "Can I offer you anything—coffee, tea?"

"Nothing, thank you." Williams lowered himself to the settee, perching at the very edge of the cushion. "I'll take up only a few minutes of your time. Also, this will be much less stressful for you than coming down to the Field Office. A quick chat in your own den is a lot more pleasant than a conversation in an interviewing room. Then there's the convenience factor. Your office and your files are just a few rooms away."

Matthew started. "Why? Is there something in them you need to see?"

"You tell me." Williams's expression never changed. "According to your partners, you keep extensive files on the sale of all your paintings, including duplicate sales receipts. Yet I don't remember your producing any of those items at our last meeting. I assume it was an oversight. Would you mind if I took a look at that file now?"

"I gave you a stack of material on *Dead or Alive* when I came down to your Field Office."

"True. But all that was related to the buy, not the sale."

"I thought Phil showed you the financial records that . . ."

"He did. I'm not asking for financial records. I'm asking for the file. Or, at the very least, the duplicate receipt. You do have that, don't you?"

Matthew was drowning, and he knew it. "I gave you all the material I had. It's possible the receipt for that particular painting was misfiled. We're talking about precomputer times."

"Right." Williams nodded, getting to his feet. "That's why I thought the proximity to your office would help. You can show me your filing system. And maybe we can locate that missing receipt."

Silence.

"You don't have it, do you?" Williams asked with quiet assurance.

It was clear that Williams already knew the answer to that question. So all Matthew could do was to try the human error approach and hope it worked.

"Honestly? No. I forgot to get one from Cai Wen. I realized it right after we completed the transaction. I felt like an idiot. So I never mentioned it to my partners."

Williams still didn't avert his gaze. "I can understand your embarrassment. So rather than leave empty-handed, why didn't you go back later and get the receipt? Or, if Cai Wen wasn't available, why didn't you ask him to mail you a duplicate, which you could have signed?"

"I guess I never thought of it."

"I find that very hard to believe. From everything I heard from your partners, you're a meticulous record-keeper. Unless, of course, that one time you were off your game? Maybe something happened that threw you enough to forget about the receipt and to get out of Dodge ASAP? Maybe that same something made you forget to mention any of this to me during our interview?"

That was it. The dam broke.

"I didn't kill Cai Wen," Matthew blurted out. "I just forgot to get the damned receipt. So if you came here to accuse me of something—"

"I didn't," Williams interrupted. "Although I am curious about how you knew Cai Wen was murdered. It didn't exactly make it to the U.S. newspapers."

"I . . ." Matthew's heart was pounding so hard, he was afraid it would explode from his chest. "We didn't leave Hong Kong until the next day. You saw that on our passports. I must have heard or read something . . ."

"And conveniently forgot to mention it when we spoke? Not likely. Oh, and for the record, Cai Wen wasn't killed until the next day—the day you left Hong Kong. So you would have had to either be at the murder scene or sitting at the Hong Kong police station to have heard about the homicide before boarding that plane. Would you care to revise your story?"

"I didn't kill him. I'm not a murderer. I didn't . . ."

"Are you covering for one of your partners?" Williams continued to drill away. "Did Leo Fox or Phil Leary kill Cai Wen?"

Matthew's mouth opened, then snapped shut. He gritted his teeth and fought to think straight. "I want my lawyer here," he managed at last.

"No problem." Williams gestured toward the phone. "Give your daughter a call. I'm sure she'll drop whatever she's doing and rush over. Oh, would you mind finding out if she's in the city or at her place in New Jersey? Because if she's got an hour-plus drive, I'll take you up on that cup of coffee."

———

Leo Fox had just decided that chili red would be the perfect accent for the spare bedroom he was converting into a small home gym for Derek when the telephone rang.

"I'll get that," Sloane told them. Scooting across the hall to the master bedroom, she chuckled as she heard Leo explain to Derek that the chili red would "pop" and energize his workout.

Her humor was short-lived.

"Hi, Dad," she greeted, having noted the caller ID and knowing her mother was at a breakfast meeting. "Everything okay?"

"No." Her father sounded even worse than he had the night he'd called to tell her about the break-in. "I need you to come to the apartment right away."

"What's happened?" Sloane sank down on the edge of the bed, a sick feeling forming in the pit of her stomach.

"That agent from the Art Crime Team, Richard Williams, is here." Her father's voice dropped to a near whisper. "He knows we're hiding information on Cai Wen's murder. He all but accused me of killing him."

Sloane went very still. "He just showed up on your doorstep and started grilling you?"

"Pretty much, yeah. And on the one morning you didn't drop by. He knows I'm calling you. But I said some stupid things . . . I—"

"Dad, listen to me," Sloane interrupted. "Don't say another word to him. Just give him a cup of coffee and a seat on the sofa. Then, go into the breakfast nook. You'll be in his sight, but you'll have distance between you. Sit there. Keep your back to him. No eye contact. Read the newspaper. Look out the window. But don't even glance his way. And don't engage in *any* conversation whatsoever. Do you understand?"

"Yes. I understand." A hard swallow. "Sloane, I'm in trouble. Please hurry."

"I'm on my way."

Sloane grabbed her purse. She was worried. She was badly thrown, not by what had happened, but by the timing. And she was livid.

She marched across the hall and poked her head into the room Derek and Leo were chatting in.

"Excuse me, gentlemen." For Leo's sake, she kept herself in check. "One of my clients has an emergency. I'm going to have to take off."

"Well, of course." Leo looked startled and a tad disappointed. Abruptly, he brightened. "Derek and I can finish up here, and then we can arrange a follow-up for all three of us once I've finalized my ideas. I have some wonderful plans for this place. Oh, and I took some photos. I'll show them to Wallace so he can coordinate the paintings he chooses for you with my design ideas."

"That would be great, Leo. Thanks for understanding." Sloane had no idea what he'd said, nor did she care. Her gaze was on Derek. "Can I speak to you for a moment before I take off?"

"Of course." Derek glanced over at Leo. "I'll be right back."

"Take your time," Leo acknowledged with exaggerated cheer. "I'll be jotting down notes."

Sloane waited until she and Derek were in the front hallway, far out of earshot. Then, she spun around and faced him, eyes blazing.

"You bastard. How could you?"

"With great difficulty." Derek issued no denial and no apology. "I hated having to divert you. But, as I told you, if it came down to protecting you or protecting your father, there'd be no choice. Not in my book. And if he's as innocent as you say, no harm was done." One dark brow rose. "Right?"

Without responding to the question, Sloane snatched up her coat and keys. "We'll deal with this later," she bit out. "In the meantime, I expect Leo to leave ten minutes after I do. You're not taking this opportunity to get him alone and subtly assess him and how much he knows—the way you have been for the past two hours. That ends now."

She reached for the door, then paused, staring Derek down. "You used me. I won't forget that. Or forgive it."

———

Sloane was more than halfway to her parents' apartment when her cell phone rang again. She clicked her Bluetooth headset to answer the call. "Sloane Burbank."

"It's me," her father said tersely, keeping his voice as low as possible.

"Dad? What is it?"

"It's bad, Sloane." His voice held that same strained sound it had the night of the robbery when he'd called her from the hospital. But now, it was muted to almost a whisper. He was clearly desperate to keep Rich Williams from overhearing him.

"I just got a call from your mother," he said. "She's in the hospital. In the Bronx. The man who picked her up this morning wasn't her driver. He was some Asian thug. He must have gotten behind the wheel while Fred was getting coffee, and Jake and Tom were changing shifts. The son of a bitch kidnapped her, broke her arm, and was taking her to God knows where—*to kill her.*"

Sloane felt ill. "How do you know that?"

"Because he told her. He said he was killing her to punish me. That the FBI was about to drop in and I'd talk. How the hell he knew Williams was on his way over here, I have no idea. All I know is that there was a traffic incident, your mother jumped out of the car, and she ran for help. I don't have specific details. She's on heavy pain meds and I don't want to grill her. But I can't leave the apartment to go to her. Not without giving Agent Williams an explanation. What should I do?"

Before clamping down on her personal feelings, Sloane asked one question. "Are you sure Mom's all right?"

"Yes. I spoke to her doctor."

"Good." The professional Sloane Burbank kicked in. "Give me her doctor's name and number. I want the hospital staff to keep Mom comfortable—and there—until after I've had my talk with Williams. My goal is to get rid of him without mentioning this—for now. We've got enough on our plate without adding Mom's attack and abduction to the mix. There'll be plenty of time to fill him in later." A pause. "Unless the cops have already been notified."

"No. Your mother's smart. She's using the fact that she's in too much pain and too woozy from the meds to provide a coherent story. So no cops are involved yet."

"God bless Mom. She's buying us time." Sloane felt a wave of relief. "Let's put it to good use. First, hang up the phone. We don't want to make Williams suspicious. I should be there in a half hour. Then we can deal with one crisis at a time."

CHAPTER ELEVEN

Xiao Long had gotten involved with the triads when he was ten. He'd done two-bit jobs and worked his way up to debt collector and muscle for local brothels and gambling parlors. But he'd spent his entire youth working to get in favor with the Liu Jian Triad and its Dragon Head, Liu Jianyu, or as he was known to the world, Johnny Liu.

The first time Xiao had laid eyes on Liu, Xiao had been eleven, and Liu had been getting out of a huge, expensive car. Flanked by bodyguards, Liu had walked into a business meeting, carrying himself with an air of authority and cold-blooded ruthlessness that resonated inside Xiao. It was as if he *were* Liu, or, at the very least, Liu in the making.

From that moment on, Liu became Xiao's icon, the inspiration for all he wanted to do and to be. And nothing would stop him from getting there.

The obstacles would be many. Xiao hadn't been born into the triad leader's world. He was a poor, street-smart kid from Fujian. The only dialect he spoke was the poorly regarded Fukienese. Liu hailed from Guangdong, as did his other triad members. Cantonese was the dialect spoken there, as it was in most cosmopolitan regions. So by the time Xiao was twelve, he'd made it his business to learn Cantonese.

He hadn't stopped at that.

Liu was from the village of Loong Doo, which was very close to Macao and just a quick hop from Hong Kong. The Loong Doo were a tight, impenetrable clan, whose loyalties extended first and foremost to one another. They were also resourceful, enterprising, and stubborn. Most of all, they were risk-takers who aspired to raise their social status and took the necessary chances to ensure that it happened. Their dialect was unique to them. It gave them pleasure to speak it to one another so that other Cantonese couldn't understand them. Conversely, they themselves spoke other dialects of Cantonese and Mandarin so that they could converse with non–Loong Doo Chinese.

Xiao Long's next order of business had been to learn the Loong Doo dialect. And he'd done so in record time.

How fitting that *Loong Doo* translated into "Dragon Society." The Dragon Head of the Liu Jian Triad was a great leader who'd established himself in society. Xiao had dug deep for every shred of background information he could find on Johnny Liu. He knew what Liu was, as well as what he appeared to be. And he knew it took a unique and brilliant mind to walk such a difficult tightrope.

To the Chinese people, Liu was regarded as a wealthy entrepreneur. Also as a philanthropist, who contributed many great works of art—pieces that had deep cultural significance—to China's museums, as well as donating large sums of money to hospitals and charities.

Those who suspected Liu of being involved in criminal enterprise were more than happy to turn a blind eye to it. And the law enforcement community had no concrete evidence of wrongdoing, so they were more than relieved to stay away.

Of course, on that score, Liu had had some help over the years. He'd been of great use to the leaders in Beijing during the Communist takeover of Hong Kong from the British in the early nineties. Thanks to the information Liu provided, prodemocracy activists disappeared. As a reward, Liu was afforded power and protection. In addition, he had a strong ally in Sergeant David Keong of the Hong Kong Police Department, also a Loong Doo. Keong was a personal friend of Liu's—and a well-rewarded one. He aided Liu in many ways—from keeping the transport of packages from Europe and the States under the radar, to ensuring that visitors like Xiao Long bypassed customs when getting in and out of the country. He served as a good, loyal associate to the triad, as well as to Johnny Liu.

Xiao was single-mindedly determined to become an indispensable part of Liu's world.

Perseverance, ambition, and results paid off. Xiao popped onto Liu's radar. Repeatedly, the Dragon Head heard the name of this smart kid from the Fujian province who'd beaten the odds and busted his ass to make something of himself. So he'd sent for Xiao—one of the most treasured, honored days of Xiao's life—and offered him a place in the Liu Jian Triad. Xiao would start small—smuggling twenty units of heroin from the Fujian province—and, based upon his loyalty and success, work his way up, handling bigger and bigger drug deals.

Xiao had followed the rules and exceeded expectations. But he was looking for a more impressive opening—one that would propel him into Liu's inner circle.

He'd found it.

Xiao's golden opportunity had presented itself in the most ironic of ways. His older brother, a small-time drug dealer, had been stupid enough to try spreading his wings by interfering with Liu's alien smuggling operation. He'd stolen one of his boats, with a cargo of over two hundred women, paid off the captain, and killed two of the crew members. Worse, one of those crew members turned out to be a cousin of Johnny Liu's.

Xiao had acted instantly, sans guilt or remorse. Killing came easy to him. It always had. Nothing gave him a greater sense of power than that of ending a life. And blood ties? They meant nothing. His family was the Liu Jian Triad.

With a surge of adrenaline fueled by that sense of power, Xiao butchered his brother and took photographs of the results. He then sliced off one of his brother's fingers—the one bearing the jade ring with their family insignia on it—and placed the cleanly severed finger and a photo of his brother's mutilated remains in a beautifully carved, ornately painted wooden box. He presented the box to Johnny Liu as a gift, as proof of the victim's identity, and as a token of his own loyalty.

Liu had been impressed. The gesture was unprecedented. Xiao had chosen his new family over his flesh and blood. His actions spoke volumes about who and what he was. Armed with guts, smarts, and unshakable drive, and unhindered by human emotion, he had his eye on a powerful future with the triad.

His reward from Liu had been fitting. The Dragon Head had significantly elevated his position and status. And the seeds of personal trust were planted.

Their relationship grew over the next four or five years, and by the time Xiao was in his midtwenties, he and Liu had forged a special bond. Xiao called him *A Sook*, or "Uncle," and Liu afforded him a special place by his side, together with a level of trust that surpassed anything he offered to any other triad member.

The clincher came when Xiao Long presented him with the beautiful painting that Liu coveted—Rothberg's *Dead or Alive*—along with the $375,000 American dollars that Liu had funded that crooked art dealer, Cai Wen, to pay for it, plus the $25,000 Xiao had brought with him, courtesy of Liu, as Cai Wen's commission for completing the transaction. The stupid dealer had tried to swindle the wrong man when he told Xiao that he was upping his commission on the valuable painting to $100,000. Xiao Long had killed him on the spot, taken back the entire $400,000 and the painting, and left without a backward glance.

He'd gone straight to the Dragon Head and gifted him with both the painting and the money. It was a meaningful gesture—the painting Johnny Liu had desired, and a large sum of cash that could have elevated Xiao Long's lifestyle tremendously had he kept it. But he hadn't.

Years of sacrifice, culminating with this latest demonstration of consummate loyalty, was more than enough. Xiao Long's future was sealed.

A month later, the opportunity had arisen for the Hong Kong–based triad to gain a foothold in the United States. Johnny Liu offered Xiao the chance of a lifetime: to go to New York, spearhead the operation, and begin expanding the triad's wealth in America.

It was the beginning of Xiao's rise to power. He'd bowed at the Dragon Head's feet, accepting instantly and vowing to make Liu proud.

With the triad's backing, Xiao had easily started his gang in New York

City's Chinatown. The Red Dragons, he'd called it, in honor of his Dragon Head. Becoming its respected Dai Lo, or "Elder Brother," was just as easy. There were street kids everywhere who were hungry for cash and even hungrier for the "family" a gang afforded. Xiao Long had capitalized on that, and the Red Dragons had flourished, surviving gang wars, police raids, and the occasional defector or informant. Over the past thirteen years, Xiao's gambling, drug, and prostitution businesses had produced a cash flow that more than met the Dragon Head's expectations.

This year they'd expanded into home burglaries, scoping out affluent Manhattan apartments through data provided by Xiao's nephew, Eric Hu, and his computer services company. From that point, the Red Dragon kids took over, bypassing uniformed doormen and deactivating burglar alarms by inputting security codes stolen through the use of Hu's hidden video cameras. The break-ins occurred at the times Hu suggested, and the kids went straight to the valuable items whose locations Hu had provided. All the stolen items were fenced, except for the valuable paintings and art pieces that Xiao shipped off to Hong Kong via the Philippine province of Cebu.

Xiao knew that Johnny Liu had a broader plan in mind. He knew Liu meant for him to play an integral part in what came next.

It was the accelerating timetable that concerned him. He had an ominous feeling as to its cause.

A limousine was waiting for him when he arrived at Hong Kong International Airport. From there, he was driven to Johnny Liu's hilltop estate on the affluent Victoria Peak. He was greeted by a servant and escorted into the main garden, which was a veritable paradise filled with exquisite arrays of flowers and cascading fountains. At the garden's center, where Liu was now seated, was a magnificent jade and marble shrine, built in honor of Liu's daughter, Meili, who'd died almost three years ago, tragically at the young age of twenty-three.

Xiao Long knew better than most how her death had eaten away at Johnny Liu.

Slowly and respectfully, Xiao approached the shrine, stopping several yards away and waiting.

The Dragon Head beckoned him forward, gesturing for Xiao to join him.

Xiao complied, ascending the steps to stand before his leader. He bowed deeply from the waist. "*A Sook*," he murmured.

He then took a seat across from the Dragon Head. "Thank you for sending for me." He automatically switched to Liu's native Loong Doo dialect.

"You look well," Liu responded in the same tongue. "Your trip was pleasant and without incident, I trust?"

Xiao Long nodded. Perhaps *he* looked well, but his Dragon Head didn't. He looked gaunt, sickly. His complexion was sallow, and his cheeks were sunken. He'd aged a decade since Xiao had last seen him, just months ago.

Liu studied Xiao for a moment, as if reading his thoughts. "You're concerned about me. We'll address that later. I'm proud of you. Your success in New York is exceptional. The time has come to expand your efforts. Providing you with the details is one of the reasons I summoned you here. But first, I want to hear about Johnson. Where do things stand?"

The question came as no surprise. Xiao knew of his leader's obsessive hatred for Wallace Johnson, and his only slightly less intense hatred for Johnson's partners. What he didn't know was when that hatred had begun or what had caused it.

Without pause, he provided the requisite answer. "Johnson continues to suffer—in all ways. As I reported, he was threatened before he spoke to the FBI, and beaten afterward. He still hasn't recovered from the bodily pain. Financially, you have things in hand. Spiritually, he deteriorates daily. Our actions cause him profound agony. He sits alone in a dungeon of his own creation. His paintings are his only companions. His anguish is acute."

"What about his partners? Is Burbank's wife dead?"

"Unfortunately, no," Xiao replied frankly. "I just received a call from Jin Huang. He followed orders. He murdered Rosalyn Burbank's bodyguard and disposed of his body. Then, he seized Burbank's wife. She would be dead, but an unfortunate traffic incident prevented it. She escaped."

Liu's jaw tightened. "Rectify that. Personally."

"You have my word." Xiao was loath to disappoint his Dragon Head. Still, he couldn't regret Rosalyn Burbank's escape. The thought of personally killing her triggered a rush of anticipation.

"Continue," Liu instructed.

"Of course." Xiao got himself back on track. "Our arrangements to ruin Burbank are in place."

"Acceptable. But, as we both know, no substitute. Burbank needs to suffer great personal loss—soon. Only then can he die. Let's move on. Where do things stand with Martino?"

"The employment agency you had me acquire continues to service Martino's clothing factory and to squeeze him dry. He's approaching bankruptcy. And his guilt and liquor consume him, body and soul. He might take his own life before we get the chance to do it for him. If not, I'll see to that personally, as well."

"Good." The Dragon Head nodded, somewhat appeased. "And the others?"

"Fox is still mourning his personal loss and ultimate rejection. Leary is drowning in debt, thanks to his addiction and his bookie. I can execute each of them whenever you choose, in whatever manner you see fit."

"Soon," Liu said. "And, again, by your hand, and your hand alone. That applies to all five men. I want them to endure brutal, agonizing deaths. Until then, escalate their suffering. Kill Burbank's wife. Target his daughter. Push Martino over the edge. Bleed Leary dry. Prepare to make Fox's loss an actual fatality. As for Johnson—no amount of torture is enough." The Dragon Head's tone was filled with such uncharacteristic venom that it caught Xiao Long off guard. Liu was a man who exhibited nothing but self-control.

The surprise must have registered on Xiao's face, because his Dragon Head studied him again before he spoke. "It's time you learned the truth about Meili's death. There are rumors that she died by her own hand. I say Johnson killed her. He didn't wield the knife. But he might as well have. Just as Burbank, Martino, Fox, and Leary might as well have twisted the blade in her heart."

"They knew your daughter?"

"Indeed they did. Especially Johnson. He knew her far too well."

This was not what Xiao Long had expected. "I thought that you and Johnson were business associates."

"And so we were—and still are, in Johnson's mind. But back then, our association was untarnished. He made many trips to Hong Kong for his investment firm. We had frequent business dealings. They were all honorable."

"So he met Meili . . ."

"Not then," Liu replied curtly. "Not until several years after she left home."

Xiao was already situated in New York when Liu's only child had run off. But he'd made the necessary arrangements to be instantly apprised about anything that affected his mentor. So he knew that Meili had left home. She'd been just seventeen at the time. And Liu had been crushed. So Xiao had respected his privacy and had asked no questions.

The answers were now being provided.

"She was so young and so headstrong," Liu murmured. "A budding artist. I saw signs of great talent. I would have used all my resources to properly educate her and to open the doors to a thriving career. But Meili . . ." A heavy sigh. "She wanted no part of it. She was naive and free-spirited enough to believe she could make it on her own. So one night while I slept, she disappeared. She took nothing but two paintings. Both Rothbergs, including the one you took such great pains to acquire for me."

"She sold them?"

"One at a time, yes. In order to eat and put a roof over her head. But she was swindled on each sale. As a result, she could barely scrape by. Her lifestyle . . . let's say it became unacceptable. I demanded she return home. She refused. I had no choice but to sever ties with her. She'd defied me, stolen from me, and brought shame to our family." A pause. "We didn't see each other again—not until just before she died."

Liu's expression remained unchanged, as did his tone, but Xiao could sense the pain and anger beneath the surface.

"She came to me then, like a trampled flower," the Dragon Head continued. "She'd been defiling herself with an older, married man. An American, who came to her whenever he was in China on business. The affair had been ongoing for over three years—ever since he and his partners tried pressuring her into selling them the second Rothberg for a price too absurd to mention. They saw how desperate she was. And they used that to their advantage."

"They *tried* buying the painting," Xiao echoed. "She refused?"

"Yes, but only because she got a slightly better offer—one that was still an insult. Worse, she sold both Rothbergs to competing triads."

Xiao knew the severity of such a betrayal. But he wisely didn't say anything about it. "And the American she was involved with?" He refrained from speaking Johnson's name.

"According to Meili, he had become totally enchanted with her. He lavished her with spending money and jewels, and professions of love. That turned out to be a facade. He'd reduced my daughter to nothing but a common whore. One night, in what he considered to be a moment of levity, he revealed to her that his friend and partner, Ben Martino, had come up with the idea of a bet. All his partners—the same ones who'd tried swindling her—had participated."

"What kind of bet?" Xiao Long was processing this onslaught of information as quickly as he could.

"The men placed wagers on how long it would take Johnson to bed my daughter." A hard swallow. "Evidently, Meili still had a shred of dignity left. When she heard that her love affair was the result of a bet, she was shamed and angry. She ended the affair at once. That bastard Johnson didn't even understand why. He would have continued their involvement indefinitely—a married man defiling my daughter, with no plans for a future with her. And all at the instigation of a bet. A bet made by thieves who'd steal from a desperate young woman who was clearly at the end of her rope."

"I don't understand. You say there was respect between you and Johnson. Yet he was dishonoring your daughter while continuing his business relationship with you."

"He didn't know Meili was my daughter. She told him only her given name." Another pause. "When she came to me, it was shortly after she had tossed Johnson aside. She was carrying his child. She was far too proud to seek him out and turn to him for help. But she was alone and penniless. She wanted my help. When I heard her story, I was so overcome with shame and rage, I turned her away. It was a mistake. By the time I went after her, it was too late. She'd slit her wrists, and bled to death all alone. It was only afterward, when I read her suicide note, that I found out Johnson was the man who'd dishonored her. From that moment, I vowed that, if it took my entire life, I would avenge Meili's death. Now you know why you're aiding me. But my revenge is not complete. I won't feel peace until Johnson has been tortured to the point where he has no desire to live, at which time I'll oblige him. And the others? The heartless animals who pushed my child into destitution, and then placed wagers on how long it would take for her to become a rich man's prostitute? They must pay as well. Have nothing. Be nothing. And then die—just as Meili did."

"I understand." This explanation was vital. It clarified much about the Dragon Head's orders over the years.

Liu was slowly killing these men. Through Xiao, he was breaking their bodies and their spirits.

And soon Xiao would be afforded the supreme satisfaction of ending their lives.

"What I've just told you remains between us," Liu stated. It wasn't a request. It was an order. "The circumstances surrounding Meili's death have been concealed. That's the way I intend it to stay."

"Of course, A Sook." Xiao bowed his head. "You have my solemn pledge."

"And you have my trust."

That was that. In the blink of an eye, Liu was no longer the grieving father. He was the Dragon Head.

"It's time to share the final phase of my plan with you," he pronounced. "The Black Eagles will soon be arriving in America. They have been paid enough to ensure we reap millions of American dollars. Thanks to the groundwork you laid with their Albanian-American relatives, everything is in order for their arrival. You will run the entire operation. It is complex, but I know you'll succeed. My niece and her amah will play key roles in the entire plan, especially in the demise of my enemies. It must unfold quickly, and with ultimate precision. After that, my personal scores will be settled, and the triad will be left wealthy and strong."

"Left?" Xiao refused to ignore the finality of Liu's statement.

Without responding, Liu rose, gripping the chair arms for support. The conversation had clearly worn him out. "I must rest now. Afterward, we'll talk again. By the time you return to New York, you will be ready."

"A *Sook*," Xiao inserted quickly, also rising to his feet. "I'm honored by your faith in me. Have no doubt that I'll make your plan succeed. I'll bring great wealth to our triad. And I'll take personal pleasure in killing your enemies. But your urgency causes me concern. Why have you so rapidly accelerated your plan?"

Liu faced Xiao without emotion. "You know the answer. My time here grows short."

"I will not accept that." Xiao had never spoken so disrespectfully to his Dragon Head. But this was one time he couldn't contain himself. "You will not leave this earth. I won't permit it. Whatever is ailing you, we'll fight it."

Rather than becoming angry, Liu looked somewhat amused. "Some fights cannot be won, my son. Not even by you. My cancer is advanced. It's spread throughout my body. I'll be dead in a month, maybe two."

Hearing the news spoken aloud, Xiao felt as if he'd been punched in the gut. His Dragon Head was his inspiration, the man he'd modeled his life after. Others died. Liu lived forever.

"There will be no mourning," Liu instructed Xiao. "Only acceptance and preparation. Live up to your potential. Put my affairs in order. Fulfill my final requests. Then I can die in peace."

There was no room left for argument. Xiao would comply with Liu's final wishes.

"All that you ask will be done," Xiao replied, the icy purpose in his soul returning to his voice, his eyes. "Everything you've requested will become reality. And afterward, I'll honor your memory. I'll make sure you live on."

"I never doubted it. If all goes as planned, the triad members will soon be addressing you as Dragon Head."

CHAPTER TWELVE

Matthew Burbank was pacing by the front door when Sloane arrived. He was sheet white, and looked ill.

"I'm here, Dad," she said quietly. "I talked to Mom's doctor. Everything is fine. They've set her arm, and she's asleep. She'll be in and out of sleep—mostly in—for a few hours anyway. So let's take care of this first. Then, we'll go pick her up. I also talked to the security agency. They're starting a private search for Fred. When I give them the go-ahead, they'll call the NYPD. But we all know the likelihood of finding Fred alive is zip. Organized crime doesn't leave witnesses."

A taut nod.

"Did you follow my instructions?"

"Yes. I haven't said a word since we spoke. Nor has Special Agent Williams. He's just sitting in the living room, like a lion waiting for his meat."

"Then let's make sure he knows he's not getting any." Sloane squeezed her father's arm. "It will be all right. Just let me do all the talking."

She walked inside and led the way into the living room.

Rich Williams was seated on the sofa with an empty coffee cup perched on the table in front of him. Quickly, Sloane sized him up. A distinguished, silver-haired man in a business suit, he was self-assured, comfortable in his own skin, and low-key in a way that suggested he'd already acquired everything he needed to call this a wrap.

An experienced agent. And a perfect demeanor to unnerve someone like her father.

"Hello, Agent Williams," Sloane said in a crisp professional voice.

"Ms. Burbank." He came to his feet at once, extending his hand to shake hers. "It's a pleasure. I've heard a great deal about you."

"I'm sure you have. Particularly while you were arranging to have me out of the picture while you questioned my father. Rather unethical, wouldn't you say?"

A spark of amusement flickered in Williams's eyes. "The D.A. must have been very sorry to lose you. I know the Bureau is. Now I know why. You're quite the steamroller."

"That's not an answer."

"It wasn't intended to be. The reason I came by this morning was to clarify a few loose ends with your father. Some interesting information came out of our talk. It obviously upset him. He requested that his attorney be present. I immediately stopped asking questions. In fact, we haven't exchanged a word since he called you—several times. I believe all that is not only ethical, it's entirely legal."

"Let's not play semantics." Chin raised, Sloane stared him down. "I want to know what was discussed."

"Gladly." Williams played back the entire conversation.

It wasn't much different than Sloane had expected.

"I want a few minutes with my client."

"By all means." Williams made a wide sweep with his arm, then picked up his coffee cup. "May I trouble you for a refill while you talk?"

"Certainly. Dad, you wait for me in the breakfast nook. I'll get Agent Williams his coffee." Sloane stopped her father as he took a step toward the kitchen. He was a wreck. The last thing he needed to do was to spill coffee on a shrewd agent who already suspected him of murder or conspiracy to murder.

She took the empty cup from Williams as her father followed her instruc-tions. "How do you take it?"

"Just black." Williams still looked amused, which infuriated the hell out of Sloane. "I appreciate it."

"No problem. You can leave a tip on the table." She was in and out of the kitchen and in the breakfast nook with her father in under a minute.

"Dad, listen to me." She spoke in a low, confident tone, keeping both their backs to Agent Williams. "You've run out of choices—especially once the NYPD finds out what happened to Mom and passes it along. It's either risk prosecution on criminal charges or tell the FBI the truth." She waved away her father's objections before he could voice them. "I have some stipulations I plan to make before you lay out the facts. I believe Agent Williams will agree to them—after he makes a few phone calls and escorts us to the Field Office so that you can't tamper with any alleged evidence."

"What kind of stipulations?" her father managed, sounding dubious and hopeful all at once.

"The kind that will get any potential charges against you dropped, and at the same time increase your level of protection. Mom's, too."

Matthew sucked in his breath. "What about Leo, Phil, Ben, and Wal-lace?"

"They'll be free of charges as well."

"How do you plan to accomplish this?"

"You let me worry about that. Call your partners. Explain the situation to them. I'm sure they'll all agree with my strategy, since none of them wants to go to prison. Once we're all on the same page, I'll present my offer to Agent Williams." She saw the flash of indecision in her father's eyes. "Trust me, Dad."

He nodded, reaching for the phone.

"Wait," Sloane instructed, holding up her index finger to indicate that it would just take a minute. She walked into the living room, standing beside the settee that was across from Agent Williams.

"In my opinion, we can fill in the blanks to your satisfaction. But, as you know, there are four other partners in my father's art investment group. Since this affects them all, he needs to get their permission before we proceed. Which means he has four phone calls to make. You have my word that this isn't a ploy, nor an attempt to devise a coordinated distortion of facts. Is that acceptable?"

Williams studied Sloane, this time with contemplation rather than amusement. "Tell your father he can make his calls."

CHAPTER THIRTEEN

An hour later, Sloane and her father were seated across from Tony at his desk in the New York Field Office. They were joined by SA Williams and—no surprise—Derek.

"So, Sloane," Tony began, leaning forward and interlacing his fingers on his desk. "I hear you have a proposal for us—along with some valuable information."

"I do." She crossed one leg over the other, sitting rigidly against the back of the well-worn chair. "As I'm sure Agent Williams told you . . ."

"Rich," Williams corrected.

"Very well—Rich. I'm sure Rich told you that my proposal has stipulations attached."

"He did. So go ahead, shoot."

"First, I want your word that neither my father nor any of his partners will be charged with a crime."

Tony's brows rose. "How can I do that without knowing what they've done?"

"Fair enough," Sloane acknowledged, feeling her father shift nervously beside her. "Suffice it to say that *if* any crime was to have been committed, the alleged charges could be withholding evidence or, if you were feeling particularly vindictive, obstruction of justice. All of which would have been done out of fear for their lives and, in my father's case, the lives of his family. Hypothetically speaking, of course."

"Of course," Tony concurred.

"The break-in was a threat?" Derek asked. "Why? For what purpose?"

Sloane pinned him with a cool, impersonal stare. "No comment. Not until and unless my conditions are agreed to."

"I can live with this one," Tony replied. "If what you're saying is true, and if your father has information that could benefit us, no charges will be filed."

"Good. On to my second stipulation. As you know, I've been arranging for private bodyguards up until now. I want FBI security assigned to my father. He, above all his partners, is in constant danger. I want that security to extend to my mother as well. Now more than ever. I'll supply an explanation for that once we have an agreement."

"You want us to put your parents in protective custody?"

"No." Sloane shook her head. "That would be a glaring declaration to the wrong people that my father had spoken to you. I want them to go on staying in their apartment—*with* an FBI agent inside. And I want agents assigned to them when they go out."

"That takes resources. But judging from the urgency of your tone—fine. It can be arranged." Tony shot her a quizzical look. "How many other conditions are there?"

"Just one." Sloane didn't blink. "Give me an operational assignment. Make me a confidential human source. I want to be fully briefed on your investigation."

Rich couldn't help but chuckle at the magnitude of her request. At the same time, he noticed that neither Derek nor Tony was laughing. To the contrary, they didn't appear the least bit taken aback.

"Am I to assume this is business as usual?" he inquired.

"We're lucky she stopped there," Tony responded drily. "I was half expecting her to ask that I order Derek to step down and make her the lead investigator." He tapped his pen against his leg, mulling over Sloane's request.

"I can justify it," he finally announced. "But only if you can explain how your involvement would benefit the Bureau."

Sloane was prepared for the standard prerequisite. Her inclusion in the process had to be substantiated for the legal department. "Obviously, I have information that I believe you want. Further, I believe that I'm a potential target for one of the top brass, maybe even the leader, of the gang you're pursuing." She turned to Rich. "Who's also a player in the art crime you're investigating. By giving me an operational assignment, you just might wrap up both cases."

"Forget it," Derek stated flatly. "That's not an operational assignment. That's using you as bait. I'm not doing it."

"No, you're not. I am." Sloane gazed steadily at Tony. "Well?"

"Well, for starters, if I were to agree, you wouldn't be calling the shots. Derek would. So answers like the one you just gave him would be out."

"Fine. But so would personal feelings," Sloane countered. "If I'm unqualified for the job, that's one thing. But if Agent Parker is reacting out of some unprofessional need to protect me, that's discrimination. You and I have worked together many times, Tony. I doubt you'd evaluate me as being unqualified."

Tony inclined his head in Derek's direction. "She's got you there. Is there some professional reason I should refuse Sloane's request?"

A tense, prolonged silence.

"No," Derek finally admitted, sounding as if the words were being dragged out of him. "I'm sure Sloane's inside knowledge will benefit us, and her skills will contribute positively to the investigation. However," he added in a no-nonsense tone, "I want it understood that I am the lead investigator on the organized crime case, and that *professionally* I make the decisions. Ditto for Rich on the Rothberg case."

"Agreed," Sloane said without hesitation.

"Then it looks like we're in business." Tony rose and shook Sloane's hand. "Welcome aboard. By the time you rejoin the Bureau, no one will realize you were gone." He turned his attention to Matthew, who, on Sloane's advice, had stayed silent until now. "The floor's yours, Mr. Burbank. Tell us what you know."

Matthew glanced at his daughter, his forehead creased with worry.

With loving support, Sloane squeezed his arm, still facing Tony. "First, I need to tell you that my mother is hospitalized in the Bronx. She was kidnapped several hours ago with the intent to kill her. Her abductor was one of your Asian gang members. Evidently, he knew Rich was on his way over to see my father. This was retaliation."

"Is she all right?" Derek asked instantly.

"Her arm is broken. The subject bent it until it snapped." Sloane reported the incident as objectively as she could, regarding Derek with a cool, impersonal stare. "Thankfully, she got out of the car before he could kill her. She's heavily sedated right now. But after you get my father's statement, I want to pick her up and bring her home, where she can be comfortable."

"Shit," Derek muttered under his breath.

"She saw her abductor," Sloane continued, her gaze shifting back to Tony. "In addition, I'm convinced that my father saw the mobster who ordered their apartment break-in—*and* who killed Cai Wen. So after this meeting, I'd suggest you call in a sketch artist. That way, we can put names to faces. I have a strong feeling you'll recognize these thugs."

"Done," Tony replied.

With that, Sloane gestured to her father, nodding for him to do what he had to.

He took her cue, producing the empty Rothberg file, the fortune cookie, and the ominous message that had been inside it.

"It'll be fine now," she reassured him quietly. "Tell them everything."

———

Cindy Liu was an up-and-coming architect with enough talent to have graduated from Cornell University's College of Architecture, Art and Planning at the top of her class. She'd done the same again two years later, earning her master's in architecture. From there, she'd been snapped up by Crawley & Foster, one of Manhattan's most prestigious architectural firms. She'd worked there for three years, learning and absorbing every nuance of the business, and making enough contacts to assure herself some clients. Then, she'd followed her dream and gone out on her own.

Her powerful *A Sook* in Hong Kong, Johnny Liu, had funded her new business, no questions asked. He'd been her guardian angel all her life, and she adored him—not only because he was her uncle or because he'd orchestrated her move to America to ensure she had the best education and future, but also because the two of them had shared a special bond since her childhood.

Johnny Liu had been blessed with only one child before his wife died. Given that fact, along with his wealth, he had spoiled his daughter from the time she was small, and she'd grown up to be a wild, reckless teenager. Her life had ended tragically several years after Cindy—Jiao was her given name—had come to America.

Cindy's own parents were very different from her *A Sook*, as were her siblings. They were traditional, content to stay within the confines of their village and their people. Her father, although Johnny Liu's brother, had none of Johnny's initiative, nor did he see any reason for Cindy, as a female, to reach beyond Loong Doo, much less to leave China to further her education and broaden her horizons.

Cindy saw life differently. She admired her *A Sook*, and often traveled with him from Hong Kong to Macao and back, watching him conduct business as he earned his fortune. She wanted the same for herself.

She'd been drawing since she could hold a crayon, and pencil sketching since not too many years after that. She always thought she'd be an artist, but her interests took a detour along the way, influenced by her structured, engineering-oriented mind and her photographic memory. So architecture seemed the perfect way to go, a marriage between her technical and creative sides.

Her true talents were in the design and creation of interior space, the very direction she pursued. Fortunately, in good times or bad, there were always a select few among New York's affluent who were adding wings to their homes or redesigning their existing living space. Consequently, there was no shortage of work in New York City for architects as talented as she.

Cindy lived on the Upper West Side of Manhattan with her amah, Peggy Sun, a close family friend and paid companion who'd accompanied Cindy to the United States when Cindy was fifteen. That was when Johnny Liu had ensured his niece a place in an exclusive private high school, and her new life had begun.

Nearly fifteen years later, Peggy was still her faithful companion—more like an older sister than an amah, since Cindy was nearing thirty. The two women had a great deal in common. Peggy, like Cindy, was a gifted artist with a keen eye for detail. She could capture and replicate almost anything on canvas. And Cindy's uncle had fostered those talents by funding Peggy's enrollment in fine arts programs that enhanced her skills.

Cindy knew that her *A Sook* had invested in Peggy so that she could be a professional asset to Cindy. And she was grateful, especially now that she was striking out on her own. Peggy's instincts for fine art rounded out Cindy's structural and conceptual skills, and her knowledge of art history and stylistic nuances helped Cindy pick out just the right design elements for each client.

They made a great team. Between that and the business savvy Cindy had in common with her uncle, her fledgling business was off to a fine start.

Still, knowing her *A Sook* as well as she did, Cindy had always suspected that he had more specific reasons—a larger plan—for training Peggy so extensively.

The phone call she now received from him confirmed it.

Her heart was broken when he told her his medical prognosis. He wasn't just ill, as he'd led her to believe. He was dying. But he wanted no tears shed. What he wanted was to get his life in order. He needed Cindy's assistance, and Peggy's as well. He needed their combined talents and expertise.

There was never a question of what their answer would be.

Up until now, Cindy had pushed many ethical boundaries, but she'd never crossed the line into criminal. It hadn't been necessary. But the conversation with her *A Sook* changed all that. She'd do anything for him. Plus, the undertaking would be challenging, exciting, and—most of all—vindicating.

So she met with his New York representative, Xiao Long, who explained the details of the individual roles she and Peggy would play.

It was a brilliant plan. Risky, yes, but what was life without risk? Cindy had learned that at her *A Sook*'s knee. Big stakes meant big payoffs—if you had the guts. Well, Cindy had the guts and the motivation. So did Peggy, who was on board with no coercion necessary.

The requisite phone calls were made. And the ball was in Cindy's court.

Her job was two-part—personal and professional. The combination would be tricky. She'd have to walk a very fine line.

It was critical that this first meeting went precisely as planned.

She spent extra time getting dressed and applying her makeup that morning. She chose a stylish black pantsuit—conservatively trendy, but fashioned by a less well known designer. Nothing that screamed money, like an Armani. She was portraying a budding professional, not the wealthy, spoiled niece of one of Hong Kong's richest business tycoons. And she was portraying it to a man who knew money.

She glanced at the photo of Meili that Xiao Long had given her. She remembered her cousin well—beautiful and vital, a turn-on for any man. There were definite similarities in their bone structure and coloring. Cindy had to make the most of those similarities.

Sitting patiently in front of the makeup mirror, she parted her glossy black hair on the right rather than the left side, letting it flow straight and loose past her shoulders. She applied a light amount of lip and eye makeup, being sure to emphasize her arresting almond-shaped eyes, dark and mysterious, and her high cheekbones.

She slipped into high-heeled pumps, since, like Meili, Cindy was petite, with a small-boned, dainty build.

Then she turned to Peggy. "What do you think?"

A smile curved her amah's lips. "I think you've more than accomplished step one of our goal."

Cindy acknowledged that statement by crossing her fingers and scooping up her purse. "Let's hope you're right."

———

They would arrive in New York on schedule.

It had taken careful planning. Smuggling criminals into the United States was far more difficult than getting them across European and Asian borders. But with the right connections and enough money, anything was possible.

It helped that no one had seen their faces. It also helped that the concentrated efforts of Interpol and the various federal government agencies that were investigating the museum heists were all focused on Europe. Criminals for hire like the Black Eagles, despite being affiliated with Albanian organized crime in Europe, didn't normally travel to the States.

But they had family in America. Family they could hide with, blend in with.

And, with one phone call, America had become the land of opportunity.

———

Wallace was in his Manhattan art gallery that morning. He'd come in early to review his finances. He was in trouble. Big trouble. But he couldn't give up the paintings. If he did, he'd be left with nothing but the cavernous hole in his heart.

He had to make more money.

He'd spend most of the day in the gallery, where business hours presented the greatest likelihood of pedestrian traffic and potential sales. Then, he'd drive out to Long Island before rush hour and spend the evening at his East Hampton gallery, when the year-round residents were strolling the streets and browsing at the local shops. The affluent often bought on impulse.

Closing time would be at nine. That would allow him the entire long, empty night in his East Hampton estate, where he'd lose himself downstairs in his private sanctuary.

His anguish wasn't the only thing that would keep him from sleeping. Nor was his escalating debt.

His entire body still ached from the beating he'd taken. He wasn't a kid anymore, and his body didn't heal the way it used to. The bruises on his throat had faded enough so he could switch from turtlenecks to buttoned dress shirts and ties. But he still flinched every time he shaved, as well as every time he stood up or made a sudden move.

He was worried sick about a repeat performance—or worse—now that

Matthew had told the truth to the FBI. Wallace had agreed that it was the only way to go when Matthew had called. What else could he say without arousing suspicion, especially after Rosalyn's harrowing experience? Only he knew that, even if Rosalyn were killed, her death would be quick and painless compared to the agonizing torture they'd inflict on him before slaughtering him for his betrayal. And there was no backing out now. He was in too deep. Plus, he *needed* those paintings. They were his lifeline.

The tinkling bell at the front of the gallery interrupted his musings, telling him that his first customer of the day had arrived. He went to the front, forcing a smile as a young Asian woman stepped inside. She brushed strands of hair off her face and raised her head, meeting his gaze head-on. "Mr. Johnson?"

Wallace felt as if his heart had dropped to his knees. "Meili?" he murmured in a choked voice.

The young woman looked puzzled. "Excuse me?"

He blinked. Her English was perfect, unaccented. And the way she was dressed, the way she carried herself—it wasn't Meili. But, dear Lord, they could be twins.

"I apologize," he managed. "I thought you were someone else."

"I hope that someone is attractive and talented." She smiled—Meili's smile—and extended her hand, palm out. "I'm Cindy Liu. I believe you spoke to my uncle?"

Liu. He'd almost forgotten. His longtime business associate in Hong Kong had called to discuss his niece, and to ask for Wallace's cooperation in advancing her career. Liu was a wealthy and influential man, whose transactions with Wallace in his prior career had escalated his success as an investment banker. Now, after Wallace had lost everything and was pouring whatever was left of his soul and his financial assets into his two galleries, Johnny Liu continued to be supportive. He had numerous affluent friends and business associates who were also patrons of the arts, and, when they were in New York, he made sure to send them Wallace's way. He'd also personally bought paintings from Wallace, and sold a few of his own through Wallace's galleries.

As a result, any favor Liu asked of Wallace was a favor done.

In this case, he'd asked Wallace to use any influence he still wielded in New York's circle of the rich and famous to promote his niece, Cindy, and her new architectural business. Since that was the world Wallace still traveled in, it would be an easy task to accomplish. Especially now that he was seeing Cindy Liu in person. Like Meili, she was beautiful and he could already tell she was charismatic. He'd have no problems getting her in the right doors, and if she was as talented as her uncle professed, she'd be an instant sensation.

"Cindy." Wallace recovered himself, clasping her hand and shaking it. "You're the brilliant young architect your uncle spoke so highly of. Please, call me Wallace."

"Thank you, Wallace. It's a pleasure to meet you." Cindy paused, eyeing him with a curious, concerned expression. "Are you all right?"

"Fine." Wallace squelched the overpowering sense of déjà vu. "You just remind me of someone. The resemblance is striking."

"I hope that's a compliment."

"It is. The woman I'm remembering was quite lovely, and obviously, quite memorable." He gestured for Cindy to come in and have a seat. "Your uncle and I have been colleagues for many years. I'm so glad he sought me out to help you. I'd like to do all I can to benefit your new business. Hopefully, I can introduce you to the right people who'll make all the difference."

Cindy gave him a radiant smile. "I have no doubt that you can."

CHAPTER FOURTEEN

Sloane ran the hounds an extra half-mile that night to atone for leaving them longer than usual.

It was eight P.M. She'd been gone since eight A.M. Between a seminar she was giving at a local police precinct, a class she taught in level-three Krav Maga, two meetings with corporate clients, and a later-than-usual occupational therapy session, the day had been packed.

And, yes, she'd also been avoiding Derek.

Last night, she'd arrived home before him, still fuming from his deception. She was also drained, having joined her father to pick up her mother and get her settled and comfortable at home, then waiting while Rosalyn provided the sketch artist with as comprehensive a description of her kidnapper as she could. Before taking off for home, Sloane had ensured that the FBI agents Tony had assigned were in place—one inside her parents' apartment, and two outside the building. She'd introduced herself and reviewed their instructions with them. Satisfied, she'd left and driven to the New Jersey suburbs.

She'd pulled into her driveway, thinking that home looked damned good. Derek's car not being there looked even better. After taking care of Moe, Larry, and Curly's needs, she'd gulped down a yogurt and turned in early.

Once she and the hounds were in the bedroom, she'd locked the door behind them, giving Derek a clear sign that he wasn't welcome.

He'd tried the door once, knocked and called her name twice, then given up and gone to the guest room.

This morning, Sloane made sure she heard him leave before pulling on her jogging gear and taking the hounds for their three-mile run. Shortly thereafter, she'd fed them, showered, and taken off.

She moved back her occupational therapy session. Connie had no problem seeing Sloane at six rather than five, since she was working at her Morristown, New Jersey, office today, rather than the Hospital for Special Surgery in Manhattan. Although, being the blunt person she was and the friend she'd become to Sloane over the past year and a half, she was quick to point out that Sloane was putting off the inevitable. Whatever it was that Derek had done to piss her off so much wasn't going away without a major blowup.

Sloane had to agree. This confrontation was going to be ugly, but it had to be had.

Finishing up her extended run with the hounds, she returned to the cottage. This time, Derek's car was already in the driveway. She went inside, unleashed the hounds so they could take off for their water bowls, and grabbed a towel, wiping her face and neck.

"Hello." Derek walked out of the kitchen with a glass of wine in his hand. "I put out some brie and flatbread crackers to go with this." He pointed at his goblet. "Care to join me? Or are we continuing our game of duck and run?"

Sloane lowered the towel. "I'm not playing duck and run. I'm just trying to calm down enough to have a civil conversation." She glanced at the wine. "Merlot?"

"Beaujolais."

"Better still. I'll jump in the shower and join you in ten minutes."

"Done."

She spent the ten minutes reining in her emotions as the spray of water hit her face and she lathered away the aftermath of her run. Then, she dried off, pulled on a comfortable nightshirt, ran a brush through her damp hair, and made her way to the kitchen.

Derek was sitting on a stool at the island that seated two. He gestured at the other stool, which he'd pulled around to the other side of the island.

"I figured we'd be less likely to kill each other with wood and granite between us."

"Smart idea." Sloane slid onto the stool and poured herself a glass of wine, taking a sip and then spreading some brie on a cracker.

"Do you blame me for what happened to your mother?" Derek asked without preamble.

"I blame you for the setup." Sloane was equally blunt. "You used our relationship, *and* the intensity of our first few nights together, to dupe me. That's not only degrading, it's a major breach of trust. Which, as you recall, is what broke us up the first time." She gazed steadily at Derek as she chewed and swallowed her cheese and cracker.

"I'm not going to pretend I don't see your point," Derek replied, although his jaw was set in that way that told Sloane he wasn't backing down. "What I was forced to do sucked. But when Rich called and laid things out for me, I had no choice. I had to protect you. *Not* from the world—I realize you're more than capable of doing that. From yourself. You love your father. If he had been guilty of something ugly, he might not have told you, and you might not have been able to see through him the way you would anyone else. And if you'd known what Rich had planned, you would have raced over to your parents' apartment and jeopardized everything Rich hoped to, and did, accomplish."

"Right." Sloane's tone was dripping with sarcasm. "So this was all about me. Not your loyalty to the Bureau."

A muscle worked in Derek's jaw. "It was about both. Yes, I did my job. Yes, I feel an obligation to put away the bad guys. And, yes, that would apply to your father if he turned out to be one of those bad guys."

"Well, what do you know? A shred of honesty. Maybe if you'd gone for that approach from the start, I would have cooperated, and we wouldn't be having this fight."

"Oh, get off it Sloane. You wouldn't have cooperated—not emotionally or legally. You'd be choosing between your father and an organized-crime investigation. That's one hell of a major conflict of interest. Worse, he's not just your father. He's also your client. You're legally obligated to protect his interests. Take a step back and view this objectively. Don't you see how irrational you're being?"

"Yes." Sloane slammed her fist on the counter, hating that Derek was right, hating that she couldn't get past this. "The logic is all there. But the way the situation was handled . . . I still feel used. And manipulated."

"I had a snap decision to make. I made it. I knew you'd be furious. And I felt like shit when I gave Rich the go-ahead. But I couldn't see any other way for him to get his answers and not put you in an untenable position. I'm sorry for how all this makes you feel. I'm sorry about your mother. But I'm not sorry for my decision. Now it's up to you. Are you going to be reasonable and work through this with me, or are you going to reerect that damned wall of yours?"

"I'm trying like hell not to. That's why I put off having this fight. I get what you're saying. But here I was, picking out fabric patterns with you, while my mother was being carted off to be killed, and Rich was grilling my father about Cai Wen's murder. Do you know what a fool I feel like?"

"The redecorating part wasn't a lie. I want to make this place ours, rather than yours. The only contrivance was the timing of Leo's appointment." Derek leaned forward. "Let's face it, Sloane. If you'd been the lead agent on this case, you would have followed the same procedure I did, and you know it. The real issue here is that you need to be the one in control—always the cat, never the mouse. Well, life doesn't work that way. This time you were the mouse. And you can't come to grips with that."

"Right back at you," Sloane retorted. "You're the biggest control freak I know. If the tables were turned, you'd be ripping mad."

Derek issued no denial. Not that Sloane had expected him to. The facts were the facts. They both hated being maneuvered like chess pieces, no matter how solid the reasons behind it were. And now Derek was waiting for her to find an objectivity that continued to elude her.

"This whole situation is impossible," she finally determined aloud. "We can't change who we are. And we can't seem to table it, not even when it comes to separating our personal and professional lives. Look at your reaction in Tony's office. You shot down my idea of becoming part of the investigation simply because you were worried that I was setting myself up as a target. Would you have done that if it had been anyone but me making that stipulation? Especially if that anyone had my experience, my credentials?"

Derek rolled his wine goblet between his palms. "No," he stated flatly. "I wouldn't have." He pinned her with his gaze. "So what's the solution? Do you want to change your mind and bow out?"

"Of what? The investigation or our living together?"

"You tell me. Which means more to you?"

There it was. Out in the open, just like the last time. Only Sloane had learned a lot since then.

"You're testing me," she replied. "I don't like it, but I know where it's coming from. So I'll surprise you. I'll answer—honestly. No, I'm not going to walk away from us. No, I won't put an investigation ahead of what we have. But I also won't bow out of this case. Not unless you force me to. In which case, it's you who haven't learned anything from the past."

She knew she'd gotten through by the expression on Derek's face.

"You're right," he acknowledged. "My being a hard-ass will only make things worse. So how do we handle this?"

"The way I see it? One minefield at a time. We'll butt heads, constantly rip each other a new one, and with any luck, come out alive and together."

A flicker of amusement. "Sounds like the story of our relationship."

"More or less."

Derek reached across the island and held out his right hand, palm out. "Truce?"

Sloane eyed him for a moment, then met his handshake. "A reluctant one, but okay, truce."

"Enough to get me out of the guest room?"

Reflexively, Sloane's lips twitched. "Barely. And only because you're so good in bed."

A broad grin. "Works for me. Want to try out our truce now? You look very sexy in that nightshirt."

"After I finish my wine and brie. And after you fill me in on this Dai Lo,

Xiao Long, and his enforcer, Jin Huang, who my parents' descriptions helped you sketch and identify."

"I'll fill you in, but on a need-to-know basis," Derek reminded her.

"Agreed. I'll take what I can get."

———————

The cemetery was quiet.

Low, moody clouds eclipsed any trace of early morning sun. But it wouldn't have mattered what the weather was. It was the same ritual each month.

The eleventh. Seven-twenty A.M.

That's when the medical examiner had declared her dead.

And when life had changed forever.

Whoever originated the phrase "time heals all wounds" was wrong. There were some wounds that nothing could heal. They remained open sores that festered as the years crept by.

He made his way across the cemetery's manicured lawns, passing headstone after headstone. Each one of them had its own story. But none of them was his.

He reached her graveside and stood reverently before it. The familiar gripping pain constricted his chest. It never got easier. It never would.

He knelt, running his fingers over the etched letters and numbers on the stone, tasting his own tears as they glided down his cheeks.

So young. So innocent. A whole life stretching before her.

Extinguished in one heinous, senseless moment.

It should have been him. If someone had to die, it should have been him.

But it wasn't.

He took the bouquet of daisies and placed it on her grave. It was always daisies. They were her favorite flower. She'd picked them from the garden on the estate from the time she was two. She'd present them to him like they were a sacred gift, rather than a crumpled tangle of stems.

To him, they were sacred. And so was she.

He bowed his head, let the grief and the guilt consume him. He didn't pray. He couldn't. He no longer believed.

Sloane panted as her sneakers pounded rhythmically on the road, the hounds racing along at her side.

The morning was gray. And so was her mood. Something was bothering the hell out of her.

Long after Derek had fallen asleep beside her last night, she'd sat up with the reading lamp on, poring over the portion of Xiao Long's file that Derek had given her access to.

Detailed accountings of the recent string of burglaries Xiao had orchestrated. The part that his nephew, Eric Hu, and his computer services company had played, electronically equipping every apartment that the Red Dragon kids had hit. All except for the Burbanks' apartment. The burglary at her parents' place didn't fit the pattern—for obvious reasons.

The facts were in order. The conclusions seemed logical.

So what was bugging her?

She'd thrashed around in bed until she couldn't stand it anymore. Then, she'd leashed up the hounds and gone out for her run, hoping it would clear her head and provide her with an answer.

It did.

Halfway through her jog, the incongruity struck home.

Rosalyn Burbank opened the front door with her good arm when her daughter arrived. She looked peaked but determined, her gaze still dulled by medication, but her power suit saying she was fighting bed rest tooth and nail. She also looked distinctly baffled, and not particularly pleased.

"Sloane." She gave her daughter a quick hug, then stepped back and glanced at her watch. "I postponed the breakfast meeting with my author for an early lunch. He wasn't too happy about it, since he's in New York only another day before he takes off for his European tour. Why did you insist on meeting here, now? What on earth is going on?"

"Hi to you, too, Mom." Sloane was used to her mother's type A directness. After all, that's who she'd inherited it from.

She walked in, hung her jacket on the coatrack, and turned to face
Rosalyn as she shut the front door. "Breakfast meeting? You're supposed to
be resting."

"I rested enough after the concussion. I'm not missing an important client
meeting because of a broken arm. But don't worry. I'm pumped full of painkillers. And I won't be at the wheel. Special Agent Carter is driving me." She
gestured at the breakfast nook, where Alan Carter was sitting, drinking a cup
of coffee. He gave Sloane a brief wave of his hand that looked more like the
wave of a white flag of defeat.

Sloane stifled a smile. Babysitting her mother was probably as taxing as
working Violent Crimes. "May I have a few minutes alone with my mother?"
she asked.

"Of course." He nearly leaped up. "I'll go out and stretch my legs, then
make sure the car's brought around."

"Thank you." Sloane waited until he was gone. "Are you torturing the poor
man?" she asked her mother.

"No, I'm just living my life—which includes meeting my client." Rosalyn
shifted impatiently. "So let's get to the point of this visit."

Sloane complied. "Ground rules," she began. "There's information I can
share with you and information I can't. So let's do this my way. No twenty
questions."

"A tall order," Rosalyn responded drily. "But, fine. I'll do my best."

"Good." Sloane pointed at the door. "I want you to reenact for me exactly
what happened the night of the burglary. Start right there, at the front door.
Pretend you just got home. Walk in. Look around. Close your eyes when you
get to the part where the thieves pulled the sack over your head. That way,
you can play it out as you remember it."

Rosalyn blinked in astonishment. "What good will it do for me to—" She
bit off the rest of her question, remembering her promise to Sloane. "I've
gone over this story a thousand times—with the police, the FBI, and you. I
don't see the point in doing it again."

"Humor me."

An exaggerated sigh. "It couldn't have been more than a minute from when I walked in and when that ape grabbed me. After that, the bag was over my head, the rag was in my mouth, and the rest happened in darkness."

"Fine. I still want you to take it from the beginning."

"Are you saying you want me to stagger blindly around the apartment in the direction I think they dragged me?"

"No. I want you to visualize it in your mind's eye, step by step, and relive it aloud."

Rosalyn shot her daughter an exasperated look, but refrained from firing any more questions. "I had my keys, but I didn't need them. As I told you and the authorities, the apartment door was ajar. I assumed your father forgot to shut it behind him when he got home. I called out to him as I walked in. That's when the first intruder grabbed me from behind, gagged me, and yanked the sack over my head. I suppose I should be grateful. If I'd seen his face, I'd probably be dead right now. No such luck yesterday."

"That's why you've got FBI protection. No one's getting near you," Sloane said fervently. "Now, I want you to freeze-frame those first few seconds when you stepped through the front door, but before you were assaulted. You had a direct view of the entire living room. What was going on? Was the place wrecked? Was there activity? Movement? Noise?"

A long, intent pause. "No. Nothing. The room looked normal."

"You also had a good view of the breakfast nook and the kitchen. Were the silverware drawers dumped? Were there pieces scattered around or were they already missing?"

"Again, no. Everything looked to be in place. I'm not stupid enough to stay in an apartment that's obviously just been burglarized."

"I agree. One last thing—what about your diamond stud? Dad found it on the floor near the door when he got home."

Rosalyn arched a brow. "When have you ever known me to overlook a diamond? That pair of studs were two carats each. Your father gave them to me for our twenty-fifth anniversary. If one of them had been lying on the floor, I would have seen it."

"Good point." Sloane made the necessary mental note. "Okay, now go on. This time from after you were grabbed. Shut your eyes."

Rosalyn complied. "I fought that son of a bitch tooth and nail. He wasn't too tall, but he was strong. He yelled out something in Chinese. Clearly, he was shouting for help from his accomplices, because one of them came running. The two of them dragged me into your father's office and tied me up in a chair—"

"Stop," Sloane interrupted. "Were both of the other burglars in Dad's office when the first one called for help?"

Another pause. "I'd say yes. The footsteps of the one who ran out to help subdue me definitely came from that direction."

"And the other guy?"

"He had to already be in there when I was brought in. No one came into the office after that. But just before they knocked me out, I heard all three of them talking and arguing. They were all definitely in the room with me."

"So while you were conscious, no one left to grab the stuff they ripped off? No sound of unplugging components from the entertainment center? No grunting as they hauled off the TV? No clanking of silverware?"

"No. Just a lot of banging and thudding that I now realize were probably the drawers and file cabinets in the office being dumped. I don't know when they ransacked the rest of the place. It had to be after that second blow to my head, when I was unconscious."

"They were certainly efficient," Sloane murmured thoughtfully. "Was there any hesitation in their motions or questions in their voices? Like they were trying to figure out where things were?"

"Not that I recall. I wasn't exactly coherent. I assume they found what they wanted, robbed us blind, and took off." Rosalyn opened her eyes and waved her hand in noncomprehension. "What are you getting at?"

"Hopefully, answers."

"What kind of answers?"

"The kind I don't think we're going to like."

CHAPTER FIFTEEN

ARMONK, NEW YORK

The total worth of multimillionaire Theodore Campbell's private art collection was not something he publicized. Personal friends and trusted business associates were the only ones privy to the elaborate art gallery he'd built as an adjunct wing to his twenty-acre estate, just thirty-five miles north of Manhattan.

His collection ranged from paintings dating back to the French Renaissance to those created by the world's greatest Impressionists, to masterpieces of the Modern age. His tastes were eclectic, and his paintings were arranged according to style, each grouping tucked in alcoves all their own. His security system was state-of-the-art, and it would take a veritable genius to crack it.

The armed team approaching the estate wasn't foolish enough to try.

They'd chosen the time for their hit after the family's routine had been scrutinized for weeks. From there, it was an easy decision to make.

It was a drizzly October dawn. Saturday morning at 6:45, before the sun and the joggers were up. Not that it mattered. The Campbell estate was set so far back from the road that the manor itself was virtually invisible.

Adhering to their Saturday morning custom, Mr. and Mrs. Campbell were still asleep, as were most of the servants, who were taking advantage of the extra few hours of rest that came with not disturbing the master and mistress. The only ones up and about were the butler, the cook, and the nanny, who was supervising the Campbells' six-year-old daughter and four-year-old son as they watched early morning cartoons in the den.

The four Black Eagles approached quietly. Three hid in the bushes on either side of the entranceway, ski masks pulled over their heads and faces, weapons loaded and ready.

The leader of the team marched up to the front door. His police uniform was authentic.

He didn't ring the bell. That would awaken the household. He simply waited until the butler was passing through the foyer. Then, he knocked—two brief, authoritative raps.

Startled, the butler came to a halt, then turned and walked over to the door. "Yes?" he asked through the intercom.

"Police," the leader replied, keeping his tone low and his words few to hide his accented English. "Silent alarm—rear wing." With that, he stood tall, directly in front of the video monitor so the butler could see his uniform.

The desired effect was achieved the moment he uttered the phrase "rear wing." The butler knew what that meant—the master's revered art collection was in danger.

Without another word, he yanked open the door. "What alarm? The security company—"

The rest of his sentence was silenced by the spray of bullets that blew through his chest.

On cue, the other three Black Eagles appeared, rushing inside as their leader yanked on his ski mask and stormed in behind them. By the time the cook hurried out of the kitchen to see what the commotion was, the assailants were in the den. The cook's hands flew to her face, and she emitted a muffled shriek as she saw the butler's crumpled body lying in the foyer, blood oozing from his chest. Inside the den, the nanny cried out in pain, as one of the gunmen dragged her away from her charges and threw her roughly onto the floor.

Two of the gunmen grabbed the two whimpering children, holding each of them in a viselike grip and pointing the MP5Ks at their heads.

"Nobody do anything stupid," the leader instructed the terrified nanny and cook as he raised his submachine gun, shifting its aim from one woman to the other. "Or my friends blow off kids' heads. And I use this"—he gave a slight jerk of his gun—"so you both end up like butler."

An utterly panicked silence filled the air, punctuated by the women's rapid breathing and the frightened weeping of the children.

A commotion erupted upstairs, and a minute later Theodore and Leona Campbell flew into the room, their bathrobes billowing out around them.

"What the . . . Oh dear God." Theodore turned sheet white when he saw his children being held at gunpoint. Leona let out an agonized scream and flew forward, instinctively trying to reach her beloved children and get them out of danger.

"Stop," the armed leader commanded, turning his subgun on Leona. "One more step and I kill kids."

Theodore caught his wife and pulled her back. "Don't hurt them," he implored. "Take whatever you want. Just don't hurt our children."

"Is up to you. Do as we say, no one gets hurt. Give us trouble, and your wife has good time watching us shoot kids. No send alarm. No call cops. Otherwise, kids will be dead before first cop car gets to house. You understand?"

"Yes," Theodore agreed.

"Good. Let's go." He nudged Theodore with his MP5K, forcing him into the hall. One of the other Black Eagles pushed the nanny and cook into chairs and tied them up back-to-back. Leona he sat directly in front of her children, still being held at gunpoint, and bound her arms behind her and her ankles together.

"Now what?" she whispered, tears sliding down her cheeks.

"You wait."

The rest went like clockwork. Twenty minutes later, a dozen invaluable paintings were carefully wrapped in the back of their van, and they were on their way to the docks.

The exchange would be made there. And the ship and its new cargo would be in international waters before noon.

The haul was a fine initiation of their American enterprise.

Wallace opened his midtown gallery earlier than usual that day. He'd stayed at his Hamptons estate last night. But he'd never gone to sleep. Instead, he'd sat up all night, staring at the paintings he so loved, and drinking his cognac.

He'd gotten a phone call on his private, unlisted line just before midnight. He knew who it was. And he knew he had to answer—for good or for bad.

This time it was for good.

There was another Renoir about to become available. And not just any Renoir. One that he'd coveted forever. It literally took his breath away, and infused a semblance of life back into his soul.

He *had* to have that painting.

But, stolen or not, the asking price was $900,000—10 percent of the $9 million it would be worth hanging in a museum or at a collector's estate.

He had only a week to come up with the money. That would mean liquidating a substantial chunk of his assets. And with his art partnership under such close scrutiny by the FBI, it was bound to raise red flags.

There had to be another way. He'd racked his brain all night, trying to come up with an answer. But it always came back to the same thing—the only way to bring in a large sum of money without arousing suspicion was to sell at least four or five of his more valuable paintings. That was called business, and no one could question its legitimacy.

As he drove into Manhattan, the sun barely peeking up over the horizon, a solution occurred to him. True, he'd dropped off the radar of the financial industry the day he'd left investment banking. Many of his former colleagues had forgotten he ever existed. But others had stayed in touch—especially those who were fellow patrons of the arts. He saw them at the Met, at MoMA, and at art auctions at both Sotheby's and Christie's. They all knew of Sophie's tragic death and how hard Wallace had taken his enormous personal loss. And they sympathized with—if not understood—his need to leave the demanding world of high finance and to reinvest his sizable assets in the less stressful arena of acquiring and overseeing his own art galleries.

In their minds, he was a semiretired rich guy with no dependents and very few financial obligations. That would work in his favor. There was no way he could compromise his reputation by going to them and asking for monetary assistance. But he could certainly invite them to an exhibit at his Manhattan gallery, and then let nature take its course.

A philanthropic gesture; a festive wine-and-cheese hour; and a beautiful, talented, and charismatic woman—one who reminded him so much of . . .

No. He couldn't go there now. He had to think of the gala scenario he'd just conjured up.

All the components added up to money. Lots of it.

The more Wallace mulled over the idea, the more he liked it.

He would introduce Cindy Liu to the highbrow world she was so eager to meet. And he'd do it by hosting a party at his gallery.

———

Cindy wasn't surprised when she received the phone call. She was gratified that Wallace Johnson had taken the bait so quickly. It was the first step toward success. Her A Sook was going to be so pleased.

She was looking forward to the lunch later today that Wallace had invited her to, so they could compare schedules and select a date for her debut party.

This enemy of her uncle's was turning out to be an easy mark.

———

Rich was almost finished packing his bag and making final arrangements for his flight to Munich, when the phone rang.

It was Jane Brennan, coordinator of the art-theft program at FBI Headquarters in Washington, D.C.

The news she had for Rich was startling. He listened carefully, taking notes as he did.

This heist was a shocker. Not the method, but the venue. Right here in the States. Rich had seen these Eurasian art-theft rings blast their way through art-rich countries in Europe, Asia, and Scandinavia.

But striking on American soil was an anomaly.

To begin with, traveling here would be a major risk. They'd have to be well funded and extremely well paid, not to mention armed with detailed plans, to make this daring act worth their while. There was no way they could pull this off on their own. Someone would have to be masterminding it.

An improbable scenario—one that made Rich suspect that the Armonk heist was a copycat crime. Well executed and grisly, but a copycat nonetheless.

On the other hand, the method, the timing, the Slavic accents, the violence, and most of all, the end goal—it was either one hell of a copycat or it was the real deal. And if it was the latter, he was operating with a whole new set of rules.

Rich hung up with Jane and abandoned his packing. The Armonk police were at the victims' estate, interviewing them in quiet seclusion, far from the media's eye. Theodore and Leona Campbell were in shock, as was the entire staff. But the Campbells were acutely traumatized, having just experienced the horror of watching masked killers hold guns to their children's heads after murdering their butler and terrorizing their staff.

It was time for Rich to get the information he needed to see what the Art Crime Team was up against.

———

Sloane spent a fair amount of time poking around, asking questions that she hoped would shed light on her suspicions that something was out of whack with regard to the burglary at her parents' apartment.

Armed with few facts and lots of supposition, she went down to the FBI's New York Field Office.

After going through security and being escorted up to the twenty-second floor, she made her way over to Derek's desk.

"Well, hi." He leaned back in his chair, arms folded behind his head. "When they called from downstairs to say you were here to see me, I was surprised. You took off like a bullet this morning. I figured you didn't want to shatter last night's afterglow by announcing you were driving to Chinatown to take on Xiao Long single-handedly."

"Very funny." Sloane sank down in the chair beside his desk. "Derek, there's a weird discrepancy in the break-in at my parents' place—besides the obvious. I sat up all night, poring over the abridged case file you gave me, concentrating on the details of Xiao Long's other burglaries. Something just didn't sit right. Then it dawned on me. We know that Eric Hu's employees were never in my parents' apartment, so Hu had no way of giving Xiao Long a heads-up on the layout of the place or what items were kept where. That includes the location of my father's office, and more particularly, his files."

"Right." Derek was no longer lounging in his chair. He was sitting up, listening intently to what Sloane had to say.

"According to the police report, the Red Dragons were inside the building for under twenty minutes—just three of which were before my mother showed up. That's twenty minutes, soup to nuts, with no input from Eric Hu's crew. No video surveillance. No electronic photos. Nothing. Let's put aside the dubious fact that, in three minutes, they ducked the doorman, got upstairs, and somehow unlocked the door. There were no scratch marks, no signs of forced entry. The NYPD's theory is that they found a way, other than through Eric Hu, to make duplicate keys. How? Which of those kids is sophisticated enough to copy keys? And, if they didn't do it, who made the copies?"

Sloane stopped just long enough to catch her breath. "Like I said, let's put that part on hold. The reason I raced out this morning was to meet my mother at the apartment."

"How is she?"

"Stubborn and difficult about accepting help, as usual. But physically on the mend. Anyway, I had her relive exactly what happened to her on the night of the robbery, from the moment she walked through the front door. Based on what she said, it's clear that all three Red Dragons were already in my father's office and in full swing when she got home."

"All that in three minutes—yeah, I'd say that timing's pretty tight," Derek agreed. "But we can't state for sure that it's impossible."

"That's because you haven't heard everything. Derek, I've seen my father's filing system. First of all, he has over a dozen file cabinets. They're all putty-colored, all unlabeled on the outside, and all organized in a unique way that works for him—grouped by art genre and project status, not alphabetical or chronological order. Finding the cabinet with the Rothberg files in it would be like finding a needle in a haystack. Yet Xiao's thugs zeroed right in on it—again, with no photos or video surveillance from Eric Hu. For all we know, they'd already emptied the contents of the Rothberg file, left that threatening fortune cookie, and were trashing the place for good measure when my mother interrupted them."

"What makes you so sure they zeroed in on the right file cabinet?"

"The timing. When my mother got home, they had to be finishing up in the office. There's no other way they could have pulled off everything else they did and been out of the apartment seventeen minutes later. It's virtually impossible. According to my mother, no other visible part of the apartment had been disturbed when she arrived. The living room, with the entertainment system and my dad's paintings and artifacts, was intact. The kitchen and breakfast nook looked perfectly normal, too—not even the silverware drawer had been overturned. Also, my mother's diamond stud wasn't on the foyer floor where my father found it, which suggests that the bedroom hadn't been rifled yet either."

"That's conjecture," Derek pointed out. "The Dragons could have dropped the earring when they fled."

"Maybe. But even if they'd already ransacked the bedroom, that doesn't explain how they took care of the kitchen and living room—yanking apart an entire entertainment unit, and making off with its contents and the rest of their haul—in under seventeen minutes. Not unless the office was a done deal." Sloane gave an emphatic shake of her head. "And let's not forget that those seventeen minutes also included an unexpected battle with my mother. She fought them like a tigress. They had to drag her into my father's office and tie her up, then knock her out. Add that to the mix, and there's no way. Not even the Flash could have pulled it off in such record time. The only explanation is that those guys knew exactly where every room and every thing was—including the Rothberg file. I'd stake my reputation on it."

"And you'd be right," Derek replied, his brows knit in concentration. "Because you're timing it only to the end of the robbery when they reached your parents' front door. After that, they still had to haul out a flat-screen TV, a painting, and a bunch of bulky art pieces, and get them downstairs and out the delivery entrance. I agree. Something here is off."

"They had help." Sloane met Derek's gaze. "It's the only answer that makes sense. Someone scoped out the place for them. Whoever it was gave them the same access and the same information that Eric Hu provided for the other robberies, and then some. The question is, who?"

CHAPTER SIXTEEN

Cindy's debut was a smashing success.

Nearly everyone Wallace invited dropped by and ended up staying for a while. Many of them brought guests—dates, friends, or colleagues—who were interested in meeting this rising architectural star who could transform their homes into unique residences that would be the talk of the town.

All the attendees had one thing in common—they had considerable wealth to spare.

When the party first began, Wallace stood beside Cindy near the doorway, welcoming his guests and introducing them to Ms. Liu. It took about twenty minutes for Cindy to take over her own introductions, and about twenty more before she was swarmed by interested patrons scrutinizing her portfolio of completed projects, while she gave out her business cards hand over fist.

Wallace's initial work was done.

With that knowledge, he turned his attention to his own situation. He began mingling among the guests, and was both relieved and gratified to see how many of them were clustered around and admiring the more valuable paintings he'd displayed. A number of guests stopped him to ask detailed questions, frankly informing him that they were in the process of deciding which painting or paintings to buy.

Considering how successful the evening was turning out to be—and how busy—Wallace was glad he'd asked both of his handpicked assistants to help out. The front desk was filled with the welcome sight of American Express cards and leather-bound checkbooks. Fine art sold well even in tough economic times, especially when there were bargains to be had.

"You've done a wonderful job of introducing Cindy to prospective clients. I'm very appreciative. I'm sure Mr. Liu will be, too."

Wallace turned to see Peggy Sun standing beside him. He'd met the attractive fortyish woman just before tonight's party and was impressed by her knowledge of art and her loyalty to Cindy. Having spent a fair amount of time in China, plus having done business with Johnny Liu for years, Wallace understood his culturally established values, including Peggy's role in Cindy's life, even now that Cindy was an adult. After all these years, and given the Lius' commitment to honor and tradition, Peggy was still looking out for Cindy, acting as her friend and constant companion. So it was only natural that she'd be by Cindy's side at an important event such as this.

"No appreciation is necessary," Wallace assured Peggy. "All I did was provide the venue, the invitations, and the refreshments. Cindy's doing all the rest herself." He smiled, gesturing in Cindy's direction.

Oblivious to the scrutiny, Cindy was drawing a rough pencil sketch on the back of a cocktail napkin for the wife of a former colleague and current racquetball partner of Wallace's. Cindy's enthusiasm was contagious, and her-soon-to-be client was listening intently, her whole face aglow.

"She really is something," Peggy agreed, following Wallace's gaze. "Her love for her work, her way with people, and of course, her extraordinary talent—once she's completed a few projects, and word of the results gets around, she'll be bombarded with clients." Peggy's smile was filled with pride. "Cindy is a rare gem. Beautiful, intelligent, gifted, and overflowing with a love of life few people possess."

"I agree." Wallace continued watching Cindy, listening to Peggy's descrip-

tion as he did. Beautiful, intelligent, gifted, overflowing with a love of life . . .
She might as well have been describing Meili.

At that moment, Cindy laughed at something one of the guests had said,
simultaneously tucking a strand of dark hair behind her ear.

That particular gesture . . . Wallace felt his chest constrict.

Meili. She'd been a bright light in his life at a time that was anything but
bright. He and Beatrice were clashing daily, fighting over their vastly different views of what being a parent meant. Given how long and hard they'd
tried to conceive, Wallace wanted to make Sophie the center of their world.
He'd assumed Beatrice would abandon everything—her weekends at the spa,
her evenings out with her girlfriends, her marathon shopping sprees—to be a
full-time mother. It never occurred to him that she'd turn out not to have a
single maternal bone in her body.

The situation had escalated to talk of divorce. At barely two years old, Sophie very much needed her mother. Wallace would have gladly traded places
with Beatrice and raised their daughter. But it wasn't feasible, not financially.
Wallace earned several million dollars a year, and Beatrice earned nothing.
She'd resigned from her job as a fashion buyer as soon as she married Wallace. That hadn't bothered him—until now. He was fifty-four years old and
way too entrenched in a career that made no allowances for throttling back.
Beatrice was thirty-nine, six-plus years out of the fashion business—and therefore out of the game—with no motivation to return to the rat race, and
equally little motivation to play in the sandbox with a toddler.

Wallace tried to make up for Beatrice's attitude toward their daughter in
any way he could. But he traveled so often, and worked such long hours, that
it made it very difficult. So he'd compensated by hiring the most qualified
and loving nannies money could buy, and augmented that by spending every
waking hour he was home with Sophie. Adult companionship, intimate or
otherwise, was shelved. For a vital, passionate man like Wallace, it was a very
lonely life.

When he'd met Meili in Hong Kong, he was at his most vulnerable and
lowest point. As it turned out, so was she. But to him, she was the epitome of
joy—free-spirited, fiery, young, and full of life. She was also beautiful—petite,

with fine, delicate features and an equally delicate figure. Looking back on it now, their love affair was like a real-life *Pretty Woman*. Except for two things.

Thankfully, Meili's pride would never allow her to resort to prostitution.

And there'd been no Cinderella ending.

The first time Wallace laid eyes on Meili was in the lobby of the Conrad Hong Kong hotel in July 2002. He and his art partners were there on business, the first time they'd returned to Hong Kong since the sale of *Dead or Alive*—even longer still since all five of them had been in this city together. Matthew, Leo, and Phil were apprehensive as hell about returning. But it couldn't be helped. The group was negotiating the purchase of a valuable painting from an elite art gallery. The owner refused to make the sale unless he met with the entire partnership. The profit made it worth the trip. Besides, they were staying in Hong Kong's affluent business and shopping district, nowhere near Kowloon, where Cai Wen's office had been.

As the established art connoisseur of the group, not to mention the investment banker with the most economic experience, Wallace made the preliminary visit to the gallery alone to view the painting and to meet with the gallery owner. While he was in the area, he stopped into a few other high-end galleries to check out the works being displayed.

He returned to the hotel to see Meili sitting in the lobby.

She clearly didn't fit in with the wealthy business crowd who frequented the Conrad. She looked like a beautiful, misplaced waif, sitting on a plush chair, wearing a pseudosophisticated suit he suspected she'd bought secondhand, and trying to act natural—as if she belonged there. Sipping at a glass of wine, she kept one hand on the canvas of a painting she'd propped up against the chair.

Wallace would have approached her, but she approached him first.

"Excuse me," she said in English. "But I understand you're an American art collector. I have a valuable painting here I'd be interested in selling. It's a Rothberg." She held out the painting, which Wallace recognized as one of Rothberg's earlier works. It wasn't worth a fortune now—but it *could* be in the future.

That is, if it was genuine.

Wallace doubted that was the case. This had to be a con. Had Wallace not seen the desperation in the young woman's eyes, he would have walked away. But he did. So he'd suggested she wait in the lobby while he went up and spoke to his partners to see if they were interested.

Of course they were interested, even though they, too, were certain this was a hoax.

It turned out not to be. Matthew had the painting authenticated, and it was indeed a genuine Rothberg.

The group had argued. Wallace didn't agree with the strategy they came up with. It might be legal, but it was damned unethical. They were going to lowball the young woman. They saw a chance to make a killing on someone who had no idea of the painting's worth but was clearly hungry for cash.

Wallace was outnumbered, and the offer was made.

Meili knew they were offering her tens of thousands of dollars less than the value of the painting. She'd told them so in no uncertain terms. And Matthew and Ben had told her to go home and think about it.

She'd called the next day to say she'd gotten a better offer. And that was that.

Except that Wallace couldn't stop thinking about her.

He'd called her the next day at the phone number she'd given them. And after hearing his apology over the group's behavior, she'd grudgingly accepted his dinner invitation.

If there was such a thing as instant, head-over-heels love, this had been it. There'd been an instant chemistry between them, and a gravitation to fill the very different, yet equally real, emotional holes in each of their lives.

They'd spent a good part of Wallace's trip together, as well as his next trip, and the next, and the next. He had taken things very slowly. Meili was young. He knew very little about her, nor she about him. They purposely kept it that way, right down to not exchanging last names. It made the whole relationship more magical, more isolated from the rest of the world.

None of it mattered anyway. All that mattered was the solace and the joy they brought each other.

She had told him merely that she was an only child, a budding artist, and that she'd left home to build her career. Other than two paintings she'd hocked for cash—including the one that had resulted in their meeting, she was living hand to mouth, working fervently on her painting. In return, he'd told her that he was an investment banker who had frequent business dealings in Hong Kong.

And he'd told her one other thing, right up front. He'd told her that he was married. He couldn't live with himself if he hadn't. She'd accepted it. She knew he was hers only when he was here. She didn't care. She just wanted him. And, God help him, he wanted her.

Right or wrong, they'd gotten involved. Wallace had told her their meeting was pure fate. Meili had teasingly informed him that it had been pure manipulation—genius on her part. Desperate to sell the Rothberg, she'd spent long hours scrutinizing Hong Kong's upscale art galleries. She'd seen Wallace visit three or four of them on several occasions. Recognizing that he was an affluent art collector, she'd bribed his driver to tell her what hotel Wallace was staying at.

She'd arrived ahead of him, and waited in the lobby with her painting and high hopes.

Wallace had chuckled at her creative ingenuity. So that was how she knew who and where he was. But it had still brought her into his life. And he'd treasured every moment they shared.

That was a million years ago.

Yet, with the exception of Sophie, for whom he felt a paternal love that was in a class by itself, Meili was the last person who'd made him feel alive, vital, and needed. Their affair had lasted three years, and it had ended because he was a stupid, insensitive fool. Countless times he'd thought of going back and trying to undo what he'd done. But what was the point? Even if he ended his marriage, he had a beloved daughter who needed him. And Meili refused to leave Hong Kong. Ultimately, there could be no future for them. It was up to Wallace to let her move on, make a life for herself, and find a man who could truly commit to her.

For so long, he had missed her. Whatever fragments of a marriage he and Beatrice still had had shattered when Sophie died, and their divorce was finalized six months later. If he hadn't been a totally broken man who had nothing left inside him to give, he might have flown back to China to see if he could find Meili and make things right.

But he was an empty shell, capable of nothing except burying himself in the memories of his precious daughter. So his thoughts of Meili faded into the past.

Studying Cindy now, Wallace was still amazed by the remarkable resemblance she bore to Meili, both in appearance and in mannerisms. Had Meili not been an only child, the two of them could be sisters. True, the similarities were purely physical. Their personalities, ambitions, and sophistication were day and night. Still, there was something in Cindy's eyes, in her gestures, in the way her face lit up when she was excited, that was a stirring reminder of Meili.

Interestingly, the differences Cindy encompassed were as compelling as the similarities. Her poise, her sophistication, and her professional drive—they created an equality for him that had never been there with Meili. Plus, now he was divorced, with no marriage to save.

"Mr. Johnson?" Peggy's voice interrupted his thoughts. "Are you all right?"

Wallace regained his composure as quickly as possible. "Yes, of course. I was just thinking how proud of Cindy her uncle will be."

"I agree." Peggy nodded. "He expects great things of her. And with your help, I know she won't disappoint him."

"I doubt Cindy could disappoint anyone." Even as Wallace spoke, he felt a twinge of something he hadn't felt in a very long time.

It might be the nostalgia. It might be the extraordinary likeness to Meili.

On the other hand, it might be something more.

Ben sat on the bar stool, shoulders slumped, tie and dress shirt damp and disheveled. Outside, horns honked, taxis whizzed by, and cars crammed the intersections trying to navigate their way through Manhattan. It was hard to believe that rush hour had ended hours ago.

Some things stayed the same. Some things changed.

It had been a half hour, and Ben was already craving his next drink. Four years of sobriety shot to hell. This whole fiasco had pushed him over the edge and off the wagon.

The situation sucked. And he was a prisoner to it.

Even the booze wasn't enough. He was drowning. And he no longer gave a damn.

If it weren't for his children and grandchildren, he'd just let the riptide take him under. He'd sink into oblivion, let go of life, of guilt, of debt. It would put an end to the agony.

"What can I get you?" The bartender walked over, drying a glass and giving Ben a questioning look.

"Scotch. Straight. Make it a double."

"Tough day?" the bartender asked.

The truth in the question almost made Ben laugh. "Yeah."

"One double scotch, coming up." The bartender turned away to do his job. At least the guy caught on. Ben didn't want to talk about his problems. He wanted to drown them in liquor.

Behind him, the front door swung open. Ben didn't need to turn around. He recognized the heavy tread all too well.

"Martino." Jin Huang loomed beside him, not even bothering to sit. "Have money?"

With a nod, Ben half swiveled on the stool and handed over the envelope. "Here."

Jin counted the bills, after which his brick-wall body stiffened. "Two thousand short."

"I know. Tell Xiao he'll have it as soon as I do."

A strong hand clamped down on Ben's arm. "Not good enough."

"Neither is business," Ben replied tonelessly. "The whole garment center is going down the toilet, in case you haven't noticed." His glance flickered to Jin Huang's grip on his arm. "If you plan to kill me, you'd be doing me a favor."

"That's why killing is later. Telling secret is now."

Ben squeezed his eyes shut, more sickened by the latter than the former. But then, Jin Huang knew that. Xiao Long had made sure of it. "Don't. Please. Give me a little more time. I'll get the money."

Jin's black eyes scrutinized him, flat and emotionless. "A week. No more."

"Fine. A week."

"And not two thousand. Twenty-five hundred. You pay interest. Plus next week's money—all of it."

Ben nodded, utter desolation pervading him. "I know the drill. I'll meet you here with everything I owe Xiao."

"You better."

By the time the bartender put the double scotch on the counter in front of Ben, Jin Huang was gone.

Ben polished off his drink in a few gulps and slammed the glass down on the counter. "Give me another. And keep them coming."

CHAPTER SEVENTEEN

Sloane's arrow whizzed through the air and struck the bull's-eye about a half inch from dead center.

Not good enough. Just like everything else that was going on.

Lowering her bow to the grass, Sloane did a few stretches, trying to ease the tension in her body. The late day run hadn't done it. The hour of archery practice hadn't done it. Nothing was going to do it.

She wiped a towel across her face, drying off the perspiration. Then, she guzzled down half a bottle of water. The sun was about to dip behind the horizon, totally eclipsing any daylight. It was time to go inside, take a shower, and review her notes.

Gathering up her archery gear, she headed back, glancing at her watch as she did.

Six-fifteen P.M.

This day had been endless. Everything was hanging in a menacing state of limbo. Fred Miller's body still hadn't been recovered, despite the FBI and the NYPD's valiant efforts to find him. Ticking inside Sloane's head like a time bomb was the fear that Xiao Long would make another attempt on one of her parents' lives—and succeed, FBI presence or not. And the rest of her father's partners? She didn't know whether to worry *for* them or *about* them.

The unnerving prospect that one of her father's oldest and closest friends had provided Xiao Long with entry to the Burbanks' apartment—it actually made Sloane sick to her stomach. She'd felt guilt-ridden that the thought had even crossed her mind when her mother was reenacting the break-in with her. But when Derek had voiced the possibility last night—that had been the straw that broke the camel's back. Rather than expanding on the conversation they'd started in the Field Office earlier that day, they'd spent the entire night hashing out the likelihood that one of the art partners had aided and abetted a criminal.

Sloane hadn't slept a wink after that. And if she had to be honest with herself, it wasn't because of the heated case Derek made. It was because of her own niggling worry that he might be right.

She'd made a valiant attempt to prove otherwise, rattling off every possible name she could think of, from neighbors Xiao might have duped, to building employees he might have paid off, to everyone affiliated with the construction and sales of the individual apartments, to employees working in the co-op office. The list was endless.

But Derek wasn't buying. The bottom line was that whoever had helped the Dragon kids break into the Burbanks' apartment didn't just unlock the door or merely know the layout of the apartment, including which room was Matthew's office.

They knew precisely where the Rothberg file was.

In a sea of unlabeled file cabinets, they knew just where to go and how to get what they needed, fast, trashing the place afterward as a cover-up.

And that meant someone who was familiar with Matthew's filing system, or someone who at least knew where he kept all the paperwork relating to *Dead or Alive.*

At the top of that list of suspects were the four most logical choices: Ben Martino, Wallace Johnson, Leo Fox, and Phil Leary.

Sloane had actually winced when Derek said their names aloud, although she'd known it was coming. She'd argued vehemently, emphasizing her father's long-term friendship, partnership, and trust with these men. To that, she added the ammo that if Matthew had been connected in any way, either to the art crime or to Xiao Long's operation, all four of his partners' butts would be on the line as well. So implicating Matthew in anything illegal would mean their own downfall.

But even as Sloane argued her case, she knew she was fighting with herself, not Derek. The fundamental basis for her reasoning was totally subjective. Friends turned on friends every day. And her argument was flimsy. If one of Matthew's partners had cooperated in a scheme like this, he would have done so only under coercion—out of fear of retaliation from a man they knew to be a killer. And that was enough motivation for anyone, close friend or not.

The truth was Ben, Leo, Phil, and Wallace *were* the most likely suspects to have aided Xiao Long with the break-in. In the guilty party's mind, it would just have involved providing Xiao with the necessary information. No one was supposed to get hurt. And no one could have anticipated that Rosalyn would interrupt the Dragon kids and wind up in the hospital.

Sloane had wrestled with this all night, wishing the pieces didn't fit.

She tried not to remember how nervous the four men had been on the night of the poker game. She tried to forget how reluctant Phil had been to leave her alone with her father at the end of the evening. She tried to forget how overly generous Leo had been about redecorating her cottage, and how hard he'd pressed her to get started. She tried to forget the untouched bottles of O'Doul's on the table, and how Ben had practically been vibrating with tension, talking a mile a minute. She tried to forget how sore Wallace had seemed when he stood up, how stiffly he'd moved, and how, with no signs of chills, he'd worn a heavy, perspiration-drenched turtleneck sweater on a warm autumn night—none of which added up to the onset of the flu.

She'd tried.

And she'd failed.

Derek had left for the office earlier than usual this morning. Sloane didn't ask why. She didn't need to. He wanted to get started running background checks on her father's friends. She could have asked to take part in the inves- tigation. Derek would have welcomed it, since Sloane could provide personal info on each of the men that wouldn't be listed in anything official that Derek could scrounge up. At some point, she might have to volunteer her services for that. But not yet. She just couldn't bring herself to do it—not until she'd explored her less likely but infinitely more tenable theories.

She'd explored little and accomplished nothing.

Her parents hadn't been available to talk to. They, and their FBI bodyguards, had been out for the day. Her mother, once again undeterred by her broken arm, was at a digital publishing seminar, and her father was meeting with the owner of an art gallery to hammer out the final details of a purchase. Not only did Sloane need the two of them to help compile her list of everyone who had access to their apartment but she also had to get their okay to interrogate all those on the list.

They weren't going to like this.

But they'd like the avenue Derek was pursuing even less—if she told them about it. For now, she had no intentions of doing that. It would only cause a lot of emotional pain, hopefully for no good reason.

Meanwhile, even after she got her parents' permission, Sloane would have to tread very carefully when digging around their neighbors and apartment staff. These folks had all been interviewed by the NYPD right after the robbery and asked if they'd seen any suspicious-looking strangers hanging around the Burbanks' apartment.

Sloane's questions wouldn't be so benign. No matter how subtly she phrased them, the implication would be that she suspected one of the interviewees of being a potential accomplice to the burglary. And the reception to that would be a far cry from the one given to the police, when they were being approached as good Samaritans.

Given her parents' unavailability, Sloane had spent the day making phone calls, finding and speaking with the architect who'd designed the building and the builder who'd constructed it, along with the real estate agent who'd sold the individual apartments. She'd also called the Manhattan Office of Land Records to determine which real estate documents, floor plans, and so on were public and which were not.

In short, she'd blown an entire day and learned nothing in the process.

Derek hadn't called.

That could mean he was swamped with work. It could mean he had nothing to report.

Or it could mean he wanted to deliver whatever unwelcome news he'd dug up in person, so he could be there to soften the blow.

Sloane wasn't sure she wanted to know which of those options was correct.

WESTHAMPTON
LONG ISLAND, NEW YORK

During the summer months, the Hamptons were hopping.

Specialty boutiques and cafés were filled with patrons. Yachts sailed the waters, polo matches and wine-tasting events were daily occurrences, and the beaches were jammed with sunbathers. At night, the clubs stayed open until the wee hours, and the wealthy and elite populated their summer cottages, which were, in fact, multimillion-dollar vacation homes.

When autumn arrived, everything changed.

The summer residents and vacationers returned to their regular lives and homes, and the Hamptons became less populated and more low-key. The trendy Westhampton shops, one of the summer's major draws, became the destinations of year-round residents, many of whom were affluent enough to keep the shop owners well compensated, off-season or not.

One of those long-standing shops was the Richtner Gallery—a pricey, upscale art gallery that had been located on Main Street in Westhampton for years. The works displayed there varied from paintings by up-and-coming local artists to paintings created by well-known modernists, to paintings considered to be one-of-a-kind masterpieces with seven-figure price tags.

There was no doubt that this gallery was the perfect location for the Black Eagles' next trial run. And closing time was the perfect hour.

Seven P.M. The browsers were gone. The joggers were home. The dusk was turning to darkness.

Karl Richtner, who'd owned the gallery since it had opened its doors fifteen years ago, was shutting down for the night.

He locked up his register, made sure all the paintings were properly displayed for the morning browsers, and told his assistant to go home.

She gathered up her purse and coat, and headed with him to the front door. As always, Richtner took out his key ring, ready to activate the burglar alarm and lock the door behind them.

It never happened that night.

The four masked gunmen slammed inside, striking Richtner's forehead with the heavy glass door and nearly knocking him down. He staggered backward, just as his assistant reached for the alarm pad.

"Don't," the leader commanded in his accented English, pointing his MP5K at her. "Or I splatter your guts on the floor."

Both the assistant and Richtner froze.

The leader signaled for his team to get moving.

On his command, two of the other gunmen strode forward, dragged their captives behind the counter, and shoved them to the floor, where they stuffed rags in their mouths and immobilized them with Flex-Cufs. The last gunman rushed by, immediately starting to remove the most valuable paintings from the walls and easels, readying them for transit. A minute later, the rest of the team joined him.

They muttered instructions to one another to expedite the process. It took no time to finish amassing what they wanted. They wrapped the specifically chosen paintings in blankets and made their exit through the back door. The van was waiting, motor running. They stashed their cushioned prizes in the trunk. Then, they jumped inside the vehicle and took off, en route to the docks off Montauk Point.

If this heist was typical of hitting an American target, this U.S. stint was going to yield the easiest cash they'd ever made.

———

Derek was still at his desk, reading through Rich's interviews with each of Matthew's partners, and combining the information there with the data he'd assembled during the day.

He had all the basics on the four men. But those were facts you could read on a résumé or find on the Internet—birth dates, schools attended, degrees earned, jobs held. He'd accessed some public records, learned how much each man had paid for his house or apartment. Nothing suspicious there. He'd found out if and when they'd been married, divorced, or started a family. Again, nothing out of the ordinary. He'd gotten his hands on any police records connected with them. The only ones that had surfaced were the tragic hit-and-run accident in April 2006 that had claimed the life of Wallace Johnson's five-year-old daughter, and Ben Martino's DWI misdemeanor, which Rich had already mentioned. The DWI had occurred in December 2004, after a holiday party. Martino had been stopped for weaving between lanes on the West Side Highway. He'd paid a five-hundred-dollar fine and lost his license for six months. Fortunately, no one had been hurt in the incident. But if Martino had a drinking problem, it was worth remembering.

Derek tucked the knowledge away for potential use.

That was it for topical info. Ben Martino's clothing manufacturing company had been passed on to him by his father, and was obviously surviving the shrinking New York garment center. Phil Leary and Leo Fox didn't have so much as a parking ticket. Both their businesses had been around for years. And Wallace Johnson was an upright citizen from a wealthy family, whose art galleries were new but well frequented, and he'd become virtually reclusive since his daughter's death.

Derek had called in a few favors and was waiting for feedback on whether any of their businesses were on shaky ground, or any of their family members were ill or in trouble. He'd love to get specific financial information for all four men, both personal and professional, including bank records showing any abrupt deposits or withdrawals. Phone records would be nice, too, as well as credit card receipts. But he couldn't get any of those without a court order—and the evidence he had wasn't strong enough to go for one. Plus, he was reluctant to go that route anyway, since it might alert his suspects to the fact that they were under investigation for more than just the Rothberg sale.

Besides, if any of them was responsible for giving Xiao Long what he needed, it was very possible that no money had exchanged hands. Xiao was a pro. These guys were rank amateurs. One "visit" by Jin Huang, along with a threat to them or their families, and they'd probably cave.

Derek wanted to speak to Rich, to tell him about this latest development and get his opinion on it. Rich had interviewed each of Burbank's partners, and while none of those interviews had set off warning bells, maybe this new piece of information would jog something in that intuitive mind of his. Maybe he could even think of a good reason to call each of the partners in again, now that they knew Matthew was cooperating with the Bureau, *and* that Rosalyn had been kidnapped and nearly killed. Maybe they'd be prompted by fear for their own lives. Rich could chat with them, the way he had with Matthew, only this time as an ally—one who was trying to keep them safe—rather than as a threat. Maybe he could finagle the guilty party into letting something slip. No one was better at playing people than Rich.

Derek was grasping, and he knew it. But Sloane wasn't about to give him anything to go on, and he had to get what he needed without arousing the suspicions of Matthew's four partners.

Meanwhile, Rich was still tied up on that Armonk art theft. Derek had dropped by his cubicle several times, only to hear Rich on the phone with the Armonk police or Interpol, as they tried to assess whether the Albanian art-crime ring that had hit the European museums was the same one that had robbed Theodore Campbell's home and killed his butler.

One more try, Derek thought, getting to his feet. If Rich was still buried in his case, the questions about Matthew Burbank's partners would have to wait until morning.

"Hey," Rich greeted Derek as he appeared in the entrance to his cubicle. "I know you've been pacing around here all day trying to talk to me. Sorry. This Armonk theft and homicide has too many similarities to the string of European museum heists. And if the Black Eagles are here, we have a national and an international open can of worms." He shoved aside the interview notes he'd taken when he'd spoken to the Campbells. "What's up?"

"Nothing as global as what you're working on. But important nonetheless." Derek explained the theory that Sloane had come to him with and the way their analysis had played out.

"Interesting." Rich leaned back in his chair, propping one leg on top of the opposite knee. "I take it that you and Sloane differ on who your prime suspects are."

"No." Derek shook his head. "What we *really* differ on is our willingness to pursue those prime suspects. Sloane's too close to the situation. Her personal feelings are tripping her up. So while she's talking to her parents' neighbors and apartment employees, I'm digging up everything I can on the likely candidates."

"Matthew Burbank's partners."

"Exactly."

"But you don't want them to realize you're investigating them." A corner of Rich's mouth lifted in a wry smile. "So you're turning to me to bail you out."

Derek blew out a breath. "It's a lot to ask, I know. And believe me, I'd do it myself if I could. But I have no basis for requesting interviews with them without tipping my hand. In your case, it's different. You're not focused on Asian organized crime; you're focused on an art crime they're smack in the middle of. All of them must be freaked out by Rosalyn's close call. Kidnapping and attempted murder are a lot more terrifying than an apartment break-in. You can capitalize on that fear. Call and say that since all the violence is obviously tied to the Rothberg, you're worried for the safety of every man in the partnership. Tell them you're trying to protect them and that the only way to do that is to solve the case and get the bad guys. Ask them to help you fill in holes on the provenance of both the fake and the authentic Rothberg. Or ask for their help in piecing together some additional background info on the gallery owner they bought the painting from—I'm not particular about the reason you provide. But I need your instincts, and your skill at getting people to let things slip they never intended to say."

"I appreciate the compliment. But this is still going to require some fancy footwork to pull off."

"It's not a compliment; it's a fact. If anyone can make this work, it's you." With a twinge of guilt, Derek glanced at the files piled on Rich's desk. "I realize how time-stressed you are, and how intricate this case is you're working on."

"True." Rich's deadpan expression never changed. "Which means that if I help you, you'll owe me one."

"Name it."

"Steaks and beer. And a cigar, if I'm successful. My steakhouse choice. Your credit card."

"Done." Derek flashed him a grin. "With pleasure."

"Don't say that. When it comes to steak, I eat like a horse. You'll be broke for a month."

"I'll risk it."

Rich was still chuckling when his phone rang. He leaned forward and scooped up the receiver, putting it to his ear. "Major Theft. Williams." He paused. "What?" Abruptly, he straightened, snatching up a pad and pen and scribbling something down. "No, that's enough for now. I'll get the rest when I get there. Where should we meet?" A pause. "I'm on my way." He hung up, jumped to his feet, and grabbed his jacket all at the same time. "An art gallery in the Hamptons was just hit," he told Derek. "No one was killed, but the MO sounds like it might be the same guys who hit the Campbells' place. Sorry, Derek, the calls to Burbank's partners will have to wait. I'm out of here."

CHAPTER
EIGHTEEN

Leo Fox had enjoyed a variety of women in his life. He wasn't the type to settle down. There was too much excitement in the discovery and exploration of fresh relationships. New faces, new interests, new sex. To commit to one person forever would be like relinquishing all the colors of the rainbow for the monotony of one single hue. It was unimaginable.

Until the May before last, when he'd met Amalie.

Whoever had coined the expression "the earth moved" understood Leo's reaction the instant he laid eyes on Amalie. He'd spotted her browsing in his design studio, running her fingers over a velvet tapestry in a delicate caress. Her beauty wasn't the kind that turned men's heads. It was the kind Leo felt in his soul.

He'd introduced himself, gazed into her eyes, and fallen in love.

The extraordinary part was so had she.

It had been like a fairy tale, one Leo never wanted to end. Amalie and her two wonderful, precocious children had moved to New York six years earlier, following a messy divorce. She'd never expected to feel such a strong bond with another man. Yet this bond was even stronger than her first.

By the end of that month, Leo and Amalie were planning their June wedding. Leo couldn't wait to begin their new life together. He'd stood at the altar that day, heart pounding with love and anticipation.

Amalie had never showed up.

Leo had panicked. He'd called her over and over—at home, on her cell. Both numbers were disconnected. He'd notified the police. They'd found nothing amiss. She'd sold her condo a week earlier—perfectly normal for a woman about to be married. To the cops, it appeared she'd simply vacated early. But to Leo, it was unthinkable. Instead of her things and her children's things being moved to Leo's place, they'd simply been packed and taken. Vanished, along with Amalie.

A week later, Leo had received a "Dear John" e-mail from her. She confessed that her last marriage had scarred her too badly to attempt another. She'd struggled to overcome her fears, but at the last minute, she'd gotten cold feet. She'd begged his forgiveness and told him to move on with his life.

He'd e-mailed her back immediately. But the account had been canceled. And Leo had never heard from her again.

His heart had been shattered. He'd never fully recovered from his pain. And he had no interest in any other women. But he had to find life again.

So he poured himself into the two other things he cared about: interior design and his friends. His four closest friends knew not to mention Amalie's name. But they also knew Leo. He had a joy for life, a heart of gold, and he needed to be needed. It wasn't hard to give him that. He'd always been their universal confidant—the one they all came to with their problems, their big news—good or bad—and yes, their secrets. He had a reassuring quality about him that screamed empathy and compassion. He was an attentive listener, an excellent judge of character, and he was smart enough to know when to keep his mouth shut. An intuitive interior designer. An equally intuitive friend.

Exactly what they all needed. Exactly what Leo needed.

Right now, his intuition was warning him that things were unraveling. Rosalyn's kidnapping had sent them all into a panic. They were all looking over their shoulders, jumping at shadows. To top that off, each of his friends was a personal mess. Ben was drinking heavily again, Phil was on the phone with his bookie more than he was with his clients, Matthew was smoking a pack a day and watching Roz like a hawk, and Wallace was coming completely unglued.

At least until that party he'd hosted for Cindy Liu.

Leo had dropped by for a while, mostly to meet this fabulous young architect to determine if there was any potential for them to work together. If she was as good as Wallace claimed, then she'd be snatched up by an affluent crowd who were eager to embark on their pet residential projects—add-ons, renovations, or total interior overhauls. And along with a superb architect, Ms. Liu's clients would need a top interior designer to complete the transitions they envisioned for their new living space.

That's where he'd come in.

He'd arrived at Wallace's gallery when the cocktail hour was in full swing. He'd glanced around the room, spied Cindy Liu—and stopped dead in his tracks. Talk about a blast from the past. She was the spitting image of that young woman Meili, who had been Wallace's heart and soul. Older and more refined, of course, plus educated and business savvy.

Still, the resemblance was astounding. And the timing couldn't be better. This was just what Wallace needed to distract him from the rapid downward spiral his life was taking. It might keep him from living in the past. It might even bring a modicum of happiness back into his life.

Leo scrutinized the expression on Wallace's face as his gaze followed his protégé around the room. Wallace was watching Cindy. But he was seeing Meili. It was there in his eyes, in his body language. Wallace might not be aware of its intensity. But Leo was. And it was palpable.

Leo picked up Cindy's business card while scanning her design samples. There was no missing her natural flair and talent. Not to mention her people skills, he noted, watching as she charmed and impressed all the guests. Yes, he could definitely foresee a long and lucrative business arrangement between himself and Ms. Liu.

And an equally long and promising personal relationship between her and Wallace.

This was good news. Three projects for Leo to work on. Approaching Cindy with his business plan. Using the time when he was redesigning

Sloane's cottage to make sure Derek was the right man for her, while making equally sure he wasn't chasing down leads that would cause problems for the art partnership.

And urging things along for Wallace and Cindy. For Wallace's sake. And for all their sakes.

Leo felt a great sense of purpose as he glanced at the phone number on Cindy Liu's business card. His own happy ending might be lost forever. But it would give him great joy to see Wallace find his.

━━━━━

Sloane was at her parents' apartment first thing in the morning.

They'd gotten her voice mail, so they were both there, waiting to hear what was on her mind. The FBI agent assigned to them that morning excused himself and went into the other room.

Over the muffins and coffee Sloane had picked up, she filled her parents in.

Matthew stopped chewing, and put down his piece of muffin. "You think one of our neighbors helped rob the apartment?"

"That's not what I said." Sloane took a fortifying sip of coffee. "I said that it's virtually impossible for the thugs who broke in here to have done so without help. The other burglaries in the neighborhood were different. There was inside knowledge of the security systems. That's not true in your case. So someone either used a key to let the thieves in, or gave them access to get in on their own."

"Gave them access—you mean this person was just waiting inside our apartment and let them in?"

"Or gave them a key to get in on their own." Sloane paused, choosing her words carefully. Not only did she not want to freak out her parents any more than she already had, but she also was limited in what she could tell them.

"The other red flag is the amount of time the thieves spent here, and how they spent it," she said. "Based on the police report, they were only here about twenty minutes, and Mom walked in less than five minutes after they did."

Sloane turned to her mother. "According to your recollections, they went straight to Dad's office. They found the Rothberg file pretty fast—no easy task, given his filing system. And they saved the rest—trashing his office, ripping off your valuables—until the end. So, other than your unexpected interruption, I'd say they had the whole burglary well planned and well timed."

Rosalyn Burbank's eyes narrowed. "So that's what our impromptu reenactment was all about. You're saying that whoever helped the burglars knew the layout of the apartment, specifically where your father's office is."

"His office and his files, yes." Sloane looked from one of her parents to the other. "I need you to compile a list of everyone—neighbors, building employees, acquaintances, you name it—who have a key to this place."

With a muttered oath, Matthew reached for his pack of cigarettes and tapped it until he could extract one. "That murderer paid someone off so his thugs could get in here, steal my records, and threaten me." Hands shaking, Matthew put the cigarette between his lips and lit it, inhaling deeply. "Hell, why stop there? What if that same someone was paid off to get their hands on your mother's schedule? What if they found out when her day and night security guys changed shifts so they could slip in their muscle to kidnap and kill her?"

"Dad, you're overreacting," Sloane said in an even tone. Not that what he'd just said hadn't occurred to her. It had. But Xiao Long had enough eyes and ears of his own to get that information. And, whenever possible, he'd much rather rely on his own Red Dragons than involve a stranger.

"Am I?" Matthew demanded.

"Yes. Gaining access to your apartment is one thing. Setting up a kidnapping and murder like the KGB is something entirely different. Let's not blow things out of proportion."

"Blow things out of proportion?" Matthew stared at his daughter, sheer panic in his eyes. "How much worse can things get?"

"Matthew, put out the cigarette," Rosalyn said in a firm, no-nonsense tone. "Destroying your lungs isn't going to make this go away."

Sloane jumped on that. "I thought you were cutting down," she grilled her father.

"I was. Until this nightmare started." Matthew ignored his wife's demand and took another long drag of his cigarette. "Does it really matter anymore? We live like prisoners, with FBI agents in our home and guarding us wherever we go. We're still part of the Bureau's investigation, one that you can't talk about, but I'm sure it runs deeper than either your mother or I know. We're dealing with a killer who almost murdered your mother, and who'll do whatever he has to to protect himself. And now we're hearing that someone we know is in on this, and had a hand in helping with the break-in. Hell, maybe for a little extra cash, they'll let themselves into our apartment one night and finish us off."

"Stop it, Dad." Sloane yanked the cigarette out of his hand and stubbed it out, tossing the butt in the ashtray. "No one's getting into this apartment, not with the FBI here. No one's going to hurt you or Mom. And no one's going to get away with this. I'll make sure of that. Now please, start compiling that list. And you can leave out the apartment's architect, builder, and real estate agent, along with the co-op office. The floor plans they have are generic, and none of them has a key to your apartment."

"So you already got started on this," Matthew said.

"Yesterday. You and Mom were unavailable, so I stuck with an impersonal list. I felt I should talk to you before I went any further. This is bound to be uncomfortable for you. No matter how tactful I am, I'm bound to piss off some people with my questions."

"I don't really give a damn." Rosalyn had already stood up and used her good arm to grab a pad and pen. "I piss people off every day. And that's just by doing my job. This is a lot more serious than negotiating a book deal. I was nearly killed. If our neighbors and the building staff can't deal with your probing, then screw them."

"I agree," Matthew concurred instantly.

"Then that's settled." Rosalyn pulled her chair close to Matthew's and put the pad and pen on the table in front of him. "It's easier for you to write. We'll break this down by categories: neighbors, service people, building staff. That'll make it easier for Sloane."

"That would be great, thanks." Sloane noticed that her mother didn't mention friends or acquaintances in her breakdown list. That meant she wasn't even thinking in that direction. If she was, she would have confronted Sloane head-on. Maybe it was better that way. Let her parents focus on the path she'd planned on them taking anyway. Later, if it came down to it, she'd hit them with the ugly possibility that one of their friends—or partners—was the accomplice they were seeking.

If it came down to it.

Sloane extracted a few sheets of paper from her tote bag. "The FBI faxed me a copy of the police report. It details all the people they interviewed after the break-in. Take a look at it, see who's applicable, and I'll start with them while you write up your list."

"We will." Curbing his apprehension, Matthew took the police report and glanced over it. "As far as I'm concerned, you can talk to all these people. Roz?" He showed the report to his wife.

She nodded. "Go for it."

"Okay." Sloane took back the list and headed for the front door. "I'll check back in a little while."

Armed with a handful of people to interview, Sloane took the elevator down to the lobby. Might as well start on the ground level and work her way up. She stepped outside to talk to the doorman, and winced when she saw who was on duty. Bernie Raskin. This was going to be tough. Given that her parents had sublet their apartment during their short-term retirement, and moved right back in when they returned, Sloane had known Bernie for a decade. He was a gentle, polite sweetheart of a guy, who always smiling and never had a bad word to say about anyone. Sloane could no more picture him aiding and abetting than she could a boy scout.

Regardless, she couldn't exclude anyone. The good news was that Bernie hadn't been on duty the night of the burglary. So she wouldn't be impugning his character with her questions. On the other hand, he had a tight friendship with the other three doormen who manned the entranceway on a rotating basis. He was bound to resent any implication Sloane made that any of them might be guilty of this.

Well, she'd known this wasn't going to be fun. Nevertheless, it had to be done.

She took a deep breath and approached Bernie.

Diagonally across the street, eating a hot dog and ostensibly scanning a college textbook, was a young Asian man. He blended right in with the pedestrian traffic, looking like every other New York college student. Except that on his right arm, concealed beneath his baggy army jacket, was a fiery Red Dragon tattoo.

Sitting against a tree, he was careful to keep his distance so he wouldn't be spotted by whatever security the FBI had guarding the place. At the same time, he had a bird's-eye view of Matthew Burbank's apartment building—and his daughter.

She'd been there for over an hour, he noted, biting into his hot dog and watching her exit the building and walk over to the doorman. Adjusting his Yankee hat, he focused in on the exchange. It started casually enough, but got real heavy real fast. The doorman was pissed, that was for sure. He stiffened up and took a step back, whipping his head from side to side in a way that said "no friggin' way" as clearly as if he'd shouted the words across the street. As Burbank's daughter continued to press her point, he stopped talking altogether, shutting her down with an emphatic gesture, his hand slicing the air with absolute, dismissive conviction.

Lucky for her that her interrogation session had gone south in a hurry. It had better stay that way.

Because if the Dai Lo heard otherwise, she wouldn't be around much longer.

CHAPTER NINETEEN

Peggy Sun took a few steps back to scrutinize her initial handiwork.

In her mind, the canvas was still primarily bare. The lush green background was well under way, in both color and texture. But the little girl, the details of her features, the fluidity of her motion—all that was yet to be captured and re-created.

A contemporary art piece would have been far easier to copy under these tight time parameters. With its broader strokes and more abstract concepts, contemporary art was more forgiving in its replication. And the process moved quickly. But a painting like this—detailed, rich with specific character expression, individualistic traits, and movement—it was Impressionism at its best, and a very tall order to replicate. At 13.5 by 10.5 inches, it was one of Renoir's smaller paintings. Also one of his lesser known—and therefore less widely recognized. But Peggy approached her job as if she were copying *La Lecture,* the breathtaking depiction of two young girls studying at their desk that was currently hanging in the Louvre and was scrutinized on a daily basis by some of the most discerning art connoisseurs in the world.

Totally immersed in her craft, Peggy didn't hear Cindy come upstairs to the loft. Tucked away on the apartment's second floor and reachable only by an inconspicuous back staircase, the loft was an artist's haven. Peggy did all her work there, both for the solitude that inspired creativity and the privacy that ensured no intruders.

"Incredible replica," Cindy praised as she rounded the top of the staircase and caught a glimpse of Peggy's canvas.

"*Partial* replica," her friend corrected, still studying what she'd painted thus far. "It's still very much a work in progress. And Renoir? It's humbling to try to emulate that level of genius."

Cindy shook her head, an expression of sheer disbelief crossing her face. "You're a genius yourself. Every brushstroke is like a caress. Watching you paint is watching a love scene unfold."

"Thank you," Peggy replied with simple gratitude. "I hope I can live up to your uncle's expectations."

"You always do." Balancing the heavy vase she was carrying, Cindy moved closer, taking in the astonishing similarities between the original and Peggy's emerging forgery. "I know how disappointed you were that you only got one of the two Renoirs to copy. But, as we both know, the other original was sold—at an exorbitant price. Especially considering it's never going to be seen."

"Except by the buyer."

"Yes, except by the buyer. Speaking of whom, look what just arrived." Cindy waited until Peggy turned around, so she could watch her reaction to the vase of magnificent pink roses. "Two dozen," Cindy clarified, placing the vase on a nearby table so they could both admire it. "From the buyer of our other Renoir."

With that, she pulled out the card and offered it to Peggy.

"'Congratulations on a stunning debut,'" Peggy read aloud. "'Let's celebrate over dinner. You choose the where and when. With great admiration, Wallace.'" Lowering the card, Peggy made a gesture of proud recognition. "In the realm of great work, you accomplished even more than I did, and a whole lot faster. From a man who's barely come out of his shell for almost two years, Mr. Johnson is certainly chomping at the bit. A bouquet worthy of a bride, and a dinner invitation with terms dictated by you. And all after one successful event that was supposedly a mere business endeavor. Brava."

Cindy shrugged off the compliment and gave the roses an appreciative sniff. "Let's not give me too much credit. You said yourself he was mesmerized by my resemblance to Meili."

"Oh, he was. I watched him staring at you and hungering over the past. But you're the one who played the part. The incentive for him is far greater this time. Meili was a reckless child. You're a shrewd and accomplished woman. And there's no wife standing in the way. So the tables will be turned. *You'll* be the one pulling the strings."

Cindy straightened up and grinned. "I think I'll start pulling now. A thank-you phone call setting our dinner date is in order. My A *Sook* already shipped the gift. It will be a lovely presentation." She lifted the vase and headed for the stairs. "We have to display these, of course. And since no one is allowed up here but us, I think the living room table would be best. A centerpiece, drizzled with sunlight."

"Moonlight," Peggy amended. "You're having dinner. The evening could run late."

"Right." Cindy paused, thinking. "Friday night is too soon. Saturday night is too intimate. Besides, he spends the weekends in the Hamptons."

"Not if you gave him reason not to. If you chose a weekend night for your dinner, I'm sure he'd stay at his Manhattan town house."

"Maybe. But I'd rather wait." Cindy's eyes twinkled. "Who knows when I might want to spend a weekend in East Hampton—after an appropriate amount of time has passed, of course."

"Of course."

"What would you think about next week, say Tuesday?"

"I'd say it's a good choice. It's enough time to make you look interested but not overeager. Oh, and I'd say wear your turquoise silk blouse. It looks gorgeous on you. He'll be captivated."

Cindy's laughter trailed behind her as she descended the stairs. "Then Tuesday and the turquoise silk it is."

Phil Leary's hand was shaking as he hung up the phone. When the call had come in from his bookie, Ardian Sava, he thought it would be routine—a hot tip on next week's race and a reminder of the hefty wad of cash he owed.

It was anything but.

Sava had gotten wind from a reliable source that someone was trying to dig up dirt on Phil's background, who he associated with and his recreational spending habits. They were nosing around at the track to find out how much time he spent there. They'd even contacted two Vegas casinos to determine his gambling habits and the frequency of his visits.

No surprise that Sava was freaked out. The hotheaded Albanian had told Phil not to contact him until this fishing expedition blew over—except to pay him his money. All of it.

Phil didn't even have half. But that was the least of his problems. If this got out, it could ruin his career. It could ruin his life.

And, depending upon who'd ordered this investigation, it could end it.

Automatically, he grabbed the phone and punched in Leo's number.

Wallace felt unusually peaceful.

Downstairs in his private haven, he sank back in his chair and soaked up the beauty of his personal gallery. The newly purchased Renoir had been well worth waiting for. He'd completed the transaction and hung it just hours earlier. And already it was enhancing the room.

The little girl in the painting was far off in the background, her features and expressions indistinct, creating a haunting, surreal effect. Her coloring was perfect, as was the hue of her frock. The full impact made it all the more effortless to lose himself in it. Especially given the focus of the painting—the breathtaking field of wildflowers spread out before the little girl, and her fascination with it. Her basket was beside her, and she was squatting down, reaching for another of the identical flowers she clutched in her hand.

Daisies.

When Wallace had first held the painting in his hands and scrutinized it up close, he'd felt that familiar constriction in his throat and chest, that pain that shot through his soul. But now, studying it as it hung in its carefully chosen spot on the wall adjacent to his chair, he felt oddly at peace.

The pain was still there. But so was an odd sense of comfort.

He shut his eyes, letting memories wash over him. He couldn't explain why the sharp agony was softened by a feeling of peace. Maybe it was because his collection was almost complete, the sole bare spot on the wall across the room waiting for the masterpiece that would be the culmination of it all.

And maybe it was because he was experiencing the unexpected and ever-so-slight longing to live again.

The vision of wildflowers in his mind transformed into a vision of pink roses—and their recipient.

Cindy had been touched by and appreciative of his gesture. She'd expressed her thanks with genuine warmth, and they'd made dinner plans for this coming Tuesday night.

He was looking forward to the evening. Yes, he understood that a portion of the conversation would be about the cocktail party invitations that had been pouring in from eager new clients she'd met at her gallery debut. And, yes, he knew that another portion of the conversation would be about the future plans her uncle had for her success.

But Wallace was hoping that they'd have more, much more, that they could talk about.

———

Sloane felt sapped in more ways than one as she drove away from the Hospital for Special Surgery and her hand therapy session that evening. It had been quite a harrowing day. Poor Connie. She'd had to work like a demon just to relax Sloane's hand enough to unclench it and massage the remaining scar tissue on her palm.

Of course she'd asked why Sloane was so wound up. And there was very little Sloane could reveal. So she emphasized the personal part. She told

Connie that she was working on a high-profile case that was pitting her and Derek against each other, and that they were fighting like cats and dogs.

The male-female bickering Connie understood well. She commiserated with Sloane about men and their pigheadedness. But she'd also reminded her how hard she and Derek had worked to find their way back to each other after their break-up in Cleveland.

Sloane didn't need any reminders of how destructively each of them had behaved after the robbery that resulted in her hand being slashed. Derek had pressured her to stay with the Bureau, injury be damned, showing the compassion of a stone wall. She, in turn, had shut him out, showing the maturity of a child.

But wanting to be together didn't mean either one was willing to take the subordinate role. And this case was a grueling test of their relationship.

Especially since the sides were unbalanced. She was operating alone, with no backup, and no time to hire the right resources. Whereas Derek had not only himself but also the manpower of both C-6 and the Art Crime Team, not to mention whatever confidential human sources he called upon to fully investigate every man in her father's partnership.

The scales were tipped in his favor.

As luck would have it, today she'd taken a detour that might just untip them.

She'd spotted the lanky Asian kid while she was talking to Bernie. After that, he'd been on her tail all day. She'd purposely tested him, overtly talking to the apartment maintenance staff outside so he could see, and hopefully hear, her. She'd also made it a point to catch most of the neighbors on her parents' list as they entered or left the building, initiating the conversations she needed to have in full view of her Red Dragon shadow.

She'd then walked three blocks at lunchtime for a sandwich, taken the long route back to her parents' place, and still the punk was half a block behind.

Finally. She'd been added to the list of Burbanks that Xiao Long considered to be a threat. He was definitely keeping an eye on her. Excellent. It was time to up the stakes and give him something real to worry about. That would make her more vital to the Bureau, and shift Xiao Long's focus from her parents to her.

The file on Xiao that Derek had given her included the police reports on all the Upper East Side burglaries the Red Dragons had pulled off. There were eight of them, not counting her parents' place. She had all the names and addresses, as well as a list of items stolen from each apartment.

Sure enough, every list of stolen items included valuable paintings. And that gave her just the in she needed.

She didn't call ahead. That way, no one could refuse to see her. She simply walked from location to location, acknowledging doormen and pressing intercom buzzers. In a clear, official voice—one that the punk tailing her was sure to hear—she introduced herself as a private consultant representing undisclosed insurance companies who'd paid claims on several of the more valuable paintings taken during their string of neighborhood burglaries. She further informed them that there were similarities between those paintings and the ones taken from their home. It was imperative that she discuss it with them.

She stopped at all eight apartment buildings, and managed to talk her way into five of them. The Dragon kid who was following her overheard only what she wanted him to. He had no idea what was being said in private. That would freak him out big-time.

Then came the pièce de résistance. Sloane exited the last building, still scribbling down a few notes. She paused a few steps away, flipped open her cell phone, and punched in a number.

"Nineteenth Precinct?" she inquired. "This is Sloane Burbank. Could you please connect me with Detective Diane Yuen?" A pause. "Hi, Diane. Listen, are you going to be at your desk for the next hour? Because I've got something on the paintings stolen in that string of burglaries you're investigating. And it's something you'll be able to act on faster and with less red tape than the FBI. Can I come by and run it by you? Great. See you in a few."

She punched off her phone, silencing the computerized voice at the other end that was providing her with the accurate time and temperature.

She headed over to the Nineteenth Precinct, had an impromptu cup of sludgy coffee with Diane, whom she'd known for years, and gave her a brief explanation of what she'd done, and what she'd presumably told Diane over the phone.

Diane started to laugh. "Very creative. Posing as an independent freelance insurance investigator. And, of course, I assume that once you got inside and actually spoke to these people, you let it slip that you're working on a contingency basis."

"You got it." Sloane grinned back. "Money is a motivator everyone understands. And I admitted that I'd collect a whopping finder's fee if I recovered the paintings." She leaned forward. "Between you and me, this was my idea. It's a little outside the lines, so I figured I'd run it by C-6 after the fact, perhaps later today. So, in the meantime, keep this between us."

"Only if, in return, you pass along anything solid that comes out of this."

"When I know, you'll know."

"You've got yourself a deal."

Sloane rose. "I've got to get going." She took a last gulp of coffee and shuddered. "Next time, let's meet for a real lunch—one where you actually sit down in a restaurant and get coffee that doesn't taste like it was pumped from the sewer."

"That sounds like heaven." Diane stood up as well, ready to get back to the mounds of paperwork on her desk. "Stay in touch."

"I will."

Sloane had stopped outside the precinct to glance at her watch, and to make sure Xiao's guy was still there.

He was. And her watch told her it was time to head over to HSS and her hand therapy appointment with Connie.

She chose to walk. He followed her all the way there.

But he was gone when she came out, and no one followed her to the garage where she'd parked her car.

Purposely, she took her time getting behind the wheel. She even slipped out of her jacket and tossed it into the backseat, giving herself an extra moment to scan the area. Nope. No shadow.

Interesting. He'd probably rushed off to fill in Xiao Long. And she'd know soon enough just how rattled the Dai Lo was.

The drive home was uneventful, although she did glance in her rearview mirror a few times just to make sure. When she was certain she was alone, she turned her thoughts to Derek, and how she was going to handle him.

He was going to be furious. Not only had she overstepped her bounds without consulting him but she'd also thrown herself right in front of the very moving train he'd warned her against. Professionally and personally, he was going to blast her. And telling him that she was fighting the odds, that she was trying to figure out who'd helped the Red Dragons break into her parents' apartment while he was working to implicate her father's closest friends— that wasn't going to fly. What she'd done today, after questioning the names on her parents' list, had been totally unrelated to her original task. Instead of hunting down Xiao's helper, she'd spent the majority of the day intentionally baiting Xiao.

She steeled herself as she drove through the wooded back roads of Hunterdon County. Connie's advice had been great—in theory. But Sloane knew that her relationship was about to take another whopping hit.

Turning up the secluded hill that led to her cottage, Sloane continued the steep climb until she was just one wide curve away from home. She spotted a row of blinking lights blocking the road and she slowed down. It was a line of sawhorses with blinkers closing off the rest of the road. Breaking to a stop, she gave an inward groan. Construction work. There'd obviously been some going on here today. And given the sparse population of the area, no one had bothered moving the barriers for the few vehicles that accessed this section of the hill each night.

Well, there was no point in bitching, silently or otherwise. At this point, all Sloane wanted to do was to get home and get this fight with Derek over with. Bearing that in mind, she shifted her car into park, put on her hazard lights, and got out. She headed over to the sawhorses to drag them away one at a time.

She'd just pulled the first sawhorse out of the way when she caught a flash of movement out of the corner of her eye.

She whirled around just as the punk who'd been following her all day got in her face. Only this time, he was carrying a long switchblade.

He didn't pause. He pivoted slightly, and his arm plunged downward in a sharp diagonal slash. The silver switchblade flashed in the night, and even though Sloane lurched backward instinctively, it managed to slice her right forearm. A burning pain shot through her.

In that fraction of an instant, she realized her assailant's intent.

Xiao Long had ordered him to go for her injured hand.

Sloane's Krav Maga training took over and she snapped into defensive mode. The blade was already on its return upward swing, this time aiming directly for her palm.

Blocking out the pain, Sloane acted. Simultaneously, she shot her feet back, arching forward and thrusting her left forearm down to block his ascending blow, breaking his momentum and halting his arm as it swung up toward her. Her left arm then wound around his blade-wielding hand, trapping it between her left shoulder and wrist.

The blade toppled from his grasp and clattered to the ground.

Sloane slammed her right elbow into his nose. He gave a hoarse shout of pain and swore in Fukienese. She ignored both. Still holding his arm immobilized, she grabbed the back of his neck with her right hand, jerking him down and smashing her knee into his groin.

He made an agonized sound. She released him, and he doubled over and staggered back. As he straightened, she drew her knee up to her chest and shot her leg straight out, connecting squarely with the center of his torso.

He flew backward from the impact, crashing to the concrete.

Sloane seized her opportunity. She rushed over, bent down, and snatched up the blade. Turning, she raced back to her car and jumped inside. She floored the gas, swerving around the miserable bastard as he half limped, half crawled toward the woods and escape. Never glancing back, she sped the rest of the way home.

It was only when she was inside the garage, the car ignition turned off, and the garage door safely down that she became aware of the searing pain in her arm. Reflexively, she glanced down—and went rigid as she saw the stream of blood trickling down her arm to her hand, coating her palm and fingers in that sickly shade of red she remembered all too well.

For one paralyzed instant she just sat there, horrifying memories flashing through her mind, waves of nausea rolling over her.

Dizzy and lightheaded, she began to gag, then to retch uncontrollably. Drenched in sweat, she scrambled out of the car and reached for the nearby trash container.

She vomited until there was nothing left inside her.

CHAPTER TWENTY

Derek was in the living room with the hounds. He saw Sloane's headlights cut the darkness as her car tore down the driveway, taking the curves at a breakneck speed.

By the time the garage door went up, Derek was on his feet, heading for the side entrance. Moe, Larry, and Curly were on his heels, their shrill barks telling him they could sense something was very wrong.

He yanked open the door. The automatic light over Sloane's car was on, illuminating the darkened garage. The door on the driver's side of her car was ajar. And Sloane was bending over the trash can, her shoulders heaving violently as she threw up.

Derek was down the steps in an instant. It wasn't until he got closer that the sickeningly familiar smell of blood invaded his nostrils. Simultaneously, he saw the thin stream of red dripping down Sloane's forearm, trickling down her wrist and hand, and sliding off her fingers onto the concrete floor. The splotches quickly increased in number.

His gut clenched.

He was beside Sloane in a heartbeat. She looked up dazedly as he reached for her, not really seeing him or even being fully aware of his presence. She was in shock, her face sheet white, her eyes huge and haunted.

Derek knew she was going to pass out even before he caught her.

When Sloane opened her eyes, she was lying supine on the sofa, her head propped up on cushions. The first thing she saw was the three hounds clustered around her, their expressive little faces filled with distress.

Recall took an instant.

Shards of pain jolted her memory.

She lurched upward, her gaze darting to her right arm, even as Derek eased her back into a reclining position.

"Sh-h-h, it's okay," he said in as soothing a voice as he could muster. "I've got it under control."

Sloane saw that he had. Her arm was elevated, resting on two sofa cushions, and Derek was using towels to apply direct pressure to the wound. The bleeding had definitely slowed down. There was a small pail with two washcloths floating in it sitting on the floor. The water was a nauseating shade of red.

None of it mattered. There was just one thing Sloane cared about.

"My hand?" she asked hoarsely.

"Not even a scratch," Derek assured her. His tone was soothing, but he looked like hell. "It was just coated with the blood from your arm." He slid his hand behind her neck and raised her head slightly so she could inspect it herself—just as he had after washing off enough blood to determine the full extent of her injury. "See for yourself."

She stared at her hand, turning it palm up, bending and flexing each finger, and feeling a surge of relief that defied words. "Thank God," she whispered. Her gaze flickered briefly over the towels, then lifted back to Derek's. "How bad is my arm?"

"It looks like a flesh wound. But we're bandaging it and getting you to the hospital." He leaned over her, scrutinizing her face. "Are you up to the ride if I carry you to the car?"

Sloane gave him a wan smile. "You don't have to carry me."

"That wasn't the question."

"Yes. I'm up for it." She paused. "Can we take your car? Mine's got blood on the seat and the steering wheel . . ."

"We'll take my car," Derek interjected. He rose, pointing at the towels. "Hold those against your arm while I get bandages." Waiting until she complied, he turned to leave the room.

"Derek?"

He stopped, giving her a questioning look.

"Aren't you going to ask me what happened?"

His jaw was set so tightly, it looked like it might snap. "Oh, I'm going to ask you lots of questions. But first I want to make sure you're all right. Because after that, and after I hear what you have to say, I have a feeling I might want to kill you myself."

Sloane leaned back weakly. "If the hospital doesn't give me some hardcore painkillers, I might just let you." She removed her left hand from the towels just long enough to scratch the hounds' ears. "Don't worry, you three. I'm fine." She kissed the tops of their little brown heads, then reached across herself again to continue applying pressure to the wound.

Derek finished the bandaging process in record time and scooped Sloane up in his arms, along with the warm fleece blanket he'd wrapped her in. Sloane would never admit it, but the truth was she was very happy to be carried to the car. She was still dizzy and nauseous, and the trembling wouldn't stop. From past experience, she recognized the signs of shock, combined with the adrenaline drop following her combat with Xiao's punk. She leaned back in the passenger's seat, her head cradled by the headrest, and tried to do some slow, deep breathing to ease the symptoms.

Just as Derek started the car, she remembered something, and her head angled toward him. "The switchblade is in my car. It's a rubber-handled automatic, maybe eight inches long, with a four-inch blade. I don't know if the prints are too smudged to make out, other than mine. But C-6 can use it any way they need to."

"How generous," Derek said wryly. "And so cooperative, too."

"Better late than never."

He shot her a sideways look. "You stopped long enough to retrieve the weapon?"

"I didn't want him grabbing it. So I did."

Derek released the emergency brake. "We'll talk later. You look like you're about to faint again."

She felt like it.

"Here. Drink this." Before Derek shifted into reverse, he handed her a can of cranberry juice and a straw he'd grabbed on the way out. "Just sip. It'll help."

She took the can gratefully. "Thank you—for everything."

"Don't thank me. I still might kill you." He grunted as he backed out of the two-car garage, then headed down the driveway. "I must be crazy to be in love with you."

"Probably." Sloane smiled faintly, taking a sip of juice. "But I'm glad you are. I was counting on it tipping the scales in my favor when you decided whether or not to kill me."

"I wouldn't get too cocky. I doubt I'll feel so magnanimous once I know you're okay, and once you've told me what happened and why." Derek shook his head as Sloane opened her mouth to fill him in. "Not now. Just drink your juice and rest. We'll talk later."

"A reprieve. Thanks." Sloane leaned back against the headrest again, shock slowly transforming to weariness. "I'm really beat. If it wasn't for the pain, I'd be nodding off."

It was the last thing she said before they reached the hospital.

She never felt Derek take the can of juice out of her hand and put it in the cup holder. She was out for the count.

Sloane hated hospitals. Particularly the ER. Nightmarish memories besieged her the minute she inhaled that antiseptic hospital smell. Fortunately, this visit was short.

Derek filled out the paperwork, and the wait wasn't nearly as long as it could have been. The doctor who treated her administered a local anesthetic. Then, he cleaned out the three-inch gash, stitched it up, and bandaged it.

"You were lucky," he informed her. "It's a nasty wound, but it only penetrated the flesh. All blood vessels, muscles, and tendons are intact. I'm going to give you a tetanus shot, just to be on the safe side. I'm also going to prescribe an antibiotic to prevent infection, and Percocet for the pain. Make sure to change the bandage daily, and keep it dry for the first three days. I'll remove the sutures in ten days, so make an appointment. And call immediately if you have any major bleeding or swelling."

"I will. Thank you, Doctor." Sloane waited while he administered the shot and wrote the prescription. Then, she slid off the table and onto her feet, so relieved that her hand wasn't affected that the pain in her forearm seemed insignificant.

"And get some rest," the doctor added.

"She will," Derek assured him. He guided Sloane out, signed whatever release papers were necessary, and picked up the two prescriptions.

Fifteen minutes later, they were in the car and on their way home.

The silence was more ominous than the impending fight.

"Are we waiting until we get home to get into it?" Sloane asked. "Because we've got a twenty-minute drive, and I'd just as soon start the explosion now."

"You've already been through one ordeal tonight," Derek replied curtly. "I figured the second could wait until morning."

"That won't work. By morning, you'll have to file a report and make some decisions. As for me, I'm tired, but I'm fine. The Percocet is starting to work, so the pain is dulling. But that also means I'll be dulling along with it. So let me fill you in now, while I'm still coherent. You can kill me later, after the narcotics kick in."

"Fine. Go for it."

Sloane started from the beginning. Her morning visit to her parents. The interviewing of those on their list. The sense that she was being followed. The confirmation that she was, and by whom. The way she'd made sure he knew what she was doing, and why.

Finally, with no apology in her voice, she told Derek about the way she'd baited the Red Dragon kid. Her ruse. Her invented role as an insurance investigator. Her talk with the other victims of Xiao's burglaries, based on the fact that they all had works of art stolen. Her pretense about going to the NYPD with some alleged information that she'd fabricated. And the subsequent knife attack by Xiao's punk in the deserted section of woods right down the road.

Derek listened to the entire story without interruption.

When he did speak, it was in that low, controlled tone that told Sloane he was beyond furious.

"Professionally, you violated every rule in the book. You overstepped your bounds and abused your role in this investigation. You're an FBI confidential human source, not a special agent. In addition, you took it upon yourself to act without prior permission from the lead case agent—that would be me—and without even clueing me in until after the fact. You did that because you knew I'd shut you down. You put your life and my investigation in jeopardy—which is precisely why I didn't want you on this case to begin with. And you nearly got yourself killed in the process."

Sloane wasn't surprised by any part of Derek's reprimand. All of it had merit. Most of it was true. The rest fell into gray territory.

"I pushed the boundaries of my role," she admitted. "But I didn't violate them. Part of the reason Tony let me in on this investigation is because my father—and his family—are targets of Xiao Long. I just used that to my advantage."

"No, you took a potential risk and made it into a certainty. There's no guarantee that Xiao would have gone after you. Now there's no way he won't."

"Point taken." Sloane took a minute to gather her strength. "As for the rest, you're right. I didn't come to you with my idea. Partly because you would have nixed it, and partly because it struck me on the spur of the moment. The situation presented itself. It was a one-shot opportunity. So I went for it."

"You have a cell phone. You could have called me."

"And been overheard by Xiao's thug? No way."

"Cut the crap. You could have gone into a ladies' room. You didn't want me to know what you were doing. You were nothing more than a loose cannon."

"But an effective one." Sloane swallowed her pride and stated the truth. "Look, I'm not going to deny your accusations. I did break the chain of command. You have every right to toss me out on my ass. But before you do, consider one thing—other than the fact that I struck a nerve with Xiao Long, maybe enough to get him to screw up."

"What is it you want me to consider?"

"You began your diatribe with the word 'professionally.' Now let's talk personally. Would you have refused any other member of your team if he or she came up with the idea I did? Remember, I had no idea my actions would result in a physical assault. My only goal was to knock Xiao off balance, get him to worry about me and our investigation rather than focusing on my parents, and at the same time, to maybe learn a thing or two about the victims of his other eight break-ins. Which, by the way, I did. But we'll discuss that later. The relevant issue here is that I've been both a special agent and a crisis negotiator. I'm a team player. My blowing off my team leader is way out of character. And, yes, I did it because I knew you'd turn me down. But I think the reasons you would have done so would have been personal, not professional. Am I wrong?"

A long pause as Derek contemplated her question and mentally ran down the list of her actions. "No. You're not wrong," he grudgingly acknowledged. "Your goal today was to question potential accomplices to your parents' break-in—which you did. Assuming a false identity is fair game for an informant. Ditto for calling on your law enforcement contacts, since the Nineteenth is the precinct of record in all Xiao's break-ins. But not coming to me first, *before* you took every single one of those steps, is a flat-out violation—one I won't tolerate."

Pausing again, Derek cleared his throat, obviously about to say something he really didn't want to. "On the other hand, your point is valid. You knew I'd say no, and that the reasons for my doing so would have been personal."

"I appreciate your honesty." Actually, Sloane was stunned. She hadn't expected Derek to make that admission, at least not until they'd had an enormous fight and she'd dragged it out of him. Reluctant or not, his acknowledgment that he was subjective, and, yes, vulnerable, when it came to her and this investigation, was a huge deal. She wasn't sure she could have done it so readily.

Sloane knew her Bureau assignment was on the line. Derek could very well fire her on the spot. Still, she felt a huge wave of love and respect for him. He really was one hell of a guy.

"Gloating?" he asked drily.

"Quite the opposite. Admiring." She left it at that. "At this point, the call is yours. You can have me removed from the case, or you can keep me on, setting new ground rules we can both live with."

"Sounds about right."

"Before you decide, I have to be as frank with you as you were with me. Other than reporting to you first, I wouldn't change any part of my actions. I'd do it all again—even if I knew about the knife skirmish."

"Of course you would." Derek shot her a dark look.

"Think of it this way. As you pointed out, I haven't rejoined the Bureau yet. The downside of that is that I have limited power. But the upside is I can bend the rules a bit. I can be creative. So give me some wiggle room. I'll be a much greater asset to you if you do."

"While putting yourself into how many lines of fire?"

It was time for *her* to make a concession. "Only those we agree upon—beforehand."

Derek blew out his breath. "Damn, you're a pain in the ass." A brief silence, during which his jaw began working. "Do you have any idea how terrified I was when I saw you bent over that trash can, vomiting, with blood dripping down your arm?"

Sloane managed a wan smile. "Not as terrified as I was. When that little weasel came at me, I snapped right into Krav mode. Focused. No time to think. No room for fear. But when I realized he was going after my injured hand, I felt a surge of panic. The good news is that that stark jolt of panic made me twice as lethal. I think I crippled the guy, or at the very least ended his sex life, broke his nose, and shattered a few ribs. He hobbled off into the woods like a quivering bowl of Jell-O."

Derek's lips twitched ever so slightly. "Now *that* I would have paid to see." Abruptly, all humor vanished. "Don't scare me like that again."

"I'll do my best." Sloane was beginning to feel the woozy effects of the Percocet. "Dammit, I'm fading. And I have more to tell you."

"It'll wait." Derek glanced over at her, saw her glazed eyes and drawn expression. "You can tell me after you get some sleep."

"Okay." Sloane blinked, trying to clear her head and failing. "Derek?"

"Hmmm?"

"About the elephant in the room . . . I know you're digging around, trying to find proof that either Leo, Wallace, Ben, or Phil were accomplices in the break-in." Her voice was starting to slur. "And you know I'm trying to prove otherwise." Slowly, her eyelids began to droop. "I don't want to . . . but I need to . . . be sure. Will you tell me . . . what you find?"

If Sloane had been alert, she would have instantly picked up on how long Derek hesitated, and she would have pressured him about it.

But she wasn't. She was halfway toward a drug-induced sleep.

Derek was relieved. She'd been through enough for one day. And given what his street contacts had started reporting late today, he had a bad feeling about the supposedly squeaky-clean members of this art partnership. If he was right, Sloane would take it hard. And it would put her in a lousy position with her father. She didn't need this dumped on her, not now, and certainly not until all the facts were in and verified, including whatever Rich found out.

When he finally did answer, Derek's reply was quiet, and, as he suspected, unheard. "When I have to, I'll tell you."

CHAPTER
TWENTY-ONE

It was midmorning when Rich strode down one of C-6's few uncluttered aisles and poked his head into Derek's cubicle. "Good, you're in. Do you have a few minutes?"

Derek swiveled his chair around and waved his friend in. "Funny you should ask. I was about to drop by your neck of the woods. I have some interesting info to pass along."

"Same here. And a favor to ask."

"Okay, you first." Derek gestured for him to pull up a chair. "What do you need?"

Rich sat down, his brow furrowed in concentration. "I've run through every detail of the Armonk burglary and homicide, and the Hampton's art gallery heist. I've interviewed all the witnesses of both crimes. It was a no-brainer that the two crimes were committed by the same team. What I needed to be sure of was that that team was the Black Eagle gang. They're the Albanian organized-crime group who hit those European museums."

"And?"

"And I'm sure. In both cases, the witnesses said the accents they heard sounded Slavic. Richtner, the owner of the art gallery, was born in Germany.

There's a large Albanian population there. He confirmed that at least two of the gunmen were conversing in Albanian."

"Then why rule out Albanian-American organized-crime groups? Why assume it's the Black Eagles?"

"Because the Albanian-American gangs make most of their money off drug trafficking. They also deal in counterfeiting and gunrunning. The crimes we're talking about here are very specific and very high profile. They also require a level of sophistication that's not everyday. The technique, the weaponry, the precision—in my opinion, that all adds up to the Black Eagles. That doesn't mean they haven't linked up to Albanian organized crime here in the U.S. The Eagles are probably hiding out, if not working, with them."

Rich paused, then gave a firm nod, as if by speaking his theory aloud, he'd intensified his conviction. "The way the crimes were carried out—the patterns are identical to the European museum heists. In all cases, there were four gunmen, all masked, all armed with subguns. They gained entry, took control, and immobilized the victims with Flex-Cufs. They opened fire and killed almost everyone who saw them, or anyone who got in their way, without the slightest hesitation. And they knew ahead of time exactly which paintings they were going after. Most of those were masterpieces worth a fortune. A few were less well known, probably the ones they could sell on the streets. The well-known masterpieces they probably shipped off to whoever hired them."

Derek had listened to every word, processing all of it. "It all fits," he replied. "Do you think it's the same 'whoever' who hired them to do the European heists?"

"My gut reaction? Yes. But I plan to find out."

"What about the weapons? They wouldn't take the risk of transporting their own. So they obviously bought them on the streets in the U.S."

"Right. That's the clincher." Rich leaned forward. "I showed a series of pictures of different types of subguns to the Campbells and their staff, and to Richtner and his assistant. At least five of them had gotten a good look at the weapons used. And they all identified them as MP5Ks—the same guns that were used in the European museum heists."

Derek whistled. "That screams paramilitary training. Also, an enterprising source to obtain the guns, and big money to pay for them, since MP5Ks are off-limits to everyone but law enforcement. These are definitely not run-of-the-mill thugs, and what you've got here is no coincidence. You've got yourself a match."

"Not just a match, but a dangerous, escalating situation. These pros didn't fly over here to just hit private collections and suburban art galleries. They're warming up. I don't know how many more practice hits they have in mind. But after that? They're going for the big-time."

"Museums."

"You bet. And between their trial runs and their grand finale, who knows how many more homicides they'd commit, and how many more multimillion-dollar masterpieces they'd make off with."

"How can I help?" Derek asked.

"I've met with C-7," Rich replied, referring to the Balkan Criminal Enterprise Squad. "And they're on board. But I'd like C-6, and you in particular, to work with them. You've got great informants for what I need. I just learned that four MP5Ks were stolen from a small-town police department in upstate New York. One of the cops caught a glimpse of the thieves as they took off. They were Asian. Their car had stolen plates, and it was dumped in a junk-yard in Queens."

"Which means the subguns were probably sold here in the Big Apple," Derek deduced. "It makes sense. Like I said, whoever bought these paid major bucks for them. We're talking twenty-five hundred apiece, which is five times the cost of most guns sold on the street. You want me to put out feelers and find out who brokered them?"

A taut nod. "And whoever's hands the subguns passed through to find their way to the Albanians. I've already spoken to Tony. He's fine with your working this part of the case. He said to come by his office and go over the details."

"Consider it done." Mentally, Derek was already running through the best scenario to get Rich what he needed ASAP. "As soon as I have something, I'll let you know."

"Thanks." Rich was clearly relieved that Derek understood they were racing the clock. "And if the Black Eagles get word they're on our radar, all the
better. It might make them nervous enough to reconsider whatever they've
planned next, giving us more time to find them."

"I hear you." Derek cleared his throat. "You mentioned having information for me?"

"Yeah, sorry." Abruptly, Rich changed focus. "With regard to the Rothberg, some additional facts have surfaced on the Dutch collector whose family consigned it to Sotheby's. Evidently, he wasn't as squeaky clean as we
thought. Seems he did business with some shady art dealers and collectors. I
should have specific details after the weekend."

"That's good news," Derek replied. "Every step we take in retracing the
sale of *Dead or Alive* is a step closer to filling in the blanks on Burbank's art
investment group. I have a bad taste in my mouth about these guys."

"You got more background info?"

"Yeah. And none of it's good." Derek shuffled a bunch of papers around on
his desk. "Ben Martino's an alcoholic whose business is in the toilet. Phil
Leary is a compulsive gambler who owes his bookie a mint. Wallace Johnson
invested most of his money in his art galleries and, before that, in high-priced
PIs, trying to find out who the hit-and-run driver was who killed his daughter.
The rest of his hefty bank account went to his ex-wife in their divorce. So he's
in rocky financial shape, too. Leo Fox is a different story. He had a fiancée
who dumped him at the altar. Now, he's all business—and, boy, is it booming.
He has dozens of rich clients, and puts in twelve-hour days to meet their
needs. Interesting how he had the time to drop everything on a dime and
rush over to Sloane's cottage to get started on our redecoration project."

"He was itching to dig around and see what you knew."

"Oh, yeah. He couldn't wait to start asking questions as we toured the cottage for its makeover. He was chomping at the bit to continue the minute
Sloane left. He was probably thrilled that she got called away. Then, she blew
a hole in his plan, since she figured out that you and I had set her up so you
could talk to her father without her being there. She assumed part of our
setup included leaving me alone with Fox so *I* could pump *him* after she took

off. So she warned me not to—in earshot of Fox. After that, he didn't dare arouse my suspicions by pushing his agenda."

"Sorry about that." Rich grimaced. "Not only did I screw up any chance you had of getting something out of Fox, I pushed Sloane's buttons. She must have ripped your head off."

"That's par for the course." Derek gave a faint smile. "Love hard, fight hard—that's Sloane's and my motto. As for Leo Fox, you'll get more out of him than I would have. Especially now."

"You mean because of what happened to Rosalyn Burbank?"

"I'm sure that scared the hell out of him and the rest of his partners, making them a lot more vulnerable to your interviewing techniques. But that's not what I was referring to. Get this. You know that hefty income Fox is making? You'll never guess where some of it's going."

"I give up."

"To his buddies. He paid off a bunch of Phil Leary's gambling debts, including a big one just yesterday. He's also helped out Wallace Johnson with financial backing for his galleries. Oh, and he went with Martino to most of his AA meetings, during the years Martino was off the booze."

"What a philanthropic guy," Rich commented drily. "And what a walking encyclopedia of dirty laundry. Seems he has the inside scoop on all his friends."

"Uh-huh. Which means he's either an extraordinary friend, or a shrewd SOB who collects smut on his buddies to store away for future use."

"Or maybe present use."

"Exactly. So, as you can see, you've got lots of juicy stuff to probe when you call each of these guys in."

"That's an understatement." Rich's lips curved in mock amusement. "It's beginning to sound like Burbank's the cleanest of the bunch."

"Ironically, yeah." Derek put aside the papers and folded his hands in front of him. "There's something else." Briefly, he filled Rich in on what had happened to Sloane last night.

"You've got to be kidding." Rich reacted with startled concern. "Is she all right?"

"Thankfully, yes. The slash on her forearm was bad. It took me forever to stop the bleeding. And when she kept passing out, I started to panic. But the ER doctor stitched her up, put her on antibiotics and heavy-duty painkillers, and assured her there was no major damage. That calmed her down. She was pretty shaken up, considering the Red Dragon kid was going for her bad hand. So, all things considered, she's doing okay. I can't say the same for her attacker. She kicked the crap out of him. I doubt he'll be getting out of bed— or off the floor—any time soon."

"Remind me never to piss off your girlfriend."

"That's a tall order," Derek returned drily. "Considering I piss her off every day."

"So now Xiao's decided to get at Burbank by going after Sloane."

"Before yesterday? Maybe. But at this point? Without a doubt. Sloane made sure to give him a compelling incentive." Derek told Rich how Sloane had baited her attacker.

Rich whistled. "You've got to admit, the woman has balls."

"Yeah, and brains, too." Derek went on to tell Rich what Sloane had alluded to last night and then relayed to him this morning—the details of her conversations with the other victims who'd been burglarized by the Red Dragons. "It seems that all of them had at least one high-profile painting stolen. Some of them had two. And they all had a couple of commonplace paintings taken as well. It's as if Xiao's guys were trying to hide the fact that the valuable paintings were what they were after. That theory holds even more water when you read over the lists of stolen items on the police reports, do the math, and figure out that the paintings were worth more than the jewelry and electronics combined."

"Which the police would have no reason to do, since they're concentrating on the burglaries as a whole."

"Exactly. But Sloane's an art dealer's daughter. She knows prices. So she zeroed in on it right away."

"Intriguing twist." Rich's interest was definitely piqued. "They camouflaged their real targets by ripping off a bunch of high-priced stuff they could fence on the streets. Between the two, they made a mint." He glanced at

Derek's desk. "Do you have those police reports? I never did see the full list of stolen paintings. You just ran a few of them by me."

"Yup." Derek passed them across to Rich. "Take a look."

Rich scanned the sheets one at a time. "Sloane's right," he concluded. "There's a definite pattern here. A few valuable paintings, a few average-priced ones. The odd part is that not all the valuable paintings are well known. Some are pieces whose value only an art connoisseur would recognize."

"Sloane said the same thing. Which, to me, says that Xiao Long is working for someone. He's a power-hungry street thug. His cold-blooded aggression and inborn street smarts are what made him a Dai Lo. The Red Dragons are a hundred percent loyal to him—and a thousand percent terrified. I've seen what he does to gang members who screw him over. It isn't pretty. But refinement? A knowledge of fine art? Xiao wouldn't know a Renoir from a finger-painting."

"But whoever's paying him does." Rich lowered the reports to Derek's desk. "I agree. Your Xiao Long case is looking more interesting by the minute. First the tie to the Rothberg, and now a string of robberies that scream art theft."

Derek nodded. "I wonder if whoever's paying Xiao to steal these paintings is the same person who hired him to kill Cai Wen and steal the Rothberg."

"Funny, I was wondering the same thing."

"It would make sense. He can't fence well-known paintings on the street. He's sending them somewhere, and to someone. I'd be willing to bet that someone is in China. Further, I'd be willing to bet he's a triad leader. It would explain a hell of a lot about how Xiao got his start, and where he's getting his financing to move up to the big-time."

"All our leads point back to the Rothberg."

Derek nodded. "Let me know as soon as you hear who that Dutch collectors' dirty dealings were with. *And* if any of them were Chinese." A pause. "In the meantime, I don't trust Burbank's partners. And that doesn't just apply to the possibility that one of them aided in the break-in at his apartment. Even if it turns out that none of his pals helped the Red Dragons get inside and grab the Rothberg file, my gut tells me that one or more of them is involved in something shady. Whatever that is, I need to know. Sloane's in enough danger from Xiao Long—and she knows he's the enemy. The last thing she needs is to be victimized by someone she considers a friend."

"I understand. And I'll get you what you need." Rich got to his feet. "Just find me my gun dealer. Then, give me a couple days to verify names of our Dutch collector's dirty contacts. After that, I'll call Fox, Johnson, Martino, and Leary. We'll have plenty to talk about. I'll ask each of them to come in—separately—for a follow-up interview."

"That'll throw them for a loop."

"Which is precisely what I want."

———

Lee Wong Kee, the skinny Red Dragon kid who'd attacked Sloane, awaited his fate.

For what seemed like forever, he'd hung in complete darkness, the back of his jacket impaled on a meat hook inside a walk-in refrigerator in Wah Chang's butcher shop. He was paralyzed with fear.

At the outside wall of the refrigerator, Jin Huang reached up, flipped on the light, and opened the heavy door for his boss.

When Lee saw Xiao enter, his insides clenched. He stammered yet another apology, and begged forgiveness from his Dai Lo for his failed mission. Xiao didn't reply. He just donned a pair of gloves, then reached into his coat pocket and extracted a piano wire with a bamboo block attached to each end.

He nodded to Jin. In response, Jin grabbed Lee's head, gripping it tightly in his big hands. Lee cried out in pain, then screamed for mercy. Xiao ignored his pleas. Silently, he wrapped the piano wire around a side of beef that was hanging inches from Lee's face, and pulled.

The powerful motion severed the carcass in two. A huge slab of meat thudded to the floor.

Xiao turned to Lee, reaching out to pat his Adam's apple. "Next time you fail, I use your neck instead." He grasped Lee's collar, and pulled the wire through a fold in the fabric to wipe off the bloody residue.

Pocketing the thin but lethal weapon, the Dai Lo nodded to Jin, turned away, and walked out. Without a word, Jin lifted the kid off the meat hook, took out a switchblade, and cut the ropes binding his hands.

Lee dropped to his knees. Jin stepped over him. As he left, he could hear the sound of the Red Dragon kid retching uncontrollably.

Cindy was in an excellent mood as she headed off to her next appointment. She'd just secured her first six-figure town-house renovation project, thanks to the debut party at Wallace's. She'd e-mailed him right away, brimming with enthusiasm over the news. He'd responded in kind. Everything was on track.

She would call her A *Sook* about this new development right away. He'd be so pleased by her escalating accomplishments—all of them.

The package he'd sent had already arrived. Now there was twice as much reason to gift it to Wallace.

Tuesday night's date promised to be an evening to remember.

CHAPTER
TWENTY-TWO

ARTHUR AVENUE
BRONX, NEW YORK

The brown sedan cruised slowly down the street. It was barely dawn, and the flow of traffic was light. The local shops were still closed. The markets were putting out their first produce. Only the bakery had a fine stream of patrons who'd come out to buy their fresh breads and rolls.

To be on the safe side, the driver of the sedan circled around the block and cruised back down the street. Satisfied by what he saw, he pulled over to the curb and parked beside a small brick residential building. Two stories high, it was old and worn, like the rest of the neighborhood, with a short flight of stairs leading to the front door. A green canopy shadowed the doorway, and the front of the building was partially blocked from view by a broad oak tree and an unusual amount of shrubbery. The house across the street, visibly unlived in, was undergoing major construction, and there were piles of two-by-fours, cardboard boxes, and plastic garbage bags strewn all over the sidewalk, half covering the house.

The area was shabby. But more important, it was deserted.

The two Red Dragons jumped out of the car, pausing only to grab their duffel bags. Then they made their way around to the back of the brick building.

One of the Black Eagles opened the downstairs door for them instantly. No words were exchanged. And none were necessary. Language barrier or not, all the parties involved knew why they were here.

The six of them gathered in the basement.

Xiao's men unzipped their duffel bags and took out the contents. Maps. A series of diagrams. Intricate floor plans. And a staggering amount of cash, neatly packaged in rubber-banded stacks of ten thousand dollars.

They handed everything over to the Albanians and waited while the cash was counted and the other contents were reviewed.

The four recipients wasted no time. Two of them counted the money. The other two, including the team leader, spread out the maps and diagrams and unfurled the floor plans, studying them intently. They muttered a few things to each other, pointing to certain spots on the designs. With a nod of comprehension, they rolled the plans back up and put the maps and diagrams aside. The leader raised his head, gazing at his other two men and waiting for a signal.

He got it.

Speaking to one another in rapid Albanian, they compared totals. Then, one of them looked up and gave the okay. The payment due them was correct. The final installment would come afterward. Everything was in order.

The team leader turned to Xiao's men and gave them a hard nod, accepting what they'd delivered and dismissing them all at once. He gestured for one of his men to show the Red Dragons out.

The entire transaction took less than half an hour.

Xiao's men exited quickly and quietly, scanning the street as they headed toward their car.

No one was around except an old man walking an equally old dog, who was currently peeing on one of the cardboard boxes across the street.

No threat there.

They tossed their empty duffel bags into the backseat of the sedan, hopped into the front seats, and drove off.

The old man glanced up, scowling as he watched the brown car disappear around the corner. "This neighborhood is going to hell, Allegro," he informed his dog in a thick Italian accent. "It's enough that the Chinese took over Little Italy. But now they're invading Arthur Avenue. Say good-bye to the good old days when it was just us. Good neighbors. Decent. Honest. Now, the whole street will be corrupt, no better than the garbage you're peeing on."

He shook his head, tightening his grip on Allegro's leash. "Like I said, this neighborhood is going to hell."

———

Sloane jerked awake and sat up as Derek sank down beside her on the sofa.

"How're you doing?" His knuckles caressed her cheek.

She blinked and looked around, realizing that, once again, she'd fallen asleep.

"You're home," she noted groggily. "What time is it?"

"Seven-fifteen."

"Dammit." Sloane tried to clear the cobwebs from her head as she struggled to sit up. "The poor hounds. They must be starved. And their evening run . . ."

"Relax." Derek gripped her shoulders and eased her back onto the cushions. "The hounds are fed, wiped out from a two-mile run, and snoozing by the fire. The only reason I woke you is because I think you should eat something before you take your meds."

"I'll take the antibiotic, but I'm not taking that damned Percocet," Sloane muttered. "I've been like a zombie all day."

" 'That damned Percocet,' huh?" Derek repeated in a teasing voice. "Would that be the same damned Percocet you were demanding at the hospital?"

"That was then. This is now. The pain's a lot better. And I don't have the time to lie around like a disoriented druggie. I have work to do." Gingerly, she moved her arm, first up and down, then from side to side. "It feels fine. And I'm not losing any more time because of a stupid scratch."

Derek didn't bother contradicting Sloane's absurdly downplayed description of her wound's severity. "Then don't take the Percocet. But you have to eat a decent meal. When I called earlier, Jerry said that all you'd eaten was tea and toast."

"Speaking of Jerry, where is he? He's supposed to provide security, not home health care. Besides, I'm not hungry. I'm nauseous."

"That's the meds." Ignoring her protest, Derek rose and walked over to the kitchen counter. "I sent Jerry home. I'm now security and nurse's aide rolled into one. So, back to food. I figure you should start with something light. I picked up chicken soup and a turkey sandwich. If you eat every bite and take your antibiotics like a good girl, then we can talk investigation—which I know you're dying to do."

Sloane shot him a disgruntled look. "Are you blackmailing me?"

"I prefer to think of it as an incentive." Derek carried over the brown bag. "There's a plastic spoon and napkins inside. Knock yourself out."

"What about you?"

"I grabbed something at work."

"Really?"

"I promise. Jeff got takeout for the squad. I ate a pint of lo mein and a ton of ribs. So I'm set."

"Okay." Sloane started with the soup, then began nibbling on the sandwich. She had to admit Derek was right. The food was not only easing her nausea but also clearing her mind and fueling her strength.

She began to eat with more enthusiasm. "Thank you," she said between bites. "This was really sweet of you. Especially considering how bitchy I'm being."

"You're entitled. You went through a harrowing experience. But I see signs of the nonbitchy-but-type-A Sloane shining through. You're on the mend." A corner of Derek's mouth lifted. "As for my being sweet, what can I say? I'm just an amazing guy."

This time Sloane didn't banter back. She simply leaned forward and softly kissed him. "Actually, you are."

He deepened the kiss for a few seconds, then reluctantly broke it off. "Get better fast. I miss you."

"Me, too. And there's no need to wait." Her eyes twinkled. "Injury or not, I'm very creative."

"Don't remind me of your creativity. I need a cold shower as it is."

"Why? I just told you—"

"Forget it," Derek interrupted. "I'm greedy. I want all your stamina back, and full use of both your hands."

She gave an impatient sigh. "That's the disciplined Army Ranger talking. Fine, we'll wait—one night. I'm a quick healer. By tomorrow, I'll be better than new."

"In that case, we can spend the whole weekend in bed."

Sloane's brows rose. "That's right. It's Friday. Are you working tomorrow?"

"Nope. I've set everything I need to in motion, and I'll keep my cell phone on. So I'm all yours."

"I like that," she admitted. "I feel as if we've been operating at warp speed, but at cross-purposes, since you moved in. We've barely had a private minute to talk, except about Bureau business. We haven't had a quiet dinner alone, or even just hung out and listened to music. I was worried that living together would hurt our relationship by cramping our independence, but instead we never see each other."

"It's time we changed that." Gently, Derek lifted Sloane's right hand and kissed her palm. "We deserve a weekend to ourselves. How about a DVD and popcorn tonight, and the next two days in bed—or wherever we happen to be when the mood strikes?" He gave her that sexy grin that made her insides melt.

"Sounds like heaven." And it did. Nonetheless, she knew Derek, knew the way his mind worked.

She gave him a you're-not-fooling-me look. "Of course, besides sharing alone time, intimate conversation, and hot sex, this is also about your acting as my weekend sentry." She reached over and popped one of her antibiotic capsules out of the foil packet, swallowing it with the water she'd kept on the coffee table. "And I don't mean a caretaker to change the bandage on my arm."

"You're right." Derek didn't bother denying it. "After the chain of events you set in motion yesterday, and what happened last night, your parents aren't the only ones who need bodyguards. In Xiao Long's eyes, you're no longer just an extension of your father—someone he needs to keep an eye on. You're a major threat yourself."

Sloane considered Derek's assessment, and nodded straight-faced. "No argument. I definitely need weekend security. Which works out fine. Because I'm dying to hook up with my bodyguard. So you're welcome to stay as close as you want."

"What an invitation." Derek leaned forward to kiss her again.

"But not quite yet." Sloane put a restraining hand on the front of his shirt.

"Let me guess. Before we start our private weekend, you want to hear all about what Rich said."

"You got it. So tell me."

Derek filled her in on everything except the discussion of her father's friends.

"Wow. So Xiao Long is dealing in valuable paintings now," Sloane murmured. "And getting paid by a triad bigwig who has both knowledge and appreciation of fine art. That would explain a lot. It might even tie back to the Rothberg and Cai Wen's murder, depending on how long Xiao's been in the art-theft business."

"Exactly. So I'm waiting for answers. We should have them soon. Rich expects to hear back from his contacts in a matter of days. Hopefully, they'll have a lot to tell us."

Sloane fell silent for a moment, her lashes lowering as she wrestled with a question she needed to ask but didn't want the answer to. Finally, she looked up and went for it. "Did you find any leads on who helped the Red Dragons break into my parents' apartment?"

"Not yet." Clearly, Derek had been expecting her question.

"Meaning you're still investigating my father's partners."

"Meaning I'm still open to any and all leads that could tell me the identity of the accomplice who got those punks through the front door of your parents' place, and straight to the Rothberg file."

"And in searching for those leads, everyone's fair game."

"Yes." Derek met her gaze directly. "Sloane, there are some avenues you're going to have to let me explore alone, at least for now. You've made it clear you're not ready to go there yet, and I respect that. If there's anything I dig up that you should know, I'll tell you right away. And if it comes down to my having to involve you or even ask you questions that are painful, I'll do that, too. But right now, I have nothing. So it's premature to jump to conclusions. Okay?"

Sloane understood exactly what Derek was saying, *and* what he wasn't. "This sucks."

"I know." He cupped the nape of her neck, stroking her skin with his thumb. "Trust me," he urged quietly. "I won't go after anyone you care about—not unless they've done something that deserves going after. Fair enough?"

She couldn't argue with that.

Reluctantly, she nodded. "I'm not happy. I realize you're more than a little suspicious of Leo, Phil, Wallace, and Ben, and that you're investigating the hell out of them. On the other hand, I know it has to be done. But not by me. I know I'm way too close to be objective. And I do trust you. So I'll let you take the lead on this one—as long as you keep me in the loop." A wry smile. "After all, you are the lead case agent. And I'm a good team player."

Derek framed her face between his palms. "I love you."

"I know," Sloane murmured, understanding the depth of what he was saying. No matter what happened or who was guilty of what, the two of them couldn't let it affect what they had. Not this time.

She wrapped her fingers around his. "I love you, too."

It was late Sunday night, and Sloane was draped across Derek, sound asleep, when Derek's cell phone vibrated on the nightstand.

He reached over with his free arm, moving gingerly so as not to disturb Sloane, and flipped open the phone. "You have something for me?" A pause. "No surprise. He's definitely got that kind of cash. Now find out who he sold them to. I want the answer tomorrow."

CHAPTER
TWENTY-THREE

Derek arrived at his desk at seven A.M. As a rule, he took Monday mornings in stride, but on this particular Monday, he did *not* want to be there—not after the weekend he'd just spent with Sloane. But life and reality had a way of intruding.

Five minutes later, his phone rang. "Parker," he answered.

"Good. You're in." Rich knew that most of C-6 started later, since their surveillance took place during the wee hours of the morning, when the drug dealing, gambling houses, and brothels were in full swing. But Derek's days as an Army Ranger still woke him up at five-thirty A.M., like clockwork. As a former marine, Rich knew the drill. "I thought I saw you pass by."

"It's just me and my coffee. What's up?"

"I just hung up with the Hong Kong police. I've got some interesting info to discuss with you on the Rothberg provenance."

"And I've got part of what you need. I'm on my way."

Derek grabbed his cup and headed down to the other end of the floor, striding into Rich's cubicle. "You work fast."

"Hey, it's dinnertime in Hong Kong. I've been on the phone since midnight."

Derek whistled. "Compared to you, I'm a slacker."

"Hardly. I slept all day yesterday. I knew what kind of night it would be." Rich glanced up, gestured for Derek to have a seat. "How's Sloane?"

"Better. I finally got her to relax this weekend. But she'll go stir-crazy if she's stuck in today. So my guess is she's back out there, chasing down leads— by herself, since she refuses to have full-time security on her."

"I get the feeling she's pretty good at taking care of herself," Rich noted drily.

"Most of the time. But if any more of her leads put her in Xiao Long's line of fire, I'm assigning her full-time security whether she likes it or not." Derek's tone was as unyielding as his words. "Anyway, speaking of leads, I've got a major one for you. The street gun dealer who's the middleman for your subgun sale is Tommy Nguyen. He's American-born Vietnamese, known for brokering risky, high-priced deals. He does a lot of business with Chinese gangs. Apparently, it was his guys who stole those four MP5Ks from an upstate New York police department. They delivered the subguns straight to Nguyen, who moved them fast to a Chinese gang. They paid top dollar for them. My informant will be calling me this morning to let me know which gang it is. That'll tell us who's working with your Albanian art thieves."

"Thanks for jumping on this so quickly." Rich was clearly relieved. "Let me know the minute you hear anything."

"I'll track you down wherever you are."

"Probably right here at my desk, on the phone." Rich pulled out his legal-size pad of paper, on which he'd scribbled tons of information. "Now for you. As I said, I just hung up with the Hong Kong police. They confirmed that the shady art dealers our Dutch collector did business with were Chinese. More specifically, they were linked to the Fong Triad."

"Interesting." Derek's forehead creased in thought. "That triad was thriving in the nineties. It's lower profile now. But it's still alive and kicking. Any proof they were in possession of the Rothberg?"

"Yup. That's one of the questions I was waiting for an answer on. Thanks to defecting triad members who are now confidential informants for the police department, we have positive evidence that *Dead or Alive* was in the hands of the Fong Triad before it was sold to the Dutch collector. And it gets better. I was hoping for a name, any name, the police could give us. That would be the starting point we needed to fill in the holes in the provenance."

"If they gave you a name, I'll fly out to Hong Kong tonight." Derek was perched at the edge of his chair.

"I was ready to do the same thing. But there's no need. Seems we caught a lucky break. The name they had was Zhang Ming, now Daniel Zhang. He's a former member of the Fong Triad, who was personally involved in the purchase of *Dead or Alive*. Evidently, he immigrated to the U.S. and turned his life around."

"Where in the U.S.?" Derek demanded.

"Right here in Queens," Rich supplied. "He's working as a youth counselor in the Chinese-American community in Flushing. And before you ask, yes, he'll talk to us. We can go over there and meet with him this afternoon."

"Yes." Derek curled his fingers into a triumphant fist and punched the air. "That's the most promising lead we've gotten since the Burbanks' break-in."

"I thought you'd react that way. So, how does two o'clock work for you?"

"I'll make it work." Derek was about to thank Rich, when his own cell phone rang. He glanced down at it and saw the familiar number of his informant's throwaway phone. "With any luck, this is the answer you're waiting for." He flipped open the phone. "What have you got?" A long, stunned silence. "You're sure?" Another silence. "Okay. Keep your ears open."

He snapped his cell phone shut, shaking his head in disbelief. "It's a smaller world than we thought," he told Rich drily. "The guy who bought the subguns from Nguyen was Jin Huang."

Rich gave him a quizzical look. "Who's Jin Huang?"

"Xiao Long's enforcer."

"You're kidding."

"Nope. My informant's description matches Jin to a tee. And the timing's right, too. Xiao had Jin buy the subguns a few days before the Campbells' house was hit. Seems our Dai Lo has bigger fish to fry than even I imagined." Derek's mind was racing. "This whole operation is out of Xiao's league.

Someone's definitely backing him. My guess is that the backer is a wealthy, prominent triad leader, and Xiao is shipping the stolen paintings to him in China."

"So it's likely that the same triad leader is behind the European museum heists. He hired the Black Eagles, and has now decided to take his operation to the U.S., with Xiao Long facilitating things."

Derek nodded. "Xiao's got a full-blown New York art-crime scheme going, stealing paintings from wealthy Manhattan residents. So why not expand it to the big time? With the backing of his Dragon Head back in China, they can score big by setting up targets for the Albanians. Come to think of it, Matthew Burbank described two Mediterranean thugs in Xiao's entourage the night of their 'chance' encounter in Chinatown. That's strong confirmation that Xiao is working with the Albanians."

"Suddenly it appears we've got one complex case here—not two separate, overlapping ones." Rich's tone and demeanor was as intense as Derek's. "Talking to Daniel Zhang just became our top priority. Our answers could all be linked to the Fong Triad."

Sloane was already halfway to Manhattan when her cell phone rang.

It was her mother.

"Where are you?" Rosalyn asked. She sounded even more forceful than usual.

"In the car, en route to the city. I've got the rest of your list to check out."

"Don't bother. Come straight here."

Sloane stiffened. "Are you okay? Is Dad?"

"We're both fine. This is about the break-in."

"Did you find out something new?"

"I'll tell you everything when you get here." A pause, as Rosalyn's maternal instinct kicked in. "Should you be driving?"

"Yes," Sloane replied firmly. "I'm off the Percocet, and my arm is more than capable of joining the other on the steering wheel. If you want to worry about an arm, worry about yours. You take lousy care of yourself."

"I'm *your* mother. Not the other way around. No lectures. Just drive to our place."

———

Sloane was both puzzled and uneasy as she stepped out of the elevator and headed down to her parents' apartment. Her mother was in full powerhouse mode. And whatever new information was causing her energy surge was critical, or she wouldn't have practically ordered Sloane to drop her investigation and come over ASAP.

"Good. You're here," she greeted her daughter, having whipped open the door when she heard the approaching footsteps.

"As summoned." Sloane slipped off her coat and walked into the foyer. She called out a quick hello to Special Agent Carter, who was having a cup of coffee in the breakfast nook. She was about to ask her mother if her father was home when the vroom of a vacuum cleaner interrupted her.

Turning, she spotted Anna, her parents' cleaning woman, manipulating the upright around the living room.

Anna had been in the Burbanks' employ for as long as Sloane could remember, coming every Monday morning since she'd immigrated to the U.S. from Poland, until the Burbanks moved to Florida. She was very good at her job and was treated with the utmost respect by the Burbanks. As a result, she'd been happy to come back when they'd returned to New York.

"Did you want to talk privately?" Sloane murmured to her mother.

"Definitely not." Rosalyn was already steering Sloane toward the living room. "In fact, I'm not going to be talking at all. Anna," she called over the noise of the vacuum. "Sloane's here."

Anna looked up, and turned off the vacuum immediately. She gave Sloane a warm, if nervous, smile of greeting.

"Hi, Anna. How are you?" At this point, Sloane was so baffled, she hardly knew what to say.

"Fine, thank you," Anna replied, her Polish accent still prominent, but her English drastically improved from years ago. "How are you?" She frowned, spotting Sloane's injury. "You got hurt, too?"

"Yes, but I'm fine now."

"Let's sit down," Rosalyn instructed. She turned to Sloane as they did. "Anna's been on vacation for the past two weeks. She went home to Poland to visit her family. Today is her first day back."

"That must have been a wonderful trip," Sloane responded.

Anna nodded. "It was. But now I find out about your parents being robbed, and your mother being hurt. I feel terrible." A nervous pause. "And responsible."

"Responsible?" Sloane's antenna shot up. "Why?"

The poor cleaning woman looked positively green. "The week before I left for Poland, I was at McDonald's. I went to the ladies' room. Two men came in, locked the door, and grabbed me. One of them held me. The other took my purse. He emptied it out on the countertop. I saw him take the money out of my wallet. Then he turned his back on me. I couldn't see what he was doing anymore. I thought maybe he was taking my credit cards. But he had something with him he was using. All I saw was that it was little"—Anna made a rectangular shape with her fingers—"and silver—like foil you cover food with."

"Aluminum," Sloane supplied.

"Yes." Anna nodded adamantly. "I don't understand what it was or what he did. They told me to shut up. I was so scared. Then they let me go, unlocked the door, and went away."

"Did you report this to the police?" Sloane asked.

Anna shook her head. "I didn't know what to say. I don't know the men. They took nothing but forty dollars. No credit cards. No checkbook. I could give police no information to catch them. I was so happy they didn't hurt me. So I told no one but my husband."

She swallowed. "Then today I come back to work. Your mother and father were out. I let myself in. I use the key your mother gave me. I see little pieces on it. Like . . ." She waved her arm in frustration. "Like bread dough, only not white. My children play with it when they make things."

"Clay," Sloane filled in. She turned to her mother. "They used a key-impression kit. They made a copy of your key. That's how they broke in here."

"That's why I called you."

"Anna," Sloane pressed. "Can you tell me what these men looked like? Did you see their faces?"

"For a few minutes, yes. Both of them from an Asian country. The one who held me was very big and strong. He was wearing a jacket. The other not. He was younger and skinny, with a cap on his head. He had a picture of a dragon on his arm. Red. But not paint."

"A tattoo."

Another nod. "A tattoo. Yes."

Sloane could see how distraught Anna was, so she spoke very gently. "If I got a special police artist to work with you, do you think you could describe the men well enough for him to draw pictures?"

"I can try." Tears filled Anna's eyes. "I'm so sorry. I never thought . . ."

"It's not your fault." Sloane reached over and covered Anna's hand with hers. "You didn't know. Besides, we owe you our thanks. You've just helped us figure out something very important."

"That's right," Rosalyn chimed in. "Mr. Burbank and I are very grateful to you for showing me your key. We're also terribly sorry about what happened to you."

"Me? What about you? You were in hospital. Now you have a broken arm. Those men almost killed you. It's my fault."

"No, Anna," Sloane corrected. "It's the other way around. You were a victim because of my family. Those men hunted you down so they could copy your key to my parents' apartment. If anything, it's *our* fault that *you* were assaulted." Squeezing Anna's hand, she rose. "I'm calling Derek," she told her mother. "Then we'll all go down to the Field Office and have a sketch artist do his thing. From Anna's description, I'll bet the skinny guy is the one who sliced up my arm. He probably also made a dry run at the apartment beforehand to scope out Dad's office and take some pictures, so they'd know which file cabinets were where."

"Yes, and the strong one might be the SOB who almost snapped off my arm and planned to do the same thing to my neck," Rosalyn replied, already in motion.

"I was thinking the same thing. Thanks for calling me, Mom. You've got great instincts. And before I forget, call a locksmith and have your door re-keyed."

A twinkle lit Rosalyn's eyes. "I already thought of that. Who do you think you inherited your smarts from?"

Sloane arched a brow. "I plead the fifth." She flipped open her cell phone. All she could think about was one thing. Thank goodness for this development. Now Derek could call off his dogs.

Ben, Wallace, Leo, and Phil were off the hook.

CHAPTER
TWENTY-FOUR

Daniel Zhang was expecting them.

He met Rich and Derek in a room at the Flushing youth group organization where he'd just finished a class for Chinese-American teens who were recently out of rehab and trying to live drug-free lives.

"Agent Williams. Agent Parker." Zhang shook each of their hands, speaking in perfect, barely accented English. He was slight, in his midthirties, with an open, friendly demeanor and a kind face. But his eyes were old, conveying the difficulty of his past. "Please, sit down." He walked over to the circle of chairs he'd set up for class and pulled three of them to the front of the room.

"Thank you for meeting with us," Rich began as they sat down. "Do you prefer Zhang Ming, or Daniel Zhang?"

"Daniel is fine." Zhang gave him a half smile. "I've been in the States for a long time now. Plus, it puts the kids I work with at ease, since most of them have English names."

"Fine . . . Daniel," Rich repeated. "You and I spoke only briefly on the phone. But you understand what we need from you."

"I do. However, first, I want *you* to understand that it's been years since I had any contact with the Fong Triad, or any triad." It was clear that Zhang wanted to clarify who he'd become, not only to avoid problems with the FBI but also because of the pride he felt for his transition. "My life is very different now. *I'm* very different now. I was lucky enough to get a fresh start. I want to share that good fortune with the kids I help. Most of them are at crucial turning points in their lives. They need hope, direction, and the knowledge that someone is there for them—someone who's been where they are and made the kind of changes I made. Someone who'll offer them the emotional support necessary to make those same changes."

"What you're doing is commendable," Derek replied. Despite his impatience to get the answers they sought, he felt a surge of genuine admiration for this man. "Let me assure you, we have no interest in interfering in your life or making any trouble for you. All we want is the information Special Agent Williams requested when you spoke."

"About the painting I bought for my Dragon Head." Zhang gave a bemused shake of his head. "The girl who sold it to me said it was a Rothberg, that it was worth hundreds of thousands of U.S. dollars, and she was only asking fifty thousand for it. She seemed pretty desperate, and since I had no idea what a Rothberg was, I assumed the offer was a scam. But my Dragon Head told me that Aaron Rothberg was a gifted artist, and that if the painting was genuine, it was as valuable as she claimed. He borrowed the painting and had it authenticated. It was real. So he gave me the money and told me to complete the transaction."

"Which you did," Derek ascertained.

Zhang nodded. "I met her at her friend's apartment and bought the painting. It was months later, when Fong and I heard there was a murder attached to it, that we unloaded the painting—fast. The Dutch guy who bought it didn't care about its history. He just wanted it, either to keep or to sell. Fong got top dollar for it. And that was that."

"Tell us about the girl who sold it to you," Derek asked, leaning forward.

Zhang sighed. "If I'd been the person then that I am now, she'd be one of the kids I helped. She couldn't have been more than sixteen or seventeen.

Straight black hair—long, past her shoulders. Petite. Pretty. And, as I said, desperate. My guess would be she was a runaway. She was way too classy to have spent her life on the streets. Her friend Lucy was another story. She was older—maybe twenty—and definitely a drug user. Her pupils were the size of saucers and she looked wrung out. Her apartment was the size of a shoebox— the rats in the hall were bigger than the room. Both girls looked as if they hadn't eaten a decent meal in weeks."

"You said her friend's name was Lucy. What about the seller herself—what was her name?"

"She never gave it to me. Neither did Lucy. I didn't know her name until later."

"So you spoke to Lucy again."

"Oh, yes. It was a good five years later. She came looking for me out of nowhere. She was in even worse shape than the last time—gaunt, so drugged up she could barely see straight, and with some ugly welts on her face. It was obvious someone was beating her. She was panicked and desperate to get out of Hong Kong. She said she'd scored a huge sum of money, and begged me to arrange transport for her to America. She was so frantic, I felt sorry for her. So I spoke to my Dragon Head. He agreed to make the arrangements—for twenty thousand dollars. She turned the money over, in cash, without a word of negotiation or protest. Fong got her on a ship to New York. After that, she was on her own."

"Where does a poverty-stricken drug addict get twenty thousand dollars?" Rich muttered to himself. "That amount of cash sure as hell didn't come from sex or drugs."

"That's for sure," Zhang agreed. "All I know is that she swore to me she hadn't stolen it. Back then, it didn't matter. I made a deal. I got a cut. I walked away."

"And that was the end of it?"

"In Hong Kong, yes. That was the last I saw of her. But I'm almost positive I saw her about a month ago."

"In New York?" Derek asked, his head snapping up.

Another nod. "In a battered women's shelter in Chinatown. I was there to bring a young girl back to her family in Flushing, where she could heal after being beaten by her drunken boyfriend. While I was there, I saw a woman I'm almost positive was Lucy. She's obviously been through hell. It's only been about three years since I saw her, so she can't be more than twenty-eight or thirty. But she looks a decade older than that. She was swollen, covered with bruises, and shivering under a blanket in the corner. I tried to approach her, but she shrunk away from me like a terrified, wounded animal. So I backed off." Zhang's brows drew together in concentration. "But her eyes, her features . . . it was Lucy. I said her name, and she startled. I think she recognized me, too, although she was too dazed to figure out from where. But I could swear I saw a flash of recognition in her eyes."

Derek whipped out a pad. "Give us the name and address of this shelter."

Zhang supplied Derek with the information. "If you find her, my only suggestion is to have a woman question her. She's visibly terrified of men, no doubt with good reason. If you two march in and approach her, you'll scare her off and lose any chance of learning what you need to know."

"I was thinking along the very same lines." Derek was already mentally laying out a plan. "We'll have a female reach out to her—one who's specifically trained to get through to people who are reluctant or unwilling to respond. The professional I have in mind is Caucasian, so I'll have a Chinese agent go with her when she pokes around in Chinatown. That'll avoid any potential cultural problems. But once the two of them are inside the shelter, my male agent will stay back, and let her do the work."

"Lucy's English is weak," Zhang warned him.

"My female investigator speaks fluent Mandarin. Communication won't be a problem. Believe me, if anyone can get through to this poor, battered Lucy, the pro I have in mind can."

"You want to send Sloane in there," Rich stated as soon as they'd left the youth center, armed with Daniel's offer to assist in any additional way he could.

"You bet I do. She's the best crisis negotiator I've ever seen. She knows how to get through to people. This is right up her alley."

"Not to mention it'll keep her mind off your investigation of her father's partners," Rich added with a shrewd sidelong glance.

Derek blew out a breath. "Look, Rich. I realize things on that front changed right before we left for Queens."

"Ah, you mean when the Burbanks' maid came in and told us her story—the one that proves none of Matthew Burbank's partners helped Xiao Long break into the Burbanks' apartment."

"Yes, right," Derek answered impatiently. "But that's the only fact that changed. I never thought these guys were hardened criminals. I thought they were involved in a cover-up. I still do. I also think it somehow links back to Xiao Long. Call it far-fetched. Call it gut instinct. Either way, I'm going to keep digging into all four men—and, yeah, Burbank, too. I'm asking you to follow through with our original plan and reinterview them. Truthfully, it's going to be easier now. Since the Burbanks' maid told us what happened, Sloane is going to assume her father and his friends are off the hook. She won't be worried that I'm still investigating them. I don't know if that investigation will link directly to the Rothberg theft. It might not. In which case, it will become my problem, not yours. And if it turns out I'm wrong and they're as clean as a whistle, there'll be no harm done—except to my relationship with Sloane. But I'm willing to take that risk. Because if I'm right, and if that cover-up is tied to Xiao Long, Sloane is still in danger. Significant danger. I know Xiao Long. He'd carve someone up like a pumpkin, and then go out to breakfast."

"I hear you. And I'll follow through using the angle of new details on the Rothberg and conduct a follow-up interview with each of the art partners. Now that we have the Fong information, it'll be a natural step to ask if any of them are familiar with the triad members or the people involved in the transaction. I'll also add a healthy dose of concern for their safety, given the attack on Rosalyn Burbank. Believe me, the way I'm going to handle it, Sloane won't get suspicious."

"Thanks, Rich."

"No problem. I'm counting on that steak dinner."

There was a team meeting first thing the next morning in Tony's office.

Squad members from both C-6 and C-7 were present, as were Rich and Sloane. Everyone was brought up to speed on the MP5K sales, the Black Eagles–Red Dragons connection, and the short-term possession of *Dead or Alive* by the Fong Triad.

The sketches of the two men Anna had described were produced, and her story was recounted. Everyone was advised that Rosalyn Burbank had verified that the solid, thickset man in Anna's sketch was the same man who'd abducted her—a man Derek and C-6 had already identified from the initial sketch Rosalyn had provided as Jin Huang.

Last, Sloane described her knife attack, and confirmed that her assailant was the other punk in Anna's sketches.

An investigative plan was laid out: Sloane and Jeff would go to the battered women's shelter in Chinatown and see if Lucy was still there, and if she wasn't, start tracing her whereabouts. With Derek at the helm, C-6 and C-7 would dig into Xiao Long's link to the Black Eagles. And Rich would continue to investigate the various art thefts, Rothberg included, and see what he could come up with.

Very casually, he mentioned his plan to call in the art-partnership members to see if they knew anything about the Fong Triad and their purchasing any valuable paintings. Also, if they'd ever dealt with Daniel Zhang—or even heard his name.

Sloane accepted Rich's announcement without surprise or concern. What he was describing was standard operating procedure.

Once again, Derek felt like a bastard. But he just couldn't let this one go— even if it meant betraying his promise to Sloane. He didn't want to keep his suspicions from her. But as of now, they had no concrete basis, and he knew that the very idea he believed otherwise—and was acting on that belief— would tear her apart. There was plenty of time to do that later—if necessary. And if it wasn't, he'd tell her anyway, fully aware that it could put a permanent chink in their relationship.

Love was a wonderful thing. Except when it wasn't.

Cindy took great pains getting dressed and ready for tonight's dinner with Wallace. As Peggy had suggested, she wore her turquoise silk blouse, which clung ever so subtly to her delicate curves. She also donned a pair of Ralph Lauren black silk slacks and classic high-heeled pumps. Wallace was tall. It was important that the two of them fit together—physically as well as intellectually.

She brushed her dark hair until it glistened, put on a minimal amount of makeup, and then dabbed some Magie Noire perfume behind her ears and on her wrists. She hesitated, then traced a tiny line of the captivating scent between her breasts. *Magie Noire*—French for "black magic."

What a fitting name for the evening she had in mind.

Derek left the office early that night. Sloane and Jeff were putting the final touches on their plans for tomorrow's visit to the battered women's shelter. After that, Sloane had an occupational therapy appointment at HSS. It was just as well. Derek needed time to think, to assimilate his thoughts, and to deal with his guilt.

Traffic was lighter than usual, and he got home in record time. As he pulled down the winding cottage driveway, he noticed there was a car parked at the foot of the driveway, near the garage. It took him a minute to recognize the red Lexus convertible and to remember that Sloane had told him she'd given Leo a key, since he'd be dropping by in the late afternoon to take some measurements and compare some color swatches.

Great. Talk about rubbing Derek's nose in guilt. It was the first night in weeks that he didn't feel like probing one of Matthew's partners for information. He just wanted to pour himself a glass of wine, go over the material he'd collected on the case—and, yes, on Matthew's partners—and figure out if it was the Fong Triad that Xiao Long had his connections to, and if so, if it was Henry Fong himself who was subsidizing Xiao's big-time art-theft crimes.

Determined to urge Leo out the door ASAP, Derek let himself into the cottage through the garage door.

Three things happened at once.

The hounds came flying out of the den, racing around the corner, and barking joyously at Derek's homecoming. A loud thud and a muttered curse emanated from the living room just as Derek appeared in its entranceway. And Leo Fox stumbled to his feet, red-faced and stuttering apologies as he collected papers off the carpet and shoved them back into the open file.

Derek recognized the contents. They were Sloane's copies of the police reports detailing the artwork stolen during the Upper East Side burglaries.

CHAPTER
TWENTY-FIVE

Wallace's taste in restaurants was impeccable.

Savoy had always been one of Cindy's personal favorites. Nestled in down-town Soho, it had a lovely main dining room on the second level. The crackling fireplace and wood-accented windows, together with the privately arranged tables and accommodating staff, created an elegant ambiance that was both homey and intimate.

It was precisely the scenario Cindy had anticipated for this all-important evening.

Wallace himself looked impeccable, dressed in a classy but understated custom-made suit and silk tie. He was carrying a small shopping bag, and judging from the glossy white color and silver roped handles, whatever was inside it was for her. And his curious glance at the slim box under her arm told her this was going to be a race to see who got the honor of presenting their gift first.

No contest. She was taking the lead here. It was a necessity to ensure that she accomplished the full impact of her presentation.

Wallace had arranged to have them seated at a quiet corner table close to the fire. As soon as the maitre d' brought them over to the table, settled them in, and discreetly left them alone, Cindy took the reins.

"I have something for you," she told Wallace. "It's a special thank-you from my *A Sook* and me. I would have saved it for after dessert, but given its size— it's not as if I could keep it hidden in my pocket." She reached down and lifted the thin, square box from where she'd propped it against her chair. "I hope it touches your heart the way we thought it would."

With a pleased but quizzical look in his eyes, Wallace took the box and opened it, peeling back the layers of tissue paper and revealing the two-foot-by-two-foot bamboo picture frame and the canvas it held. His breath caught for a moment as he lifted it out and gazed at the master oil painting in his hands.

The room in it was a muted shade of green, and dim lighting haloed the closed door. Standing there, with one hand on the doorknob, was the room's sole occupant.

The little Asian girl was about four years old. She was laughing, her other hand clapped over her mouth as if to keep the subject of her mirth private. Her hair was in two braids, a bright pink flower tucked behind each one. Her robe was a traditional Chinese silk with ornate trim at the wrists and neck. The way the pale aura captured and illuminated her, it was as if she was right there with you, her dark eyes dancing, the very essence of life emanating from her youth and beauty.

The signature, in the painting's lower right-hand corner, belonged to a well-known Chinese artist.

Wallace swallowed twice before he spoke.

"This is exquisite," he finally managed. "I can't tell you how moved I am."

"You don't have to," Cindy replied softly. "Your expression just did."

He raised his head. "'Thank you' doesn't do justice to what I'm feeling right now. But it's all I have. So thank you, to you and your uncle." He reached across the table and took Cindy's hand, half rising from his chair so he could bring her fingers to his lips.

"You're very welcome." Cindy kept her gaze fixed on his. "It's as much a gift for me, to see such appreciation for a fine work of art, as it is to you. I hope you'll hang it in your home and think about me every time you look at it. That way, you'll know how grateful I am for all you've done for my career—and for me." She let her fingers linger in his hand for an extra moment, as her warm expression caressed his face. "Your support has made all the difference."

Reluctantly, Wallace released her hand, and sank back down into his chair. "All I did was open the door. Your talent took over from there. And I should warn you—even though we're celebrating your first big project, a deluge of them is about to follow. I've received a dozen cocktail party invitations for the next two weeks alone. Every one of the invitations is for the two of us, and every one of them is from an eager perspective client. Between that, and the word of mouth you'll receive on this first design project you're undertaking, you'll barely have time to sleep."

"How exciting!" Cindy lit up.

"Does that mean I can accept the invitations on your behalf?"

"Of course. I'm thrilled. It will give me the chance to line up new projects, and equally important, it will give us the chance to get to know each other better."

"Nothing would please me more." Wallace carefully rewrapped the painting and set it aside, then handed Cindy the package he'd brought. "This is just something that made me think of you—a small congratulations gift. It pales in comparison to the painting—and to you."

Cindy lowered her lashes. She was beginning to enjoy this game of romantic cat and mouse. "You've already given me my career start," she murmured as she opened the bag. "That's more than enough congratulations." A soft laugh. "But I have to confess, I love presents." She unwrapped the tissue paper, revealing a black, buttery-leather briefcase. It was classy yet high-styled, feminine and at the same time professional, with enough room for her sketches, portfolios, and even her laptop. It was clearly handmade by an Italian designer, and it had that wonderful new-leather smell that screamed success.

"Wallace, it's stunning," she murmured, taking it out and inspecting it, then opening it up and running her fingers over the soft suede interior. "And it's so very—me."

"My thoughts exactly." He smiled, leaning back in his chair and squinting, as if picturing her walking down the streets of Manhattan, carrying his gift in her hand. "I have a minority interest in an Italian leather goods manufacturer. The overseas reps were in New York for Market Week, and I got the chance to see their new designs. This was the showstopper. The moment I saw it, I knew. It won't even be available until next season. You're the very first person to have one, which is fitting."

A minority interest in an Italian leather goods manufacturer? For a fleeting instant, Cindy wondered if her *A Sook* knew about Wallace's gift to her, and its source. If so, he was probably amused.

"I'll bring it with me on the first day of my new project," she declared. "Once my clients see it, they'll have to hire me. They'll assume that anyone who can afford something this exclusive and pricey must be earning a fortune—which could only mean that her work is superb."

"And they'd be right to be impressed. But not about your wealth. About your talent and you. You're a very special woman, Cindy."

This was going even better than she'd hoped.

She leaned forward. "I'm glad you'll be escorting me to all those cocktail parties. Frankly, I find this sudden notoriety a little overwhelming."

"You shouldn't. But not to worry. We'll tackle the parties together."

"You're very kind." Cindy paused, as if weighing her words. This next part of the conversation was crucial. She had to handle it just right, or things could fall apart very quickly and *very* prematurely.

"I don't mean to be presumptuous," she said, "but I feel as if we're far more than casual friends. So I'm going to risk overstepping my bounds. My *A Sook* told me about your daughter's tragic death. I'm so terribly sorry. A loss like that . . . I can't even imagine how devastating it must be. I want you to know my heart goes out to you."

The expression that crossed Wallace's face was so tragic that Cindy almost felt guilty for bringing up the subject.

"If I'm violating your privacy . . ." she heard herself say.

"No." Wallace shook his head. "You're not violating anything, nor are you being intrusive." A veil of tears moistened his eyes. "Losing Sophie was crippling. It still is. Talking about it is something I seldom do, but not because it makes the pain any worse. Mostly because there are no words to say, and no one I care to say them to." He met her gaze. "I've been dead inside for a very long time. I know I'll never fully recover. Part of me died with Sophie, and that part is gone forever. But the rest . . ." He drew in a breath. "Truthfully, I thought all of me might be dead. That's why meeting you has been such a breath of fresh air. For the first time in ages, I feel a tad of hope, a possibility that someday I might have the impetus to get out of bed in the morning."

"I'm glad." Cindy's conscience couldn't take any more. Neither could her stomach. She understood all the reasons why she was doing what she was doing. But theory and reality weren't the same.

She was tough. But apparently not as tough as she thought. She couldn't pursue this subject. If she wanted to accomplish what her A Sook wanted her to, she'd have to accomplish it without discussion of Sophie. A five-year-old girl being killed by a hit-and-run driver was not something she could rub in Wallace's face, whether or not his anguish satisfied her A Sook's sense of equity.

"I hope I'm not scaring you off," Wallace said in a rueful tone, clearly interpreting her silence as a sign that he was pushing too hard too soon. "I have no expectations. I try to take life a day at a time; it's the only way I've survived. But if I'm overwhelming you, please let me know. You're young, you're vibrant, you're beautiful, and you're talented. You've got your whole life ahead of you, and the whole world at your feet. You deserve to share that life with a circle of people, particularly a man, who can offer you that same anticipation and exuberance. I have no delusions that I'd ever be able to rally enough to be that man. But, selfishly, I enjoy your company, and I find your energy infectious. So if you're willing, I'm very happy to just enjoy this time together, and take things as they come."

"That works perfectly for me," Cindy replied, feeling on more comfortable ground. "My own life is so up in the air, and everything is happening so quickly, that I'm not in any position to plan long-term relationships. I enjoy your company as well—and I think you underestimate your assets. You're self-assured, you have an aura of success, and you're distinguished and handsome. Those qualities hold equally as much impact as youth and enthusiasm. So I

agree, let's just let things unfold as they're meant to." An impish grin. "I realize that being spontaneous is contrary to both our natures. We're planners.
We like being in control. From what I hear, playing the role of a free spirit
has its merits."

Cindy's last comment had the desired effect, and an odd expression flickered across Wallace's face. "Sometimes you remind me so much of that
woman I mentioned to you. And I assure you, that's a high compliment. She
was unique, beautiful, and a free spirit, as you mentioned. Only in her case,
it came naturally."

"Was this woman significant in your life?"

"For a long time, yes. But we were very different. We eventually went our
separate ways. It was best that way."

Best for whom? Cindy asked herself, picturing Meili as the joyful girl she
remembered, and reminding herself that this man was the reason she'd taken
her own life.

That reminder was enough to strengthen her resolve. That, and the fact
that avenging Meili's death was one of her beloved *A Sook*'s dying wishes.

Cindy would continue her charade to its rightful conclusion.

That night was a sleepless one for Derek.

He'd let Leo walk out without a confrontation. What good would accusing
the man have done? At this stage, it made more sense to let things slide than
to open Pandora's box. Derek would do that *when* he had the evidence to
back up his suspicions that some or all of Matthew's art-partnership members
were involved in something shady.

But tonight, he'd pretended to accept Leo's stammered explanation about
looking for a missing sketch when he upset Sloane's file.

Both men knew Derek wasn't buying it for a minute.

But neither of them pursued it. Instead, Leo had gathered up his decorating books and swatches, brightly announced that he'd be in touch soon, and
blown out of there.

What in the hell had he been searching for?

Any way you sliced it, rummaging through Sloane's file smacked of the kind of desperation innocent men don't possess.

Which only added to Derek's guilt about not sharing his suspicions with Sloane. But how could he? He was in no stronger of a position than he'd been in before. What could he add—that he'd come home to find Leo cleaning up papers from a file he claimed to have knocked over? Describing Leo's flustered reaction wouldn't help. Sloane would only remind Derek how intimidating Leo perceived him to be, and how very badly he wanted to impress Derek and create the perfect love nest for them.

No. Derek couldn't say anything to Sloane. Not yet. But tonight's little escapade made him even more certain that something was going on with these guys, something they wanted to keep hidden.

He wasn't giving up until he figured out what it was.

At a little after nine in the morning, Sloane and Jeff arrived at the battered women's shelter in Chinatown.

As planned, Sloane let Jeff take the lead as they walked through the front door and sought out the woman who was in charge. Jeff showed her his Bureau ID, informing her in Mandarin that they were with the FBI and needed to see a resident named Lucy. The woman started, and closely examined his ID. Then she introduced herself as Mrs. Chin, and asked if he knew Lucy's last name. Fully prepared for that question, Jeff told her he didn't, but he rattled off a full description of the Lucy in question. Still, Mrs. Chin was very leery and very protective. She asked several more questions of Jeff, all of which Sloane understood, none of which she responded to. When Mrs. Chin sent curious glances her way, Sloane bowed her head and kept her mouth shut, showing overt respect and awareness that she was the outsider, and that it was not her place to intrude on this community, not without permission.

Jeff assured Mrs. Chin that their interest in Lucy was strictly to get information that would help others in trouble. They had no intentions of revealing her identity or her whereabouts to anyone, most significantly to the husband whose abuse had resulted in her being there. Last, he urged Sloane forward and told the administrator that his partner was fluent in Mandarin, had traveled extensively in China, and that, Caucasian or not, she'd been selected to accompany him here out of consideration for Lucy, to alleviate any fears she might have by speaking to her woman-to-woman.

His final statement caused a definite thawing in Mrs. Chin's attitude. "I'm not sure Lucy will talk to you," she said to Sloane in Mandarin. "She's been badly traumatized, and speaks to only a chosen few."

Sloane nodded. "I understand," she replied, also in Mandarin. "But I'd like to try. I'm not unfamiliar with situations where men have taken advantage of their strength and brutalized women."

"Very well." Sloane's candor and empathy caused the woman to agree. "Come with me."

She led them down a hall to what appeared to be a pleasant, if worn, living room, where a handful of Asian women were gathered. Some were sitting quietly; some were talking among themselves. A number of them were visibly bruised. Others had haunted expressions in their eyes that spoke volumes.

Sloane's heart went out to them.

"Lucy?" Mrs. Chin had walked over to a corner of the room, where a disheveled Asian woman was crouched on the floor with a blanket wrapped around her shoulders, trembling as if she were ice cold from the inside out.

Mrs. Chin leaned forward, touching her arm gently and speaking in a soft, soothing voice. "There's a woman here who'd like to talk to you."

Lucy's head snapped up and her gaze found Sloane. "Why? And who's the man with her? Did my husband send them?" She cringed against the wall. "I won't go back."

"Lucy, you don't have to go back." Sloane stepped forward, speaking Mandarin in a comforting tone. She squatted down beside the shivering woman, but made no move to touch her. "I'm a friend. I work for the FBI. I'm just trying to find another friend of yours—one who might be in trouble. Your husband has nothing to do with this. He doesn't know where you are, or that I'm talking to you. You're safe."

"Safe?" Lucy looked up at her, white-faced, which only served to emphasize the yellowing bruises on her cheeks and throat. "I'll never be safe. Not as long as he might find me. You're American," she blurted out, as that fact registered.

"Yes, I am. And I've helped other women who've been hurt by men. Women of all different cultures and nationalities. I've never betrayed any of them. And I never will. So, yes, you're safe."

"How do I know? Just because you say so?"

"Because you're in a warm and caring place. Because Mrs. Chin won't let anyone through that door she doesn't trust. And because I'm going to give Mrs. Chin my business card, so that if she ever feels you're in danger, she can call me. I'll make sure that that danger is taken care of so you can continue to feel safe. Does that sound fair?"

Lucy was quiet for a moment. "What do I have to do in return?"

"Just think about the fact that, by talking to me, you can help keep other people safe." Sloane rose. "My partner and I will leave you now, and let you consider what I've said." She reached into her pocketbook and pulled out a business card. "This has my personal contact information on it. Mrs. Chin will have it, so you can call if you ever feel threatened." As she spoke, Sloane handed the card to Mrs. Chin. "We'll come back tomorrow. I hope you'll decide to talk to us."

With that, Sloane gestured to Jeff that they should leave. "Thank you, Mrs. Chin," she murmured. "We'll be back in the morning."

"That was pretty impressive," Jeff commented as they stepped outside.

"What? My Mandarin or my technique?"

"Both." He grinned. "But I was talking about your technique—right down to your timing. Knowing how far to push, when to call it quits, and when to give her space by saying we'll come back tomorrow. The way you handled that woman was amazing. She was in bad shape. I never thought she'd say a word to us. You're a natural."

"Thanks, but it's not just innate ability. It's training. I was a crisis negotiator when I was with the Bureau. I was taught how to coax people who didn't want to talk to open up. It takes trust and patience. Hopefully, those skills will pay off with Lucy."

"You've also worked cases with victimized women. I haven't forgotten the one earlier this year with that goddess-obsessed psycho."

"Neither have I . . . although I try to." A shudder. "So let's not go there. Let's just—" Abruptly Sloane broke off. An instant later, she casually opened her purse and began rummaging through it until she found and extracted her sunglasses. "The punk who attacked me with the knife," she murmured to Jeff, as she slid on the sunglasses. "He's diagonally across the street—at eleven o'clock—watching us."

"Xiao Long's kid?" Jeff asked, intentionally keeping his gaze on Sloane and not turning to look in the direction she was referring to.

She nodded. "I guess he's reporting our activities to his boss."

"Let's grab him before he does." Jeff glanced at his watch. "Talk to me as we cross the street. We won't pick up our pace until we're closing in on him."

"Better idea—why don't we split up and close in on him from opposite directions?"

"No dice. You're not an agent, remember?"

Sloane rolled her eyes. "Jeff . . ."

"You know the rules, Sloane. It's my way, or no way."

She gave up with a sigh. "Fine."

The two of them turned left and crossed the busy Chinatown intersection at the corner, then crossed to the opposite side of the street, heading straight for their target.

He spotted them just as they picked up the pace.

He saw Sloane coming at him first. Before she could blink, he was sprinting away, shoving through the crowd to escape.

Jeff and Sloane broke into a run. They tore down one street and then another, weaving their way through the pedestrians. It didn't help that Sloane was Caucasian and the kid she was pursuing was one of their own. Several produce vendors stepped directly in her path, and a few shopkeepers chose that exact second to step outside to pick up their newspapers or to smoke a cigarette, totally blocking her way.

By the time Sloane broke through the human obstacle course, Jeff was a solid half block ahead of her.

It didn't matter. As she caught up with him, Jeff came to a grinding halt. Disgusted, he gazed up and down the cross street. "I lost him."

"I never had a chance. I was sabotaged from the get-go. Talk about being an outsider." Sloane made a frustrated sound. "Jeff, I know it was him."

"No question about it. He matched the sketch to a tee. And the look on his face when he saw you closing in on him . . . yeah, it was him." Jeff scowled, looking distinctly uneasy. "Xiao Long never shoves his gang in our face, not unless he wants to make a point or issue a threat."

Sloane got Jeff's message loud and clear. "You don't think it's the Bureau Xiao is threatening."

"Nope. I think it's you. And if he doesn't like what he hears from his punk kid . . ." Jeff gave a hard shake of his head. "This isn't good."

"You're right. It's not." Sloane's brows drew together in irritation. "And not because I'm intimidated. I'd love to be the one to lure the bastard out and expose him for the killer he is. But after this, I won't get the chance. Not once you tell Derek."

CHAPTER TWENTY-SIX

Derek's reaction to Sloane and Jeff's report was not what Sloane had expected.

All he did was sit silently at his desk, fingers interlaced behind his head, and listen to what they had to say.

When they were finished, he unlinked his hands and leaned forward, scribbling down some notes on a piece of paper.

"Jeff, type up the report and e-mail it to Tony and to me. Sloane, nice work at the shelter. Both of you go back tomorrow as planned. With any luck, Sloane, you'll get some solid information out of Lucy." He rose. "Just so you know, Fred Miller's body was pulled out of the East River an hour ago. No surprises. Estimated time of death is consistent with your mother's kidnapping. Cause of death—one lethal stab wound to the back. Sloane, I'm putting full-time security on you until your involvement in this case is over. Right now, I've got a meeting with Tony."

Without another word, Derek headed off.

Jeff and Sloane stared after him and then exchanged glances.

"That was weird," Jeff commented. "No explosions. No lectures. And he didn't pull you off the case, or confine you to desk duty. He was almost eerily quiet. When do you think the volcano's going to erupt?"

"I don't know." Sloane was puzzled. She shared Jeff's opinion that there was a lot more brewing beneath the surface than Derek had displayed. But she knew Derek better than anyone. The emotion he was repressing wasn't anger. It wasn't even frustration. It was something more.

———

She broached the subject that night when they were getting ready for bed. It was the first time they'd been alone all day. The hounds were snoozing in a pile of blankets they'd arranged at the foot of the bed, and Derek was in his gym shorts, doing his nighttime push-ups.

Sloane came out of the bathroom, pulling on one of Derek's Colorado State T-shirts that she used as a nightshirt. Then, she slid between the sheets. "Do you want to talk about what happened today?" she asked, sitting up, arms wrapped around her knees.

"Not particularly." Derek reached his fiftieth push-up and rose.

"Well, I do."

"Fine. Which part of what happened today did you want to discuss?"

"Your reaction, or lack thereof, when Jeff recapped what happened."

"I did react. There's FBI security posted outside the cottage. You should be used to that by now. It's not the first time I've assigned security to you. I'm sure it won't be the last." Derek took a few gulps of water and got into bed.

"That's not what I meant, and you know it. Something's going on in that nonstop mind of yours. You're not pissed, which I expected. You're not threatening to take me off the case, which I also expected. You're not even raving about my impulsive way of putting myself in danger."

"Would there be a point?"

"That's not the question, not in this case. I know you, Derek. This isn't about your resigning yourself to who I am. It's about something else. Whatever that something is, I want you to share it with me."

"I'm not sure you do." Derek propped his back against the headboard, staring straight ahead. His expression was sober, and his jaw was tight.

"Let me be the judge of that."

"This isn't a five-minute conversation, Sloane. Let's shelve it."

"For when? When we have hours of free time? That's not going to happen. If we have to lose a night's sleep, so be it. We've done it before, for pleasure and for work. So talk to me."

Derek was silent for a long moment.

"What's going on inside me is complicated," he said at last. "I'm not even sure I can sort it out myself, much less explain it to you."

"Try." Sloane slid down and rolled over to one side, propping herself up on her elbow. "I might surprise you."

A hard swallow. "Our lives are spinning out of control. I need some sense of order. I thought living together would resolve that. It hasn't. And I'm not sure it ever will."

Whatever Sloane had been expecting, it hadn't been this. An odd knot formed in the pit of her stomach. "What is it you want to change—our living arrangement, or us?"

"It isn't that simple. I love you—the kind of crazy, forever, deep-in-my-gut love I thought existed only in books and movies. I'd go to hell and back for you."

"As I would for you," Sloane replied quietly.

"I know. We've got all the vital feelings down pat. And that's supposed to make everything right. But it doesn't. That's the part that stops me cold."

"Why, because we're different? Because we don't do anything half-measure—love, fight, make up, back down? Is that it?"

"It's not *that* we're different. It's *how* we're different." Derek exhaled heavily. "Sloane, I want you to be everything you want to be, everything I know you can be. I want you to go back to Quantico and kick ass. I want you to re-join the Bureau and be the special agent you've been deprived of being for so long. I want you to leave your mark on the world."

"I never doubted that." Sloane was studying Derek's expression, trying to read his thoughts. "Is it my ambition? The pressures of the job? Are you worried that we'll lose sight of each other once I'm back, working under the same Bureau constraints as you do? Because I'm out now, and I'm still working my ass off."

"That's not it—although both of us being workaholics makes it twice as hard to prioritize our relationship. But that's life. Neither of us does anything halfway. We'll find a way to make time for each other. With regard to your rejoining the Bureau, if I have to be honest, I hope you'll go back to white-collar crime. Given what a stubborn, fearless ball-breaker you are, I'll have less to lose sleep over if you're out of Violent Crimes. Plus, there's no way we can ever work together. Our objectivity is compromised. Our feelings get in the way. We'd clash at every turn. Frankly, I'd either kill you or myself."

Sloane gave a soft laugh. "That won't be a problem. The FBI wouldn't put us on the same squad. Hopefully in the same Field Office, but never on the same team. It was hard enough when we collided in Crisis Negotiations where I was the lead negotiator and had to deal with you on SWAT. Our styles are different. Our wills are both like steel. Top that off with our emotional involvement, and, yeah, we'd kill each other if we were on the same squad. But we'll be working separately. So what's the problem?"

"Our long-term goals. *Personal* goals. The ones I try never to bring up. I can't live like that anymore. I can't ignore my own needs, waiting for yours to change. Life is too short. Guarantees are nonexistent. We have to treasure what we have, and fight for what we could have."

"I agree." Sloane now understood Derek's reaction to what had happened to her and Jeff this morning. He'd been rattled by the fact that she'd come face-to-face with danger again. It had happened to her far too often these past few years, starting with her near-death experience with the bank robber who'd carved up her hand. All these incidents had impacted Derek, and together with the fragile aspects of their relationship, had brought on this philosophical frame of mind.

"I know how precious life is—*and* how precious we are," she assured him. "I never want you to compromise your goals or your needs." She reached out, caressed his arm. "You're not the only one who's grown and whose perspectives have changed. Mine have, too. I'm sorry if I scared you today. I'll do my best to minimize those situations."

"How do you feel about kids?" Derek blurted out.

That one caught Sloane totally off guard. She startled, her hand jerking off Derek's arm. "Excuse me?"

"Children. Babies. How do you feel about having them?"

"Wow." She breathed. "Talk about coming out of left field."

"Does that mean you've never thought about it? Or that you've thought about it and decided motherhood isn't for you?"

"Derek, we just moved in together."

"I didn't ask for a recap. I asked if you wanted kids."

Sloane was still reeling. "Okay, yes, I want kids—someday. But I've got a lot to accomplish before then." She searched Derek's face, totally bewildered by this radical leap into the future. "Where is this coming from?"

"From day-to-day life. From risks that appear out of nowhere. From my feelings for you. From the fact that my job is great, but that I want a family. From the knowledge that a family is the only true legacy one leaves behind. From the fact that I see you fighting to protect your father, and I recognize that family means more to you than you realize. And from the fact that, despite my determination to give you space, it isn't working—not for me. This baby-step stuff is crap. I want more. I want you. Not just as my girlfriend. Not just in a halfway, live-together mode. I want you as my wife, as the mother of my kids."

Derek's pronouncement just hung out there, like a finely suspended thread of silk that could either be broken or caressed.

A wealth of emotion swelled inside Sloane—one that was more intense than she'd expected. "I've got to hand it to you," she managed. "When you warned me this conversation would be a biggie, you really meant it."

"So, am I packing my things and moving out tonight, or can I wait until tomorrow to break the news to Leo that he won't be finishing his redecorating job?"

Sloane didn't smile at Derek's attempt at dry humor.

"When you started talking, I thought you were about to call it quits," she said with stark candor. "The pain I felt was excruciating. When I realized you were talking about the total opposite, about making us permanent, official—I didn't feel trapped. I felt moved, overjoyed, and so relieved, you have no idea. I don't think I realized until this very instant just how much I want to spend my life with you. The space I needed—at some point, I stopped needing it. As for kids . . ." This time, Sloane smiled, picturing the adorable little tyrants they'd make together. "That's going to take some mental preparation. It's also going to take some time, some planning, and a fair amount of juggling, given our careers. But I'd love to have children—*our* children. I just hope they don't line up their booties in neat little rows beside their cribs."

Sloane's eyes were sparkling with mirth and misty with tears as Derek pulled her into his arms and rolled her onto her back.

"I love you," he said hoarsely, tunneling his fingers through her hair.

"I love you, too." Too choked up for words, Sloane resorted to actions, wriggling out of her T-shirt, tugging it over her head, and tossing it aside.

Derek kicked off his gym shorts, then blanketed her body with his.

"Mental preparation, yeah," he murmured in a husky tone. "But physical preparation, too. Making just the right babies is going to take hard work and practice." He took her mouth in slow, deep kisses. "Lots of practice."

"Then we'd better get started right away." She wrapped her arms around his neck. "From what I hear, boot camp is one hell of a challenge."

———

Xiao Long sat alone in the back room of his gambling house, gripping his bottle of Tsingtao Dark Beer. Every now and then, he took a swig. Most of the time, he was absorbed in his thoughts.

He was closing in on his prey. A little more toying with them. Just till he got the word. Then came the kill.

The toying was losing its luster. He'd upped the ante, as his Dragon Head had directed. And, yes, it pleased him to torture Burbank by going after his family. To tighten the noose around Martino's neck. To have Leary's bookie threaten him, not only with cutting him off, but with bodily harm. To get closer to locating Fox's fiancée. And to dig a deeper and deeper grave for Johnson, while Cindy enticed him like a sheep being led to slaughter. All that pleased him, mostly because he was doing it for his Dragon Head.

But none of it provided him with the rush he craved.

He had to focus on the prize. He'd honor his Dragon Head's dying wish, punishing his enemies and killing them with the maximum amount of suffering possible. It was a gift he'd savor.

He shut his eyes, visualizing how he would wring the life out of each man. Different methods. But the same sense of exhilaration as he watched their expressions, the emotions mirrored in their eyes. The transformation from realization to fear. To panic. To a frenzied struggle for survival—one that lessened and weakened as it faded into glazed resignation.

And then froze in the empty vacuum of death.

He could feel the sweat as it soaked their skin. The blood as it oozed from their bodies. Their heartbeats pounding with terror. Beating unsteadily. Then faintly.

Finally, not at all.

The rush of power was indescribable. He always had to be a vital part of the closure. He'd wrap his fingers around his victims' throats and squeeze, squeeze—even though they were already gone. That moment belonged only to him.

This time, he'd have multiple such moments. Including the added gratification of forcing Burbank to watch his wife being brutally murdered before his very eyes—and dying with that as his final memory. The same fate awaited Fox, once they located his precious Amalie. Martino and Leary were so weak, it would be enough to see them die in their own excrement.

He'd squeeze until he heard bones crunch. Until he felt rings of cartilage crumble. Until he . . .

Xiao Long winced as a sharp, cutting pain sliced through him. He looked down, surprised to see he'd shattered the beer bottle in his bare hand. He eased his grip, noting he'd pierced his flesh in numerous places. Shards of broken glass clung to his palm, some embedded in his skin, the larger, jagged pieces falling off, tumbling to the floor.

The blood began to flow. Rivulets trickling down his hand, converging at his wrist, and dripping onto the tablecloth.

Pain and blood.

A promise of things to come.

CHAPTER
TWENTY-SEVEN

Jeff and Sloane arrived at the women's shelter the next morning promptly at ten.

Crossing her fingers, Sloane sought out Mrs. Chin and asked if Lucy had made a decision.

"Actually, yes." Mrs. Chin nodded. "I was surprised. But she said she'll speak to you. But *only* you," she added, glancing at Jeff. "She still cowers when a man approaches her."

"I understand. I'll wait out here." He motioned for Sloane to go in.

She followed Mrs. Chin, who guided her through the living room and into a cafeteria-type kitchen, meagerly stocked with a toaster, a microwave, and a basic sink, stove, and refrigerator. Lucy was sitting at one of the kitchen's round tables, sipping a cup of tea, and staring off into space.

"Lucy?" Quietly, Mrs. Chin got her attention. "The woman from the FBI is here."

Lucy's gaze darted straight to Sloane. "You're alone?"

"Yes." Sloane waited for an overt invitation to join her.

"Sit down," Lucy said at last. She gestured to Mrs. Chin that it was okay to leave them alone, and the older woman nodded and left.

Slowly, Sloane walked over and pulled out the chair across the table from Lucy, sitting down and sliding in. She instantly switched over to Mandarin. "Thank you very much for seeing me. I won't take much of your time."

"I'm not sure I can help you."

"And I'm sure you can. This is as personal for me as it is for you." Very slowly, Sloane held out her arm, showing Lucy the knife wound that was now stitched but still very visible. "When I said I understood, I do. I was attacked myself, just recently. The man who did this wasn't finished. He wants to keep hurting me. I was lucky to get away—this time. But I know he'll try again. He could also hurt many other women. Please, I need any information you can give me."

Lucy's gaze flickered to the knife wound, and she winced. "I'm sorry," she said softly. "My husband doesn't use knives. He uses fists. Sometimes he choked me. I thought I was dying." A shaky swallow. "What do you need to know?"

Sloane leaned forward, but only slightly. "Do you remember a man named Daniel Zhang? You probably knew him as Zhang Ming."

Lucy stiffened. "Zhang was a thief."

"Back in China, yes. He's changed. He came to America and is helping kids stay away from gangs." Sloane went on to explain how Daniel had spoken about the painting he'd bought from Lucy's friend. Sloane made sure to add that he'd spotted Lucy here at the shelter and expressed great concern for her before pointing Sloane in her direction.

Lucy looked dubious, but didn't reply.

"According to Daniel, he bought the painting at your apartment," Sloane concluded. "He said you were there."

"Did he also tell you he cheated Meili out of lots of money? He paid her only fifty thousand American dollars for that painting. It was worth much more."

Sloane's ears had perked up at the mention of a name. "Meili—that was your friend?"

A nod.

"What was her last name?"

Lucy shrugged. "She didn't tell me. I didn't ask. It didn't matter. We were friends. Six years. Maybe more."

"You said Daniel cheated Meili. According to him, fifty thousand dollars was what she asked for the painting. Is that not true?"

Lucy gave a bitter laugh. "Oh, it's true. But she was desperate. She'd stolen the painting from her father when she ran away. That, and another one. She knew they'd both been painted by a famous artist and that they were worth a lot, because a man who worked for her father had killed someone to get the first one. But she had no idea how much a lot was. Neither did I. Zhang did. He also knew how bad Meili needed money. And he still cheated her. She was young, naive, and way too trusting. She owed money to everyone, including me. And I'm ashamed to admit that I took it—every last jiao. I needed my drugs, and they cost a lot. By the time Meili paid back all her debts, she was left with less than half of what Zhang gave her for the painting. It was only a matter of time before she had to sell the second one."

"Did Meili work?"

"She wanted to be an artist. But that took time and money. In between trying to sell her work, she waitressed at a bar. She earned almost nothing. That's why she was so excited when that rich American came into her life. She was crazy about him. I warned her not to care so much. But she didn't listen." Lucy's voice quavered, and she stared down at the table. "Why should she? I wasn't so smart. Every man I knew robbed me, beat me, and walked out on me."

This time Sloane took the risk, reaching over to cover Lucy's hand with her own. "You were alone. You were desperate. And you were lonely. The men who abused you—it wasn't your fault."

Lucy raised her head, wiped the tears from her eyes. "Thank you."

"Can you tell me more about Meili's rich American? His name? What he looked like?"

"I never met him and Meili never said his name," Lucy replied, shaking her head. "She was protecting him and his precious reputation. I know she met him when she was trying to sell her second painting. He and his partners offered her next to nothing for it. She ended up selling it to some other triad swindler like Daniel Zhang. But the rich American pursued Meili, if not her painting. He was an important businessman. He was much older than she was, and he was married. He came to Meili whenever he was in China, and she ran to be with him. This went on for three years. She ended it all the night the pig got drunk and told her he'd first slept with her to win a poker bet."

"What a bastard," Sloane muttered, revolted by the all-too-common story.

"Wait." Lucy's fingers stiffened under Sloane's hand, and her trembling started anew. "Meili came from a very traditional family. Honor was everything. She was humiliated by the rich American. She cried all the time, and wouldn't talk. She was still like that when she found out she was pregnant. She didn't know what to do. It took all her courage, but she went crawling back to her father. She knelt at his feet and begged for his forgiveness. He threw her out and said she was no longer his daughter. Three weeks later, she slit her wrists and died alone."

"Oh God." Sloane felt bile rise in her throat. "Lucy, I don't know what to say. I'm so very, very sorry."

Lucy was weeping. "Meili was my best friend. I miss her so much. But I betrayed her."

"Betrayed her? How?"

"The man I was with when she died—he was worse than the others. He beat me hard every night, held me down and choked me until I blacked out, then threatened to kill me if I told anyone about it. I was so scared. I had to get away. So I took the rest of Meili's money, paid a Dragon Head for safe passage, and had him smuggle me into the U.S. I stole my best friend's money. And for what? To end up with another violent animal? One I was stupid enough to marry?"

"Stop it," Sloane commanded, meaning every single word. "You didn't steal Meili's money. She was gone. And if she'd been alive, she would have gladly given it to save you. You needed help. You're getting it here. You won't ever make the same mistakes again."

"No, I won't," Lucy said emphatically. She wrapped her blanket more tightly around her trembling shoulders. But she managed to meet Sloane's gaze, and there was a tiny flicker of pride in her eyes. "No more drugs. Four months now."

"You should be very proud of yourself, Lucy. You're traveling a long, hard road. But you're making it. You're strong. Meili would be so proud of you. I know I am. And I meant what I said yesterday. If you ever need anything—to talk, to find your way once you've left the shelter—call me. I'll help in any way I can."

Lucy just stared. "I gave you everything I know. Still you'd help me? Why?"

"Because you're a good person."

"So are you." Lucy reached under her blanket, rummaging in the pocket of her pants until she found what she was looking for. "Maybe this will help," she said, extracting a folded photo and handing it to Sloane. "It was taken a few months before Meili died. I've carried it with me ever since."

Sloane glanced down and smoothed out the lines of the photograph. It was Lucy and a smiling, dark-haired girl with the very love and joy on her face that Lucy had alluded to. "Meili?" Sloane confirmed.

"Yes. Stop these men from hurting other women. It will make me very happy. Meili, too—happiness and peace."

"I'll do everything in my power to make that happen," Sloane vowed, rising to her feet. "You have my word. And when I see you again to return this photo, I'll tell you all about what I've done, and you'll know you helped protect others."

CHAPTER

TWENTY-EIGHT

Leo was a wreck.

It had been almost a week since Derek had caught him hastily reassembling Sloane's FBI file. And while he'd perceived no overt changes in either Sloane's or Derek's behavior toward him, he knew the incident hadn't been ignored or forgotten.

If Derek hadn't been suspicious before, he sure as hell was now. Thanks to his own carelessness, Leo was probably right up there at the top of Special Agent Parker's suspect list.

What had possessed him to go through Sloane's file? What he was looking for wouldn't be in there, even if the FBI had compiled full dossiers on each of them. He was a stupid, blind fool, searching for answers that didn't exist.

Even so, if the FBI suspected them of anything more than being in the wrong place at the wrong time and keeping quiet about it out of fear . . . he had to know what that something was, and how deeply and personally each of them was involved.

The tinkle of a bell and the sound of a door shutting at the front of his studio nearly made him leap in the air. His head snapped around in that direction.

He sagged with relief when he saw Phil walking toward him—until he saw the panicky look on Phil's face. Then, the relief vanished.

"What's wrong?" Leo demanded. "Did Derek Parker contact you?"

"Derek Parker?" Phil stared blankly at him, oblivious to everything except his own stark fear. "Why would he contact me?" Awareness penetrated his agitated state. "Are you still obsessing over that stupid file he saw you putting back together? What could he think—that you're clumsy? You are. That you're nosy? You're that, too."

"Or he could think I was searching for incriminating evidence that could land our asses in jail."

Phil gave an impatient wave of his hand. "You've been watching too many spy movies. The FBI is finished with us. Besides, if that file contained anything that pointed in our direction, do you think Sloane would have been stupid enough to leave it in plain sight when she knew you'd be alone in the cottage?" Shifting nervously, Phil wiped beads of perspiration off his forehead. "Leave it alone, Leo. There's enough going on without you inventing more."

"Obviously." Leo turned his attention to his friend. "You look like death warmed over. Is your bookie on your back again?"

"He's not just on my back." Phil drew a shaky breath. "He's threatening me. He says he has friends who could hurt me if I don't pay him by next week."

"Why is he pushing so hard? I just loaned you ten thousand dollars to give him. That should be more than enough of a down payment to calm him down."

Silence.

"Wasn't it?" Leo asked.

"No." Phil was sweating again. "That was a drop in the bucket. You have no idea how much I owe him."

"Well, I'm about to. Give me the grand total."

More silence.

"Phil?" Leo prompted.

"A hundred and twenty-five."

"Thousand?" Leo gasped. "You owe that Albanian crook a hundred and twenty-five thousand dollars?" He slapped his hands on his desk. "Are you out of your mind? None of us has that kind of money lying around. Not even Wallace—not anymore. Plus, you, better than anyone, knows that a withdrawal of that size would have the FBI in our faces in a minute."

Phil sank down on a chair, lowering his head into his hands. "Leo, I don't think he's bluffing. He said his boss is a big shot in an organized-crime group. God knows what they'd do to me. And if you think a huge bank withdrawal would put the FBI on high alert, imagine how they'd react to my being worked over by the Albanian mob."

"Fine. Okay. I hear you." Leo's mind was racing, searching for solutions. "Let me talk to Wallace. He's going to a bunch of cocktail parties with Cindy Liu. I'll be there, too. So will a crowd of rich guests. Maybe if Wallace and I put our heads together, we can come up with something."

Phil's head came up, and a flicker of hope lit his eyes. "When are you going to these parties?"

"They started last week. I've got a half dozen more this week and next. Stall your bookie. I'll come up with something." Leo sighed. "I always do."

"Thanks. I can't tell you how—"

"Save it," Leo interrupted. "After this, I'm dragging you down to a twelve-step program. You're a gambling addict. It's time to confront it once and for all."

"I know." Phil nodded, resigned and utterly depleted. "You won't have to drag me. I'll go."

"And I'll go with you. I won't leave until I'm sure you're sticking it out." Leo glanced over as his cell phone rang. "Now go home and get some rest," he advised, reaching for the phone. "You're about to keel over. Hello," he said into the mouthpiece.

"Mr. Fox?"

"Yes."

"This is Special Agent Williams. New information on the Rothberg provenance has just come to light. I'd appreciate your coming down to the Field Office so we can discuss it."

Leo felt his heart drop to his feet. "What new information?" he asked, wildly beckoning Phil to come back to the front of the studio.

"We'll go over the details when you're here. How does ten o'clock tomorrow morning sound?"

How did it sound? Like an order, not a request. "Ten o'clock is fine. Will all my partners be present?"

"I'll be interviewing you one at a time. It's easier to keep my facts straight that way. I appreciate your cooperation. I'll see you tomorrow at ten A.M."

Click.

White-faced, Leo stared down at his cell as he snapped it shut.

"Was that the FBI?" Phil asked in a tight voice.

"None other." Leo's breath was coming in a nervous, uneven rhythm. "Agent Williams wants to reinterview us. *All* of us. But individually. It seems he has new information on the Rothberg provenance."

"Why individually? And what could he possibly have?"

"I don't know," Leo snapped. "But we're back on his radar again. And that means trouble, any way you slice it."

Just as Phil opened his mouth to reply, his cell phone rang.

He and Leo stared at each other, then at the phone as Phil fished it out of his pocket.

They both knew who was calling.

Cindy slid on a pair of high-heeled shoes and gave a weary sigh.

She was exhausted. A week of cocktail parties. A week of being "on" every evening. And a week of manipulating Wallace to fall even more in love with her.

Peggy had her hands full, too, working 'round the clock on her forgeries so that both the handpicked originals and their identically created fakes could be shipped to China.

The plan was coming together nicely. Xiao Long was putting the information Cindy provided to good use. There'd already been two burglaries since the steady stream of cocktail parties had begun. Both burglaries took place at the private homes of some of the wealthy guests who'd attended the parties, and who'd discussed their art collections with Cindy after hiring her to redesign their manors.

Cindy chose her victims carefully. Never the host and hostess's place. Never a couple who spent an extensively long time alone with her. And never a couple whose collections weren't valuable enough to be worth the trouble.

Leo was both an asset and a pain in the ass. His talent was undeniable, as was his reputation as a world-class decorator. The newly acquired clients practically drooled when they managed to hire Cindy and Leo as a collaborative team.

On the flip side, he never went away. He always had projects to go over with her, or personal conversations he *had* to have with Wallace for just a few minutes—which always turned into a half hour. Cindy needed time alone with Wallace. It was imperative to solidify his feelings for her.

Sighing, she rose and zipped up her dress. Tonight she'd invite Wallace in for an after-party drink. She'd let things progress—gradually. Depending on how avid Wallace was and how much headway she'd made, she might accept his invitation for a weekend in the Hamptons this week or next.

The odd part was she was actually looking forward to sleeping with him.

———

Rich went to see Derek the minute his last meeting with the members of the art partnership was finished.

"Okay, so the results are in," he announced, sitting down across from Derek's desk.

"And?"

"And we've got an interesting potpourri of reactions. They're all nervous wrecks, especially since Rosalyn Burbank's bodyguard was pulled out of the river with a fatal stab wound in his back. That's to be expected. But there's definitely something going on beneath the surface. I'm still convinced it doesn't relate to a dirty deal or a switcheroo on the Rothberg. But the integrity of the players involved—that's another story."

With that, Rich pulled out his notes. "Burbank is the one I have the least problems with. He wasn't surprised by the fact that Xiao Long's criminal activities might be tied to a Chinese triad. He agreed that it would explain Xiao's determination to keep his murdering Cai Wen quiet—to protect whoever he's working for. Burbank himself offered up the theory that in the final hour, Cai Wen probably tried to squeeze Xiao for more money, which got him killed."

"What about Fong? Had Burbank heard of him? Had any dealings with him?"

Rich shook his head. "He drew a blank. And he wasn't lying. The name Henry Fong meant nothing to him. Neither did Daniel Zhang or Zhang Ming."

"So he has no idea where *Dead or Alive* went after Xiao Long stole it." Derek shot Rich a quizzical look. "You didn't get into Lucy's story, did you? Because I promised Sloane we'd keep her out of this. As it is, I put security on both her and Zhang. If Xiao is tied to the Fong Triad, and if he sees either Lucy or Zhang as a threat, he won't hesitate to eliminate them."

"Lucy's name never came up. All I said was that the Rothberg was stolen from whomever Xiao Long got it for, after which it was sold to Zhang. That's all that Burbank, or any of his partners, needs to know."

"Good. What about the others?"

"Ah, the others. Leo Fox was flying on so much caffeine that he was practically on the ceiling. He kept waiting for me to bring up the file you found him rifling at Sloane's. Of course I didn't. It's better to keep him squirming. He didn't react to any of the names I ran by him, either. But he's sitting on something. I'm just not sure whether it relates to Xiao Long or to his partners. He's definitely the Dear Abby of the group. So if anyone has secrets, he knows them."

Rich turned the page and continued. "Phil Leary's an interesting fellow. His professional books are impeccable, but when I brought up how erratic his personal financial statements are, he fell all over himself. After that, he was a basket case. He looked dazed and clueless when I brought up the Fong Triad and Zhang, and when I brought the interview to a close, he spilled his coffee in a race to get out the door. Whatever he does or doesn't know, his actions are certainly consistent with your findings that he's a compulsive gambler."

"Not just compulsive. An addict," Derek corrected. "I verified the extent of his problem through a half-dozen sources. And, yeah, he's loyal to his partners, but you and I both know that addicts sacrifice a lot more than just friends to support their habit. I'm on the verge of finding out his bookie's name. Once I do, I'll get the scumbag to talk, even if I have to throw his ass in jail."

"Sounds like a plan. With regard to Leary, I'm tapped out at my end."

"Fair enough. What about Johnson and Martino?"

"That's where things get more intriguing. Both Johnson and Martino reacted when I mentioned Xiao Long's name. I found that to be fascinating, considering they're the only two partners who weren't in Hong Kong when Cai Wen was murdered. That's why we didn't bother showing them our sketch. And since Xiao is under FBI investigation, we never mentioned his name before now. So any interactions either Martino or Johnson had with him had to be under different circumstances, probably right here in the U.S."

Derek was all ears. "Did you get the feeling they were in this together or separately?"

"Not sure."

"Under what contexts did each of them react?"

"Martino wasn't totally sober. When I asked him about Fong and Zhang, he claimed not to know them. But then he went on to slur a bunch of stuff about being sick to death of all this Chinese organized crime. That's when I slipped in Xiao's name. He started shaking and sweating, and looking around like he'd kill for a drink. So I dropped the bomb that Xiao Long was the one who stole the Rothberg and killed Cai Wen. I thought he was going to either vomit or pass out at my feet. He definitely knows the guy. Does that association relate to the Rothberg? It's possible. As for Zhang and the triad, I'll run Martino's name by Daniel Zhang and see what he says. Either way, Martino warrants further investigation."

"He's at the top of my list." Derek's hands balled into fists. "What about Johnson?"

"Wallace Johnson is a complicated man. Smart. Polished. Quite adept at keeping a poker face. But he made no secret of the fact that he was displeased about holding our follow-up interview, or discussing the ongoing art thefts at all."

"Any reaction to Fong's or Zhang's name?"

"He said he vaguely knew of the Fong Triad, that he'd heard of them during his numerous business trips to China. But he added that he'd never met any of the members personally, Zhang included. I doubt he's lying. He's too shrewd not to know I could easily check out his story with Zhang. Then I dropped Xiao Long's name. Despite his best attempts to cover up his reaction, he was taken aback. He asked me if Xiao was suspected of being part of the Fong Triad. I evaded the question, but told him that Xiao had killed Cai Wen and stolen the Rothberg. Again, he tried to take it all in stride, but he was thrown for a loop. It could be personal. Maybe Xiao screwed him over in an art deal."

"Maybe. Or maybe Johnson and/or Martino are involved in something illegal."

"Yeah." Rich blew out a breath. "Between this information, and the recent home invasions and art thefts, we certainly have our work cut out for us."

"You've done your job with Burbank and his partners. The next step's mine." Derek picked up the reports he'd been reading when Rich came in, then tossed them across his desk in disgust. "Three damned break-ins in one week. All at affluent homes. And even though Xiao Long organized them, these robberies were definitely *not* committed by the Red Dragons. Windows smashed to gain entry. Burglar alarms ignored. Home owners all present, with no attempts made by the intruders to wait for the houses to be empty. All residents held at gunpoint and restrained with Flex-Cufs. Thieves who wore masks, spoke with accents, and were in and out by the time the cops arrived—in under ten minutes, according to the victims. And nothing taken except valuable paintings. Your Black Eagles strike again. With one charming addition, courtesy of Xiao Long."

"Yeah, the empty fortune cookie left at each home." Rich scowled. "This burglary ring is not only practicing for their pièce de résistance, they're taunting us, demonstrating our ineffectiveness at stopping them."

"Xiao Long knows we've linked him to the Albanians. But he's flaunting our lack of proof."

"We'll get some," Rich vowed. "We'll nail our triad, and connect them to the Albanians and to Xiao Long."

CHAPTER
TWENTY-NINE

Derek started with Ben Martino.

His gut instinct had always been that Martino was the weakest link. So Derek had decided to save his visit to Wallace Johnson for later, and see if he could rattle Martino and get some information.

He waited until two o'clock. That meant lunchtime was over, and Martino had doubtless had his share of drinks, and then some. The consequence of that would be lowered defenses and a looser tongue.

Wearing jeans and a T-shirt, Derek hung out near Martino's manufacturing factory on East Broadway until a delivery boy finally exited the building.

Derek approached him, jerking his thumb in the direction of the factory. "Hey, I have to see Martino about an order for my company. Is he in there now?"

"Yeah," the teenager replied, barely breaking stride or glancing up. "He's in the front office."

"Thanks." Derek had his answer. He also had the very thing he'd hoped for going for him—the element of surprise.

He headed inside.

Ben Martino was right where the delivery boy had said. Through the office's glass pane, Derek could see him standing up and throwing papers around on his desk. He was in a visibly agitated state, and pretty loaded, too, judging from the uncapped, half-empty bottle of whiskey on his desk that he was taking repeated swigs from.

Derek gave a brief knock and walked in.

"What?" Martino snapped, not abandoning his paper-hurling, not even glancing up.

"Mr. Martino, I'd like a few minutes of your time."

Now, Martino's head snapped up. He gazed at Derek through glazed, bloodshot eyes. "Do I know you?" he asked in a slightly slurred voice.

"Special Agent Derek Parker," Derek replied.

It took a minute. "Sloane's boyfriend. Right." Martino shook Derek's hand. His palm was shaking and sweaty, and his expression reminded Derek of a nervous rabbit at the wrong end of a shotgun.

"I'm here in my official capacity." Derek wasted no time, getting to the point and utilizing the intimidation factor. "I'm sure Matthew Burbank told you I'm working the Chinese organized-crime angle of the Rothberg case."

"Yes, he did. So did that other agent—Williams. He asked me all about some triad leaders in Hong Kong. I didn't know what the heck he was talking about. I'm not exactly an expert on what goes on in China."

"Good point. Now that I think about it, you weren't even there when your partners sold *Dead or Alive* to Cai Wen—or after the transaction, when he was killed and the painting was stolen."

Martino shook his head. "My father had just had a stroke. I was here in New York with him." An awkward laugh. "I sure missed all the excitement."

"You sure did. You and Wallace Johnson. He was away on a business trip when the ugly mess went down." Derek went out on a limb and feigned knowledge he didn't have. "But he did check in on you when he returned— you and your father."

Sure enough, Martino nodded. "He was concerned. He dropped by the hospital."

"Very considerate." A quizzical look. "Are you two close friends?"

Martino swallowed so hard his Adam's apple visibly rose and fell. "We're all good friends. We have been since college."

"True. But I get the feeling that you and Johnson have a unique bond."

"We do . . . We did . . . We don't talk about it anymore." Although Martino was stumbling on his words, he was clearly providing a lot more information than he would have if he were sober. "Wallace desperately wanted a child. No one understood that better than me. My family, my kids and grandkids— they mean everything. But Wallace and Beatrice had a rough time conceiving. I introduced them to a specialist. He performed a procedure. It worked. When Sophie was born, Wallace made me her godfather. She was the sun, the moon, and the stars to him." Tears glittered in Martino's eyes, and, disregarding Derek's presence, he took a gulp from his whiskey bottle. "I'm sure you know she was killed in a hit-and-run accident."

"Yes, I did. She was only five. That's a tragedy no parent should have to bear. I'm sure you rallied around Johnson, gave him your time and emotional support."

"I tried. We all did. But Wallace has never been the same." Martino took another drink, then deposited the bottle, now two-thirds empty, onto his desk.

Derek's gaze followed its path. "Do you always drink during the workday?"

"What?" Martino started, and then a flush crept up his neck as he struggled to switch gears. "In case you missed it, the garment center's dying. I've got a business I'm fighting to keep alive—one my father started years ago. So, yeah, I have a couple drinks now and then to calm my nerves."

"A couple?" Derek arched a pointed brow at the near-empty bottle. "I'd say you have a lot more than that."

"Fine," Martino snapped. "I drink. I doubt that comes as a big surprise to you."

"You're right. It doesn't. Based on your police record, you lost your license for six months after a DWI back in 2004. And the bars in midtown have been seeing quite a lot of you these days."

Martino turned a sickly shade of green. "So I have an on-again, off-again drinking problem."

"It's certainly on-again these days," Derek observed.

"I just told you, I'm under a lot of pressure." There was no doubt that Martino was unraveling—fast. "Why are you here? Am I being accused of something because of my drinking? Because I haven't gotten behind the wheel of a car after having even one drink—not in years."

"You're not being accused of anything," Derek assured him, making a mental note of Martino's paranoia about his drinking. "I was just acknowledging the challenge you face. Especially since the garment industry is shifting to China big-time."

"It's their cheap labor," Martino muttered, glancing through the glass window that overlooked the floor of his factory. "It's hard to come by here."

"Especially when the workers you hire are legal," Derek probed with a pointed statement, having followed Martino's stare and noting the rows of Asian women hard at work on their sewing machines. "You seem to have that problem well covered. A factory full of hard workers, who probably command little more than minimum wage."

"It's a win-win situation," Martino responded quickly. "They work hard, and, you're right, it doesn't cost me an arm and a leg to keep them. But their pay is more than fair. There isn't exactly a slew of job opportunities waiting for them. Most of them can't speak a word of English."

"Really. So how do you find them?"

Martino was sweating. He shot a sidelong look at the whiskey bottle, clearly itching to take another drink. "The usual. Word of mouth. Referrals. Employment agencies."

Interesting that employment agencies was the last thing Martino had mentioned—and he'd done so with great reluctance. He was looking at the whiskey bottle again, this time his gaze flickering nervously to its base.

Derek's gaze followed suit. Currently acting as a coaster for Martino's whiskey bottle were a couple of business cards. They were identical, both with the words SIH FU EMPLOYMENT AGENCY printed on them, along with some other information Derek couldn't make out, half of which was in English, half in Chinese.

Sih Fu Employment Agency. That name rang a bell. And for good reason. Xiao Long owned it.

One thing was for sure. Xiao never formed a business relationship that

didn't earn him a hefty profit. So there had to be more to this arrangement than met the eye. Xiao had to be bleeding Martino dry, using either
the threat of having Martino's bones broken by Jin Huang, or the threat of
an anonymous tip being made to the cops that Ben Martino was hiring
illegals.

Either way, Martino was screwed.

And either way, it was no coincidence that Xiao Long had chosen him as a
victim, any more than it was a coincidence that Xiao was involved with Wallace Johnson in some capacity as well.

There was an underlying pattern here, one that Derek was determined to
unravel.

Next stop, Wallace Johnson.

———————

Derek was heading toward Johnson's midtown art gallery when he flipped
open his cell phone and called Jeff on speed dial.

"Hey." Jeff recognized Derek's cell phone number. "What's up?"

"A lot. Most of which I'm still putting together. But get this. Ben Martino
is hiring his workers from the Sih Fu Employment Agency."

Jeff whistled. "There's your tie to Xiao. Rent-an-illegal."

"More like rent an illegal today, get squeezed and threatened tomorrow."

"Threatened with what—violence? Bringing down the business?"

"Or something bigger. I'm on my way to Johnson's gallery. I'm sure he's
expecting me, since Martino probably called him the minute I walked out
the door. Could you do a little digging for me?"

"Not a problem. I'll find out how long Martino and Xiao have been doing
business, and how the relationship got started. Also if Johnson is part of the
equation. And speaking of digging, Rich and I have both talked to our contacts at the Hong Kong police. There's no record of a suicide involving a
woman in her early to mid-twenties matching Meili's description—not as
Meili Somebody or Jane Doe."

"So someone's covering it up."

"That's our take. We're pushing to find out who. I'm also putting some of
our informants out on the streets to see if Xiao Long's name is linked to a girl

named Meili. He's been running his gang here since the mid-nineties, slowly growing his empire. Now we're pretty sure it's triad-funded. In which case, he'd be tight enough with the right people to find out if the Rothberg he'd killed for had been ripped off and sold to Henry Fong."

"Or *resold* to Fong," Derek amended. "If the Fong Triad is the one Xiao's working with, this Meili could have gone to Zhang because she knew Fong would want his stolen painting back. But you're right. We've got to follow up on this Meili lead. She's our tie to the Rothberg, and to whomever Xiao gave it to."

"And whoever that is is now funding Xiao and the Black Eagles."

"Right." Derek glanced up as a group of pedestrians crossed the street. "I gotta go. Let me know what you dig up on Martino and Xiao's employment agency. I'll see what I can find out from Johnson. I know this case seems like a giant can of worms. But my gut still tells me it's all part of one big puzzle. We've just got to get our hands on the right pieces, and then figure out how they fit together."

———

Derek was right about Ben grabbing his cell phone the instant Derek left.

But he was wrong about who Ben called.

His first call was to Xiao Long. He had to warn him that the FBI was piecing things together, or Xiao would send that big ape Jin Huang over to break his legs. Or worse—do it himself. Jin Huang was a hefty, menacing guy. But Xiao called the shots. And he had an icy coldness about him that was eerily terrifying. It was as if the man had no soul.

Ben wasn't pushing him any more than he had to. Besides, he'd find out about Derek Parker's visit anyway; Xiao Long had eyes everywhere. Better the news should come directly from him.

Xiao wasn't happy. But he wasn't surprised either. In broken English, he told Ben to go on as usual, keep his mouth shut, and leave the rest to him.

Ben didn't even want to know what that meant.

His second call was to Phil. He'd never wanted to make this call, but the time had come. His choices were nil. And he was just drunk enough to get it all out before he changed his mind.

Almost all of it.

"Phil, I need your help," he began, the minute his friend answered.

"You're drunk," Phil replied.

"And getting drunker by the minute. Listen to me. You're the numbers genius. I don't know where else to turn. I'm being squeezed, and I can't get out of it."

Phil gave an ironic laugh.

Ben didn't even hear it. "I've been getting my workers from the same Asian employment agency for years. A couple of years ago it was taken over by another company. Their prices were great, so I stuck with them. Then I found out why they were so cheap. Without my knowing it, they'd been sending me illegals. When I tried to break off the relationship, they tripled their prices and threatened to tip off the cops if I opened my mouth. They've been upping the prices ever since. I've sold off everything I can. I'm about to go bankrupt."

"You've got company. I'm in a major financial hole. So if you're looking for a loan, there's no way . . ."

"I don't want a loan. I want a solution. Because it gets worse. Sloane's boyfriend just left the factory. Besides mentioning my DWI and asking questions about Wallace and me not being there when you sold the Rothberg, he spotted the agency's business cards on my desk. He must know they're dirty. So I'm going bankrupt for nothing. I'll end up in jail or dead on the street anyway."

"Did he actually say he saw the business cards or knew the agency is crooked? Or are you just overreacting because you're wasted?"

"I don't know . . . I don't know." Ben dropped his head to his hands. "But I'm not kidding about being dead on the street. If Parker keeps poking around, the crooked bastards I'm dealing with are going to kill me. Without batting an eye, they'll cut me into little pieces, toss me in a Dumpster, and go out for noodles."

"Slow down, Ben. Get a grip. And let me think." A long, drawn-out pause. "Actually, I might have an idea."

"What?"

"Give me a little time to work this through. I'll call you back in a couple hours. I might just have the answer to both our problems. Now go drink some coffee and sober up."

Ben flipped his phone shut. He should be relieved. And on some level, he was. But the answer to all his problems? Not a prayer. There were some things that could never be fixed.

He didn't need coffee. He needed absolution.

Derek left Johnson's gallery an hour later. The man was smooth. Derek might have learned nothing if Jeff hadn't called right after the meeting, as Derek was wolfing down two hot dogs. But now he had two solid links.

It wasn't the whole picture.

But it was enough to convince him that it was time Sloane knew what he was up to.

Sloane let herself into the cottage, automatically squatting down to greet the hounds as they came tearing around the corner, leaping and yipping with pleasure. It had been a fine evening for them. Derek had come home early and romped with them in the den for a good half hour before taking them out for a jog. Now, Sloane was home, also earlier than usual, which meant another round of attention. Life was good.

"Hey, you." Derek walked out of the bedroom, wearing only a pair of jeans, a towel wrapped around his neck. His hair was still damp from the shower he'd taken. He leaned down and kissed Sloane hello, holding her for just a minute before letting go.

"Okay, that shoots my first theory to hell," Sloane commented. "When you called and asked me to come home early, I was half expecting a candlelight dinner, or at least another lovemaking tour of the house. But that kiss and the look on your face tell me it's neither."

A rueful smile. "I only wish." He gestured toward the living room. "We need to talk."

Sloane followed him, a wary expression on her face. "I don't like the sound of that."

"You're going to like it even less once I'm finished," Derek replied as they sank down on the sofa. "Just hear me out, think objectively like the professional you are, and leave our feelings for each other out of it."

"In other words, you did something to protect me, and never said a word."

"Sort of, yes. But it wasn't only about protecting you. It was about working this case and getting answers to the anomalies that have been bugging me."

Sloane eyed him shrewdly. "Those anomalies don't happen to be my father's partners, do they? Because I thought we'd put to rest any involvement on their part once Anna came forward with her information."

"*You* did. *I* didn't. There were too many questions still unanswered."

"And now you've answered them?"

"In part. Enough so that I felt it was time to come to you and fill you in. It's still very much a work in progress."

Sloane folded her hands in her lap. "Is Rich in on your theory? Is that the reason he questioned my father and each of his partners again? Because I was told those interviews pertained to any knowledge they might have of the Fong Triad."

"It was. I just asked Rich to throw in a few extra questions, mentioning Xiao Long's name and an implication of his involvement in this case—just to gauge their reactions."

"And?"

"And both Johnson and Martino reacted. Odd, considering they weren't in Hong Kong when their partners sold the Rothberg and Cai Wen was killed. When Rich told them the name of the killer, they were visibly taken aback. The name Xiao Long struck a chord. So I paid each of them a visit today."

Sloane listened silently as Derek relayed his entire conversation with Ben to her. He omitted nothing, including Ben's drunken state, his defensiveness about his relationship with Wallace, and his agitated reaction to Derek's reference to hiring illegal workers. Derek concluded with the business cards, the fact that Xiao Long owned the employment agency, and the probability that he was squeezing Ben.

Then came Wallace, who, during his interview with Derek, claimed that he was appalled by the whole idea of his art partnership inadvertently dealing with organized crime, and who'd fervently said he wished he'd been in Hong Kong during the Rothberg transaction, since he was the one most likely to smell a rat.

Afterward, Jeff's phone call revealed the interesting fact that both the computer systems at Wallace's galleries were serviced by none other than Eric Hu's company. Further, Hu had been referred to Wallace by an art appraiser who—surprise, surprise—worked for Xiao Long.

Sloane was quiet when Derek finished, her gaze lowered as she fidgeted with her hands.

"Sloane?" Derek prompted.

"I wish I could say I'm shocked," she surprised him by saying. "But I'm not. It occurred to me more than once that Xiao Long was holding something over my father's friends. When Anna came forward and exonerated them from aiding Xiao in the break-in, I was so relieved. I assumed my suspicions had been wrong. I *wanted* them to be wrong. But I couldn't stop thinking about the night of the poker game. Ben was such a wreck. I could tell he'd started drinking again. And Wallace . . ." Sloane swallowed. "He was in physical pain. Stiff. Wincing. Sweating. He claimed he was getting the flu. He looked like he'd been in a brawl—and lost." Another pause. "Answer me honestly—do you think it's more than Ben and Wallace who are involved?"

"It's possible." Derek went on to tell Sloane about walking in and finding Leo shoving papers back in her FBI file last week. "That's not necessarily a sign of personal guilt," he qualified. "Maybe he was looking for something that would protect his friends. As for Phil, he's a gambling addict. I don't know how far he'd go to support his habit."

"Including fraternizing with organized crime," Sloane said tonelessly. Her chin came up, and she met Derek's gaze head-on. "What about my father?"

"Rich and I see no sign that he's done anything illegal. I can't speak to what he knows, only what he's done."

Sloane nodded. "I understand why you kept this from me until now. I've been in denial. But no more. I want to know how Xiao Long inserted himself into each of their lives, and why."

CHAPTER THIRTY

Phil had thought through everything long and hard.

His plan was a winner. It would get Ben out from behind the eight ball, force the employment agency to stop squeezing him, and rattle them enough to accept Phil's proposal and pay his fifty-thousand-dollar consulting fee.

It wouldn't cover his entire debt, only a third. But that was just the beginning. Having found the right Achilles' heel, he'd capitalize on it, expand the creative services he provided. And that would mean subsequent payments.

In the meantime, fifty thousand dollars would be a healthy first installment—enough to keep Ardian Sava, his bastard of a bookie, from giving the go-ahead to break a few of his body parts.

Phil glanced at his watch. Nine-thirty P.M. Too late for even Ben to still be at work.

He called him at home.

Ben answered on the first ring, dropped the receiver twice, then put it to his ear. "Hello?" he mumbled.

"It's me," Phil said, wishing Ben's garbled tone meant he'd been sleeping, not drinking. But no such luck.

"Phil—finally. I've been waiting for you to—"

"Here's what I want you to do," Phil interrupted. "Go stand in the shower under a cold spray of water until you sober up. Then call that new owner of the employment agency who's bleeding you dry, and broker a meeting between him and us."

"*Us?*" Ben might be drunk, but he wasn't unconscious. "I can't do that."

"Why not?"

Silence. Whether it was because Ben had a legitimate basis for his objection, or he was trying to clear his mind, Phil wasn't sure.

"Why can't you do that?" he pressed.

"Because . . ." Another pause. "What do you want me to say—that my accountant wants to have a nice chat with him about bringing down his prices so I don't go bankrupt, and so he holds off sending over a thug to bash my head in?"

"Just tell him I'm your partner, that I handle the company's finances, and that I have a winning business proposition for him that'll settle your debts and benefit his agency."

"Phil, this isn't a guy you want to screw over."

"I'm not screwing him over. I'm proposing a deal. He'll either take it or leave it. But I have a feeling he'll take it. The fact that he keeps raising your prices tells me so. He needs the cash. And he's a shrewd operator who'll look out for his own best interests. We'll use both to our advantage."

"His English sucks."

"He'll understand the universal language: money." Phil talked over Ben's continued objections. "Just trust me and do it. Tell him he can pick the time and place—so long as it's private. Let me know the details once he decides them."

"It isn't that simple."

"Actually, it is."

"Phil, he doesn't *need* the cash. He *wants* the cash."

"Fine. So he's not hurting, he's greedy. That works, too. I'll offer him a strong incentive—a couple of them, in fact. Now go take that shower. And don't come out until your mind is crystal clear. Then make the call."

Ben stared at the receiver long after the dial tone signaled that Phil had hung up.

He should have told him. He'd tried to, several times. But Phil had cut him off.

Who was he kidding? If he'd wanted to tell his friend, he would have found a way. But Phil had seemed so damned confident that he could make his plan work.

Ben squeezed his eyes shut. He was a fucking coward. Phil deserved to know that the mob leader he was asking to negotiate with was the same one who'd killed Cai Wen and stolen the Rothberg. Ben hadn't been in Hong Kong that day. But Phil had. He might have gotten a good look at Xiao Long. He might recognize him.

Or he might not.

Even if he'd clearly seen Xiao as he left the crime scene, the murder had happened fourteen years ago. People's appearances changed. The only reason Matthew had recognized Xiao Long that night in Chinatown was because Xiao had planted himself in Matthew's face for the sole purpose of being recognized. Otherwise, they might have walked right by each other and never batted a lash.

And if Phil *didn't* recognize Xiao Long, and if this plan of his really did work, it would be a godsend. It would free Ben from both financial and physical demise. No more debt. No more terror of being dismembered by Jin Huang. And it would mean a pretty penny for Phil, as well.

On that thought, his decision was made.

God help him if it was the wrong one.

Peggy waited until she heard Wallace leave before she came downstairs to talk to Cindy.

"It looks like we've both been busy tonight," Peggy commented drily, noting Cindy rearranging her clothes and combing her fingers through her hair.

Cindy gave a faint smile. "Things are definitely heating up on all fronts. I got two new projects tonight. I met a charming couple from Bronxville who collect Picasso and Matisse. And I agreed to accompany Wallace to his East Hampton estate this weekend. So I've got more commissioned jobs than I know what to do with, Xiao Long has another profitable target to hit, and Wallace is so captivated by me he can't even see straight." She finished buttoning the top of her blouse. "He's more like an ardent teenager than a middle-aged man."

Observing the sparkle in Cindy's eyes and the high color on her cheeks, Peggy said, "This game with Wallace is becoming less of an act and more of a reality. You're starting to care for the man."

Cindy's fingers paused on her collar. "I find him attractive and intelligent. I doubt any woman would object to the gifts, adoration, and attention he's lavishing on me. And truthfully, I feel a little sorry for him. I know what he did to Meili, and I don't blame my A Sook for despising and wanting to ruin him. But in all fairness, it was *she* who dumped *him*. Wallace has no idea how hard she took their break-up, or that she found out she was pregnant after it was over. I believe he would have taken care of her and the baby. He's an honorable man. And losing his five-year-old daughter—isn't that punishment enough?"

"He didn't just lose her," Peggy amended quietly. "She was killed. By an anonymous hit-and-run driver. Three months after Meili took her own life. Do you really believe that was a coincidence?"

Cindy's fingers faltered for a moment, and then continued smoothing her hair off her face. "Of course not. I'm not a fool. I know my A Sook. It's an eye for an eye. But we've never spoken about Sophie's death. I never intend to ask him outright. Because, frankly, I don't want to hear the answer."

"It was easier when Wallace Johnson was a faceless name, wasn't it?"

"Yes." Cindy nodded. "Now he's a flesh-and-blood human being. But I'll do what I have to. I gave my word. It's my A Sook's dying wish."

"I know." Peggy dropped the subject. "When I said we were both busy tonight, I meant it. The Renoir is complete. I finished it while you were at the cocktail party."

"Excellent. I'm sure it's a flawless duplicate. They always are." Cindy hurried to the stairs. "I can't wait to see it."

"Do you want me to make the arrangements?"

Cindy paused on the first step, considering the situation from every angle. "Not yet," she decided. "I'll call my *A Sook* and give him an update. It has to be his decision. With the FBI sniffing around, he might want to wait until Xiao gets his hands on all the outstanding paintings, and then send the entire shipment together. On the other hand, he might want the original Renoir out of the U.S. right away. Everything has to be timed just so. The pièce de résistance is coming up fast."

Outside the Jaspar Museum of Art on Crosby Street in Soho, the Albanian art student shot a few additional pictures with her still camera. She'd already taken a ton of digital photos inside the museum, and written notes to accompany each photo.

Soon her assignment would be complete.

Phil met Ben at two A.M. outside a hole-in-the-wall gambling dive in Chinatown.

"That was fast," Phil commented, looking very pleased. "Four hours after your phone call. Evidently, your employment company owner is eager to do business."

Once again, Ben opened his mouth to tell Phil the truth. He probably would have gone through with it this time. They were already walking into the lobby, and he doubted Phil would turn back. But an Asian teenager with a scar on his face approached them and wordlessly beckoned them to follow.

The back room was dimly lit and consisted of a few round tables, all of which were empty, save one.

Xiao Long was wearing a jacket, no tie. His hands were folded on the table, and his face, cloaked by shadows, was expressionless.

Ben shot Phil a sideways glance. No reaction. Good.

"Sit," Xiao said without preamble. "Martino said you take care of money and that you have business deal. Describe."

Phil and Ben each pulled back a chair and sat.

"It's very simple," Phil explained. "You're right. I handle the money. Ben handles the day-to-day business. In checking our books, I saw that, each month, he's been paying you more and more for your workers. That's hurting the business. So I came to the factory to see why. I figured out the girls are all illegals. That's a big problem. ICE is conducting major investigations to crack down on illegals. And they're taking action. Not just deporting the girls. Putting the employers in jail."

Xiao barely blinked. "You are employers. Your crime."

"Partly." Phil didn't dispute Xiao's claim. "There's no doubt we're at risk. But so are you. You hire the help. My partner rents them. We could all go to jail. I doubt any of us wants that."

"You bring solution?"

"Yes. I'm not just a certified accountant. I'm also a certified financial planner. It's like a business adviser. I'm good at protecting my clients and increasing their profits. You could become one of those clients. I know lots of people. Rich people. I'd send you to all the right customers. Customers who need many hard workers. Customers who don't need their workers to speak English. Customers who pay top dollar and don't ask questions. And I could fix your financial records so everything looks legal. You'd make a fortune. And you'd make it fast."

Again, no change in expression. "And you get?"

"To start with, a fifty-thousand-dollar consulting fee, to be renegotiated based on your profits. And a receipt saying that all Ben's and my company debts have been paid in full. Of course, you'd keep charging us for our workers, so everything looks legal. But you'd reduce your rate—a lot. We'd call it a bulk discount."

Phil stopped, waiting for a reaction.

"Fifty thousand," Xiao Long said thoughtfully. "You very confident."

"I'm very good at what I do."

"So am I." Xiao pushed back his chair and rose. "I think. You hear from me."

"Fair enough." Phil stood up as well. Ben was already on his feet, eager to get the hell out of there.

As Phil reached out to shake Xiao's hand, the teenager who'd showed them in opened the door to escort them out.

A shaft of light flashed across Xiao's face.

Phil's hand paused, and his brows drew together. "Have we met? You look familiar."

A hint of a smile. "Not met. Seen. Ask any of your partners. Ask Burbank."

All the color drained from Phil's face, and his arm fell limply to his side. "Oh my God."

Xiao's smile didn't waver. "Also, word to the wise. Fifty thousand not nearly enough to pay Ardian Sava. You owe lot more. Albanians no like to wait for money. Good-bye, Mr. Leary."

CHAPTER
THIRTY-ONE

Xiao Long's gaze bore into Leary's and Martino's backs as they walked rigidly out of the back room.

He was livid. Even so, the white-faced shock that had registered on Leary's face had been worth the wasted time he'd spent listening to Leary's bullshit and looking at that pathetic, drunken partner of his who hadn't even had the guts to tell Leary who he was meeting with.

Xiao had taken care of that forgotten detail himself.

He might as well enjoy the results.

With that goal, Xiao made his way out of the back room and slipped into a far, dark corner of the gambling parlor. Silently, he watched Leary and Martino make their exit. Sweat was pouring down Leary's face and neck. The back of his shirt was drenched. And Martino looked like a chicken about to get its neck wrung.

Martino's neck would come later.

But Leary—he was another story. He'd just made Xiao Long angry. Very angry. Xiao, who was next in line to head the Liu Jian Triad. Xiao, who had more power than Leary could begin to imagine. Xiao, whose brains and ambition were second to none, save his Dragon Head.

No one squeezed him for money. No one issued ultimatums, not to him. Especially not some stupid, ego-inflated accountant with a gambling problem and no backbone.

This meeting changed everything. Xiao would push up one element of the timetable. Revise the order he'd planned for the executions. The Dragon Head would agree. Leary's mental torture was complete. The final blow had been dealt when Xiao let him know that Sava was in his pocket. Now, Leary had outlived his usefulness. It was time for him to endure an agonizing death.

Xiao felt the familiar surge of adrenaline and excitement.

This was what he'd been waiting for.

He retraced his steps into the back room and made the phone call.

Phil went straight to his office. He sure as hell wasn't going home. God only knew who was waiting for him there.

He poured himself a drink and wiped the sweat off his neck and face with his sleeve. What the hell had Ben been thinking? Dealing with Xiao Long, and not telling Phil—not even after he knew who Xiao really was? The animal wasn't just a bloodsucking mobster. He was a killer. A killer who was after their entire art investment partnership. Not to mention arranging a hit on Rosalyn Burbank and stabbing her bodyguard to death in the process.

Phil had to call the FBI—now. His gambling debt didn't matter. Nothing mattered. His life was on the line. Xiao Long knew Ardian Sava's name. That meant the slimy Albanian bookie was in his pocket. There was no way out.

He sat down behind his desk and picked up the telephone receiver.

He'd barely pressed the first button when the door to his office was kicked open. Two armed men with stocking masks burst inside, submachine guns raised. Phil didn't have time to make a sound. Both men opened fire instantly.

Phil's body jerked from the impact as the spray of bullets riddled through him.

His chair toppled backward, and he was left sprawled on the carpet, dead, blood oozing everywhere.

Removing the silencers from their weapons, the Albanian killers checked to be sure their target was dead. Then, they turned to his desk. They took what they needed, planted what they'd brought, and altered what needed to be altered.

Calmly, Xiao Long strolled into the office in their wake, and walked directly behind the desk. He stood over Leary's dead body, watching his blood ooze out and pool on the floor. An annoying, high-pitched beep echoed from the telephone receiver dangling from the desk. Xiao had no doubt that Leary's attempted phone call was being made to spill his guts to the FBI.

So much for that plan.

After pulling on his gloves, Xiao picked up the receiver and replaced it in its cradle.

Then, he reached in his pocket and yanked out the piano wire he carried with him. He squatted down and wrapped the wire around Leary's limp, blood-soaked neck. He pulled on the bamboo handles. Tight. So tight he felt as if he were killing the guy all over again.

He closed his eyes, savoring the sense of power for himself and retribution for his Dragon Head.

Long moments passed. Having wrung every last drop of satisfaction from his victory, Xiao released Leary's neck, letting his body slump to the floor. Blood was spreading out everywhere.

Xiao rose and took a few steps backward. One of the Albanians took some quick digital photos and handed the camera to Xiao. He would share the photos with his Dragon Head immediately.

Then, he turned and walked away, giving a terse nod to the Black Eagles as he exited the room.

A minute later, they followed suit. Having carried out their orders, they left the scene—and what was left of Phil's body—shutting the office door behind them.

CHAPTER
THIRTY-TWO

Derek left the cottage at dawn the next morning, heading straight to midtown Manhattan. He planned on marching into Phil Leary's office, unannounced and unyielding, and planting himself in the man's face until he got answers.

He and Sloane had been asleep when Derek's cell phone rang at two forty-five A.M. It was the members of Derek's C-6 team who were assigned to surveillance that night. Ben Martino and Phil Leary had been spotted in Chinatown, exiting a gambling house that belonged to Xiao Long. Both men were visibly upset. They'd walked half a block, then halted, arguing vehemently. A short time later, Leary had stormed off, and Martino had trudged, head lowered, into a nearby bar.

This was one gambling casino Leary hadn't visited to place bets, Derek had thought grimly. He'd gone to help get Martino out of the hole he was in. Interesting that Martino had chosen Leary to run to. Derek had expected it would have been Johnson.

On the other hand, Leary was a logical choice. He might be a walking financial disaster personally, but professionally he was sharp as a tack. And he was Martino's accountant.

Armed with a slew of questions and a gut feeling he was getting closer to the truth, Derek left his car in a parking garage and walked the three blocks to Leary's office.

He slowed down as he reached the building, his brows drawing together as he saw the bustle of activity going on outside. A bunch of spectators were standing around on the sidewalk, and there were two NYPD cars blocking traffic. As Derek watched, a body bag was carried out, transferred to the back of an Emergency Medical Services vehicle, and driven off.

He jostled his way through the crowd and up to the entranceway, where a cop was posted to keep everyone out.

"FBI," Derek said quietly, displaying his ID to the officer.

The cop stepped aside so Derek could enter.

"What floor?" Derek asked.

"Twelfth."

Leary's floor.

"Thanks." Derek opened the door and made his way through the lobby.

He rode the elevator up, then strode down the hall to where all the activity was taking place.

The yellow tape sealing off Leary's office told Derek it was the crime scene.

There were three or four NYPD detectives at work, and CSI was inside, gathering evidence and examining the room with a fine-tooth comb.

"Special Agent Parker, FBI." Derek flashed his ID to the first detective he ran into. "What's going on?"

The detective glanced at Derek's ID and blinked in surprise. "Detective Hill, Midtown North," he identified himself. "Why was the FBI called in? It looks like we've got a routine homicide here."

"Not so routine." A second detective corrected his partner as he ducked out from under the tape and stepped into the hall. "The victim was pummeled with bullets. The spray pattern identifies the weapon as an automatic." He turned to Derek. "Agent Parker, you said? I'm Detective Kramer."

"Kramer." Derek shook his hand. "I'm not here to step on your toes. It's likely this homicide is part of an FBI investigation. If not, the case is all yours."

"I'm not worried." As a seasoned NYPD detective, Kramer waved away Derek's clarification. "The victim's name was Philip Leary. An accountant and financial adviser. Looks like he was working all night—or planned to. According to the M.E., the time of death was between three and five A.M. The whole thing must have happened in seconds. The victim barely had time to look up. His door was kicked in. The killers opened fire from the doorway, probably using silencers. Based on the angles of penetration, there were two shooters. And one of them was a psycho besides being a killer. He choked the victim with a piano wire, so hard it sliced open his neck. And he did it posthumously."

Derek recognized the calling card. "Was anything taken?" he asked.

"Not that we can tell so far. We've only been on the scene for an hour. The call came into the precinct at six-ten. A couple of guys from the early morning cleaning crew found him. They were smart enough not to touch anything." Kramer's forehead creased in thought. "Personally, I'd love to know why *two* guys with automatic weapons would murder an average accountant, and then choke the hell out of him afterward."

"Yeah, so would I."

<hr>

It was midmorning when Derek called Sloane. He knew she didn't normally listen to the local news, but he wanted to get to her just in case.

She was in the backyard, doing major damage to her archery target while racking her brain trying to think of ways to find Meili's American lover, when her phone rang.

She was fully aware of where Derek was, and with whom, as well as what he hoped to accomplish. Quickly, she put down her archery equipment and flipped open her phone.

"Hi. Any news?" she asked.

"Where are you?" Derek answered her question with one of his own.

Something about Derek's tone formed a knot in Sloane's stomach. "In the backyard. On the archery course. Why?"

"Because I have some tough news. I wanted to make sure you were alone when I shared it with you. Especially since you'll want to be the one who tells your father."

"Okay."

Derek didn't try to sugarcoat it. There was no way to cushion this kind of blow.

"Phil Leary was killed last night in his office. Some time between three and five A.M., a couple of guys kicked in his office door and shot him with automatic weapons. After that, he was choked with a piano wire. I've been with the Midtown North detectives and my squad the whole morning."

"Oh God." Sloane sank down on the grass. "Do we know who ordered the hit?"

"All signs point to that bookie of Phil's I was trying to hunt down. Name's Ardian Sava. As it turns out, he's part of an Albanian crime syndicate in the Bronx. With regard to specific evidence linking him to the murder, Phil's gambling records were found in a locked drawer in his desk. The numbers showed he owed Sava over a hundred and twenty-five thousand dollars. There was a scribbled note in Phil's pocket, written in Sava's hand, threatening Phil if he didn't pay up. And there was a money clip just inside the office door, which, it turns out, belonged to Sava. He must have dropped it when he and his friend broke in. It had his fingerprints all over it."

"That sounds a little too tidy," Sloane managed, her voice quivering a bit. "Motive, means, and opportunity, all neatly at the crime scene."

"Yeah, isn't it? Anyway, we tracked Sava down. He was in his apartment, asleep. It took him a good five minutes to figure out what we were talking about. When he did, he freaked out and started shouting in half-Albanian, half-English, that he was innocent and that he was being framed. The cops brought him in for questioning. He was more than willing to talk, once he realized how bad his ass was on the line."

"And?"

"And the case is now officially ours. Take a guess who paid Sava off to make sure Phil's gambling debts multiplied big-time by giving him more bad tips than good—and on the good ones, shaving the point spread so that Phil's losses far exceeded his wins?"

"Xiao Long," Sloane replied woodenly.

"You got it. Not that I needed the proof. The whole posthumous choking with a piano string until the victim's neck is sliced open is Xiao's trademark. He doesn't get his hands dirty too often. But when he does, he loves his job. And he takes great pride in letting us know it."

"The man's a sociopath."

"No arguments there."

Sloane lowered her head, rubbing her temples with one hand while she processed everything she'd just learned. "Derek, this is a vendetta, pure and simple. My father and his partners are all being targeted by Xiao. But why? Nut job or not, this can't all be a plot to shut them up about what they saw in Hong Kong. It doesn't make sense, especially after fourteen years have passed."

"Agreed." Derek paused. "Are you okay?"

"I'll be fine." Sloane wasn't about to give in to her personal feelings. Not now. "How do you want me to handle this?"

"Give me a half hour. Then call your father. Tell him only the facts. That Phil was killed. That Phil's bookie is in custody. And that we're investigating the murder. Your dad can notify his partners."

"Why a half hour?"

"Because I'm on my way over to Martino's factory. I want to be the one who breaks the news to him—face-to-face. I plan on finding out every detail about the meeting he and Phil had with Xiao Long. Martino's going to tell me why Xiao wanted Phil dead."

"Call me when you're done." Sloane had already jumped to her feet and was gathering up her archery equipment. "I'm driving into the city. That'll give you more than enough time to grill Ben, and me the chance to tell my dad about Phil in person. This news is going to hit him hard."

Martino was walking the factory floor when Derek strode in.

He didn't see Derek right away. He was pointing something out to one of his Chinese employees at her sewing machine. She seemed to have understood his gestures, because she nodded and went back to work. Martino turned, and Derek got his first good look at him.

He looked like death warmed over. Bloodshot eyes, disheveled clothing—probably the same clothes he was wearing last night—and a haggard expression. He was a trifle unsteady on his feet, but definitely not staggering drunk.

His expression turned even sicker when he spotted Derek, who motioned for him to join him in the front office.

It took Martino a few minutes to make his way up front. But when he finally did, he glanced nervously at Derek and shut the door behind him.

"You're back," he said, his gaze flickering to the newly opened bottle of whiskey on his desk. "Did you come up with more questions for me overnight?"

"I didn't have to. They came up on their own." Derek jerked his thumb in the direction of Martino's gaze. "Go ahead. Get it. This is one drink you're going to need."

"I'm all right." It was a bald-faced lie, and they both knew it. "What's this about?"

"Did you have a productive meeting last night?"

Martino started. "What?"

"Your meeting with Xiao Long. Did it go well?"

Martino's mouth opened and closed a few times, but nothing came out.

"I sure hope so," Derek continued. "Because the price was steep."

"Price? What price?"

Derek stared him down. "Your partner, Phil Leary, was shot dead last night."

Martino sagged backward, every drop of color draining from his face. "Phil's . . . dead?"

"Very. Whoever did it was thorough. They used submachine guns."

"Oh my God." In a trancelike state, Martino reached over and grabbed the bottle of whiskey, tipping it back and gulping at it. When that didn't help, he stumbled behind his desk and dropped into the chair, burying his face in his hands. "Oh my God," he repeated over and over. Tears seeped down his cheeks and between his fingers. "I was just with him . . ." he managed. "When . . . ?"

"Some time between when the two of you finished arguing outside the gambling parlor and five A.M." Derek couldn't help but feel sorry for Martino. He was a scared, weak man, and any guilt on his part stemmed from that fear and weakness. But he had a heart. He cared about his friends. And he was crumpling before Derek's eyes like a demolished building.

"It happened in his office," Derek continued. "Apparently, he went there directly from your meeting with Xiao."

"He was probably afraid to go home." Martino was babbling aloud, half to himself. "I knew he might recognize Xiao Long . . . but I so hoped . . . and I never expected Xiao to confront . . . but if I'd known Phil's plan sounded like blackmail . . ." Martino broke off, choking back a sob. "I should have told him. I knew he needed money. But he was also trying to help me. I should have told him. If I had, he might have walked away. He might still be alive. I got him killed."

Derek was trying to assimilate the bits and pieces Martino was spewing. "In other words, you never told Leary that Xiao Long was the person you were meeting with, or that he owns the employment agency you get your help from."

"I tried. I couldn't. But I told myself it's been fourteen years. I hoped. And I prayed."

"That Leary wouldn't recognize him," Derek supplied.

A shaky nod.

Derek pulled up a chair. "I need to know the whole story. Why Leary went with you. What this plan of his was. What happened between the two of you and Xiao Long. Everything." Studying the top of Martino's bowed head, Derek added, "You can call a lawyer if you'd like."

Martino's response was an ironic laugh. "What lawyer—my own? He handles wills, real estate—not criminal cases. Sloane? She works with you. Besides, once she knows about this, she'll never speak to me again. Neither will her father. He'll hate me. And I don't blame him."

Slowly, Martino raised his head, and the raw pain on his face was almost too agonizing to see. "I don't want a lawyer. What I want is never to have been born. You can't give that to me. No one can. So ask me whatever you want to. Any way you slice it, I'm going to hell."

CHAPTER
THIRTY-THREE

Phil's wake was held that Friday at the Thomas Mackie Funeral Home in Rockville Centre, Long Island. He had grown up there, his family was there, and his two grown children had made all the arrangements. He was to be buried at a local cemetery beside his wife, who'd passed away ten years ago after a long bout with cancer.

Given the circumstances of Phil's death, it was a closed casket, and the attendees were markedly solemn. Many of them were still in shock.

Matthew and Rosalyn were already there when Sloane and Derek arrived.

Sloane went over and squeezed her father's arm, blinking back her own tears. She'd spent a lot of time with her father these past few days, comforting him and explaining as much as she could—which wasn't much. He knew that Phil's bookie was in custody and that a search was being conducted for the killers. He knew—from Ben himself—that Ben was under investigation for hiring illegals, and that Xiao Long owned the employment agency he dealt with. He also knew that the FBI had upped the security on all the remaining partners in his art investment group.

Matthew wasn't stupid. With or without further in-depth explanation, he knew that Phil's death had something to do with Xiao Long and that the whole group of them were in danger.

The partners hadn't talked, except by phone, since the murder. Each of them needed to grieve alone, and in his own way. The wake was the first time they'd all be together since Phil's death.

Leo was the next to arrive. He was pale and grim, with dark circles under his eyes. He went over to Matthew, and the two men hugged in mutual sorrow. Then, Leo went wordlessly over to pay his respects to the family.

Watching everyone's suffering, hearing the quiet weeping that accompanied the loss of a loved one, Sloane felt more tears dampen her lashes. Maybe if she'd solved this damned case by now, Phil would still be alive. Maybe if she'd put together just a few more pieces . . .

"Don't even go there," Derek murmured in her ear. "There's nothing you could have done to prevent this. All we can do is try to stop it from going any further, and bring the right people to justice."

"I know," Sloane replied. "But we'd better hurry up and do that. Because my gut tells me time is running out."

———

Wallace and Cindy were en route to the Hamptons for their weekend alone. Part of Wallace wanted to block out the reality of Phil's murder. Still in shock and denial, he wanted nothing more than to escape to the Hamptons with Cindy and make the world go away. But there was no way that he could do that without stopping first to pay his respects to his longtime friend. Much as he cared for Cindy and as much as he tried to squelch his pain, he was sick to his stomach about Phil's murder. And scared to death about its ramifications. A forty-year friendship among five men. Slowly being destroyed, along with the decent men who composed it.

God help him.

God help them all.

Cindy was very understanding. She was even supportive. She could have waited in the car. But she agreed to go in with Wallace and offer him the comfort of her presence.

He felt humbled and grateful as he pulled off the Southern State Parkway and headed toward Rockville Centre. Losing a close friend was painful enough. Grieving alone would have been even more painful. He knew. He'd done it before.

He'd just parked his car and was opening the door for Cindy when Ben's sedan came careening around the corner and zigzagged into the parking lot. He swerved diagonally, then slammed on the brakes and turned off the ignition, taking up two parking spaces. He practically fell out of the car.

As soon as Wallace saw the drunken state Ben was in, he rushed forward, trying to head his friend off before he caused a scene.

"Ben, wait." He grabbed his arm. "You can't go in there in this condition . . ."

"I've got to see Phil," Ben slurred, shaking off Wallace's grasp, "before it's too late." He was up the stairs and inside the funeral home before Wallace could stop him.

"*Phil!*" he bellowed, shoving his way into the room. "I need to talk to you. I need to explain. You're my friend. I have to make you understand."

"Ben, for the love of God." Matthew clenched the sleeve of Ben's rumpled jacket, blocking his path as Ben struggled to get past. "This is a wake. Phil's wake. It's not the time for you to bare your soul at the top of your lungs."

Ben gazed at Matthew as if he were some nebulous object. "I can't talk to you now," he announced. "I have to find Phil."

"*Phil!*" he shouted again, oblivious to the sea of shocked faces staring in his direction. "Remember the cockroach races in college? The all-night cram sessions that got me a C in accounting? I was flunking the course. I would've failed. You made sure I passed. I won't fail you either. I'm here. I'll fix things. You have to let me fix things . . ."

By this time, Leo had crossed over and reached them. He met Matthew's frazzled stare and grabbed Ben's other arm. "Come on, Ben," Leo said in a soothing tone. "There are a lot of people visiting Phil right now. Let's sit down somewhere and wait."

"But I have to . . ."

"You will—soon," Matthew assured him, following Leo's lead by speaking in a low, calming voice, while helping Leo guide Ben into the director's office. "You'll talk to him in just a few minutes." He glanced back over his shoulder at Sloane, as if asking for her assistance in righting the situation.

Sloane stepped forward immediately. "Please forgive Ben's unfortunate outburst," she said respectfully, addressing Phil's family, but making certain the rest of the guests heard her as well. "You know how close he and Phil were, ever since college. He's taking Phil's death very hard. I know he meant no disrespect. I apologize on his behalf."

As Sloane was speaking, Wallace hurried into the room, accompanied by a young Asian woman. His gaze darted around, trying to see where Ben had gone. He visibly relaxed when he saw Matthew and Leo leading him into the office.

"Thank you, Sloane." He quietly addressed her as soon as she'd finished issuing her apology, and the activity in the room had started to normalize. "I tried to stop Ben in the parking lot. He shoved right past me. He's even worse off than I realized."

Sloane was only half-listening to Wallace's words. She was staring at the young woman Wallace was escorting—a woman who'd now come over to stand by his side.

She was the spitting image of the woman in the photo Lucy had given her—older, but a dead-ringer for Meili.

At first Sloane thought it actually *was* Meili. Then she recognized the subtle differences in features and face shape. But, dear Lord, they could be sisters.

Wallace noted the expression on Sloane's face, and took it to be curiosity.

"Forgive me. You two haven't met," he said. "Sloane Burbank, this is Cindy Liu. Cindy, this is Matthew's daughter, Sloane. We've all known her since she was born."

"It's a pleasure." Cindy shook Sloane's hand. "And please accept my sympathies over Phil Leary's death. Wallace has told me how close he and his friends are—your father included. This is a tragic loss."

"Thank you so much." Sloane had recovered herself by now. She was dying to ask Cindy if she had a relative named Meili. But now was not the time.

Clearly, she and Wallace were an item. Sloane would find another opportunity—soon—to find out what she wanted to know.

For now, she placed a comforting hand on Wallace's arm, offering her compassion and support. "I'm so sorry. You know that Phil will always be remembered, honored, and loved." She stepped aside as her mother walked over, giving Wallace a warm hug and some kind words.

The timing couldn't be better.

"Would you excuse me?" Sloane asked, glancing from Wallace to Cindy. "I want to go inside and see if my father and Leo need some help."

"Of course." Wallace nodded his understanding, then turned to introduce Rosalyn to Cindy.

Sloane slipped away and headed back over to Derek.

"Everything okay?" he asked as she reached his side.

"I'm not sure," Sloane murmured. "Would you mind staying out here and keeping an eye on Wallace and his lady friend? I'm going to see if my dad and Leo need help with Ben. Afterward, you and I have to talk."

Derek shot her a quizzical look, but held off asking questions. "Not a problem. I'll be here if you need me."

"Thanks." Sloane crossed the room and went into the office.

Both her father and Leo glanced up when she entered. Ben was slumped in a chair, looking totally out of it.

"We can't get through to him," her father told Sloane in a low tone. "It's like he doesn't even hear our voices. He just keeps saying that Phil is outside, waiting to talk to him. I'm afraid that if we shove his nose in the truth, he'll start ranting and raving again. The last thing Phil's family needs is another scene."

Sloane nodded. Stepping forward, she squatted down in front of Ben and took his hands in hers. "Hi, Ben."

He blinked. "Sloane," he slurred her name in surprise. "Is it poker night? Are you here to join the game?"

"No, Ben. It's not poker night. And we're not at your apartment, or at Leo's, Wallace's, or my dad's." She squeezed Ben's fingers. "We're in a funeral home. Underneath all that pain you're feeling, you do know that, right?"

He looked around, as if noticing his surroundings for the first time. "A funeral home," he repeated. "Yes, I know that. I drove here. I had to . . . for Phil."

"That's right—for Phil," Sloane agreed, keeping her tone even and quiet. "His passing is a terrible loss. We all feel it. I know how much you loved him. And I know that you're grieving. But please don't tarnish his memory by expressing your grief through shouting. It won't bring him back. And no amount of liquor will make the pain go away. That's why you're with friends. We're all here to help one another—to help you. We're honoring Phil together."

"Phil's dead." It was as if Sloane's words of comfort had penetrated Ben's alcohol-induced stupor. Tears filled his eyes. "Phil's dead."

"I know." Sloane stood up, kissed Ben's cheek. "I know he is."

"Then you also know why."

Dangerous territory. Sloane pondered her answer carefully.

Ben answered his own question before Sloane could speak. "Because I killed them. They're dead. And they're dead because of me. Everything . . . all of it . . . it's my fault."

Them? Sloane turned to shoot her father a questioning look.

He seemed as bewildered as she was. So did Leo, who shrugged at Sloane in noncomprehension.

"I doubt he knows what he's saying," Leo muttered. "I'll take him home. It'll be fine now. Thanks for calming him down."

"Leo—wait." Sloane delayed him for a minute as her father went to help Ben to his feet. She kept her voice down so that only Leo could hear. But if there was anyone who'd know the lowdown on Meili's look-alike, that someone would be Leo. "Are you acquainted with the woman who Wallace brought with him? I think her name is Cindy Liu."

"Sure," Leo acknowledged. "That's Wallace's architectural protégé, the one I've been collaborating with on design projects. She's a natural." Leo's expression softened. "She's also become more than a protégé to Wallace. I think he's fallen for her—hard. Not a surprise. He's always had a thing for Asian women. And this one's beautiful, smart, and talented. It's good to see him alive again. I was really afraid his soul had died with Sophie."

Sloane's investigative mind had already kicked into high gear. "You said she's his protégé. How did that happen—did they meet at one of his galleries?"

"No, actually her uncle's a longtime business associate of Wallace's. He's a big wheel in Hong Kong—rich and influential. His name's Johnny Liu. He and Wallace worked on deals together back in Wallace's investment-banking days, when he did a fair amount of traveling to the Far East. I also think that Liu is an art connoisseur and that he buys paintings from Wallace's galleries. Anyway, Liu asked Wallace to help Cindy kick-start her own architectural firm here in New York. And the rest, as they say, is history." Leo's lips curved slightly. "Or, in this case, history in the making."

Sloane smiled back. "Thanks. I'm glad Wallace is finding some happiness, too." She moved aside as her father guided Ben over and transferred him to Leo, who took Ben's arm and looped it around his neck in order to haul him out of the office.

"You sure you don't need help?" Matthew asked.

"No. You stay here with your family. I'll drive Ben home and stay with him until I'm sure he's okay on his own." He half led, half carried Ben to the door.

"Tell Phil I'm sorry," Ben begged Sloane and Matthew in a tear-clogged voice. "I'm so sorry."

"He knows, Ben," Sloane assured him. "And he'd want you to go home and get some rest."

Ben was placid when he and Leo left. But he was also totally broken.

"I can't help hurting for him," Sloane admitted to her father.

"You'd have to be made of stone not to." Switching gears, Matthew turned to his daughter. "You handled that really well. Talk about crisis negotiation. You're every bit as good as the FBI claimed. I'm proud of you."

"But?"

A heavy sigh. "But I'm not only hurting for Ben. I'm really worried about him. He's drinking himself to death. And now ICE is coming after him for hiring illegals. I don't know how much more he can take."

Sloane absorbed that and gave her father a questioning look. "Why do you think Ben used the plural when he talked about everything being his fault? He kept saying *they're* dead because of him. You don't think he did something for Xiao Long we don't know about, do you?"

Matthew shook his head emphatically. "I know the world is upside down these days. But Ben is *not* a killer. He's many other things, clearly more than I knew about, but he wouldn't hurt a fly. He's just so loaded that he doesn't know what he's saying."

"You're probably right." Sloane dropped the subject at that point. She could always pick it up again later, but right now she was nagged enough by her reaction to seeing Cindy Liu and absorbing Leo's comments about Wallace's propensity for Asian women to pursue something entirely different with her father.

"Dad, have you met Cindy Liu?" she asked.

"Wallace's Cindy? Not in person, no. Why?"

"Do you know anything about her background?"

Matthew shrugged. "Only that she has some great educational and professional credentials, which I'm sure is why Wallace agreed to sponsor her. I don't know much about her personal life, except that she's brought a little of the old Wallace back, for which I'm grateful. Any reason why you're interested in Cindy?"

"I just met her a few minutes ago. She so closely resembles another woman I've seen, it caught me off guard." Sloane paused, then went ahead and tested her theory. "Dad, does the name Meili mean anything to you?"

Matthew looked startled. "Meili? That's a name I didn't expect to hear again."

"Then you know her?" Now it was Sloane who was surprised.

"We met once. As for knowing her, for several years, she's all Wallace talked about."

Wallace.

Sloane's theory was beginning to seem a lot less far-fetched.

"Were they romantically involved?" she asked.

Matthew glanced uneasily at the door. "Can we have this conversation later? I feel uncomfortable isolating ourselves in the office when Phil's wake is taking place right outside. Actually, I feel uncomfortable having this conversation at all—especially with my daughter."

"I'm sorry, Dad. We can't delay this talk," Sloane surprised her father by saying. "As for feeling uncomfortable, pretend I'm an agent, not your daughter. The information you give me might be crucial. So I need to know. Tell me everything you recall about Meili. After that, I promise we'll go right back in and rejoin the others."

Puzzled, Matthew drew a deep breath, mentally backtracking six years. "Yes, Wallace and she were romantically involved. After Sophie was born, Wallace's marriage went rapidly down the drain. His and Beatrice's fidelity to each other went with it. Wallace had a slew of affairs. Then when Sophie was almost two years old, Wallace met Meili. He called her his free-spirited angel—beautiful, lighthearted, filled with laughter, and refreshingly impulsive."

"And was she?"

"I suppose. She was also half Wallace's age, so she saw life through very different eyes. But she was just what Wallace needed at the time. So, if anything, her youth was part of her charm."

"And how did you happen to meet her?"

"The same way Wallace did. She tried to sell the group of us a painting. An early Rothberg, actually. Not one of his more valuable ones, but still, a Rothberg."

"When did this happen?"

"July 2002. I remember because it was the first time since Cai Wen's murder that Leo, Phil, and I took the risk of setting foot in Hong Kong. And we only went because we were negotiating a major deal with a Hong Kong gallery owner who insisted on meeting all five of us in person. This young woman—Meili—spotted Wallace during one of his solo visits to the gallery and followed him back to our hotel. She brought the Rothberg with her. She was clearly desperate for money."

"And?"

"And she ended up selling it elsewhere."

Sloane's eyes narrowed. "You lowballed her."

"We tried to make a healthy profit. That's what the art-dealing business is about."

"I'm not naive, Dad. And it doesn't matter whether or not I approve. I'm just trying to establish the facts."

"The facts are, yes, we lowballed her. Wallace was against the decision. After the deal fell through, he got in touch with her and took her to dinner. By the time we left Hong Kong, he was already head over heels in love. His feelings only got stronger each time he visited. Which was often. Wallace did a lot of traveling in his previous life. Especially to the Far East. So there was lots of opportunity for him to be with Meili. The rest of us ribbed the hell out of him. We were already calling him Casanova Johnson. This just gave us more ammunition. One night in August . . ." Matthew broke off, his neck turning red. He was visibly embarrassed by getting into this story with his daughter.

"Go on," Sloane prompted. "I don't shock easily. And remember, I'm FBI, not your little Sloane."

"Okay," Matthew conceded. "One night in August, during a weekly poker game that involved way too much alcohol, we actually set up a pool on how long it would take Wallace to get Meili into bed. The idea was Ben's, of course. He was always the clown—and the instigator. Look, we all acted like juvenile asses, and we knew it. It was just one of those stupid, throwback-to-college days."

"Who won the pool?"

"Actually, Ben did. He counted on Wallace being gallant. And he was right. Wallace held off until November. The ironic part is that Meili didn't want to go slowly. But Wallace has that decent streak in him. He was so afraid of hurting her."

"He obviously got over it."

"Not without a huge surge of guilt," Matthew assured Sloane. "Trust me, this wasn't just a fling or even an affair. It lasted three years. And it was serious. *Too* serious."

"Meaning?"

"Meaning that Wallace's marriage might not have been a priority, but his daughter was. He would never, ever have left Sophie. And Meili would never have left Hong Kong. So the relationship wasn't going anywhere. But Wallace couldn't let it go. He bought Meili jewelry, expensive clothes, you name it. And he visited her every chance he could."

"What happened?"

"Like I said, Wallace's decency always prevailed—which, in this case, backfired. During a playful moment when he and Meili were together, he stupidly told her about the bet. He assumed she'd be amused. She wasn't. What he considered to be a silly game, she considered to be the ultimate betrayal and humiliation. I don't know all the details. Nor did I ask. I only know that Wallace was a wreck when he came home. He briefly told us that Meili had ended things between them, and why. Then, he went off like a wounded bear—cut himself off from everyone. He spent the week before the holidays holed up in his town house. He wouldn't talk to a soul. The only reason he went home to East Hampton the following week was for Sophie. He'd never let her spend a Christmas without him."

Sloane was mentally calculating dates. "You said the affair lasted over three years, and ended before the holidays. So that was December 2005."

"That's right."

"Did Wallace say anything else, describe anything else, that you can remember? Anything about Meili's background, her family, her life when they weren't together?"

Matthew frowned. "I remember him saying she didn't like to talk about her past. I think she had some kind of major falling-out with her family, after which she severed all ties with them. She was a struggling artist when he met her, working in a bar. He put a stop to that right away, and helped get her a job as a hostess in an upscale restaurant while he tried to kick-start her art career. He said there was a fineness about her that smacked of good breeding." A hint of a smile. "That's old-money Wallace for you. Always a keen eye for class. Anyway, other than that, all he talked about was the present."

"Thank you, Dad."

Sloane had all she needed—well, *almost*. Her father's story dovetailed perfectly with Lucy's. Wallace was the rich, married man Meili had gotten involved with and, ultimately, committed suicide over. And the tragic aftermath of their relationship, which Wallace probably knew nothing about, all stemmed from an idiotic bet about Meili's virtue. There were pieces to the equation still missing—like what the connection was between Meili and Cindy Liu—but those could be uncovered. As for Cindy's sudden appearance in Wallace's life—now *that* was no coincidence. Not with them being so physically similar. But her father had met Meili. And she wanted a qualified opinion. A picture might be worth a thousand words. But there was nothing like the real thing to confirm the facts.

"Do you want to tell me what this is all about?" Matthew was asking.

"I can't. Not yet. But I do need one more thing from you." Sloane clamped a hand on her father's arm and led him to the door. "I need you to take a quick look at someone and tell me what you see."

"What I see?" Matthew looked utterly baffled.

"Don't ask questions. Just wait till I tell you. Then, look." Sloane eased the door open a crack and peered out, scanning the room. She spotted Wallace and Cindy, talking quietly to each other. An instant later, Wallace nodded, crossing over to get their coats, and leaving Cindy standing alone.

Sloane waited until Cindy was turned in their direction, her face visible from their angle.

"Now," she directed, pointing at Cindy through the narrow slit in the doorway and urging her father's focus onto her.

Matthew complied, and started in surprise. "That's Meili. I don't understand. When did she get here? Why didn't Wallace tell me that—"

"It's not Meili," Sloane interrupted. "It's Cindy Liu. So you do see the resemblance?"

"A dead man could see the resemblance." Matthew stared as Wallace rejoined Cindy, a tender expression on his face. "Unbelievable." Shutting the door, Matthew turned to Sloane. "What does all this mean?"

"As I said, I can't supply the details. Not yet." Sloane held her father's gaze. "But, Dad, you can't say anything about this to Wallace. Don't even mention our conversation. There are things I need to verify first."

"How does this relate to Phil's murder? Or to the Rothberg sale? Or to Xiao Long?"

"Let's go back to Phil's wake." Sloane's nonresponse was intentional. "Keep this discussion and what you just saw between us. I'll answer your questions as soon as I can."

A few minutes later, Sloane returned to the wake. She glanced around until she spotted Derek, who quickly disengaged himself from one of Phil's sons, to whom he'd been expressing his condolences.

"I was beginning to think you'd slipped out the back door," he muttered as he joined her.

"I'm sorry I vanished for so long," Sloane replied. "But it was critical."

"I saw Leo haul Ben out of here a while ago. He was docile as a lamb. I'm sure you had something to do with that."

Sloane shrugged. "I eased Ben back into reality as gently as I could." Her gaze darted around, searching for Wallace and Cindy.

"If you're looking for Wallace and his girlfriend, they just left," Derek informed her. "I tried to go over and engage them in conversation. But she clearly wanted no part of chatting. She avoided me like the plague. And she wasn't too much better with everyone else. She expressed her condolences, stayed as long as Wallace felt it was necessary, then urged him out the door. I'm sure she felt out of place. So do I. But I got the distinct impression it was me she was avoiding. Maybe she saw my gun and got nervous, or maybe I'm imagining things."

"You're not imagining things. If Wallace told her you're FBI, it's possible she has reason to avoid you."

Derek's brows drew together. "It sounds like you accomplished a lot more at this wake than just calming Ben down."

"I did." Sloane slipped her arm through Derek's. "Let's say our good-byes. You and I *really* have to talk."

"Done."

They were in the car ten minutes later, and then drove to an empty parking lot to talk in private.

"Let's hear it." Derek turned off the ignition and turned to face Sloane. "You look like you're about to burst."

"I am." Sloane sucked in her breath, then began. "Wallace's girlfriend's name is Cindy Liu. She's an architect in Manhattan. I need you to run a background check on her."

"Fine. Why?"

Sloane fished in her pocketbook and pulled out the photo Lucy had given her. "This is Meili, the girl who sold the Rothberg to Daniel Zhang." She pointed. "See any resemblance?"

Derek let out a low whistle. "Add a few years, and she and Cindy Liu could be twins."

"Exactly. My father said pretty much the same thing after he got his first glimpse of Cindy a few minutes ago—and he's met Meili. I'll tell you the whole story. But first, I have one question. Do you happen to know a rich, influential man in Hong Kong named Johnny Liu?"

The stunned expression on Derek's face gave Sloane her answer.

"Johnny Liu's been on our radar for years. But no one can get anything on him. To the world, he's a successful businessman. In China, he's a beloved philanthropist."

"And to the Bureau?"

"He's a kingpin in Asian organized crime. Both American and Chinese law enforcement suspect that Liu heads up the Liu Jian Triad. The triad has major illegal operations going on in Hong Kong and Macao." Derek paused. "But Liu is a very common name, Sloane. So if you're trying to link . . ."

"I'm not trying. It's a fact. Assuming it's the same Johnny Liu, he's Cindy's uncle. And if he is, the story I'm about to tell you could take us in a whole new direction."

CHAPTER
THIRTY-FOUR

There was no doubt that Johnny Liu had members of the Hong Kong Police Department in his pocket.

It took Derek and Rich all weekend to dig up what they wanted to know. Fortunately, they had their own contacts—honest Hong Kong police who wanted to cooperate and who were willing to work hard to get at the truth.

When the truth was finally unearthed, it dropped the central piece of the puzzle into place.

Johnny Liu had fathered one child, a daughter.

Her name was Meili.

Meili had left home in August 1999, at seventeen years old. A death certificate for a Jane Doe matching Meili's description did indeed exist, but it had been so deeply buried, it had been virtually impossible to find in Rich and C-6's first attempt. This time, with the right people at the other end researching, the death certificate was located in a pile of very old, very cold cases.

It was dated January 2006, cause of death unknown.

The dates matched up with Lucy's story.

Liu had covered things up well. But after additional digging, it was determined that it was he who had identified Meili's body, and that the cause of death had been suicide. His daughter had slit her wrists and been found alone in a broken-down apartment with a note to her family—one that had mysteriously vanished after being confiscated by the police.

"Sloane's right," Derek announced to Rich, after they'd met to compare notes. "This changes everything." He reached for his half-empty, lukewarm cup of coffee. He'd lost track of how many cups he'd consumed in the past forty-eight hours. "The pieces all have to be rearranged. Your case. My case. Motives. Victims. You name it."

"My cases," Rich corrected. "As for *Dead or Alive*, everything Daniel Zhang told us was true. But we've been headed in the wrong direction. Henry Fong's involvement with the Rothberg began and ended with Meili. The *other* Rothberg, however, began with Burbank's art investment group and ended with Meili getting screwed over, staying destitute, and turning to Johnson. So the key here is who Meili stole the paintings *from*, not who she sold them *to*."

"Her father—Johnny Liu."

"You got it. He's the common denominator."

"We also think he's the Dragon Head of the Liu Jian Triad. So it's Liu Xiao's working for, not Fong. And he's skyrocketing his way up the ladder. Liu probably sent him to the States right after Cai Wen's murder. That got Xiao out of the country, and gave Liu the opportunity to expand his illegal operations to the U.S."

"It all fits. Liu's got a reputation of being a huge patron of the arts," Rich added, rubbing the back of his neck to get out the kinks. "A generous benefactor to Chinese museums, donating artifacts and pieces of great cultural significance to landmark museums. He's also an avid collector. And he's got more than enough capital to fund the Black Eagles, both internationally and here in the U.S."

"So he's paying the Black Eagles to rip off valuable paintings for him. He's probably keeping some of the works and selling the others, making a killing in the process. And he's got Xiao Long running the show, at least here in the States. It's a win-win. Liu adds to his fortune, and Xiao takes a giant step into the triad's inner circle." Derek blew out a frustrated breath. "You gotta give Liu credit. He's smart. He does so much good and in such a public way that he's a folk hero in the Far East, so legendary that law enforcement doesn't dare touch him. Not to mention he's buried every shred of evidence so deep, no one could find it anyway."

"Cai Wen must have been Liu's front man in the deal with Burbank's art investment group," Rich deduced. "That way, Liu could keep a low profile. Cai Wen would seal the deal and get a percentage. Xiao Long would pick up the painting and bring it to Liu. But Cai Wen got greedy. During the exchange, he tried to squeeze more money out of the deal. So Xiao killed him, grabbed the Rothberg and the money, and brought it all to Liu, who'd probably still own the painting if Meili hadn't taken off with it four years later."

"Talk about getting into Liu's good graces," Derek muttered. "That was quite a gift from Xiao, not to mention a huge display of loyalty. It probably raised Xiao up about three rungs on the organizational ladder. Which is another reason for Liu to designate him the chosen one and to send him off to New York with the backing and resources to become the Dai Lo of the Red Dragons—and who knows what thereafter."

Rich took another belt of coffee. "Now I understand why Xiao Long was so freaked out when the identical Rothbergs surfaced and I started tracing the provenance of the real deal. It wasn't just himself he was protecting. It was Johnny Liu. Xiao knew there was a chance that Burbank, Fox, and Leary could identify him from Cai Wen's murder scene. He had to get his hands on Burbank's receipt for the Rothberg sale—*and* he had to scare Burbank and his partners off. He must suspect that C-6 has him and his gang on their radar screen."

"Oh, he more than suspects. He's been playing cat and mouse with us for months now. But you're right. Between his high visibility here, and his involvement in the Rothberg—if the Bureau started connecting the right dots, it would lead them straight to Johnny Liu. And he was protecting his Dragon Head at all costs."

Rich's brows drew together. "But the rest of it; Liu's personal agenda . . ."

"Sloane was right about that," Derek broke in. "Her father and his partners are all victims. Xiao's the long-distance enforcer of Liu's vendetta. Leary's dead. Martino's on the verge of bankruptcy. Burbank's wife and daughter were both assaulted. Fox I'm not sure about, but I will be after I grill him and find out what he was looking for in Sloane's files. And Johnson . . ." Derek sucked in his breath. "Wallace Johnson is the prime target. Having Cindy Liu work her way into his heart and then break it is only a small facet of what her uncle would regard as an eye for an eye. God only knows what else Liu has in store for Johnson."

In the office of his palatial Hong Kong mansion, Johnny Liu's private telephone line rang.

He lifted the receiver and, as was his custom, said nothing. If the person at the other end was one of the select few who'd been given this number, he or she would know to speak first.

"Liu? It's Keong."

It was Sergeant David Keong, Liu's best and most loyal contact at the Hong Kong Police Department.

"Yes. Go ahead," he said, using the Loong Doo dialect the two men shared.

Keong followed suit, stating his business in the same prided dialect. "The FBI has been on the phone with our department all weekend. Many questions about Meili were asked. Answers were supplied by others beyond my influence. The death certificate was located. They are on the verge of figuring things out. I thought you should know right away."

"You thought correctly. My thanks."

Liu disconnected the call.

Then he dialed Xiao Long on his throwaway phone.

Xiao answered instantly, greeting his Dragon Head with the utmost respect and, as always, in Loong Doo.

"I just heard from Keong," Liu said without preamble. "The FBI has made the connection to Meili. It's time to finish what we've begun. You did good work with Leary. Go on to Martino."

Sloane met Derek at a small café near her parents' apartment.

"You summoned. I obeyed. Here I am." She sat down across from Derek at the private corner table he'd requested—but not before giving him a long hello kiss and scrutinizing his face. "You look wiped," she noted.

"Nothing a little rest won't fix."

A teasing smile curved Sloane's lips. "I have to admit, the five o'clock shadow is kind of sexy." She reached across the table and rubbed her knuckles against his jaw. "In fact, all of you is kind of sexy. I missed you this weekend."

"Don't tempt me. Or we'll be banished from this café for life." Derek kissed her fingertips. "The good news is I'm coming home tonight. So you'll have a chance to show me just how much you missed me. Plan on an allnighter."

"I'm up for it." Concern flickered across Sloane's face. "But I'm not sure you are. Did you get *any* sleep since Friday?"

"A catnap here and there. But Rich and I finally got our answers."

"I'm all ears."

Derek leaned forward, speaking in a hushed tone despite the fact that they were very much alone. "You were right. There's a major connection between Cindy Liu and Meili. They're cousins. Meili was Johnny Liu's daughter."

Sloane let out a whistle. "That puts things in perspective."

"Yeah. Also, I ran that background check on Cindy. She's squeaky clean, from top grades at the best schools to a prestigious job at a major architectural firm. Interesting side note—she and her uncle are very close. As a kid, she traveled with him, grew up at his knee. She was more interested in his world than in the traditional one her parents wanted for her."

"So she and her uncle planned this." Sloane gave a rueful shake of her head. "Cindy is part of the retribution Liu has planned for Wallace. He capitalized on his niece's striking resemblance to Meili, asked her to play it to the hilt and make Wallace fall in love with her. And it worked. What's more, I doubt it's more than the tip of the iceberg. If Liu's hatred has been festering for two and a half years, a broken heart for Wallace is only the beginning."

"I agree. There's no doubt that, in Liu's mind, Wallace is the villain in this tragedy."

"Liu seems to have selective memory," Sloane responded drily. "He's the one who turned his daughter away and virtually disowned her when she came to him, pregnant and alone. I'd say that played a major role in her suicide."

"No argument. It's much easier for a proud, stubborn man like Liu to put all the blame on Wallace than to assume any of it himself. But Wallace's affair with Meili isn't the only issue here. It's what Liu sees as instigating it."

"My father's art partnership's lowballing her on the second Rothberg, and forcing her to sell it way below value. Pushing her closer to destitution." Sloane sighed. "And then the icing on the cake—that stupid bet they made about when Wallace would get her into bed."

"You got it." Derek spoke gently but candidly with Sloane. "All five partners were involved in the two events that, in Johnny Liu's mind, pushed Meili over the edge. We've already discussed what he considers to be Wallace's sins. Ben and your father were the most vocal when it came to intentionally undervaluing the worth of the Rothberg Meili tried to sell them. To top that off, Ben initiated a bet that centered on Meili's virtue. The sum total of results? Your father's office has been ransacked, your mother has been beaten up, then kidnapped and nearly killed. As for Ben, he's been pushed to the point of self-destruction. Phil was killed. That leaves Leo and your father."

Anxiety tightened Sloane's features. "You don't think that what Xiao's thugs did to my mother, and the knife assault on me, were enough retribution when it comes to my father?"

"Not compared to Ben's bankruptcy, total alcohol dependence, and possible jail time. Not compared to Phil's cold-blooded murder. And not compared to whatever vile plan Liu has in store for Wallace. Your mother's assault at the apartment wasn't planned; she interrupted the break-in at their apartment. As for her kidnapping, it was aborted before Liu could have her killed. The fact that she's still alive is a thorn in his side. And the SOB Xiao sent to slash your palm? That was Liu's idea of a warning for you to back off. Otherwise, he would have sent Xiao himself, or Jin Huang, not some scrawny kid.

No, none of those incidents targeted your father's core, or destroyed him in the fundamental way Liu seems to be aiming for."

"You're right," Sloane replied grimly. "Liu is going for each man's Achilles' heel and using it to destroy his life. Especially Wallace. I shudder to think what Liu considers brutal enough for Wallace . . ." Sloane broke off, all the color draining from her face. "Oh God."

"What is it?"

For a long moment Sloane didn't speak. And when she did, it was in a strained, sickened tone. "My father said Meili ended the affair with Wallace around Christmastime 2005. What's the date on Meili's death certificate?"

"January 2006." Derek's eyes narrowed as he tried to figure out Sloane's anguished reaction. "The dates make sense."

"Maybe too much sense." Sloane squeezed her eyes shut, and when she opened them, there was pain reflected in them. "Derek, the unknown hit-and-run driver who killed Wallace's daughter, Sophie . . ." Sloane swallowed hard. "The crime was committed on April 11, 2006. Three months after Meili killed herself."

"Shit." Derek felt bile rise in his throat. "That sounds like a hell of a coincidence to me."

"It sounds like an eye for an eye. Or, in this case, a daughter for a daughter. And if it's true . . . Derek, I'm not sure Wallace can survive this."

"And Liu's not finished. His plan seems to be coming to a head."

"Why now?"

"I'm not sure. But I intend to find out. Meanwhile, Phil was just murdered. Cindy Liu is about to tear out whatever's left of Wallace's heart, with God knows what to follow." Derek seized Sloane's hands. "Listen to me. I've already arranged for extra security on Ben, Wallace, Leo, and your father. But they've got to be warned that their worlds are about to be blown apart."

"I agree." Sloane met Derek's gaze. "I'll talk to my dad. I'll also *try* to get through to Ben. For Wallace, this news also has to come from me. I'll see how he handles the part about Meili before I decide if I should mention my theory about Sophie's death. Right now, it's pure speculation. But he has to be prepared just in case it turns out to be fact. How and when I tell him . . .

I'll have to play that one by ear. In the meantime, I don't want any of the other men to know."

"I agree." Derek nodded. "In the meantime, leave Leo to me. He's met Cindy, and I'm sure he's seen the resemblance to Meili. So don't be surprised if, once I fill him in on the kind of danger he's up against, he figures out that she's part of this plot. In the meantime, I want to confront him head-on about what he was searching for the night I caught him rifling through your file. I'm hoping that my warning about Liu and Xiao Long, together with what he figures out about Cindy, will rattle him enough to tell me. And if we're lucky, his answer will give us a clue about Liu's agenda."

"Are you heading over to Leo's studio now?"

"Right after you promise me you'll be careful. You should know that I also put extra security on you."

"Over and above what you've already provided—why?"

"Because it's probable that you and your mother are Liu's ultimate targets when it comes to punishing your father. You're both what means the most to him. I'm not taking any chances—especially since I'm sure Xiao's still keeping an eye on you and will be alerted by his punk kids the minute you walk into Wallace's gallery. Wallace is back in the city, by the way. He and Cindy drove in from the Hamptons a few hours ago. They're each at work. So you can catch Wallace alone."

Sloane was quiet for a moment. "Even if I don't tell him about Sophie, the rest of this is going to tear him up. Not just Cindy's betrayal, but that Meili was pregnant with his child, that her father disowned her when he found out, and that she committed suicide. Wallace was deeply in love with her. And he knows nothing about her life since the day she ended their affair."

"If it's too much for you, I can talk to him," Derek offered.

"Thanks, but no. This is something I have to do."

CHAPTER
THIRTY-FIVE

Ben was slumped over his desk, head lolled to one side.

One eye cracked open. The whiskey bottle was almost empty. It didn't matter. He couldn't reach it anyway. His arms wouldn't work. None of him would work. Except his goddamned mind. Dulled to the point of unconsciousness, it still refused to shut up.

Murderer. He was a murderer. Directly. Indirectly. He was killing the people he loved.

Flashes of memory. Blanks he couldn't fill in. Images he'd never forget.

Is this how Phil had felt when the spray of bullets tore through him? No. Phil hadn't had time to remember anything. No cherished memories. No moments of joy. Unlike Ben, Phil had never harmed anyone but himself. His soul had been free of guilt, and yet Ben had deprived him of the precious flashbacks that defined his life. So what had Phil felt? Pain. Sharp, life-draining pain. Then, death.

All Ben's fault.

And Sophie. Beautiful, little Sophie. With the purest of souls, and not enough years behind her to have begun forming the priceless memories she deserved. At the very start of her young life. Gone in an instant. Had she been afraid? In pain? Had she called out for her daddy? Or had death come quickly?

If the gates of heaven were strewn with stars, then Sophie was the brightest star in the sky.

The daisies. Had he picked the daisies? Was it the eleventh yet? Or had it slipped by while he was inside a bottle? He'd never missed that date, not since the first one. He couldn't see the calendar, couldn't remember what day, what month, what year it was.

Dear God, why couldn't he just die? Hell could be no worse than this.

"Martino."

He heard the voice, but it was muted and very far away.

"Martino." This time it was accompanied by thick hands around his neck, and a powerful jerk, yanking him up. "I come for money."

The face swam in front of Ben's drunken gaze. Jin Huang.

"No money," he croaked out. "No girls. No work. No money."

Jin Huang's emotionless gaze flickered across the factory floor below. It was unnaturally still. No workers. No activity. No production.

No surprise. Xiao Long had pulled his girls from Martino's place the day the government found out Martino was employing illegals.

"Take whatever you want," Ben muttered into the desk. "Take it all. There's nothing left."

"Xiao Long not happy."

"Tell him he's welcome to kill me. I wish he would."

"Good idea. He'd enjoy. But maybe he not come in time. Maybe you kill you first," Jin Huang replied, his words as stilted as his English. "Or maybe Johnson kill you. Xiao. You. Johnson. All have reasons. No matter what, you die. Soon."

———

Sloane felt physically ill as she opened the door to Wallace's gallery and stepped inside to the tinkling of the bell.

Talking to her father had been a cinch compared to what she had to do now. And talking to Ben hadn't happened. He'd been so out of it when she called, she'd given up and agreed to let her father try getting through to him.

But Wallace. Poor Wallace. This was going to be one of the hardest conversations Sloane had ever had.

Thankfully, his gallery was quiet, with just two or three patrons browsing around. One of Wallace's assistants was helping them. When he saw Sloane, he held up his index finger in a "one minute" gesture, then excused himself from his potential customer and went into the back office.

When he returned, Wallace was with him. He was tan and relaxed, looking happier than Sloane had seen him in ages.

She was about to blow all that newfound joy to bits.

"Sloane, this is a pleasant surprise," he greeted her. "Are you ready to select some paintings for the cottage?"

"I wish that's why I was here," Sloane replied soberly. "Unfortunately, it's not. Can we please talk privately?"

Wallace's smile vanished, and his forehead creased in concern. "Is it Ben? Did something happen over the weekend?"

"No, nothing like that." Sloane's gaze flickered to the rear of the gallery. "Is your office empty?"

"Yes. Come in. Let's talk there."

Once they were inside the office with the door shut, Wallace gestured for Sloane to take a seat. "What can I offer you—coffee? Water? Soda?"

Sloane glanced over at the small fridge in the corner. "Water would be great, thank you." Requesting the water served two purposes. To ease the mounting tension. And to give her something to keep her hydrated so she didn't pass out during what promised to be a long, draining conversation.

Wallace got out two bottles and handed one to Sloane.

He uncapped his and stood beside his large teak desk, watching her.

"I think you should sit down," Sloane suggested.

An odd expression crossed his face, a mixture of apprehension and worry. "All right." He walked around and sat down behind the desk. "This sounds very serious."

"It is. And I wish more than you could ever imagine that I didn't have to tell you this."

"Go on."

"It concerns Meili."

Wallace started. Clearly, it was the last thing he'd expected. "Your father told you about Meili?"

"He didn't have to. I found out about her from her closest friend. The friend is here in New York, recovering in a women's shelter from an abusive marriage." Sloane pulled out the photo of Lucy and Meili and handed it to Wallace.

He studied it for a long time, his gaze growing soft and faraway. "Meili. Beautiful and unique." His head came up. "You said her friend is in New York. Is Meili here as well?"

"No." Sloane uncapped her water and took a fortifying gulp.

Something in Sloane's tone must have served as a warning, because Wallace tensed. "She's still in Hong Kong then," he decided aloud. "What did her friend tell you?"

"About your relationship. About what happened once it ended. Everything except your name, which Meili never revealed. I only learned it was you Meili's friend was describing this past Friday. At Phil's wake. After I met Cindy. I dragged the background story out of my father. He didn't want to tell me. But the situation was critical, far more than even he knew. He still doesn't know everything. You had to hear it first."

"What situation?" Wallace demanded. "Why is it critical? And what is it about Meili that I have to hear?"

Sloane steeled herself. "There's no easy way to say this. Meili is dead. She died three weeks after she broke things off with you."

Wallace winced, lowering his gaze to stare at the floor. "How?"

"Suicide." Sloane made it as short and devoid of details as possible.

"Suicide?" Wallace's head snapped up. "Impossible. Meili was a survivor. Strong and independent. She'd never take her own life. You must have the wrong woman or the wrong story."

"I wish that were so. But it's not. Wallace, Meili was pregnant," Sloane told him quietly. "It was your child. She didn't realize it until after she'd sent you away."

"Pregnant . . . oh dear Lord." Wallace's water bottle struck the desk with a thud. "And she didn't even contact me . . . "

"She was too proud to contact you. She went to her father. But he turned her away. The shame and dishonor were too much for her."

"So she killed herself." Wallace's voice was choked. He was also still clearly in shock. "She killed herself and our child. All because I wasn't there for her."

"Wallace, you couldn't have known—"

"How?" he interrupted, not even hearing Sloane's words.

"How what?"

"How did she kill herself? Pills? Drowning? How?"

Sloane gritted her teeth. "She slit her wrists."

Wallace shuddered, and his Adam's apple began furiously going up and down as he choked back emotion. "Sloane, I'd like to be alone now."

"I understand. But I can't leave yet. There's more."

"More?" He stared at her. "How much more can there be?"

"Quite a bit." Sloane was gripping the water bottle so tightly, the plastic was buckling. "Meili's family name was Liu. Johnny Liu was her father."

This time, Wallace jerked backward as if he'd been punched. "What?"

"Johnny Liu. Meili was his only child. That explains her strong resemblance to Cindy. They were cousins. And Wallace, Meili left a suicide note. Her father knows everything—your name, the way your art investment group offered her an absurdly low price for the second Rothberg, the bet you guys made during your poker game, the fact that Meili ended your relationship when you told her about it—everything."

Wallace had gone so still and was staring so intently into space that Sloane wondered if he was absorbing all her information.

When he spoke, she realized he was, and that he'd been processing everything she'd said and all the ramifications associated with it.

"If Liu's known all this time, he must despise me. I don't blame him. I'm not sure I don't despise myself. But the pretense he's kept up . . ."

"It was planned. Liu has spent these past few years obsessed with getting revenge."

"All our business dealings, the favor he asked of me when it came to Cindy . . ." A painful pause. "Cindy's appearance in my life isn't a coincidence. And the relationship is all a facade. Liu wanted to rub my nose in her resemblance to Meili, and then make sure I relived our break-up as painfully as possible."

"Cindy and her uncle are very close," Sloane confirmed softly. "I haven't confronted her, but my guess is you're right."

"I am. The way she said good-bye to me today seemed oddly final, considering we'd just spent the weekend together. And in the car, she apologized for how her priorities would affect us. I assumed she meant her being a workaholic. I told her that I understood, that I'd been there. She averted her gaze and said she doubted that. Now it all makes sense. And that exquisite painting she gave me of the little Chinese girl—she said it was a heartfelt thank-you gift from her uncle and herself. I assumed it was meant to be a tribute to Sophie. Now I know it wasn't. It was a reminder of Liu's loss, a way of taunting me about my own, rubbing salt in wounds that will never heal. My precious Sophie. And the unborn child I never even knew existed . . ."

Sloane saw where this was headed. Wallace's thoughts were turning in the exact direction she'd feared. Soon he'd come to the logical conclusion about Sophie's death that would send him into a murderous rage. She had to tell him the truth. She had no choice.

"Wallace, this is even bigger than you realize," she began. "Liu isn't just a wealthy entrepreneur. He's head of the Liu Jian Triad. He has loyal members helping him with this plot to avenge Meili's death. And that plot doesn't just involve you, although you're his prime target. All your partners are on his victim list. He's slowly destroying each of them because of the slimy way the group did business with Meili, topped off by that ludicrous bet you all made. He's going for everyone's jugular—especially yours. Which brings me to Sophie . . ."

Sloane was interrupted by the ringing of her cell phone. She was tempted to ignore it, but given the precarious state of the investigation, she couldn't.

"I have to take this," she apologized to Wallace.

Vaguely, he nodded. His mind had already returned to processing mode.

"Hello?" Sloane said into the phone.

"Sloane? Thank God you answered. I just got it. It's a year and a half later, and I just got it. They made sure I got it. I read it three times. Then I saw the Post-it they attached. They're going to kill her. I'm sick to my stomach. And I don't know who to call—the police, the FBI. Tell me what to do."

It was Leo. His voice was tear-clogged. And he was distraught to the point of hysteria.

"Leo, calm down," Sloane directed. "You're not making sense. What is it you just got and read, and what Post-it was attached? Who's going to kill who, and how do you know the information is authentic?" She covered the mouthpiece with her hand. "Something's happened at Leo's end. I need a few minutes."

"Take them. I need time to think, anyway." Wallace crossed over and left the office. He looked ill.

Sloane was just finishing up with Leo, assuring him she'd take immediate action with regard to his situation, when Wallace stormed back into the office. He was positively shaking with rage, out of control in a way Sloane had never seen him.

"A messenger service was here," he announced, ignoring the phone in her hand. "They delivered these."

He opened the manila envelope, pulled out the contents, and flung what turned out to be some photos and a newspaper clipping across the desk at Sloane.

She glanced down at them and froze.

The photos were of Ben. Passed out drunk at the wheel of his white Mercedes. His front fender was badly dented. Blood was splattered all over the front grill and hood of the car.

The date stamp on the photos was April 11, 2006. And the newspaper clipping was Sophie's obituary, dated a few days later.

The nightmare had just exploded into a hellish reality.

"Leo, I've got to go," Sloane said into the phone. "Don't touch the letter, the Post-it, or the envelope again. I'll have someone at the FBI pick them up.

The Evidence Response Team will check for fingerprints. But we both know who's responsible. I'll call you back."

She snapped her phone shut and reached for the photos, holding them gingerly at the very edges in case there were prints to pull off. But there wouldn't be. Any more than there'd be prints on Leo's letter.

"Ben killed my child," Wallace said tonelessly. "Ben. Sophie's godfather. My lifelong friend. He helped make her birth possible. He was there the day she was born. He was there the day she died. He stood by my side at the funeral. He puts daisies on her grave every month. She adored him. He killed her. Then he drove away. He didn't even stay to help her or to see if she was alive. He didn't turn himself in. He didn't come to me. He ran and hid, passed out in a drunken stupor. And when he came to . . ."

"Wallace," Sloane tried. "Johnny Liu is the one who arranged . . ."

"I know who sent me these pictures," Wallace snapped. "I'm not an idiot. But that's irrelevant." His index finger jabbed at the images. "Ben killed Sophie. The evidence is staring us in the face. I'm sure Liu's been blackmailing him. None of that matters. My friend killed my little girl."

"No. He didn't." Sloane gave a hard shake of her head as she finished scrutinizing the photos. "Wallace, this is a setup. Ben didn't kill Sophie. Xiao Long did."

That name made Wallace go very still. "What the hell does Xiao Long have to do with this?"

"He's Liu's henchman, a valued member of his triad. He's loyal to his Dragon Head. And he's the instrument Liu's using to carry out his vendetta."

A spark of realization flashed in Wallace's eyes, and Sloane could see his wheels turning. What he was thinking, she wasn't sure. Nor did she have time to ponder it.

"But it's Ben who's behind the wheel," Wallace maintained. "The car is definitely his. I recognize the Saint Jude medal hanging from his rearview mirror. How do you explain that?"

"I can't speak to how Xiao pulled it off. Only Ben can. But I can tell you that these photos have been doctored. Look. Ben is posed. He's completely unconscious, literally drooling. His head is propped against the headrest, yet his hands are on the wheel."

Wallace was staring at the photos. Sloane didn't know if he was buying her explanation. But at least he was hearing her. She was thankful for that.

"See the background here behind the car?" she pressed on, pointing. "The sun is barely up. That means these photos were taken at the approximate time Sophie was killed. There's no way Ben would have been cognizant enough to drive. But even if he had been, he'd be out of control, physically and mentally. He could never have made the rational decision to speed off after plowing into the car Sophie was in. It doesn't make sense."

"Your points are well taken. But . . ."

"Think about it. The accident happened on Eighty-ninth Street, near Sophie's school. That's a busy residential neighborhood. Ben would have swerved all over the road. Cars would have been bashed in. Pedestrians would have been injured or killed. And Ben would have ended up crashing into a tree or causing a pileup at the intersection of Eighty-ninth and Park. The cops and PIs who investigated the accident were convinced that the hit-and-run driver was fleeing from something or racing to something. He was purposeful, deliberate. So much so that not one of the dozen witnesses interviewed managed to identify his vehicle as anything but a white Mercedes sedan. They didn't catch the model, or make out even a few letters or numbers off his license plate. The driver was too quick and too focused." Again, Sloane pointed at the photos. "Does that man look like he's either of those?"

Wallace shut his eyes and sucked in his breath. He was clearly desperate to believe her.

"Coincidentally, Leo just told me he got a delivery about the same time you did." Sloane went for her trump card. "It was from a courier service. Inside was a handwritten letter from his fiancée. The envelope it came in was addressed to Leo and was postmarked June 23, 2007—their scheduled wedding day. It had clearly been stolen from his mailbox. In the letter, she begged his forgiveness and understanding. It seems that some Asian thugs had just left her condo, having held guns to her two children's heads, threatening to kill them. She was informed that the only way her children would remain alive and unharmed is if she packed her bags immediately, took her children, and moved away. Her orders were to disappear and to never contact Leo again. If she did, or if Leo discovered her whereabouts and tried to contact her, her children would die. She had no choice but to run. But I don't need to tell you what her leaving Leo standing at the altar did to him."

"No, you don't," Wallace replied, still hovering between shock, anger, and pain.

"There's more. Evidently, Liu is having Xiao Long track down Amalie. Because there's a cryptic Post-it attached to the letter, telling Leo as much, and informing him that once Amalie's been found, he'll have the luxury of watching her die."

Wallace swore, squeezing his eyes shut.

Sloane gripped his arm. "Don't you see what's happening here? Liu has ordered Xiao to destroy every member of your group. His timing is based on circumstances, some of which I can't share with you, some of which I don't even understand. But I will tell you that Phil's bookie was paid off by Xiao—and now Phil is dead. Ben's employment agency was purchased by Xiao in March 2006—and Ben is about to self-destruct. My mother was kidnapped and almost killed, and I was attacked at knifepoint. And you? You've had your soul torn out. Sophie died a few months after Meili committed suicide. Cindy—who's a dead ringer for Meili—came into your life less than a month ago. Now, these photos of Ben arrive. Don't you see the pattern?"

Slowly, Wallace nodded. "I see the pattern. I see what Liu is doing. But all that proves is that he's trying to destroy us. It doesn't prove that Ben wasn't driving the car that killed Sophie."

"There's only one person who can confirm my theory—Ben. I'm heading over to his factory now." Carefully, she slipped the photos and news clipping back into the manila envelope. "I assume I can borrow these?"

"There's no need. I'm going with you." Wallace grabbed his sport coat. "Whatever the truth is, I have to hear it directly from Ben."

CHAPTER
THIRTY-SIX

Ben crawled out of the bathroom and back to his desk. That was the third time he'd been sick in the past hour. This time he'd stayed inside the toilet stall forever, kneeling on the floor, his head against the cool wall. He was just too damned weary to get up. Besides, there was nothing to get up for.

Finally, his legs had started to cramp. He'd crept out of the stall, dunked his head under the faucet to drench his face and head with cold water, then grabbed a wad of paper towels to dry himself off. His hair was still wet and his shirt was sticking to his body. He didn't give a damn.

Now, he dropped heavily into his chair and let the chill permeate his body. Maybe if he stayed cold, he wouldn't puke again.

He opened his top drawer and pulled out a stale pack of peppermint Life-Savers, popping one in his mouth. A sucking candy. It was the first solid food he'd had since yesterday. Or was it the day before? He'd lost count.

The door to his office swung open. He didn't bother glancing up. With any luck, it was Xiao Long, here to blow his brains out. It was exactly what he wanted, but he was too spineless to do it for himself.

Jin Huang had said something about that when he'd been here earlier. Something in response to Ben's plea that Xiao put an end to all this and just kill him.

He'd enjoy. Jin Huang's taunt drifted through Ben's groggy mind. *But maybe he not come in time. Maybe you kill you first. Or maybe Johnson kill you . . . Johnson kill you . . . Johnson kill you. . .*

Abruptly, the implication of Jin Huang's prediction struck home.

He didn't have time to react. Wallace was standing in front of him, with a deadly expression that told Ben all he needed to know.

"Shit," he muttered, dropping his head in his hands and starting to tremble. Bile rose up in his throat. "He sent them to you. That son of a bitch sent them to you. Why? *Why?* Just to twist the knife in your gut? To kill you altogether? Because it's not me he's punishing. I'm already dead."

Sloane had followed Wallace in. Now she went around to the side of Ben's desk, spoke to him quietly. "So you know about the photos?"

His head came up when he heard her voice. "How could I not? They've been shoved in my face a dozen times. And each time, another piece of my soul gets eaten away." Ben forced himself to look at Wallace. "Go ahead. Do what you have to. God knows, I deserve it."

Wallace's breath was coming fast, and his fists were clenching and unclenching at his sides. Exerting this self-control was clearly the hardest thing he'd ever done.

"If it comes down to it, I will," he answered, his steely tone rife with suppressed rage. "I'll kill you with my bare hands. But not until I get some answers."

"I don't know what to say." Ben spread his hands wide, palms up in helplessness. "I don't remember anything. I didn't then. I don't now. All I know is that I must be the lowest form of scum on earth."

"Ben, listen to me." Sloane touched his sleeve, intervening before the scene turned far uglier than she believed was necessary. "I need to know if you're sober right now."

"Unfortunately, sober enough. I donated a day's supply of booze to the toilet, and stuck my head under a faucet of cold water."

"Good. Then I want you to tell me everything you remember about the morning Sophie died. Every single detail."

"Why? The photos say it all. Certainly more than I can."

"No, they don't. They only say you're in your car, after it clearly was in a violent accident. What memories do you have about that morning *before* the hit-and-run? Do you remember getting into your car, or what your destination was?"

A hard shake of his head. "I've spent two and a half years racking my brain. I remember the night before. I'd just been given a new monthly rate by Xiao Long's employment agency. I was frantic. He'd doubled prices since he bought the agency from its previous owner the month before. I couldn't make the payments. So I called him. He said that we should discuss terms, that he'd review my previous contract and sit down with me in the morning. I agreed. I met him at six A.M. so we could talk alone."

"Where?" Sloane asked.

"Some sleazy dive in Chinatown that Xiao owns. I think it was off Mott Street, south of Canal. It didn't matter. I wasn't hungry. All I cared about was that no one was around except him and me."

"So you two talked."

"Not that it did any good, but yes. He was nauseatingly solicitous—buying me drinks, explaining how the cost of labor had gone up since my previous contract with the old owner. But in the end, nothing changed."

"In other words, he said he wasn't budging on the rates."

"I don't know what the hell he said. I can't remember that part. But it turned out to be moot. The next day, he showed me those vile photos. We both knew he had me. I'd pay anything to keep him from sending them to Wallace. So the rates, and the threats, remained the same."

Wallace's jaw was working furiously. He opened his mouth to say something, but Sloane held up her hand to silence him.

"Let's back up," she instructed Ben. "You met Xiao at six A.M. He'd reviewed your contracts, but brought nothing new to the table. Clearly, he'd decided he wasn't bringing down his rates. So what was the point of the meeting?"

"To make me feel like an even bigger ass? Who knows? Does it matter? With the ammunition he wound up getting to use against me, any chance I had of negotiating a compromise was over."

"It matters. Xiao Long doesn't waste time. He always has an agenda. You said he bought you drinks. A little odd at the crack of dawn."

Ben's laugh was hollow. "Maybe. But with the state of mind I was in, booze sounded good at any hour."

"What kind of drinks were they?"

"Some traditional three-flower Chinese liquor called Sanhua Jiu. It was so strong, so bitter and nasty, I could barely choke it down. But Xiao Long made it sound like some kind of ritual. And I sure as hell didn't want to offend the guy. So I drank it—two shots, in fact. I passed out right on the table. That's why I don't know what I did or where I went."

"Who served you the drinks?"

"One of Xiao's girls. She was there when I came in. She must have been finishing up her late-night shift."

"I'm sure she was. I'm also sure she followed instructions—two rounds of Sanhua Jiu spiked with God knows what."

"Huh?" Ben looked utterly lost.

"Xiao Long set you up, Ben. I suspected it the minute I saw those photos. And everything you just said confirms my theory. You didn't kill Sophie. Xiao Long did." Sloane went on to tell Ben the deductions she'd made at Wallace's gallery—and why, including the whole story about Johnny Liu and Meili. She even took the time to fill him in on what was going on with Leo.

"With regard to you, let's add one more thing to the mix," she concluded. "You were in Chinatown at six A.M. You had a meeting there. You had two hard-core shots of booze. You passed out. I'd say you were out of commission for a good couple of hours. But your car was in a nearby parking lot. And your keys were probably right there in your jacket pocket. How incredibly convenient for Xiao. Think about it. Even if you passed out before seven, there's no way you could have come to, sobered up, and made it from downtown to the Upper East Side in time to hit the car Sophie was carpooling in. She was officially gone at seven-twenty. The accident happened a little after seven. Ben . . ." Sloane took both his hands in hers. "You weren't driving that car. You didn't kill Sophie. Xiao just made you believe you had so he could blackmail you."

Shock, disbelief, pain, realization—they all registered on Ben's face simultaneously. "Oh my God. Oh my God." He stared at Sloane, unable to absorb what he was hearing. "Are you sure?"

"Positive," she responded without hesitation. "You had nothing to do with Sophie's death. You were a victim of a different kind, thanks to Xiao Long."

"I'm innocent?" Ben needed one final word of affirmation.

"Completely."

He drew a long, ragged breath, as the weight of the world was lifted from his shoulders. "Thank you, Sloane. With every fiber of my being, I thank you."

With that, Ben turned to Wallace, tears streaming down his cheeks. "I'm sorry . . . I'm so sorry. I should have come to you. I should have told you. But you were dying inside. And I was paralyzed with guilt and consumed with pain. I loved Sophie as if she were my own. The thought that I could have hurt her, taken her life . . . but, thank the Lord, I didn't. I didn't."

He rose, walked around the desk to where Wallace was standing with tears trickling down his own cheeks.

"I was a coward," Ben choked out. "A pathetic, drunken coward. I don't deserve your forgiveness. I'm not even going to ask for it. But you can't know what it means to me that I can mourn Sophie as she deserves to be mourned, offer her the tribute she deserves, knowing that I have the right. That I wasn't the one who robbed her of life. That I . . ." He broke down completely, bowing his head and openly sobbing.

The well-bred, always self-contained Wallace Johnson stepped forward and grabbed his friend, hugging him tightly as they both continued to weep.

"You have my forgiveness," Wallace managed. "Do I have yours?"

"For what?"

"For doubting you. For believing those photos. For believing you could ever hurt Sophie and not remember. Not rush to her side. I'm sorry, Ben. From the bottom of my heart, I'm sorry."

Watching the scene unfolding before her, Sloane felt her own eyes grow damp. It was impossible to witness this emotional exchange without being affected.

"That son of a bitch," Ben burst out, pulling away. "That fucking son of a bitch. Him and his boss. Destroying people because of a bet? Because of a suicide you couldn't have prevented, since you knew nothing about Meili's pregnancy or her state of mind? What kind of monster does that?"

"A monster who can't get away with this," Sloane inserted in an adamant tone. "This or any of the other atrocities he's guilty of. I've got to get over to the FBI Field Office. I want ERT to examine these photos and the news clipping. I need to bring Derek up to speed. Then, we'll . . ."

She was interrupted by the ringing of her cell phone. When she saw the caller ID, her heart sank.

"Dad? What is it?"

"Sloane, you've got to get over here now." Matthew sounded shaken to the core. "The police are here. They have a warrant to search the apartment. They're tearing my office apart. I heard them say something about the anonymous tip being good. That they'd found a valuable painting that was stolen during that string of neighborhood burglaries. And my phone rang thirty seconds ago. It was Xiao Long. He said he'll have just enough time to kill your mother while I watch, before I went to jail. What's happening? What should I do? Should I tell the cops about the phone call? Should I tell Special Agent Carter?"

Dammit. Xiao Long had dropped all the bombs at once.

"No," Sloane said adamantly into the phone. "You know the drill. Don't say a word to anyone. Not even Agent Carter. Just tell him I'm on my way. And give Mom the same instructions. No talking. Does she know about Xiao's call?"

"Yes. She's right next to me."

"Good. Tell her to hang in there. I'm at Ben's factory. I'm on my way."

———————

En route to her parents' apartment, Sloane made two phone calls.

The first one was to Derek. She reached him, no problem, providing him with the lowdown, together with a few requests.

The second call was to Detective Diane Yuen of the Nineteenth Precinct Burglary Squad.

"Diane?" She was relieved as hell when her friend answered the phone. "You wanted me to keep you up-to-date. Well, I'm about to. But first, we have a problem. It's urgent. And I need your help."

CHAPTER
THIRTY-SEVEN

Sloane rested her head on Derek's shoulder.

It was midnight. The cottage's living room was peaceful. The fire Derek had kindled was crackling rhythmically in the fireplace. And the hounds were enjoying the warmth, stretched out near the fireplace screen, snoozing.

With a contented sigh, Sloane tucked her legs under her, curling up on the sofa. She reached for her glass of merlot and took a few sips. She'd earned it. Talk about a long, draining day.

"Tired?" Derek murmured into her hair.

"From the insanity of the day, or the three hours we just spent in bed?"

His chuckle brushed her ear. "Take your pick."

"Bonelessly, wonderfully tired from the latter. Wiped out from the former."

"Good answer." He combed his fingers through her still-damp hair. They'd taken a leisurely, soapy shower together, and were now wrapped in terry-cloth robes. "This whole thing is coming to a head. My gut tells me it's about to blast wide open."

"Mine, too. What I worry about is who's going to get caught in the cross fire, and how bad the damage will be." Sloane took another sip of wine, then placed her goblet on the coffee-table coaster. "I keep asking myself why. Why now? Why the urgency on Liu's part? Why everything at once? He's wiping out his enemies in one frenetic, simultaneous explosion, at the exact same time as he's funding the Black Eagles to pull off big-profit, high-visibility art thefts. Why take the risk?"

"Good question. I'm stumped by the same thing. Liu's smart. He always keeps a low profile. He always acts with meticulous care. And he always keeps a major trump card hidden away—just in case. None of that seems to apply here. Other than acting through Xiao Long to keep his name clean, he's going full force, guns ablazing. There's got to be a reason. I've got my feelers out. I'll find out what that reason is."

Sloane nodded. "Liu's done his worst with all the men—except Wallace. He's still exacting revenge on him, and he has been for two and a half years. First, he had Xiao kill Sophie. Then, he framed one of Wallace's dearest friends for the crime. Next, he stayed in Wallace's life as a supposed business colleague helping him get back on his feet. And now, he brought in his niece—a Meili look-alike—to emotionally torment Wallace and break his heart. He's building up to some sick grand finale. But what? And how do we stop him? We have no jurisdiction in Hong Kong, and Liu's influence runs deep and wide."

"I can't answer that one either—yet. But C-6 is building a strong case against Xiao Long. And if we can provide the assistant U.S. attorney with some hard-core evidence connecting him to Liu and the Liu Jian Triad, maybe we can get Xiao to flip on Liu. In the meantime, I'm trying to second-guess Liu. The final ways for him to go after Wallace are financial ruin and personal humiliation."

"And then death," Sloane concluded quietly. "Killing Wallace after stripping him of everything would be the only way Liu could settle the score enough for him."

Derek didn't dispute the obvious. "Let's see what my feelers turn up. I should hear back tomorrow. Until then, the FBI agents we assigned to Wallace have been advised of the escalated danger. They're on high alert."

Sloane chewed her lip, worry creasing her brow. "Wallace is scared. He'll never admit it, but he is. Now that he realizes the full extent of Liu's hatred, and how far he'll go to carry out his vendetta, he's pretty shaken up. Especially with Xiao Long breathing down his neck, ready and waiting to do Liu's bidding. I tried to reassure him. I reminded him that we put extra security on him and that we're working with the Hong Kong police to establish solid evidence against Liu. I even tried to divert his mind by giving him something to look forward to. He has a big fund-raising event at the Jaspar Museum in Soho tomorrow. He's one of the museum's major sponsors. I urged him to go."

"And?"

"And he said he'll think about it." Sloane sighed. "I wasn't going to lie to him, Derek. I don't blame him for being scared."

"Neither do I. But if anyone can reach him, you can. You have a way with people that's amazing."

"I hope that holds true in this case. After Wallace left Ben's factory, all he wanted to do was have it out with Cindy—which I doubt was pretty—and then lock himself in seclusion. I told him I'd get his partners to gang up on him and drag him out if need be." Sloane raked her hands through her hair. "I feel so damned helpless."

"You're not. You're getting answers. So am I. We're closing in on this case. We'll get there."

She twisted around to gaze up at him. "Speaking of which, if I haven't said it enough times, thank you for what you did for my father."

"I didn't do it alone," Derek reminded her. "Your friend Diane worked with me every step of the way. Your dad's technically in custody. So's your mom, on trumped-up charges of obstructing justice. All that's only for Xiao's benefit. This way, if his Red Dragons poke around to make sure the cops found the stolen painting where they planted it, they'll find out that your father's been arrested and is being held at the Nineteenth Precinct—along with your mother, so Xiao doesn't try going after her. But don't worry. They're in a comfortable break room, not a cell. The charges are pending until we wrap up the case. But we all know the anonymous tip was an obvious setup."

"And a scare tactic. That phone call Xiao made nearly gave my parents heart attacks. As for the setup, Xiao might as well have hung up a neon sign."

"Yeah." Derek made a derisive sound. "Out of the blue and at the exact same time that Wallace and Leo are getting their packages and Ben is being pushed over the edge by Jin Huang, the Nineteenth Precinct gets a call from one of the victims of Xiao's Upper East Side burglaries, claiming he'd gotten an unsigned note saying he could have back his priceless painting *The Bird*— for a finder's fee of twenty-five thousand dollars. Of course, when he called the phone number provided, he got a voice mail message saying he'd reached Matthew Burbank and Associates. Then, low and behold, when the cops ransack your father's office, they find *The Bird* shoved behind one of his office file cabinets."

"Not to mention that *The Bird* just happened to be stolen a week before my parents' place was ransacked. Now I know why my mother said Xiao's guys spent a long time shoving things around in my father's office, when they already knew damned well where the Rothberg file was. Could there be a more obvious plan to frame my father for art theft?"

"Nope. Then again, Xiao wasn't going for subtlety."

Sloane frowned. "You're sure the police will drop the charges?"

"Positive." Derek counted off on his fingers. "Your father has an alibi for the night *The Bird* was stolen. Johnny Liu has a vendetta against your father and his partners—one he unleashed on all of them simultaneously. And the FBI has a solid case against Xiao Long, who we'll try to establish has a connection with Johnny Liu. Trust me, there'll be no problem. All the charges against your father will be dropped. Diane and the Bureau are already working on it."

"I owe both you and Diane a huge debt of thanks for jumping on this and getting it resolved so quickly."

"You can thank Diane by buying her lunch. As for me, I have other ideas for how you can express your undying gratitude."

Sloane smiled. "With pleasure, Agent Parker."

"Oh, one more thing I forgot to tell you. When I talked to Leo, he told me he was rifling through your file that night in the hopes of finding the dossier the Bureau had compiled on him, and that it might contain something that would give him a clue as to where his fiancée was. He realized it was a long shot, but he saw the file and acted on impulse. I can't blame the guy."

"Neither can I. I'd move heaven and earth to find you."

Derek gave her a deep, slow kiss. "You won't have to. I'm right here. And I'm not going anywhere."

"Derek, let's get married."

Sloane's proposal came out of the blue. Derek was so stunned he nearly fell off the sofa. "What did you just say?"

"I said let's get married. Soon. Before I reapply to the FBI, and hopefully am accepted. Before I go down to Quantico and put in my time at the Academy. This way, when I graduate, the Bureau will be more apt to place me in the New York Field Office with you. We'll be married, but there'll be no conflict of interests. You handle Violent Crimes, and I handle White-Collar Crimes. Different squads, same Field Office. This way, when I start my new professional life, my personal life will already be exactly where I want it."

Derek was still staring at her. She'd obviously given this a great deal of thought. Even so, he had to be convinced she was a hundred percent certain.

"You're sure this is what you want?" he asked bluntly. "That you're ready to make this official? To commit to a lifetime? It's a huge step."

"Unless you're not ready, or it's not what you want." Sloane's tone was teasing, but her gaze was serious as she searched Derek's face.

"Are you crazy?" Derek gripped her shoulders. "Say the word, and we'll get a marriage license tomorrow." He frowned. "If we lived in New York, we could be husband and wife the next day. In New Jersey, there's a three-day waiting period. But, okay, we'll be married this weekend."

Sloane laughed. "I see you've done your research. But let's slow down, just a little. And not just because of this Johnny Liu case that's about to explode wide open. Although, truthfully, I'd like to put it behind us so we can enjoy our day."

"Fine. What else?"

"I'm not a big fan of traditional weddings, but I'd kind of like to have our families there, and a few close friends. And I'd also like a little time to savor the thought of becoming your wife. How about a December wedding, right before the holidays? That'll give us six weeks to plan."

"Done. Let's pick a date."

CHAPTER
THIRTY-EIGHT

Sloane and Derek drove into the Field Office together the next morning. Once inside, they went their separate ways. Derek headed off to fill Rich in on *The Bird* and all the other happenings of yesterday. And Sloane went into one of the conference rooms for her morning's first order of business: calling the Nineteenth Precinct to check on her parents.

They were both hanging in there. So, Matthew reported, were his friends, all of whom he'd spoken to. Everyone was strung out, but holding it together. Each in his own way was taking steps to put his life back together. Leo was welcoming the bittersweet knowledge that Amalie had never stopped loving him, but had left him to protect her children. He was worried sick about her, but convinced, thanks to the FBI, that Xiao Long hadn't yet located her. If he had, she'd be dead, killed right before Leo's eyes. So Leo was focusing on a plan, once this crisis was behind them, to hire a PI to find her—hopefully so they could enjoy the happy ending they'd been deprived of.

Ben was calling his AA sponsor and arranging to attend a meeting. And to Sloane's pleasure and surprise, Wallace had decided to take her advice and attend the Jaspar Museum's evening fund-raiser.

The details of her father's update lifted a huge weight off Sloane's shoulders. All these fundamentally decent men she'd known all her life had been through hell. All of them were at their breaking points. And all of them were fighting their way back.

Relieved beyond measure, Sloane shifted her focus to checking out a completely different extraneous detail that had been bugging her.

The background check that Derek had run on Cindy Liu had been so clean that it practically sparkled. It had also been superficial, the only personal detail being her close relationship with her uncle. Something about that didn't sit right. It was almost as if the details of her life had been scrubbed clean.

Which usually implied there was something to hide.

Maybe they were all underestimating Cindy Liu. They'd relegated her role in Liu's plan to wreaking havoc on Wallace's emotions. But she was a very intelligent, very talented woman.

So maybe there was more to it. Maybe Cindy's talents were being used in a more diverse fashion.

Sloane logged on to one of the conference room computers and began her search.

———

Sloane lost track of time as her search took on a life of its own. She started digging deeper, and the slight niggle she'd been feeling going into this escalated into a full-fledged suspicion. The information she was uncovering wouldn't interest only Derek. It would also interest Rich. It smacked of being a major link connecting all the tentacles of this complicated and diverse case.

She'd just printed out some pertinent pages when the conference room door swung open and Derek strode in.

"There you are," he said, the frustration in his tone telling Sloane he'd been searching for a while. "I was getting a little antsy. You vanished hours ago."

Sloane glanced at her watch, startled when she saw the time. She'd been in the conference room for over three hours. "Sorry. I had no idea I'd been in here so long. I checked in with my dad, and then got involved in some online research. I want to run my findings by you and Rich . . ." She broke off when she saw the intense expression on Derek's face. "You struck pay dirt. What did you find out?"

"More than I expected." He sat down beside her, crackling with as much energy as a live wire. "I got those phone calls I was waiting for. The first was from a former Army Ranger buddy of mine who's working in the U.S. Embassy in Beijing. He did enough digging to get us our answer as to why Liu's hell-bent on executing all his plans urgently and simultaneously. He's dying. He's only got a month or two to live."

All the pieces fell into place in Sloane's mind. "Of course. Now it all makes sense. Liu wants to settle all his personal scores and fill the triad's coffers with a ton of cash before he dies." A pause. "And I suspect he's getting a lot more cash than even we're aware of."

"Meaning?"

"I'll get into that in a minute." Sloane wanted to hear the rest of Derek's news first. "Who was your other phone call from?"

"One of my contacts at the Guardia di Finanza."

"The Italian special police force?"

"Yup. My kind of outfit—military corps *and* law enforcement all in one."

"I've dealt with them. They serve the Ministry of the Economy and Finance and investigate financial crime like credit card fraud and money laundering."

"*And* anti-Mafia operations," Derek added.

Sloane's brows arched. "Go on."

"It turns out they're investigating Wallace's leather company—which, incidentally, is totally controlled through a complex web of legal entities, several of which are located in Hong Kong, all with Cayman Island bank accounts. The ownership is so convoluted that only Wallace is traceable."

"Why?"

"Good question. Even better answer. The Guardia di Finanza suspects that the company has been manufacturing counterfeit high-end leather goods and that it has strong ties to Albanian organized crime."

"Damn." Sloane exhaled sharply. "So Liu is not only robbing Wallace blind *and* setting him up to take the fall for a dirty business but he's also setting him up so the authorities will believe he has ties to Albanian organized crime."

"And you and I know exactly why. Liu's planning things so that when Rich and his squad close in on the Black Eagles, he'll miraculously discover that their funding leads straight to Wallace. Johnny Liu will have extricated himself entirely, and Wallace will be stripped of everything and charged with every crime in the book, including conspiracy, racketeering, major theft, and murder."

That prompted a question in Sloane's mind. "How long has Wallace had an ownership interest in this leather goods company?"

"A year. Why?"

Sloane shrugged. "I'm just surprised that Wallace didn't take on a more active role in the purchase. He was an investment banker before Sophie died—a pretty brilliant one. It's out of character for him to blindly trust someone else to handle all the details on such a sizable transaction. Even if Wallace didn't have the wherewithal to take the reins in the acquisition, he'd at least do some due diligence. Clearly, he didn't. If he had, I'm sure he would have spotted something fishy."

"What are you getting at?" Derek asked.

"I'm not sure." Sloane studied Derek uneasily. "Could there have been a different motivating factor—one that would keep Wallace from asking any questions?"

"You mean like blackmail?" Derek mulled over the possibility. "Liu certainly pulled it off with Wallace's partners, through Xiao Long. But what would they have on Wallace to blackmail him with—other than those things Liu was unwilling to make him aware of?"

"You're right. I'm probably overthinking this."

"Maybe. Maybe not. We've spent a lot of time exploring Liu's ties to Wallace as they relate to Meili. We really should broaden the spectrum, investigate the entirety of their history."

"And while we're at it, I think we should include Cindy in that investigation. She and her amah."

"That woman Peggy Sun? Why?"

"Because she came to the U.S. with Cindy fifteen years ago. Since then, she's attended some very prestigious art programs—at Johnny Liu's expense, I'm sure. There's no way a governess could afford training like this. And the direction of the training . . ." Sloane held out the pages she'd printed right when Derek walked in. "Take a look at this."

Derek scanned the first page, then the second. He raised his head. "I have to make a quick phone call. But I think we should get this right to Rich."

"I agree."

Instantly, Derek punched in Rich's extension. Then he stepped out to make his call.

———

Liu motioned for his trusted adviser to enter his private library.

"Zhezhi." One word, uttered as a command.

His adviser understood. Literally, *Zhezhi* was the Chinese art of paper folding, a predecessor to origami. But in this case, Liu was instructing him to collapse all traces of his involvement—ties to the Italian leather goods company, to any paintings bought from and sold by Wallace's galleries, to shipping manifests for the stolen and forged paintings, and to his orchestration of the plan to destroy all the members of the art partnership.

In response, his adviser nodded. "It will be done at once," he said in the Loong Doo dialect.

"And my family?" It was phrased like an inquiry. It was anything but.

"As we speak, steps are being taken so that Cindy and her amah will have nothing to hide. Their home, their characters, will be beyond reproach. As for Xiao, he's ready to assume the role of Dragon Head as soon as he's needed. He'll leave for Hong Kong on your command. He knows that, as a precaution, a special bank account in the Cayman Islands has been arranged for him, to be used in the future should he miss his window of opportunity to escape and end up going to prison. He is humbled by your generosity. Your name will never be uttered."

"Excellent," Liu replied. "Then I can bring my life to a close, and join my daughter."

Derek was back from making his phone call when, five minutes after being summoned, Rich came striding through the conference room door.

"I had *The Bird* authenticated," he reported. "It's genuine. Unfortunately, it's also devoid of fingerprints or anything else that could link it to the Red Dragons." He looked intently from Derek to Sloane. "I doubt that's the reason for your urgent call."

"Read these." Derek gave Rich the pages of Sloane's research. "We want your opinion."

With a great deal more thoroughness than Derek, Rich pored over the sheets of information. Then he let out a low whistle. "My opinion is that we'd better do an exhaustive profile on Peggy Sun. Ditto for Cindy Liu. And *fast*. I agree with Sloane—these two are doing a lot more to assist Cindy's uncle than manipulating Wallace Johnson's emotions."

Derek's cell phone rang. He flipped it open and glanced at the caller ID. PRIVATE.

He punched the receive button. "Yes?" he said cautiously.

"Hello, Special Agent Parker," a polished voice with the slightest hint of an Asian accent greeted him. "Your extreme interest in me is flattering. I thought it was time I contacted you directly."

Derek's eyes narrowed. "Who is this?"

"I think you know. But if you need confirmation, that's fine. This is Johnny Liu."

"Johnny Liu," Derek repeated, his hard, pointed stare meeting Sloane's startled gaze, then flickering to Rich's intrigued one. Quietly pressing the speakerphone button, Derek placed the phone on the conference table and pulled his chair up close beside it. "How did you get this number?"

"I would think by now you'd realize I'm a resourceful man. There's very little I can't acquire."

"Including the most efficient and devout followers," Derek replied. "Xiao Long has really proven himself to be a worthy Dai Lo. You must be very proud."

"By nature, I am proud. What I'm not is stupid. Don't insult my intelligence with pathetic attempts to bait me."

"Fair enough." Derek gripped his phone more tightly. "No games. Just tell me why you're calling. Are you hoping to make some kind of deal before we have enough on you to make that impossible?"

"Again you insult me." Liu didn't even flinch at Derek's pointed question. "I make deals every day, Agent Parker. Business deals. I set the rules. I profit by them. What you're referring to isn't a deal. I believe it's what you Americans call bartering. That kind of negotiation is beneath me."

"I see. But criminal acts are not."

"That's actually the reason for my call." Once again, Liu evaded the question and led the conversation in the direction of his choice. "I have some helpful information to pass along to you. It might provide the answers you're looking for."

"I'm listening."

"One of the gentlemen you're investigating has an estate in East Hampton. It's been brought to my attention that he has his own private art collection buried deep inside his manor. No one is permitted to enter. He keeps it under lock and key. I've been told he has good reason for that secrecy. The paintings he owns are all valuable, many of them priceless masterpieces. Sadly, they're also stolen. I'm assuming that Special Agent Williams is with you now, being that you've put me on speakerphone. Am I correct?"

Rich didn't miss a beat. "I'm right here, Liu."

"Good. Then Agent Parker doesn't have to waste time relaying my message. I know how eager you both are for justice to be done. It would be a shame for others to be sent to prison for the crimes of one. Especially Matthew Burbank. He's already under arrest and suffering great strain—possibly beyond his endurance." A poignant pause. "How is his daughter holding up? The poor woman must be at her breaking point. I know how close you two are, Agent Parker. Losing her would be tragic."

Derek heard the underlying threat loud and clear. He gritted his teeth, fully aware that Liu wanted to get a reaction out of him. He wasn't going to get it.

Sloane opened her mouth to cut Liu off. Rich silenced her with a hard shake of his head.

"Thank you for your concern," Derek said in a calm, even tone. "Although I think you should reserve it for your own health. From what I understand, your time here is very limited."

The barest hint of a pause. "I'm at peace. I've accomplished all I set out to. And my honor will be my legacy."

"Good to know." Derek didn't pursue the point. "As for your tip about the East Hampton estate, I'm sure Special Agent Williams will take the necessary steps."

"I doubt a phone call from me will suffice. But my sources tell me a package should be arriving at your desk within the hour. It will give you more than you need for a search warrant."

"How considerate of your sources—and of you."

"I'm glad I could help. Have a nice day, Agent Parker."

The connection was broken.

"Unexpected," Rich commented drily.

"Desperate," Derek amended. "Liu knows we're getting close. He wants Wallace to go down—fast."

Sloane, who had remained unusually quiet, now spoke up. Her tone was strained as she strove for objectivity. "It's no news flash that Liu wants to destroy Wallace. But he can't fabricate a roomful of stolen paintings. We were just questioning what could be used to blackmail Wallace. It's possible we just got our answer."

Both men looked at her. "Why would Wallace associate himself with stolen paintings?" Derek asked.

"I don't know. But Liu does. We've got to follow up on this lead."

"I intend to." Rich's wheels were already turning. "I'll call the assistant U.S. attorney and alert him to the fact that we're going to need a search warrant fast. As soon as we see what's in Liu's package, we'll act." A quizzical look at Sloane. "You know Johnson better than we do. How hostile a reception should we expect when we march into his house with a search warrant?"

Sloane glanced down at her watch. "No reception at all. My father convinced Wallace to go to a museum reception in Soho. Other than possibly whizzing by each other on the parkway, we won't be seeing him." She swallowed. "We also don't have to go through a whole production to gain entry. My parents have a spare key to his house. They go out to the Hamptons a lot over the summer. Wallace insists they stay at his place."

"Sloane, this is going to be hard on you," Derek said gently. "You don't have to go."

"You couldn't stop me if you tried." Sloane gave him a wan smile. "I appreciate your compassion. But I need to see this through."

"Understood."

"Then I'll make that call so our warrant will be ready when we are," Rich said.

"Make that *two* warrants," Sloane corrected. "Liu's sources weren't just Xiao Long and the Red Dragons. Not this time. Xiao had outside help. I vote for Cindy Liu. Between what we're beginning to piece together about the roles that she and Peggy are playing in Liu's operation, and the fact that Cindy just happened to have returned from a romantic weekend at Wallace's place . . ."

"As an architect, she'd remember the layout of the manor well and make a mental note of any rooms that were locked tight and off-limits," Derek finished for her.

"Exactly." Sloane was already back on the computer. "Rich, you go make those phone calls. Derek, stick to your desk till that package arrives. I'll call Diane and ask her to find out from my mother where in their apartment she keeps Wallace's key. Someone from the precinct can pick it up and drop it off here at the security desk. I'm not leaving this computer until I find something—*anything*—on Peggy Sun. Digging for information on Cindy won't do any good. Liu will have covered her ass in every way possible. But Peggy's another story. He won't have been as thorough with her. Which makes her vulnerable—especially since she's up against me."

Rich regarded Sloane with amused admiration. "I don't envy Peggy Sun. She doesn't stand a chance." His gaze shifted to Derek. "Neither do you."

"Not to worry. I give as good as I get. Plus, I love a challenge." Derek shot Rich a quick grin. "Besides, I don't know why you're surprised. Tony warned you she'd end up being this case's lead agent."

CHAPTER
THIRTY-NINE

The package Johnny Liu had described arrived twenty minutes later.

With Sloane and Rich peering over his shoulder, Derek tore it open. Inside were spreadsheet printouts detailing specific assets that Wallace had liquidated and their selling price, and matching receipts documenting monetary deposits made to a numbered bank account in the Cayman Islands.

A copy of the original account application confirmed that the numbered account, along with all transactions connected to it, belonged to Wallace.

"Bribery goes a long way," Sloane commented, trying to keep her tone light.

"It sure does. All it takes is one greedy bank employee to bypass the veil of secrecy. Or a bank manager desperate to keep his biggest customer—a customer who's threatening to withdraw all his money to force the bank manager's hand." Rich reached across the desk to grab Derek's phone and used it to notify the assistant U.S. attorney that they were armed with the grounds they needed and on their way to secure their search warrant. "Did someone from the Nineteenth Precinct drop off the key to Johnson's place?" he asked Sloane.

Sloane held it up.

"Good. Then let's pick up the warrant and get on the road. As it is, we'll be fighting rush-hour traffic."

"We'll have to take two cars," Derek informed him. "My SWAT gear fills my entire trunk, and my backseat is loaded with boxes of personal stuff I've been meaning to clean out."

"Not a problem. My trunk's jammed, too, between my firearms bag, vest, shotgun, and MP5, plus all the changes of clothes I keep in there for under-cover work."

Derek's brows shot up. "You still carry a Remington and MP5?"

Rich's lips twitched. "I may be a decade older than you, and no longer on SWAT, but I'm in better shape than you are," he retorted. "I was doing Major Theft and Enhanced SWAT when you were still in high school using Cleara-sil. Oh, and remember, I'm a former marine. You're just a former Army Ranger—what we call a marine wannabe."

"My mistake." Derek snapped off a mock salute. "Didn't mean to insult your abilities. Although when we have more time, I plan to challenge you over that snide remark. Loser buys dinner, drinks, and cigars."

"Make that *two* steak dinners, drinks, and cigars. You already owe me one. I'll be glad to relieve you of another. So bring your wallet and you're on." Humor faded as Rich's mind returned to the matter at hand. "Time to head out. I'll follow you and Sloane."

"That's a given." Derek couldn't help it. Rich had set himself up for this one. "Rangers lead the way."

———

A half hour later, with the sun setting behind them, the two cars were en route to East Hampton, search warrant in hand.

As Derek drove, Sloane contemplated the intriguing pattern that had emerged during her research. There was a distinct correlation between the dates of Cin-dy's recent cocktail party appearances and the equally recent burglaries carried out by the Albanian art-theft team. In addition, every one of the burglary vic-tims had been a guest at the cocktail party Cindy had attended just before their homes were burglarized, and, from the specifics Sloane had acquired from the follow-up calls she'd just made, they had spent time chatting with Cindy about potential renovations to their homes and the existing layouts.

Interestingly, not one of the hosts and hostesses' apartments had been robbed, even though there was a wealth of valuable paintings in each of their homes. Cindy was far too smart to be so obvious.

Timetables were lining up. Sequences of events were making more and more sense. And ultimate connections, and conclusions, were being drawn.

"You're awfully quiet," Derek commented. "Are you concentrating on your notes, or worrying about what we'll find at Wallace's place?"

Sloane looked up. "Honestly? I've laid out what I think is an ingenious addition to Johnny Liu's plan. I'll give you the details later, and the bottom line now. Short and sweet—Cindy is scoping out homes to rob, the Black Eagles are carrying out the crimes, and Peggy is forging copies of the stolen paintings. It's all being shipped to China, and Johnny Liu is selling them and making a huge profit. My guess from what I've learned hearing my dad talk about the art dealing world? Liu is selling the forgeries on the open market, and the originals to private collectors—quietly and secretly."

"Getting paid twice, along with the security of knowing that the valuable original will never see the light of day. And even if it does, and it's identified, there'll be no trail leading back to him." Derek let out an admiring whistle. "Smart plan. Smarter analysis. Great work."

A half smile. "I aim to please." The smile vanished. "The one thing I'm missing, which is the most important part, is how to turn this theory into enough probable cause to get our warrant to search Cindy's place. But I'm working on it."

She glanced around, tensing as she realized they were nearing their destination. "As for your question about Wallace, I'm not looking forward to what we might find at his house. But I'll deal with it. There's no choice. Although I still can't figure out his motive. Liquidating his assets to buy stolen paintings? It just doesn't fit."

"I can't disagree with you." Derek turned onto Wallace's street. "I'm hoping we'll find answers."

They maneuvered down the long winding driveway, Rich directly behind them. As Sloane had predicted, Wallace's BMW wasn't in the driveway or the garage.

Still, they gave a procedural knock on the front door.

"FBI," Derek called out. "We have a warrant to search your house." A pause, then a second knock, this one louder than the first. "Johnson, it's Agent Derek Parker of the FBI. If you're in there, open the door."

No movement or reply.

Derek gave Sloane a terse nod.

She took out her parents' key and opened the door. The rhythmic, warning beeps of the burglar alarm sounded, and Sloane punched in the code her mother had given her. The beeping stopped, telling them that there'd be no tripping the alarm.

The foyer was dark.

Rich flipped on the light just inside the door. Automatically, Derek pulled out his pistol, raising it in a defensive motion.

"He's not home," Sloane stated tonelessly. "And he wouldn't know how to hold a gun, much less fire it."

"It's procedure, Sloane," Derek replied. "You know that as well as I do. This manor is way too big to assume no one's here just because the car is missing and Wallace didn't answer the door. As soon as we're sure all's clear, I'll holster my weapon."

Sloane nodded.

"Rich, you and Sloane start looking around," Derek instructed. "I'll cover you."

They made their way through the foyer and stepped down into the sunken living room. Sloane paused, reaching over to slide up the light dimmer until the room was illuminated enough to make out everything in it.

The first object they saw was the painting of the little Chinese girl. Wallace had put it on an easel just inside the room, so the eye would be drawn directly to it.

"That's beautiful," Sloane murmured, approaching the painting and studying the innocent quality of the little girl.

"It should be," Rich responded drily, walking up close to the painting and studying the details of its design and frame. "It's a costly painting, created by a highly successful Chinese artist. It was stolen from a private collector in Beijing six months ago."

Sloane's head jerked toward Rich. "Stolen?"

He nodded. "So we've already got grounds for Wallace's arrest."

"What we've got is grounds for that second search warrant," Sloane corrected him. "Wallace didn't steal or buy this painting. He told me that Cindy gave it to him as a thank-you gift from her and her uncle."

Derek had already flipped open his phone. "I'll call Jeff and have him get started on the warrant right away. I don't want to give Cindy Liu an extra minute to clear out any evidence she's hiding at her apartment. If we can tie this stolen painting to Johnny Liu, it will be a real coup."

"It'll get you the warrant. But it won't get you Liu," Rich apprised him. "He'll deny knowing it was stolen property when he bought it. He's probably already fabricated a paper trail to make the provenance as murky as possible."

"Plus, he'd never send us here if he knew we'd find something to use against him or his niece," Sloane added. "But right now, I'll settle for the warrant."

"You'll have it." Derek called Jeff and set the wheels in motion.

After that, Sloane, Rich, and Derek made their way through the seven-thousand-square-foot manor, room by room. The starkness of each room revealed a man whose emptiness had consumed him. The furniture was minimal, the accents nil. Any remaining space that was richly decorated and highlighted with complementary colors was clearly the work of Beatrice's elite European interior designer, and had been done ages ago.

The one bedroom that emanated personal warmth and a sense of light and life was, without question, Sophie's. Painted a soft pastel pink, it had ruffled white curtains at the windows and a matching bedspread on the four-poster bed. The bed and one entire wall was filled with dolls and stuffed animals, and the dresser held a DVD player, a color TV, and a lineup of Disney and other family-oriented DVDs. The way the room was arranged, the exact lineup of toys and movies, told Sloane that, other than keeping the room immaculate, Wallace hadn't changed a thing since Sophie's death.

She felt a lump in her throat as she turned away.

"Let's move on" was all she said.

Exploring the multitude of rooms took an inordinate amount of time. But even though the doors were shut, none of them was locked, not even Wallace's bedroom, which was masculine but minimal—a place to sleep but not to live.

They checked the basement, which would be an obvious choice, but it was nothing more than a storage room. Ditto with the attic. They checked the wine cellar, which was stocked only with bottles of fine wine. They even checked the garage, which had two additional pricey sedans in it, but no paintings.

"Do you think Liu was lying?" Sloane asked.

"No." Rich shook his head. "There'd be no point. Besides, if Johnson's collection is not only hidden but also extensive, I haven't seen a room yet that would fit the bill as a gallery."

"So it's time to play *Nancy Drew: The Hidden Staircase*," Sloane murmured. "I'd suggest we start looking for places in the main section of the house that might lead to an inconspicuous stairway. Maybe an area with wood panels, where a doorway made of the same wood would blend in and go unnoticed."

"There are wood panels in the breakfast room, the den, and the media room," Derek reported.

"Fine. Let's each of us take one of those rooms and explore it inch by inch." Rich jerked his thumb in the direction of the kitchen. "I'll take the breakfast room. It forms an L-shape with the kitchen, but it juts out to the rear, so it's not visible to arriving guests. It's also a place where Wallace would probably spend time when he was here—reading the paper, eating his meals."

"I'll take the den," Sloane announced. "Wallace's leather wingback chair is in there; he's had it forever. His brandy's also in there. So are his books and his photo albums. It's the most personal room in the house, other than Sophie's."

"Then the media room's mine," Derek said. "It's fully wood-paneled. And, with all the electronic components in there, it would be easy to conceal a doorway."

The three of them scattered, each taking a flashlight with them to minimize the number of lights they had to turn on, but maximize the illuminated areas they were searching.

Sloane walked into the den and swept the room with her flashlight. The wingback chair was kitty-cornered on the left at the front of the room, flanked by small wooden side tables. There was an enormous bookcase that covered the full extent of the far wall. But the shelves were constructed of solid mahogany. They weighed a ton, and Sloane doubted that she'd find a spring-activated secret panel, like in the old movies, that would allow her access by pressing the correct shelf.

The rear left side of the room had a fireplace. Beside it was a sideboard, and a full liquor cabinet to accompany it. Again, heavy as a rock, and not a practical spot to conceal a door for a man who wanted frequent access to a gallery of stolen paintings.

Sloane crossed over to the right wall. There was a bay window spanning most of it, so that area was out. But there was a space between where the window ended and the adjacent wall where the bookcase began. The only thing filling that spot was a low table, which contained a vase of daisies, a photo album, and a framed picture of Sophie, smiling at her nursery school graduation.

Gently, Sloane tugged at the table. It moved easily, so easily that it surprised her. She looked more closely and saw that the table was made out of plywood, painted to match the rest of the red-brown furniture, but light as a feather.

She lifted it out of the way and stepped into the barely noticeable corner, which was hidden by the depth of the bookcase. She aimed her flashlight at the three-foot section of the now-exposed wall.

The outline of the door was clear. So was the dead bolt that stood between Sloane and her goal.

"Guys," she called out. "I've got something."

The sound of thudding footsteps came from two different directions. An instant later, both Derek and Rich appeared, shining their flashlights around the room.

"Over here," Sloane instructed.

They joined her, and Derek gave a triumphant grunt. "This is it. Sloane, your instincts come through again."

"Except I have no clue how to get past that dead bolt."

"The old-fashioned way." Derek walked over to the fireplace, picked up one of the heavy andirons, and carried it back to use as a battering ram. He began whacking at the lock. The door shuddered with each strike. It took time and patience, but at last the wood around the lock began to give—more, a little more—until finally it gave out.

Derek shoved open the door and groped on the inside wall until he found a light switch. He flipped it on, revealing a long, winding staircase. "Let's go."

They trekked down the stairs, Derek leading the way.

At the foot of the stairs was another light switch. Derek flipped this one on, too, just as all three of them reached the base of the stairs.

The room was flooded by a soft, iridescent light, revealing the entirety of Wallace's private sanctum—and all of its contents.

"Holy shit," Derek blurted out, staring around at the wealth of paintings covering the walls.

It was a full, private, and very personal art gallery.

There were over two dozen paintings, some of them incredibly valuable—masterpieces by Renoir or Cassatt—others far less pricey, whose signatures labeled them as up-and-coming artists, plus a few Hamptons locals.

Every painting depicted a little girl, ranging in age between two and six. Each child emanated joy and exuberance—some of them running through fields, others picking flowers, splashing in the ocean, or chasing butterflies.

All of them celebrating life.

The gallery Wallace had created was devoid of furnishings, with the exception of a wingback chair in the dead center of the room with a small end table beside it. On the table were a bottle of bourbon, a lowball glass, and a neatly stacked pile of snapshots. The leather chair was identical to the one upstairs, with the additional feature of being able to swivel 360 degrees—obviously to allow Wallace full viewing options.

There was one bare spot on the far wall directly across from the staircase, clearly awaiting the painting that would put the crowning touch on Wallace's collection. Once it was hung in its place of honor, the tribute would be complete.

Wordlessly, Sloane scanned the room, her gaze lingering on certain paintings. Then, she picked up the snapshots and sifted through them, feeling tears sting behind her eyes. They were all photos of Sophie. They all captured her at different moments, in different settings.

But they all captured her sense of pure joy.

Raising her head, Sloane walked over to one painting that reminded her so much of one of the photos in her hand. It was a Cassatt, and the little girl in it was laughing, frolicking outdoors, eyes bright with wonder. Her hair was streaming out all around her as she dashed about with all the delight and innocence of childhood. God, she looked so much like Sophie. The same golden brown hair and dancing eyes. The same exuberance. Alive, vital, filled with a love of life and the promise of tomorrow.

A promise she'd been deprived of. Just as her father had been deprived of sharing it with her.

Rich was already across the room, examining the paintings. "Astonishing masterpieces," he murmured. "There's a work by Bouguereau, one by Rembrandt . . . unbelievable. The value of the paintings in this room—I can only begin to imagine." He walked over to the one empty space on the wall. "This is obviously meant for the final painting in Johnson's private gallery," he concluded, half to himself. "I wonder which one he has in mind. Which work of art would belong here? Johnson wouldn't settle for anything less than the perfect choice."

"It's probably a moot point," Derek reminded Rich. "I doubt he and Johnny Liu are doing any more business, so Johnson won't be getting that final painting after all."

"True." Rich continued to closely scrutinize the paintings. "I recognize several of these masterpieces as being among those stolen by the Black Eagles at the recent museum heists in Spain and Germany. The Cassatt over here and that Miró belong to the Museo de Arte Moderno. And the portrait of the little girl in a field of wildflowers is a Renoir that was displayed at the Kunsthalle in Munich."

"What I recognize is that we have our motive," Sloane stated, trying to separate emotion from fact. She recognized that Wallace had bought stolen paintings, knowing full well that it was a crime. On the other hand, she understood why he'd done it. She could only begin to imagine the pain that was still tearing him up inside.

"This gallery is a father's ultimate memorial for his daughter," she determined aloud. "A five-year-old innocent child whose murder was ordered by the very man who orchestrated the selling of these paintings to Wallace. Liu was using Xiao Long as a conduit to prolong Wallace's agony and to keep alive the paralyzing pain of Sophie's death—probably in the hopes of driving Wallace over the edge."

"And having the perfect ammunition to blackmail him with," Derek added. "Wallace had to be terrified of going to jail, more terrified of what Xiao would do to him if he opened his mouth, and most terrified of losing his link to the paintings that were his obsession."

"Now we know why Johnson flipped out when I mentioned Xiao Long's name in connection with the Rothberg." Rich dropped another puzzle piece into place. "He was learning that the same man he'd been buying valuable stolen paintings from was the killer who Burbank, Fox, and Leary had seen in Kowloon and was now threatening their lives. That realization must have blown his mind."

With a shudder, Sloane turned away. "This whole plot makes me sick."

"Liu's a bastard. That doesn't change the fact that Wallace is guilty of buying and harboring stolen property," Derek replied quietly. "We have no choice but to arrest him."

"I'm not arguing," Sloane returned.

"And we'd better move fast," Rich informed them. "Remember, once Sloane talked to Johnson, he figured out that Liu was behind the sale of the paintings and that he means to bring him down at all costs. If Johnson is as smart as I think he is, he's going to get this merchandise out of here as soon as possible."

"And hide it where?" Sloane asked, spreading her hands wide. "There must be thirty paintings here."

"I have no idea what his plan is. I only know we've got to get him into custody before he or the evidence disappears." Rich's brows drew together, and he glanced quizzically at Sloane. "Didn't you say he was at a museum reception tonight?"

"Yes." Sloane nodded. "At the Jaspar Museum of Art—on Crosby Street in Soho."

"We can grab him there," Derek concluded. "Rich, call the Major Theft Squad from your car. Work out whatever details you have to. I'll call C-6 and have them seal off this manor until ERT can catalog and take the stolen pieces into evidence. When I talk to my squad, I'll also check on the status of the warrant to search Cindy Liu's place."

Rich nodded. "Agreed."

Derek was already climbing the stairs, taking them two at a time. "Let's move."

CHAPTER
FORTY

It was dark.

The business day had ended hours ago.

The team's targeted industrial area was empty except for a few delivery trucks parked behind fenced-in loading docks and surrounded by tall razor-wire fences.

With its close proximity to Manhattan, Long Island City had been bustling with activity just hours ago. Now, it was deserted.

The beat-up white van turned off its lights and crept toward the rear of the two-story industrial building with a painted metal sign that read ALL-CITY SECURITY, INC. The driver pulled into a spot that was sandwiched between two trucks. It couldn't be more ideal. Ensured concealment. An unlit area. Close proximity to their target. A clear path to get away.

Now, they'd wait. It wouldn't be long. As their ongoing surveillance had shown, the younger guy, maybe in his early twenties, was a nicotine addict.

Sure enough, not fifteen minutes later, the metal door swung open and the kid stepped out. He reached down for the brick he kept alongside the concrete wall and wedged it between the doorjamb and the door. He double-checked to make sure the brick was secure so the door couldn't lock behind him. Satisfied, he strolled into the cool night air, lighting up his cigarette.

It took a drag or two, but he began to visibly relax. Twice, he succumbed to a hacking cough, cursing under his breath. It didn't seem to deter him. He returned to his smoke, totally unaware that the four men in the hidden van were watching him with keen interest.

"He smokes so much he's going to die of cancer," the driver said wryly to the others, speaking in Albanian.

They chuckled.

With that, the leader, who was in the front passenger seat, motioned to one of his men in the rear to get out of the van and get started.

The designated member of the team followed orders, exiting the van behind one of the trucks and walking nonchalantly toward the building. He placed a cigarette between his lips, simultaneously fumbling in his pocket for a pack of matches. Coming up empty, he scanned the area and pretended to catch his first glimpse of the smoker just outside the back entrance.

He slid a large knife out of his other pocket, gripping it behind his back as he headed in the kid's direction. Approaching him, he asked for a light in heavily accented English.

The kid was happy to oblige, pulling out a cheap disposable lighter. In one smooth motion, the intruder bent over to accept the light, reached behind his victim, and plunged the knife in his back. Before the kid could react, the killer slapped a hand over his mouth, muffling the inevitable cries of agony.

The struggle was over quickly. The young guy dropped to the ground, dead.

Without so much as a second glance, the killer bent down and ripped the key fob holding the victim's car keys off his pants. He then signaled for his colleagues to join him.

The leader and one other team member jumped out of the van and headed toward the building, while the driver remained at the wheel, ready to take off the instant the job was done.

The three Black Eagles dragged the lifeless body into the building. Shutting the door with a loud clang, they rushed upstairs to the main command center where a technician was huddled over a bank of monitors.

The guy spun around, expecting to see his buddy back from his cigarette break. Instead, he was greeted by the business end of an MP5K.

"Where's John?" the terrified technician stammered, his gaze darting around frantically for his smoker chum.

"Dead," the leader replied calmly. "He died"—a quick mental search for the right English word—"unexpectedly. Now I ask you question. Tell me administrative password."

The technician hesitated. The leader veered sharply to the left, aiming his subgun at a nearby chair. He blew its back to bits in a hail of gunfire, transforming the plastic molded chair into a stool. Ejecting the empty magazine and inserting a fully loaded one, he turned back to the technician and moved in, holding the barrel of the subgun so close to his face that the man's nostrils burned from the smoking barrel and the hot, acrid smell of spent gunpowder.

"Password!" the leader shouted.

The technician needed no further convincing.

"'Mortal Kombat,'" he blurted out instantly, his voice quaking with fear as he spelled the password. "The M and the K are capitals. The rest of the letters are small. It's all one word: 'MortalKombat'—no spaces."

The leader smiled, motioning for the technician to move over and sit in the chair he had just blasted with gunfire. The second gunman forced the technician's hands behind his back and secured them with Flex-Cufs. Then he rifled his pockets, confiscating his car keys.

At the same time, the third gunman sat down at the console, expertly navigating the menus and logging in to the administrative application. With a clear knowledge of how the alarm-monitoring software functioned, he located the museum's account and quickly changed all the alarm dispatch codes from "immediate" to "call first." With a chuckle, he replaced the series of phone numbers for key museum personnel that were listed in the system with Phil Leary's office number and Ben Martino's factory and home numbers.

That done, he placed the entire museum account on "test" for the next twenty-four hours. Everything he had completed would ensure that all alarm signals received from the museum would be ignored. No police. No fire department. Even if someone at the alarm-monitoring company tried to contact the museum, all they would reach was the disconnected number of a dead person or a drunk. As a final mocking gesture of what was about to take place, he changed the administrative password to "JOHNSON."

"Finished," he announced in Albanian, rising from the console and giving the thumbs-up sign to indicate the task was complete.

Nodding, the leader turned and opened fire with his subgun, obliterating what was left of the stool-chair along with its struggling occupant.

"Finished," he echoed, smiling as he led the others back down the stairs, past the corpse, and out the rear entrance.

The van driver spotted them the instant they appeared.

He shifted the van into drive and eased out from between the trucks to pick up the team leader. In the meantime, the other two men raced through the lot, splitting up as they neared their arranged goals. Each one of them located one of the dead technicians' cars, unlocked it, and climbed in. Seconds later, they turned over the motors.

"Done. No problems," the leader was informing the driver in Albanian, as he settled himself in the van.

He glanced in his rearview mirror and saw the two other cars pulling up behind them. "Go," he commanded.

The three vehicles swerved out of the lot and through the streets of Long Island City, on their way to Manhattan.

———

The Jaspar Museum was the brainchild of billionaire venture capitalist Edward Jaspar. With Jaspar supplying the seed money, and the help of some affluent sponsors who were patrons of the arts, the new SoHo museum had been built on two adjoining properties on Crosby Street. Millions had been spent to create a small but effective space for exhibiting Jaspar's eclectic art collection, as well as showcasing the talents of new, unique, and gifted artists.

Tonight was an invitation-only soirée intended to tap into Jaspar's rich friends and raise additional funds for the museum's aggressive expansion plans. In honor of the occasion, Jaspar had filled the museum with some of his most cherished artwork, including *Innocence*, which was the talk of the elite art crowd. *Innocence* had been painted by Christian Arlington, a newly discovered young American artist with incredible talent. His paintings were already commanding six figures. And *Innocence* was worth even more.

Unfortunately, Jaspar wasn't willing to sell it.

Wallace Johnson sipped at his champagne, strolling through the connected exhibition rooms. He'd already stopped three times in the central viewing room to stare at *Innocence*. No one could appreciate or want it as much as he. He'd be willing to pay any amount Jaspar asked. But Jaspar had made it abundantly clear that this particular painting was not for sale.

The piece of art itself surpassed the description *breathtaking*. But that wasn't the main reason Wallace wanted it.

The little girl who was the centerpiece of the painting was the spitting image of Sophie.

It wasn't just a strong resemblance. It wasn't only similar features, facial expressions, or body movements. It was as close a rendition of Sophie as any actual portrait of her could convey—from her flowing golden brown hair to the sparkle in her wide, velvety dark eyes, to the impish grin and the dimple she always flashed that had Wallace wrapped around her little finger. The little girl in the painting had Sophie's stubborn chin, upturned nose, and soft peaches-and-cream complexion. In all ways but in reality, she *was* Sophie.

Wallace had saved that final central spot on his gallery wall for this painting. A painting that he'd originally been promised by that street scum Xiao Long. That transaction sure as hell wasn't going to happen now—not since Wallace was fully aware that it was really Liu who'd been selling him the paintings out of some sick desire to torture him.

Once again, rage knotted his gut. What an idiot he'd been. Missing all the signs. Mistaking Liu's support of his galleries for compassion. Bartering his investment-banking services for a minority stake in that Italian company, only to learn that the Mafia was involved with the business. Missing Liu's reasons for introducing Cindy into his life, even after seeing her strong resemblance to Meili. And missing the fact that Xiao Long, that low-class thug, was fronting all along for Johnny Liu.

Liu blamed Wallace for a negligence that was, in fact, his own.

Wallace had loved Meili. He'd never intentionally hurt or abandon her. If he'd had even the slightest inkling that she was desperate and, of all things, pregnant with his child, he would have been by her side, taken care of her and the baby.

To Liu, it would still have been a disgrace he couldn't abide. He still would have cast Meili aside. And he still would have hated and resented Wallace. But Meili would have been alive today.

None of that could be undone. But Liu's retaliation—to maliciously, deliberately rob a five-year-old child of her life? No one short of a monster could do that.

And the bastard wasn't finished.

Wallace might have been blind before, but his eyes were wide open now. He knew Liu's plans for him were building steam. He'd already stripped him of everything he held dear. The only thing left to bring Wallace to his knees was criminal prosecution. Liu would find a way to alert the authorities to the stolen paintings in Wallace's private collection. Then, he'd manage to keep his own name out of it and frame Wallace for stealing all those works of art.

Johnny Liu wasn't a patient man. Time was of the essence.

Wallace's entire collection would have to immediately be disassembled and moved to the rustic little cottage in the Catskills that he'd purchased some fifteen years ago. The cottage was set on twenty acres on top of a rolling hill. He'd originally bought it for investment and recreational purposes. But after 9/11, he'd carved a hidden underground bunker into the beautiful hillside. At the time, he'd been thinking of preservation of life and the salvage of his most precious possessions.

Now he was fighting for his freedom.

He'd clear out his collection later tonight, pack up his car, and leave at dawn for the drive to upstate New York.

He'd be home before any suspicions were raised.

The three vehicles turned onto Crosby Street and paused.

No traffic ahead.

The van and one of the cars proceeded down the narrow street, while the well-worn gray Honda Accord stayed behind, maneuvering itself perpendicularly, blocking all vehicles from passing. The driver shut off the vehicle, yanked out the ignition key, and tossed the key fob belonging to the dead alarm-company employee under the front seat and out of sight.

The van continued down the block. The leader scanned the area, ensuring that the security provided by the FBI had been neutralized. Satisfied, he gave the driver the go-ahead. The van accelerated rapidly, parking at the end of the block near Prince Street. Its driver and passenger exited and watched while the second car wedged itself sideways, scraping its bumpers against cars parked on either side of the street. With the block inaccessible, the team convened on foot in the middle of the street, carrying their duffel bags.

The leader nodded.

Two members of the team responded by pulling out cell phones and dialing two different numbers. They watched as the vehicles at either end of the street exploded, bursting into flames.

The four well-trained Albanian killers headed for the door of the Jaspar Museum of Art.

They reached the entrance and pulled on their masks. The leader pointed at his watch. The other men nodded. Then the four Black Eagles stormed the museum, guns drawn.

With Rich's car close behind, Derek turned east on Spring Street. As he approached Crosby, he and Sloane spotted a burning vehicle blocking the street.

"What the hell . . . ?" Derek slammed on the brakes, and he and Sloane jumped out.

"Derek!" Sloane yelled, pointing. "There's another car on fire at the other end of the street!"

"The burning cars are buying them time," Rich announced, having abandoned his car to run over and join them. "They're hitting the museum—now."

"Not just the museum. Wallace, too." Sloane grabbed Derek's arm. "This isn't just a museum heist. It's an execution. Liu's sending them to kill Wallace."

"Yeah. I know." Derek turned. "Rich, call for backup," he shouted as Rich raced back to his car.

"Already on it," Rich called over his shoulder, his cell phone pressed to his ear.

Derek opened his padlocked trunk, yanking out his enhanced SWAT gear. He had finished suiting up when Rich returned wearing his bulletproof vest and carrying his shotgun.

"The New York Field Office is sending reinforcements and coordinating tactical operations with the NYPD."

With a hard nod, Derek turned to Sloane. He'd already geared himself up for an argument—one she was going to lose. And there was no time for niceties.

"Here's the deal," he stated flatly. "You're not FBI. You have no authorization. You don't even have protective equipment. You're a sitting duck. And I'm the lead case agent. So I'm ordering you to stay out here. That's nonnegotiable."

Sloane wanted to argue. It was written all over her face. But she didn't. Every second counted. Lives were at stake.

"Fine. I'll sit this one out." She gripped his sleeve. "Derek . . . be careful."

He covered her hand with his and squeezed her fingers. "Don't worry. I've got a wedding to look forward to."

Releasing Sloane's hand, Derek joined Rich, and they inched their way carefully toward the museum, using parked cars and trucks for cover. They shifted impatiently as they waited for SWAT to arrive.

Every minute seemed like an eternity.

The security guard leaped to his feet as the four armed thugs marched into the second-floor reception area. Reflexively, he grasped for a silent alarm beneath the front desk and pressed it. He then raised his quaking arms and informed the intruders that the alarm had been tripped. He half suggested, half begged them to flee before the police arrived.

They laughed in his face. The leader sent a volley of bullets from his MP5K, killing the guard instantly.

———

Somewhere in Long Island City a panic signal appeared on an alarm monitor. Programmed to respond as if the museum were testing its alarm system, the automatic-monitoring system ignored the call for help.

No alarm-company technicians responded to the problem. Both were lying dead, in rivers of blood, on the building floor.

The museum and its patrons were at the mercy of the intruders.

———

Derek and Rich heard the burst of gunfire and the shattering of glass. A heartbeat later, shards of the large window rained down on the street below.

Waiting was no longer an option.

Derek grabbed his M4, and he and Rich tore across the street and into the museum.

Inside, Derek could hear the screams of hysterical people coming from upstairs. He and Rich carefully made their way up the circular staircase and past the dead security guard. They paused on each floor for a quick search. Nothing. The first two floors of the museum were devoid of people.

On the third floor, they edged down the narrow hallway. All the gallery areas seemed empty. But on the way back, they passed a small room where the catering company had set up. Hiding beneath the conference table was a terrified server, crouched on the floor in her black-and-white uniform. Derek lowered his weapon and went into the room, bending down and reassuring the sobbing young woman that she'd now be safe.

"Did you see how many men there were?" he asked.

In a state of shock and unable to speak, she held up four fingers.

"Good." Derek continued to press her. "Do you know where they went?"

She pointed upward, indicating they were on the top floor, just one flight above.

"Thank you." Derek helped her to her feet, and Rich escorted her to the doorway.

"Just leave now. Quickly and quietly. Don't even look back."

The young woman needed no second invitation. She ran out the door, pausing only long enough to whisper, "Thank you."

Then, she was gone.

Derek and Rich left just as fast, proceeding to the end of the hall and toward the stairway that led to the top floor.

Upstairs, almost all the patrons had been located and seized. They were crammed into one storage room and ordered to get down on their knees, hands in front of them.

"Shut up. Cooperate. Then no one dies," the leader warned them.

Instantly, their captives did as they'd been commanded, lowering themselves to the floor and flattening their hands in front of them, keeping their heads down.

Cell phones were confiscated, together with any items that could be used as weapons. The gunmen removed valuable pieces of jewelry from their captives and stuffed them into their duffel bags—Patek Philippe and Rolex watches from the men, and diamond rings, bracelets, and earrings from the women.

After that, the victims were shoved back against the wall and forced into a sitting position. Flex-Cufs were used to immobilize their hands.

The gunmen scanned the room. Almost all the patrons were there.

Wallace Johnson was not.

Infuriated, they zeroed in on a group of men who were whispering among themselves. The Albanians demanded to be told where Johnson was. Most of the men didn't know. Their captors didn't care. They used whatever means necessary to learn Johnson's whereabouts. One profusely sweating hostage who kept averting his gaze became their target. A punishing blow with the stock of an MP5K to his groin produced the necessary information.

Johnson was in the central viewing room, admiring *Innocence*.

The leader barked out for the other Black Eagles to follow him, pointing toward a concentric circular hall leading to the inner exhibition space.

In the hallway, the four gunmen spoke rapidly in Albanian. Each team member checked his walkie-talkie. Assured they were picking up one another's signals, they pocketed the communication devices, locked the storage room door, and split up into groups of two. One group raced off to locate and collect the paintings they'd been ordered to steal. The other group, which included the leader, rushed straight to the central viewing room.

———

Sloane was pacing near Derek's car.

As soon as she saw the catering employee burst out of the museum and start running down the street, Sloane rushed forward and grabbed her arm.

The young woman whipped around like a frightened deer.

"It's all right. I'm with the FBI." Sloane wasn't wasting any time playing semantics. "What's happening in there? Two of my agents are inside. Did you see them?"

The young woman glanced fearfully behind her. Then, she blurted out that the security guard was dead, that four armed men had taken everyone hostage, and that the two FBI agents had saved her life and were on their way to capture the killers.

With deliberate calm, Sloane asked her name, thanked her, and let her go.

With that same deliberate calm, she decided it was time to take matters into her own hands.

Reaching into her handbag, she pulled out the Glock 27 that was her personal weapon. Slowly, cautiously, she eased her way toward the museum entrance, using the line of parked vehicles as cover.

———

Derek and Rich kicked open the storage room door.

Assault rifle raised, Derek burst inside, his gaze and weapon quickly sweeping the room. "Clear," he called out to Rich. He turned his attention to the frightened hostages. "FBI. You're safe now," he told them as Rich crossed over to begin offering assistance.

As Rich snipped the Flex-Cufs on the first few victims, Derek spotted the small group of men trying, despite their bound hands, to do what they could for their friend, who was doubled over and vomiting from the trauma he'd endured.

"We'll get you medical attention," Derek assured him, squatting down and cutting his Flex-Cufs to free his wrists. Quickly moving on to free the other four men, Derek asked about the gunmen.

"They're after Wallace Johnson," one man told him. "They went to the central exhibition room to find him."

Leaving the freed victims to help the others and make their escape, Derek and Rich moved cautiously toward the center of the museum—until they heard Wallace's screams of agony. Then they rushed the room, taking cover behind a larger, decorative column.

Wallace was tied to a chair. One of the gunmen was gripping his hair at the scalp, yanking back his head with punishing force. Wallace's face had been beaten practically to a pulp. The other gunman was taking photos with a digital camera, purposely documenting the torture for someone's pleasure. It didn't take a scholar to figure out that that someone was Johnny Liu.

Spotting the FBI agents, the leader dropped his grip on Wallace and reached for his gun. "Behind you!" he shouted in Albanian, warning his accomplice.

In one motion, the second gunman dropped his camera, grabbed the subgun slung across his chest, and pivoted around to the agents.

Before he'd completed the semicircle, Rich fired a blast from his shotgun at point-blank range, ripping a hole in the assailant's chest and sending his mangled body flying.

The leader had squatted down behind Wallace, using him as a human shield while preparing to fire. During those brief seconds, Derek was quickly sizing up the situation to determine how to deliver a lethal shot without hitting Wallace. It was virtually impossible.

Wallace knew it.

With a burst of adrenaline, he used his legs to push off, toppling the chair sideways and to the floor. As he went over, he managed to send an elbow into the face of the leader. It was a glancing blow, but it knocked the Albanian off guard for an instant.

That's all Derek needed. With the skill of an Army Ranger, honed by years of FBI SWAT training, he fired a burst of ammo from his weapon, striking the leader in the chest, neck, and head.

In a matter of seconds, two gunmen were dead.

The two remaining Albanians heard the gunfire. They abandoned their assignment, grabbed their walkie-talkies, and began barking questions into them, demanding to know what had happened.

There was no response.

Panicked, they snatched up their partially full duffel bags and headed toward the staircase that would take them down to the museum entrance.

Derek and Rich rounded the top-floor corner just as the last hooded killer was about to disappear down the stairs. Rich fired his shotgun, the blast taking out a chunk of the wall and shattering the trailing gunman's leg.

The wounded man fell to the ground, shouting out in pain, while his colleague raced on, desperate to flee the museum.

"Rich, secure him," Derek called, gesturing at the maimed Albanian as he stepped over his body and kicked his subgun out of reach. "I'm going after the last guy." With that, he raced down the staircase.

Sloane had inched her way across the first floor of the museum and was at the base of the staircase when she heard the shotgun blast. She halted, waiting for what came next.

Pounding footsteps, descending the stairs in a frenzy and heading in her direction.

She retraced her steps at a run, reaching the museum's entranceway, then crossing over and hiding in an alcove near the door. The staircase was at the far end of the hall, a full length away from the entrance, but Sloane still had a full view of its base.

A hooded man, dressed in a black turtleneck and tactical pants, rounded the bend and hit the ground floor, turning sharply and racing toward the entranceway. Sloane's gut clenched when she saw who was flying down the steps in close pursuit.

Derek.

The gunman sensed that Derek was closing in on him. He stopped—about thirty feet from where Sloane had taken cover—and pivoted. Derek wouldn't be able to see him until he reached the ground floor, where he'd be standing like a human target on a shooting range.

The gunman realized his advantage at the exact time Sloane did. Seizing the opportunity, he wrapped the sling of his subgun around his arm and prepared to open fire.

No matter how fast Derek's reflexes were, he could never take the gunman down first.

Instinct. Training. Muscle memory. They all kicked in, and Sloane edged her way out of the alcove. No time to aim for body mass. If she succeeded only in wounding the SOB, he'd still get off a round of fire that would blast Derek.

No. This situation required a kill shot.

She raised her weapon, focusing on the back of the gunman's head, and aimed at the exact spot that would be her bull's-eye.

Then she squeezed the trigger.

EPILOGUE

"I'd forgotten how much paperwork has to be done after a big case."

It was a week after the thwarted museum heist, and Sloane was perched at the edge of Derek's desk as he typed up yet another FD-302. "Or maybe I just blocked out the memory."

A corner of Derek's mouth lifted. "You mean you don't find 302s the high-light of being a special agent?"

"Nope." She tucked a strand of hair behind her ear. "But I'd suffer them if it came with the rest of the package."

"So I gathered, Bull's-Eye Burbank."

Sloane's lips twitched at Derek's form of address. The story of her dead-on shot that had killed the Albanian gunman at the Jaspar had quickly spread through the New York Field Office. Somewhere along the line, one of the agents had come up with the nickname "Bull's-Eye Burbank." And it had stuck.

"Like I told you, I aim to please." Sloane's voice was teasing. "But I also aim to win."

"I believe the aim-to-win part. But aim to please?" Derek stopped typing and sat back in his chair. "We've been so bombarded with follow-up, I haven't had the chance to reprimand you. When you left the car, you disobeyed my direct orders. That's not aiming to please. That's aiming to defy."

"You're right. And in this case, an apology is not forthcoming. So tell me, Special Agent Parker, do you plan to take disciplinary action?"

"Actually, I had a different kind of action in mind." Derek stood up, leaned forward, and kissed her. "Like another bedroom marathon tonight, and an announcement about our wedding tomorrow."

"That works." Sloane ran her fingers over his jaw. She was still so grateful he was alive and all right. The museum gun battle had been a little too close for her. She gave him another slow, deep kiss, then eased away. "I think this behavior counts as a breach of protocol, too."

"Screw protocol."

Sloane laughed. "That's my guy. Bending the rules to suit his needs."

"Sloane." Derek caught her hand, his tone and gaze turning abruptly serious. "In case I haven't said the words, thank you. You saved my life."

"I love you," she answered simply. "No other alternative existed."

"I love you, too. And believe me, I know how that love compels you to protect me at all costs. I've been there, too, remember?"

"I remember," Sloane replied, thinking back to the life-or-death situation she'd found herself in this past spring.

"But you know what?" Derek continued. "You would have reacted with those same instincts, done the same thing, for any fellow agent. That's just who you are. *And* why you belong with the Bureau." An insightful look. "By the way, how's that right hand doing?"

With a twinge of surprise, Sloane glanced down at her scarred palm. "It's fine. But how weird. I haven't thought about it. Not since last week when Connie checked it out and gave me the thumbs-up. No pain. No muscle weakness." A grateful sigh. "I never believed this day would come."

"Well, it has." A cocky grin. "And now I can say I told you so—since I always knew it would."

Sloane sighed. "I'm going to hear about this for a long time, aren't I?"

"You bet. Arrogant guys like me love to gloat."

They were both laughing when Rich poked his head into Derek's cubicle.

"Good. You're both here. I wanted to fill you in on a few things. Is it a bad time?"

"Not at all." Derek gestured at the chair across from his desk. "Have a seat."

Rich complied. "First and foremost, our agent who was assigned to Johnson is stable. It was touch-and-go for most of the week. But he's going to make it."

"That's the best news you could have delivered," Derek said fervently. Protecting their own was a Bureau priority. And this time they'd gotten lucky. The Black Eagles couldn't afford to make a scene by whipping out a subgun and pummeling a guy with bullets outside the Jaspar, so they'd dragged him into an alley at gunpoint, beaten the crap out of him, and clubbed him over the head with a two-by-four. He'd been in bad shape when he was rescued.

"Thank heaven," Sloane said. "We've all been praying for him."

"Well, the prayers worked." Rich looked as relieved and happy as Sloane and Derek did. "So that's the positive update on that front. As for the Black Eagles, I dropped by the hospital again and interviewed the wounded team member—the only one of them who's still alive. He's still waffling about talking. But he's being released into our custody today. Trust me, a day with me will be a lot more grueling than a day in a hospital bed. Give me one interview with him at our Field Office and I'll have him chattering like a magpie. And you'll have Xiao Long on all kinds of new counts."

"That's great." Derek's brows drew together in a frown. "It would be better if we nailed Johnny Liu. But he destroyed every link between himself and all the criminal activities he's involved in, including the Italian leather goods company that funded the Black Eagles. Xiao handled everything for him. And from the looks of things, he's not giving Liu up."

"Of course not. And without Xiao's testimony, you could never touch Johnny Liu," Rich stated factually. "There's no concrete evidence, and no extradition between China and the U.S."

Derek shrugged. "The point's moot. Liu will be dead in a few months, anyway. I just wanted to strip him of his precious honor beforehand. But I'm not complaining. He won't be hurting anyone again."

"You know Wallace is innocent of everything Liu framed him for, especially funding the Black Eagles," Sloane inserted quickly. "He'd never—"

"I know," Derek interrupted. "I don't think we'll have any problems proving that Johnson was in the dark on that, just like he was on so much of what Liu did. But buying those stolen paintings—that's another story. Extenuating circumstances or not, he purchased them knowing they were stolen."

Reluctantly, Sloane nodded. "I know. I just wish we could use emotional hardship as grounds to reduce the charges."

"Don't give up on reduced charges. Remember, Johnson bought those paintings directly from Xiao Long. He met with him, paid him, and was threatened and beaten by Xiao's enforcer. I'm pretty sure the assistant U.S. attorney will consider a deal if Wallace testifies against Xiao Long."

"*If?* You couldn't stop him." Sloane's tone vibrated with anger. "Xiao Long killed Sophie. I'm sure Wallace would prefer to respond in kind. But at least he can feel a small sense of vindication if he helps put the bastard away. The only thing better would be putting him right beside Liu, six feet under."

"That might not be doable, but I can arrange an insurance policy. Just in case Xiao Long manages to slip away from us. He's smart and he's well connected. But his loyalty to Liu—even posthumously—will always be his Achilles' heel. Let's use it." A smug expression accompanied Derek's cryptic statement.

"How?" Rich asked. "As I said, we've got nothing on Liu or his loved ones. By the time we got our warrant and had Cindy Liu's apartment searched, there wasn't a shred of evidence there. Nothing to incriminate her or Peggy Sun."

"Does that really surprise you?" Derek leaned forward to shuffle through a pile of material on his desk. "I figured that finding anything was a long shot. By the time Liu called us, he'd probably made sure that all physical evidence and documentation tying Cindy and Peggy to anything illegal was long gone or destroyed."

"But you pushed for the search warrant anyway," Rich pointed out.

"Of course. We needed it to get into the apartment, just in case. That doesn't mean I relied on it. A contingency plan is always a good thing to have."

"Meaning . . ." Sloane folded her arms across her breasts, leveling an anticipatory stare at Derek. "Okay, Mr. Cat-that-swallowed-the-canary. Out with it. What did you do that we don't know about?"

"Something that will keep Liu and Xiao in line. And keep them from going after your father or his partners again."

With that, Derek found what he was looking for on his desk—a padded mailing pouch that had arrived for him a few days ago, with no return address on it. He opened it as he spoke. "You know, it's amazing what can be found right out in the open, no search warrant needed, if you know where to look." He pulled out the contents of the mailing pouch—a few photos and several Ziploc bags. "Take these, for example."

He laid out the two high-quality photographs, taken with a sophisticated digital camera and a zoom lens.

Photo #1: Cindy Liu meeting with Xiao Long on a busy Chinatown street under the canopy of a local produce store. Time stamp: 3:35 P.M., three days before Cindy's debut at Wallace's art gallery.

Photo #2: Cindy and Xiao in heated conversation outside Cindy's apartment. Time stamp: 6:45 A.M., just after dawn on the day Johnny Liu had called Derek.

While Sloane and Rich were staring at the photos, Derek placed the Ziploc bags in front of them. "These were removed from the trash outside Cindy Liu's apartment." He pointed to the first bag. "Oil paints and varnish. Made out of some very unusual ingredients. The kind used a hundred and fifty years ago. None of the commercial pigments and finishes made today. All natural-based." He indicated the second bag. "Swatches. Specific color mixtures of oil paints. Colors I'm sure Rich can match to one or more specific masterpieces—paintings that only a top-notch forger would want to reproduce." He moved on to the third bag. "Finally, brushes. Very small brushes, the ones used by the masters more than a century ago. All natural horsehair. I've been told that DNA testing, done by the right expert, could reveal the approximate time period when the horse this belonged to lived. I'm sure we'll find Peggy Sun's fingerprints all over every one of these bagged items."

Derek leaned back in his chair, arms folded behind his head. "And that, as they say, is that. Other than the phone call to Johnny Liu I'm about to make while I e-mail him pictures of all the evidence. You're both welcome to stay. It should be fun."

"You've outdone yourself on this one." Rich shook his head in disbelief. "You even one-upped me. How in the hell did you arrange this in time?"

"The phone call you ran out to make right before we took off for Wallace's place," Sloane remembered aloud. "You were giving instructions to your informant."

"Yup. He knew just what to do."

Restudying the photos, Sloane narrowed her eyes in a quizzical look. "What about this first photo?" She indicated the one taken outside the produce store. "This meeting happened before we were on to Cindy Liu. How did you know to have it taken?"

"That was pure luck," Derek replied. "C-6 has dozens of photos of Xiao Long taken during our investigative surveillance. We ran through the ones that fit the right time period. This one turned up. Handy, don't you think?"

"I think your whole plan was a stroke of genius," Sloane stated flatly. "It doesn't matter what's admissible in court. What matters is what Johnny Liu believes. And what he's willing to do, or order Xiao Long to do, to protect Cindy."

"Exactly." Derek sat up, his hands going to his computer keyboard. He clicked on "New," opening up a fresh e-mail message. To: Johnny Liu's personal e-mail address. From: Derek's FBI e-mail address. In the subject box, Derek typed: "Interesting Acquisitions." Then, he clicked on the paper clip and attached his digital photos of all the evidence.

He pressed "Send" as he flipped open his cell phone.

The connection went through. Derek was greeted by silence.

"Hello, Liu," Derek began. "It's Special Agent Parker. I thought it was time I contacted you directly." Purposely, Derek parroted the same words Liu had used with him. Only this time the tables were turned.

"Parker." Liu's voice was emotionless.

"Were you about to ask how I got this number?" Derek inquired. "I would think by now you'd realize I'm a resourceful man. There's very little I can't acquire."

"What is the purpose of your call?"

"To give you a heads-up. Check your e-mail. I just sent something your way. I'll wait while you open it."

Another silence, this one longer than the first. But Derek could hear Liu clicking buttons to open the e-mail, followed by several additional clicks as he viewed each attachment.

"I have fingerprints and DNA evidence to go along with those," Derek informed him. "I could have copies of the analysis forwarded to you."

"That won't be necessary," Liu said at last. "What is it you want?"

"For now? Only that this ends. Permanently. Even after you're gone. No more special-skilled colleagues relocating to the U.S. No more interaction, direct or indirect, with Burbank, Fox, Martino, or Johnson. Whatever punitive steps need to be taken will be taken by the U.S. judicial system. Not by you, Xiao, or anyone else in your trusted circle. Otherwise . . . let's just say it would be a shame for your loved ones to be imprisoned or embarrassed because of your overzealous need for payback." The same poignant pause that Liu had given him. "Which reminds me, how is your niece, Cindy, holding up? I know how close you two are. The poor woman must be devastated by her breakup with Johnson. On the other hand, thanks to him, she now has such a promising future ahead of her. A successful architect. Right here in the U.S. Losing that opportunity would be tragic. And humiliating."

Liu's tone didn't change. "I understand your requirements."

"I thought you might. So we're clear on what you and your colleagues will and will not do?"

"Perfectly clear, Agent Parker. The terms are acceptable."

"Excellent. You take care of your health." Derek flipped his phone shut and turned to Sloane. "Tell your father that he, your mother, and his friends are no longer in jeopardy. Also, tell Leo he can feel free to hire that PI. I'm sure his fiancée will be delighted to know she can sleep easy." Derek's eyes twinkled. "And maybe with him."

"I will." Sloane's expression spoke volumes. "They'll all be very grateful. As am I."

"Hey, my pleasure, Bull's-Eye. I'm sitting here today because of you."

"That reminds me . . ." Rich glanced at his watch. "Tony asked us to meet him in the conference room at ten-thirty. It's already ten thirty-five."

Reflexively, Sloane jumped to her feet. "Let's go. Tony's not big on tardiness."

As she hurried off, Derek and Rich exchanged grins. Then, they followed Sloane to the conference room.

———

Sloane was startled when she opened the door and stepped inside.

Not only was Tony there, but Gary Linden, the assistant director in charge of the New York Field Office, was there as well.

"Hello, Ms. Burbank," he greeted her.

"Sir." Sloane glanced around, uncertain if she'd interrupted a meeting. "I hope I'm not intruding. I was told . . ."

"You were told correctly." He waited while Derek and Rich joined the small group, shutting the door behind them. He then indicated a spot at the conference table across from where he and Tony were standing. "Have a seat," he instructed Sloane.

Totally baffled, she complied, sitting down and interlacing her fingers in front of her.

"I've been brought up-to-date on the investigation in which you've been a confidential human source," Gary began. "I've also been made aware of the part you played in saving the life of Special Agent Parker, and of possibly helping to prevent future incidents like the one at the Jaspar Museum. You have my personal thanks, as well as the thanks of the entire Bureau."

"I appreciate that, sir," Sloane replied.

He passed a manila envelope across the table to her. It was labeled BULL'S-EYE BURBANK.

Sloane glanced at the title, then her chin came up, her gaze studying the now smiling ADIC.

"I like the nickname," he said. "It suits you. I have a feeling it will stick." He gestured at the envelope. "Open it."

Sloane followed orders, wondering what was going on. Maybe it was a certificate of acknowledgment, signed by the powers that be. If so, she'd be really touched.

It turned out to be a lot more than that.

Sliding the pages out of the envelope, Sloane saw the first document and recognized it as an application for reinstatement to the FBI. It had her name on it. Behind the application was a printout of a letter of recommendation from Tony, detailing her service and contributions to the FBI during her time as a special agent. He specified her outstanding work with the Crisis Negotiation Unit, adding that he'd rarely seen a newcomer with so much promise.

And last, there was a glowing letter of recommendation from Gary himself, itemizing her post-Bureau work with C-6 and several other squads, calling special attention to the two huge cases this year that she'd had a big hand in solving.

Sloane was blown away by the praise, and honored that so much of it had come from the ADIC himself—head of the New York Field Office.

"That letter you're reading is a follow-up to a call I made to Headquarters," Gary apprised her. "Both Supervisory Special Agent Sanchez and I agree that your talents, both as a crisis negotiator and as a multitalented, dedicated agent, combined with your proficiency at numerous foreign languages, dictate that you're a necessary asset to the Bureau."

Sloane sat quietly, unblinking, her insides clenched with anticipation.

"I advised Headquarters that you'll be submitting your application for reinstatement within the next few days," Gary concluded. "Barring unforeseen circumstances, you should be leaving for Quantico right after the first of the year. Understand that, even though it's been only two years since you left the Bureau, you will have to put in the full twenty weeks at the Academy to be current on your training."

A twinkle. "I suspect there will be aspects of it, like firearms, that you'll breeze right through." Gary cleared his throat, finishing up on a serious note. "As I'm sure you're aware, your background for the two years you were gone will have to be updated to ensure you receive a top secret security clearance. If you had a full polygraph before you left, that's good for five years, presuming you didn't have any overseas travel. And, obviously, you won't have to go through the interviewing process again. So, Bull's-Eye Burbank, I'd say that by next summer, you should be a special agent again." A pause. "*If* that's what you want."

Sloane blew out a long breath. The truth was that even *she* hadn't realized how much she wanted it until now. "Yes, sir. It's *definitely* what I want."

"Good. Then that's settled." He rose, and extended his hand. "Congratulations. I look forward to your rejoining the Bureau, where you clearly belong."

"As do I. Thank you so much." Sloane shook Gary's hand, then leaned forward to shake Tony's. "I can't begin to tell you what this means to me."

"From what I've heard about your fierce struggle to heal, I'd say I have a pretty good idea," Gary replied.

"Congratulations." Derek spoke up for the first time, giving Sloane a very quick, professional hug. "And welcome home. Being that I'm the grateful agent whose life you saved, and that I've worked with you in the past, I think I can confidently say the Bureau is lucky to have you."

"You forgot to finish that sentence," Rich informed him, straight-faced, as he shook Sloane's hand and wished her the best. "What you meant was 'The Bureau is lucky to have you, and so am I.'"

A collective chuckle went through the room.

"Speaking of which," Tony added. "Derek, you can take those two weeks' vacation in December you asked for."

Derek flashed him a grin. "Thanks, boss."

"Anything special planned?"

"As a matter of fact, yes." Protocol be damned, Derek looped an arm around Sloane's shoulders. "A wedding and a honeymoon. When Bull's-Eye leaves for Quantico, she and I will be husband and wife."

"That's great news." Tony slapped Derek on the back. "Congratulations to you both."

Everyone else echoed the sentiment.

"Life's finally coming together," Sloane declared. "New marriage. New career. That leaves only one unresolved question."

"What's that?" Derek asked, turning to gaze quizzically down at her.

Sloane met his gaze, her lips twitching. "Between the two of us, which one is going to be the lead case agent in life?"